Dragon Tamers

DIGITAL TEMPEST

Copyright details

Dragon Tamers 2
by
Emma Maree Urquhart

First published in Great Britain by
Aultbea Publishing Company in 2005,
28 Church Street, Inverness IV1 1HB

Second Edition

ISBN 0-9549340-6-7

Printed by Highland Printers Limited
Henderson Road, Inverness IV1 1SP

"A computer lets you make more mistakes faster than any invention in human history…"

To my family, friends, publisher, teachers and readers.

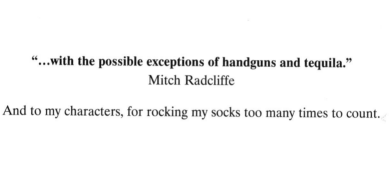

"…with the possible exceptions of handguns and tequila."
Mitch Radcliffe

And to my characters, for rocking my socks too many times to count.

Contents

The Plot

After the events of Dragon Tamers 1, the Dragon Realms are finally at peace once more. Or at least, that's what they want you to think. Last summer, the game's Creator – a mere teenage boy - was freed from the clutches of the Spirit, a demonic tyrant who had possessed his body, planning to take over the game and use it as a path into reality. However, on the night after his release, an NPC (Non-Player/Playable Character) was let loose in Destro Castle, where the computers that contain all of the virtual world's data are found. Purely by glitch, it managed to activate a program that had been dormant for many, many years… Now, a few months later, the game is in chaos. Areas are becoming unstable, players are finding ways to access forbidden areas through these glitches, and all dragons are in danger of destruction as the world begins to crumble. Now, it's up to the players to discover the secrets behind the hidden game, and the source of the game's trouble – but will they be able to succeed, when the game and its characters begin to turn against them?

Meanwhile, in an ancient world, a lost Princess makes a plea to all humanity – to stop the Dragon Realms from being destroyed, as hers was before. As worlds collide, she reaches out to our world, and makes contact – a contact with this world that could save it, but could also destroy it.

Her name is Opal, Princess of the Cat Folk, and she will do anything to make sure history doesn't repeat itself…

WARNING: THE DRAGON COUNCIL CANNOT ACCEPT ANY LIABILITY WHATSOEVER FOR ANY INJURY, ACCIDENT, MISHAP OR DEATH OR OTHER LOSS, HOWEVER CAUSED, ARISING FROM A PLAYER NOT FIRST READING AND UNDERSTANDING THE FULL DRAGON TAMER'S RULE BOOK AND GUIDE, A COPY OF WHICH CAN BE FOUND AT THE BACK OF THE BOOK IMMEDIATELY AFTER CHAPTER 37

Chapter 1:

An Error Has Occurred

As the party went on, celebrating the Dragon Tamer's last adventure, a single motorbike left the site of the festivities and appeared in the Destro Plains. The Creator pushed the bike harder and harder, enjoying the high speed and the wind that blew through his hair. After almost a year possessed by the Spirit, this was his way of celebration.

…But it couldn't last long. After all the damage the Spirit had caused, he had a lot of work to do. He'd already had a dozen or so Killimario pestering him as he tried to organize the party and a quick check of his e-mail had revealed almost five thousand messages for him to read. Clouds of dust filled the air, as he skidded to a halt in front of Destro Gardens.

'This place hasn't changed much,' he said with a smile, walking through the garden and examining the plants. Most of them still stood, bright and colourful – refusing to comply with the Spirit's dark world. A few still wilted though, bright leaves now slowly dying. 'He really should have remembered to water the plants.'

In one swift movement, he leapt on top of the wall, before jumping back down onto the springy grass. Under his breath, he allowed himself a quiet 'ta-da!'

'Massssster?' The Snake Guardian hissed hopefully, raising his head and untangling his two tails.

'Who d'ya think?' He answered, unintentionally sharply.

'No need to be sssssssnappy!'

'I'm not snappy. The rest of the world is, and I have to take the blame.'

Staring at him curiously, the Guardian sighed with relief. 'You haven't changed.'

'Now I have.' The teenager said, snapping his fingers. His biker suit changed into a more comfortable long sleeved black shirt and trousers – both of which showed his unnaturally thin body – and soft, rubber-soled shoes. His hair and face also changed – the dust from the plains and dirt from the garden disappearing.

'And sssso hassss the resssst of the game,' the giant snake said dejectedly, bowing his head. The Creator patted him comfortingly, a move that would have resulted in a slow and painful death if he had been a normal player.

'For better or for worse?'

'For worsssssssse.'

'Then I'd better have a look,' he muttered reluctantly, turning towards the castle. Then he stopped, turning back to the Guardian.

'Wait… that doesn't look like your original character design, Guardian, has it been altered?' The Guardian was well known for his thoughtful attitude, and tendency to stay quiet and listen to what others had to say. But when you got on to a topic he had something to talk about, you'd have a hard time shutting him up again.

'Yessss....' The Guardian hissed, with rising anger. 'That ssssstupid sssssspirit altered my desssdign! He sssseemed to believe I would look more sssssssssscary with an extra tail.'

'But... that doesn't make sense, an extra head, I understand, but an extra tail?'

'I know, it'ssssss ssstupid!' The snake spat. 'He didn't even read the dessssignnotesssss – I'm not basssed on a hydra, or any mythological creature! I'm a giant cobra, the fool!'

As the snake ranted angrily, the Creator placed a hand on his scaly body, gently running it down the dark surface. That Spirit had no right to harm his game... his creations. But why did he have the feeling that the Spirit had done a lot more to the game than just change character designs... and why did he have the feeling he wouldn't be able to sort all of it?

'And the sssssecond tail issssssn't even much ussssse! All I need isssssss one tail to catch mosssssst partiessssss! All the sssssecond tail doesssssss is trip me up! It'ssssss like having two left feet!'

Pulling out a cable, the Creator silently slotted it into the snake. For a second, he flickered slightly.

'I mean, even if it wassssssss an extra head, it would be sssssstupid! I'm the Sssssnake Guardian! Not the Hydra Guardian! Ssssspeaking of which, why am I called that? Ssssssnakessss don't need guardiansssss...'

'I'm aware of that fact. The 'Snake' title is there to make it clear you're not a human. Actually, I think I just put it there because it sounded better. Most people just call you the Guardian anyway...' The Creator muttered thoughtfully, completely losing his current train of thought. Shaking his head, he returned his attention to what he had to do. 'Anyway, your design's fixed.'

'It issssssss?' The guardian said, blinking as he looked down at his now normal tail. 'Thanksssss....'

'Don't mention it. Now if you excuse me, I've got some work to do,' the Creator said, setting off towards the castle with feline speed and care, his footsteps muffled.

He stopped by the door, avoiding most of the security measures, and pausing to hiss a password to the monitor. As he passed some sort of weight sensor, there was a soft 'click'. He froze, watching the door uneasily. The whole path was silent as the Creator tried to remember any blind spots the security cameras had. He couldn't think of any.

Swallowing, he looked down at his shirt. Red spots danced on the dark material.

A single 'pow' echoed through the still air, setting off a barrage of lasers, melting the ground where the Creator had stood. Ducking down with seconds to spare, he rolled sideways, watching as the door closed. He allowed himself a slight smirk. You could always count on video games.

'This is more like it!' He said, punching the air in a short moment of joy, before rolling under the door. 'Some action!'

He cried out, as the door closed too quickly, catching his leg. As its weight threatened to crush it, he pulled a black pistol from one of two holsters on his belt, before jamming it upright between the door and the ground.

The door creaked loudly, accompanied by the slamming of metal feet on the ground behind him. The gun was almost split in half by the weight on its centre, but held strong as he freed his leg, before turning to look at the small army of poorly made robots behind him. He glanced down at his chest, as dozen of red dots found their target. 'This is starting to get a little old...'

As the gun was snatched away, the door slammed to the ground, cracking the stone floor.

As lights flashed all over the castle, the boy ran up the stairs, shooting every one of the Spirit's own robots that tried to stop his advance.

Eventually, he arrived at his destination – a door, with a plaque on it reading 'Clix CCTV'. Finding the door closed, he turned and faced the robots that filled the corridor. Some were coming from above, others below, but they were all coming towards him.

It was one of those awkward situations when godlike powers would come in handy. It was convenient that the Creator had just those.

'Now, this is rather stupid,' he sighed, tapping his foot on the ground and glaring disapprovingly at the army in front of him. 'I have a lot of work to do, and I'm busy running from robots.'

The robots paused, uncertainly, as the Creator surveyed them.

'Well, what are you waiting for?' He asked. 'I can't be the only one sensing the impending DOOM here, can I?'

As if waking from a dream, the robots burst into life, crying out as they scrambled over each other in a desperate bid to escape.

'Go rot with the rest of your pathetic kind, in the floating tower of Destro.' He growled, raising his hand. A replica of the cyberglove (from the virtual reality equipment used to play the game) appeared on his hand, as he waved at the crowd of confused robots.

They disappeared, and an uncomfortable silence filled the castle. It was broken only by the reluctant droning castle security alarm, which itself seemed uneasy about continuing.

'Stupid Spirit's minions.' He muttered. 'Worst robots ever to enter this game; and enough of that stupid wailing! Despite being a stupid castle and having no A.I. whatsoever, you know just who I am!'

The alarms abruptly stopped, and the door to the CCTV room was unlocked. He walked in, sitting down on a chair and spinning round before turning to the monitors.

The first screen showed the inside of a cave...judging by the earth walls, an underground one. A cave? But... that's a breach of the privacy rules...

'Computer. Give me a location.' He commanded, staring at the screen.

`We cannot. We have no A.I. whatsoever.`

'Oh, stuff you.' He growled sourly, shooting a dark glare at the monitor. 'Anyway, I was right – it's not the castle with the A.I., it's the computer system that runs it. Now, give me the blinking location.'

`The Castle feels offended.`

'Ack, cut this rubbish out, will you? It's been a hard day. Let's go with argument number two, then – if you have no A.I., how are you talking with me?'

`Good point.`

'I'm a genius. What did you expect? Now give me a location.'

`The Cave of player Ceirin, one of the Dragon Tamers.`

'Him…?'

`The Destroyer's Apprentice, or the Snake.`

'You're kidding me, right?' He said, frowning. The computer didn't answer. It didn't lie. That kid was the Spirit's apprentice?

His hand hovered uncertainly over the keyboard. Using his computing skills was fair enough…but using his raw power and unique weapons was much more fun. Besides, he needed the practice.

Pressing a single key, he was teleported inside Ceirin's cave.

His bright blue eyes scanning the room intensely, he pinpointed the spot where the camera would be positioned. He held out his right hand, and his gun appeared in it. With deadly accuracy, he took aim and fired.

There was a flash, as a silver bullet shot out of the gun and hit the tiny, invisible camera. It flashed into sight, falling to the floor.

Checking for any visible wires, the Creator picked it up in a gloved hand, crushing it, before returning to Destro.

'Masssssster! You're back!' The Guardian said, standing at the door to the room.

'Yes, Guardian. Why are you in the castle?'

'Don't worry,' he said reassuringly. 'The game'sssss offline, there'sssss no chance of intruderssssss. And anyway, I have a reassssson. Dragon Tamer Ceirin ssssssent you a Killimario.'

'He did?' The Creator said meekly. How had he known? Hadn't that boy been at the party? Did he have a spy in that cave?

'He's gone onto the Destro computer system. He says there's a problem with the system covering Clix.'

'Really?' The Creator said, breathing a sigh of relief. He looked up at the CCTV. 'There doesn't seem to be anything wrong with the CCT-…shoot.'

He froze, staring at the screen showing an area called Fear Fork. The screen was strangely blurred, hiding one of the figures.

'What isssss it?' The Guardian asked. The Creator ignored him, changing quickly back to his biker suit.

'Attention Destro Computer System! We have an identified user in Fear Fork, Clix. Block that area from all normal players, and allow no one to leave.'

'That'sssss Ellen.' The Guardian said, looking up at the screen. 'The tamer with no dragon…'

'I know who she is,' he snapped. 'Computer, play and record the audio from that area.'

'Who are you?' Ellen asked. 'What are you doing here?'

'It is not important. But I know who you are, Ellen. And I can help you.'

As the Guardian listened, confused by all the sudden action, the Creator leapt out of the window, landing cat-like on the ground. Pulling out his gun from his belt, the same he had used to shoot the camera, he shot once into the air, before rolling to the side as a large, heavy duty motorbike came crashing to the ground. It looked slightly tougher and more hard-wearing than the previous one.

It roared into life as he got onto it, pulling the front wheel into the air in a wheelie before speeding away across the plains. The tires spun wildly as the bike picked up speed. The screen on the dashboard flashed, as the Creator kept gaining speed. They were nearing the edge, and he showed no signs of stopping. As the bike roared on, he was going at over 180 miles an hour.

On a small, private area somewhere on Clix, the party was continuing long into the night. Maree stood apart from the group, staring out at the black sky and running a hand down the window. She'd spent a lot of time recently working on outfits, and tonight she stood as a dark figure among the colourful partygoers, in a black suit and crimson top, with black, polished shoes and her sword hidden inside the outfit. Better safe than sorry.

As the party went on, Nick raised his head and gave a low growl.

'What's wrong, Nick?' Ceirin asked, in charge of the party's music system. Instead of operating them manually, however, he'd programmed the MP3 equipment to play random tracks. It was working well, but in doing so he'd picked up on an error in the Destro Castle Computer System, and it worried him.

'Listen!' He barked. Ceirin stopped the music, and everyone listened as a faint, but still noticeable, roaring sound was heard. Everyone turned accusingly to one guest in particular.

'IT WASN'T ME.' Sphinx Ten said angrily, his sandy-coloured face turning crimson. There was laughter from the guests, and some shouts of 'What's so funny?' from the people in the pool outside. Ceirin played the music, and the party continued.

'WOO HOO!' The Creator yelled, as the bike roared through the air. 'I haven't had this much fun in a year!'

'What are you doing?' The Guardian exclaimed, his worried face appearing on the bike's dashboard.

'What do you think I'm doing? Having fun!' He yelled.

'You could die!'

'I know, isn't it great!' He shouted, grinning psychotically into the monitor. 'I love it when I'm hyper!'

'You're going to land in the loch!'

'I am?' He asked, pausing and looking down. His grin instantly faded. '...Oh. that's not so good.'

As he tried to point the bike towards land, he became aware of just how out of place the woods looked. He remembered programming the loch...it had been there quite a long time. He also remembered the woods, but they had never stretched past the areas were the caves were. That Spirit had extended them out to the edge of the lock...but why? And why had he named the area Fear Fork?

Turning his attention back to his current predicament, he realized how close the bike was getting to the ground.

Two flaps opened at the back of his jacket, and out of them burst two black raven wings. They fluttered madly in the wind, and he had to fight to control them and stop them from being snapped straight off by the wind. As they spread out around him, he struggled to stay seated on the bike.

He could fly off… but he hated flying. The wings were only to slow his landing, and make it a little bit softer.

* * *

'Simple. I need your help…and your amulet…' The mysterious figure in the trees said. It was covered completely in a stormy blue cloak, hiding its face and body from view.

'You need my help?' Ellen asked, raising a hand to her neck and clutching the amulet. 'Why?'

'There isn't much time to explain.' It said, a note of desperation in its voice. 'I need that amulet.'

'I have to know why.'

'Please!' It begged, as the roaring around them grew louder…and closer.

'What's that noise?' Ellen asked, looking round.

'You have to give me the amulet now! Hurry!'

'Where's it coming from?'

'Give me it!' It said, its voice slowly becoming less vague and more distinct… Ellen could tell it was male. And he was panicking. Looking up, he could see the black motorbike and he knew where it was going to land.

'Look, can't you just tell me what's wrong? Maybe I can help without my amulet.' Ellen offered. 'I'm sure my friends could help out, too.'

The hood was tilted up lightly, as the wearer stared up in alarm at the falling vehicle. Grey eyes turned wide, indecision mixed with the fear they showed.

'I…can't…' He said quietly, bowing his head. There was a flash of metal, and he leapt at Ellen. 'Get out of the way!'

The blonde-haired rider cried out, as the shadowy figure ran into her, pushing her to the side as a huge black shape fell through the trees. She caught a glimpse of paws and tail, and a dagger was pressed against her throat. 'Don't move.' It was pulled away, and the figure vanished in a whirl of blue. A gust of wind blew through the branches of the trees around her.

As the bike smashed into the ground, the Creator was flung off. He lost his wings as he flew, trying to avoid getting tangled up in the branches, and was instead thrown flat against the trunk. Barely conscious, he fell to the forest floor.

Ellen screamed, as the tree the bike had smashed into was torn from its root, crashing into the ground inches away from where she sat.

There was a sudden silence, followed by another scream as the bike lost its balance and fell sideways. Getting up shakily, Ellen walked over to

8

where the Creator stood, rubbing his head and gasping in pain. She could see blood on his palm.

'Are you okay?'

'If I'd done that tree, it would have been harder.' He muttered, getting up unsteadily. 'Stupid spirit…couldn't even design a tree right.'

His head spinning and vision blurred, he scanned the forest. 'Where is he?'

'Who?'

'Don't mess with me, Ellen.' He growled. 'He was here a few seconds ago. The cloaked figure.'

'He left when the bike came.'

'I expected that. Coward.'

'Who was it?'

'You don't need to know. The important thing was, he shouldn't be here.'

'Why don't I need to know?'

'You're not a programmer.' He said simply, struggling to try and make sense of his own words.

'Are you?' Ellen asked. The Creator turned to her, raising an eyebrow.

'Well, what do you think?' He asked. She didn't answer. 'Of course I'm a freakin' programmer! I created this game, I have to be!'

'Can you teach me?' Ellen asked.

'…Pardon?' The older teen asked.

'I'd like to learn. Could you teach me?'

'In theory…but, it's difficult….and you see-' He stammered, taken aback.

'That's great! You teach me how to program, and I'll help you with your anger management problem.' She said, walking away.

He froze, blinking, before glaring at her.

'I DO NOT HAVE AN ANGER MANAGEMENT PROBLEM!'

'Yes you do.' She said, grinning. 'I'll see you soon for our first lesson!'

Sighing in exasperation, the Creator banged his already aching head against a tree.

'That's right! Get rid of all your pent up aggression!' She yelled, waving cheerily at him.

'I don't believe that girl…' He sighed, watching her disappeared into the large, dark forest.

'Look'ssss like the beginning of a beautiful friendsssssship.' The Guardian hissed, as he slithered into the clearing. Dry leaves rustled under his thick, scaly body, leaving a trail of flattened undergrowth in his wake.

'Oh, you're going to get it for that…' The Creator hissed, his eyes narrowing as he stared at the snake. Swallowing nervously, the Guardian slithered away, back along whatever route he had used to get there in the first place.

'Hey, get back here!' The Creator yelled, running after him. 'I'm not finished with you yet! Wait up! I STILL NEED A LIFT BACK TO DESTRO!'

* * *

In the now deserted castle, a small black and silver creature ran across the corridors, looking all around with childish amazement.

'Why did all the alarms stop?' He wondered, opening the door of a room and looking inside. 'Hey! Computers!'

Grinning, he tried to climb up onto the chair. Finding himself too short, he kicked his heel into the ground. There was a small whirring sound from the metal pads on his feet, only audible to the big-eared imp, and blasts of air issued from the pads and let the imp hover up onto the chair, then onto the keyboard. Grabbing the mouse, he started clicking madly.

'Games! Games! Games!' He yelled, clicking everything he could see. A message appeared, and his ears folded flat against his head as it was read out by Reresan, the main computer – who somehow seemed to know the imp couldn't read.

'Serious error? That sounds bad. I wonder what happens if I press a button...'

'ERROR - UNIDENTIFIED USER.'

'Um....my name's Beta. Does that help?'

'PLEASE LOGIN.

PLEAZELOGGIN.

PLEEEAZLOGGGIN.'

The screen blurred, and Reresan's voice became stuttering and slurring the words.

'Maybe I should just go now...' Beta the Imp said, backing away from the keyboard.

'ACCESS DENIED TO INSTALL/GAMES/WOTC SETUP

COMPUTER IS SHUTTING DOWN

ALL PROGRAMS WILL BE TERMINATED

DTLOGIN HAS BEEN TERMINATED

DESTROCCTV HAD BEEN TERMINATED

WOTC IS CLOSING...

AN UNEXPECTED ERROR HAD OCCURRED.

RECOVERING DATA...

AN UNEXPECTED ERROR HAD OCCURRED.

DATA CORRUPTED.

UNABLE TO FUNCTION.

SHUTTING DOWN.'

'Uh oh...' Beta said. 'Why's the screen go black? Um...there's gotta be an on switch around there somewhere, isn't there? Oh, come back on Mr. Computer...please... Yay! Buttons!'

Opening a panel at the side of the computer, Beta found an array of power switches and lights. So, he started pressing every single one until the screen came back on.

'Welcome, user. Please log in.'

'I already told you who I am! I'm Beta, Beta the Imp.'

'User Beta Beta the Imp is not a registered user.'

'Not Beta Beta the Imp! Beta the Imp!'

'User Beta the Imp is still not a registered user.'

'Hey, do you have any games? I wanna play a game!'

'You must log on to continue.'

'Okay!' He said, nodding. 'Do it!'

'Logged on as TamerTec (Guest/Demo Account).

Searching…One Match Found.

WOTC is loading

…An unexpected error has accorded. WOTC had to close. Some Data may be lost. Tell the Dragon Council about this problem?'

'No! Don't tell anyone!' Beta said quickly. 'Uh…um…It's a secret! You can't tell anyone, Okay?'

'Command Received.'

'…I should go, before anything else goes wrong.' Beta said, as the log in screen appeared and the computer returned to normal. 'I just hope nobody finds out…'

Chapter 2:

Starting Over

It was hard, having to start life all over again. Now that there was almost no chance of them returning to their old world, the tamers were working on making their new one better. When the group was together, they often worked on Silver Leaf City, Clix's capital city, and a meeting point for the players of Dragon Tamers.

But without a challenge to keep them together, they were slowly drifting apart...

In his spare time, Ceirin liked to do sports, and was working on adding some new mini games to the worlds, like bungee jumping in Fabrico, hide and seek in Dite, and water hockey in Tropica.

Maree was rebuilding the valley, replanting the trees that had been burned down, fixing the caves that had been destroyed by the Destroyer, expanding the fishing pond, and trying to bring wild dragons from other planets back to Clix.

Before, her game play was based on battling. But now, it was getting hard to bring herself to kill characters she knew were real, and could feel. Instead, she occupied herself with working to help out the game in a variety of ways.

Ellen stayed her normal, carefree self. She didn't forget the promise she made to iZ, but quickly discovered she had absolutely no idea how to fix a robot. So she asked for help from an old friend...

'How's it going?' Nick asked, as Ceirin crouched over iZ's still body. The underground cave was lit only by candles, most of which had blown out, but Ceirin hadn't noticed. Nick was curled up in the corner, his wings wrapped around him.

'Not too good.' He sighed. 'I'm pretty good with normal machines, like toasters, cars, roller coasters...you know, that kind of stuff. But this is an android. That's the Creator's field, not mine.'

'So why don't you ask him?'

'Me? Ask the Creator? No way!' Ceirin exclaimed, offended by the very suggestion. 'I don't trust that guy.'

'Why not?'

His tamer paused, ramming a screwdriver into a hole in his wooden workbench. Sighing, he stared up at his partner.

'How do we know he's a different person, Nick? He hasn't done anything to prove it. He could still be the Spirit, or... he could be someone even worse. How are we supposed to be sure?'

'I don't know. Ellen seems to get on well with him.'

'He's just taking advantage of her. He's probably still after her amulet.'

Nick paused, ears flicking up at the mention of the item. 'Why is everyone after that thing?'

'I have no idea.' Ceirin said, shrugging. 'Power, I guess.'

Nick paused, one ear flopping down and one eyebrow rising. 'Why power?'

'Why not? Everyone wants power, don't they?'

They both turned, as footsteps came from outside, and a player entered the underground cave.

'Hey!' Maree said, jumping down the last few steps onto the wooden floor. She paused, staring at the cloth-covered body, and raised an eyebrow in an uncanny impression of her partner. 'What're you doing?'

'Trying to fix iZ.' Ceirin muttered. 'I don't know where to start.'

'I recommend starting with the big hole in his chest.' Maree suggested, grinning cheekily at her old friend.

'And how do you suggest we fix it? He's gone and destroyed his own power supply, and most of the cables have been severed.'

'Sounds…painful,' Sam said, looking at the android curiously with her large, round eyes, before poking her nose under the sheet and sniffing his still body. 'Where's Ellen?'

'Away with the Creator.' Ceirin murmured, searching through a toolbox for something, 'I think she mentioned programming lessons.'

'She what?'

'Didn't you know? The Creator's been teaching her.'

'But…she's a noob! She doesn't know anything about computers.'

'No she's not, and you know that. She just needs to learn a bit more about computers and video games, that's all. And what better way than to learn programming?'

'I know.' Maree sighed, finding a still lit candle and using it to light the ones that had gone out. *I didn't mean for it to come out like…*

But it does seem strange. Ellen's really close to him, and Ceirin often has business with him because he was once the destroyer's apprentice. But what about Sam and me?

He rarely talks to us. Most of the missions he gives us are just simple errands.

…What if he thinks we're useless? What if he decides it would be best if he just deleted us?

'Hey, don't you think Ellen's spending too much time at Destro?' She added after a pause, frowning.

'I think it's because she doesn't have a cave.' Suggested Sam, rubbing her nose after turning and colliding with a shelf.

'But she does…'

'She won't go back to it, though. I think she spends the night at Destro.'

'She's the only one who's allowed. I can't believe the Creator lets her have access to the castle when none of us do.' Ceirin muttered bitterly. Their accommodation in Clix wasn't bad, and it was in a good location, but… come on, he had a CASTLE. Everybody wanted to sleep somewhere that cool.

'Who? Me?' Ellen asked, coming down the stairs into the cave.

'Oh…Hi, Ellen.' Maree said, turning as she came round.

'Couldn't you have knocked?' Asked Ceirin, irritated. 'Especially you.'

'I let her have access to the castle because she requested it.' The

Creator said, glaring at Maree and Ceirin as he came down into the cave. 'If you two want access, all you need do is ask.'

'I didn't say you could come in here.' Ceirin growled, glaring back at the Creator, annoyed his previous demand had been ignored.

'This is my game. I go where I please.' He replied mockingly, walking over to iZ. 'Anyway, I only came here to see the android.'

He sat down, running a hand over the android's metallic surface. His hand hovered over the claw Alfie on his chest.

The sign of the Destroyer…and also of the Spirit. iZ's one of his robots now, he should be destroyed. It's not as if there's much chance of repairing him, anyway.

'I promised I'd try to fix him…' Ellen said quietly. 'But I don't know how. So I asked Ceirin to try and help.'

'Why did you not bring him to me?' The Creator said, examining the bullet wound.

'Well…um…you see…' Ellen stammered. '…It's just…well, Ceirin…'

'There's no reason for any of you to fear me,' said the Creator. 'Just because I created this game, doesn't make me different from you all. I'm still a kid, I'm still human. And I don't abuse my power.'

He sighed, looking at the Dragon Tamers.

'Because I created this game, everyone treats me like I'm different to everyone else. But I guess the same goes for you three…everyone else is just playing a game, but for you, this is real. Which is why I've prepared a separate world for you all?'

'You what?'

'You heard me. A separate world, just for the Dragon Tamers – right now it's empty, but once you decide what you want to do with it, I will help you make it that.'

'But what about the Tamer-only areas?'

'They're nothing. The only difference between tamer-only areas and the normal areas – the Tamer-only server, to use the correct terminology - is that in the former, there are no normal players. But this can be much, much more.

I owe you all – you saved both me, and the Dragon Realms. I believe this is a fitting reward.'

'Really, I don't think that's necessary.' Ceirin said his gaze still unwelcoming. 'We may be different to ordinary players, but we shouldn't have a separate world.'

'But it's good to be different, isn't it?' The Creator said sharply. 'Better to be a Snake than an ordinary player, isn't it?'

'Just what are you implying?' Ceirin demanded. The Creator paused, about to give an answer, then decided against it.

'…It doesn't matter.' He said quietly, before looking back to the tamers and smiling. He passed one hand along the android, and it departed to Destro, where his enemies couldn't tamper with it.

'Come on, humour me! I could be using that space for something much more useful, but instead I'm offering it to you. The least you could do is go and have a look.'

14

Now that he came to think about it... what had been in that space? It had just showed up as blank space, but he shouldn't have had an area that large spare...

'I think it sounds good.' Ellen said. 'It was really nice of you to do this for us.'

'It's no trouble,' he said, slightly embarrassed. He'd expected a reluctant agreement, but not thanks. The tamers weren't usually like that.

But Ellen knew more about programming now than any of the others, so she had a better idea of how hard he worked on the game.

'I think it must have been, especially because you could have used some of that space to create new areas for the game. It's really kind.'

'Suck up.' Nick growled, sticking his tongue out at Ellen.

'What have you got against the Creator?' Sam asked, surprised by Nick's attitude.

'Plenty.' He hissed back, voice low.

'I agree with Ellen.' Sam said loudly. 'I think we should go.'

'Sam!' Nick barked. Sam stuck her tongue out at him in turn.

'If Sam's game, then so am I.' Maree said, nodding.

'Looks like you're outnumbered, Master Ceirin.' The Creator sniggered, too quietly for the others to hear. 'Right, everyone. Follow your leader.'

* * *

Not far from their destination, the Creator paused, evidently troubled. 'I... have to go.'

'Why?' Maree asked, glaring at him warily. 'Is something wrong?'

'Perhaps.' He said simply, evidently eager to leave. Relaying some instructions to Maree and Sam, he summoned his motorbike and fled the area.

They followed the creator's directions and found that a new trapdoor had appeared in the ground of the area they had found when with the fire imp, with trapdoors leading to all the different worlds.

'Wow...' said Ceirin with a low whistle. 'I didn't think you could get anything duller than the trapdoor...' The hatch had taken them to an area almost exactly like the area above, but without any trapdoors.

'Maybe I'll practice my programming on that area,' commented Ellen. 'I think it's meant to be some kind of portal. It should be fun seeing what I can do with it.'

'You know, the way you find playing with our world 'fun' is kind of scary,' said Nick, glaring sharply at her.

'Don't worry, Nick. I'm not doing any harm, I'm doing good things!'

'I sure hope so. Before we know it, you'll be the Creator's new apprentice.'

'I'll take that as a complement,' said Ellen proudly, grinning. Nick didn't reply, turning away at Sam's voice.

'Hey everyone, there's something over there!' Said Sam. Not far away there was something small and square.

'Oh my!' Gasped Ellen. 'I hope it's not a dead pixel!'

'It's good to know newbie Ellen's still in there,' grinned Maree. Ceirin nodded, watching her rush over to the object and pick it up.

'It's a box.' She said, frowning and turning to the others. 'An expansion pack for Dragon Tamers.'

'Wow! Can I see that?' Shouted Nick, running over. Without waiting, he grabbed it, and soon everyone was crowded round it except Ellen. When Nick had grabbed the box, something had fallen out, a slip of paper.

'What is this? Some kind of note left by the Creator?' Asked Ellen, picking up the envelope. Strange markings covered the sealed parchment, in a language she'd never seen before. They were vaguely Celtic in design, with an odd resemblance to chicken scratchings or the marks cats leave on curtains.

Frowning, she tore it open, picking up the disk that fell out. Seeing her shirt glowing, she yanked at the chain around her neck, pulling out the amber amulet.

The last time it had glowed that brightly had been on the night of the party, when Ellen had gone to the Fear Fork clearing and met that cloaked figure. He'd fled when the Creator had found her, but hadn't given up.

Every time she had went to the clearing after that, her amulet would start glowing, and she would know he was hiding in the trees.

Meanwhile, the box had been torn open. Inside was a booklet marked 'Imp Instruction Manual', and a disk.

'How are we meant to use that?' Asked Sam.

'We'll have to ask the Creator if he can program it in, I guess. I never knew he was working on an expansion pack.' Ceirin shrugged, glancing at the disk. 'You'd think one of those fan sites would have found out about this by now.'

'Maybe it has something to do with that planet that's closed off,' suggested Ceirin, before turning, startled by a bright flash from Ellen's amulet.

'Ellen, are you alright?' Asked Maree. She didn't answer.

Ellen's eyes were glazed, her pupils wide, and her body limp. The last thing she heard were her friend's cries, as she crumpled to the ground.

'Get up! Get up, you have to hurry!'

'What?' Ellen asked, clutching her head and looking up at the speaker. It was a tall cat, standing and talking like a human as he pulled her to her feet. He was draped in dark blue robes, and wore a heavy golden collar around his neck. 'Come on, Opal, you have to get to shelter!'

'Why? What's going on? Where am I?' Ellen said, clutching her head. She paused, as white fuzziness blocked her view. She took away her hand, and it left.

Staring at her fingers, she realised she had a paw. A white cat's paw.

'...What in the realm?'

'Come, to the temple!' The stranger yelled, pulling her through a pale, stone archway and into some kind of passageway.

'Where are we going?'

'The humans, daughter! You must remember!' Said the old, grey haired cat, gripping her paw tightly. 'They are attacking us once more.'

'They're attacking?'

'Medics! To the temple! Princess Opal's fallen ill!'

'Yes. They mean to destroy us all.' The cat spat, slamming a staff into the ground. 'But we shall be the victors, Opal. We shall be the ones who defeat them; we shall be the ones who rule this world.'

Chapter 3:

Boys will be Boys

When Ellen awoke, she was lying in Ceirin's cave at the edge of the new city, on a neatly made bed.

What happened… did I pass out?

She frowned, staring at her hand. It was just the same as always – she was human. She wasn't some kind of cat-girl from an ancient world. At least, she wasn't anymore…

What a weird dream.

Ceirin was asleep on the couch, in a black shirt and jeans. Ellen smiled slightly as she saw him – he looked so normal. In a world filled with colourful outfits and extravagant clothing, he managed to keep his air of normality, wearing what felt comfortable instead of what looked the most magical.

Unfortunately, that air of normality was frequently shattered when he mistook stars for alien spaceships, tried to convince every dragon he met that the Council were hiding things, and prophesized the end of the world in cockney rhyming slang.

Maree, by comparison, was wearing an unusual outfit – but mostly because Ellen was not used to seeing her in a dress. She had to climb halfway up the steps back to ground level before she saw her, sitting silent on a branch of the cherry blossom tree outside the cave's entrance.

She was wearing a long, flowing black dress, with loose sleeves that billowed in the warm breeze. Her knee length, high heeled boots were decorated with silver, and her dress was covered in lace of the same shining colour. Her hair fell loose around her; much longer than it had been when she began playing.

Sam was circling the skies above, hunting, enjoying the breeze, or sharing her tamers sadness. If she felt the latter, it was likely she also shared in her confusion – why were they sad? Neither knew.

Quickly, Ellen changed into a different outfit – a French maid design to annoy the Creator, who had been born in France but spent most of his life in England. It was a simple black dress that fell down to her knees, with a white apron, black silver-buckled shoes, knee-high socks, and one of those strange hat-things she could never find a name for.

Giggling slightly, she walked through the valley and along the portal area, and out into the plains of Destro. By now, night had fallen, bathing the castle in moonlight.

The Guardian lay curled up in the gateway, and rose up to look at Ellen as she entered. 'Good evening, missssssssstressssss.'

'Same to you, Guardian,' she said, smiling. 'Having a good night?'

'Yesss, actually. Very few player dissstractionsssss, as my master's sssstopped perssssssonally taking part in the final battle for a while.' He said, before frowning. 'But I am worried about him, Misssss Ellen.'

'Why?'

'There have been problemsssss in the game – problemsssss he will need to ussssse Vermal to fix. He issss the only one in thissss game capable of working with it and fixing the sssscript, but hissss memory has not quite returned – I am worried the challenge may prove too much for him.'

'Vermal?'

'VRML. Virtual Reality Modelling Language. It's the coding that makesssss up thissss game, data ssssssstored asssss a text file. All the 3D graphicsssss, every curve, all ssssstored in sssssssimple writing. It issss… complicated.'

'Sounds like it, too,' Ellen said. 'Alright, I'll get right up there!'

'Wait!'

'What?' She asked, turning. The Guardian stared down at the ground, tail curled around him.

'Be careful, Miss Ellen.'

'Why?' She said, frowning.

'There is ssssssomething not quite right about my masssssster tonight.'

Hard-soled shoes clattering on the stone floor, Ellen ran through the castle, up spiral staircases, past workshops and computing rooms of various names. Eventually, she arrived in the area where the CCTV footage was recorded, and the Creator spent a large amount of his time monitoring the game. It was empty, but the adjoining room, where he answered the many thousands of e-mails he received daily, wasn't.

He was sitting in a small bunk in the corner, up above one row of monitors. His legs were crossed underneath him, as he sat and stared into the darkness.

The monitors below him cast the floor in a pale white glow, displaying pages of text Ellen couldn't read.

Smiling, Ellen walked over to him, standing in front of the bunk. 'Hey there. What're you doing?'

'Don't talk like you're innocent.' He snarled, taking a swig out of a glass bottle. 'We're all sinners.'

Ellen blinked, shaking her head slightly and staring at the bottle. 'Is that alcohol?'

'It's cola. Spiked cola.' He muttered, finishing the bottle and tossing it over her head. It smashed against a wall, littering the floor was glass. 'It's all spiked. Nothing's safe to drink anymore.'

'Uh… yeah.' Grinned Ellen, resorting to the tried-and-tested strategy of nodding and smiling.

'Stop smiling. You're giving me a hangover.' He muttered, pulling a Satsuma out of thin air and tossing it idly. 'Saaaatsuuuummmaaaaa.'

'…You sure it's not alcohol?'

'I wish. I need Sake[1].' He muttered, leaning against the wall. 'Your outfit offends me.'

'Sorry.' She said, switching to a dark denim dress that clung as tight as a corset around her chest, covered with a white leather jacket. She kept

---

1 Sake (Sä´ké), a traditional Japanese wine made from rice, usually served warm.

her knee-length socks and shoes though, more for ease than any particular liking.

'You're getting good with the designs,' he said, nodding approvingly, 'It's sexy.'

They both froze, staring at each other.

'OHMYGAWSH! I SAID SEXY! THE CENSORS ARE GONNA KILL ME!' He yelled, diving beneath a pillow. 'THE GOVERNMENT IS COMING! GODMODDERS IN THE FRONT RANKS! AHHHH-HHHH!'

'Good council, it really was spiked.' Ellen whispered softly.

The Creator burst into tears.

Her amused smile dropped away into a frown. Mood swings were bad enough, but crying? 'Hey, what's wrong with you?'

'Huh?' He said, poking his head from out of the pillow. 'Miss Mariah, there is nothing wrong with me! I regret that accusation!'

'The term is resent.'

'NOOO! MY IQ! IT'S SHRINKING!'

'No, seriously. There are tears in your eyes.' Ellen said, hopping up onto the bunk next to him. 'What's wrong with you?'

'THE RODNEYS ARE COMING! THE RODNEYS ARE-GMPH?' The Creator mumbled, as Ellen slammed a thermos into his mouth, before tipping the contents down his throat. His screams were muffled, and his eyes grew red.

'A couple of litres. That should do it.' Said Ellen, before pulling away the thermos.

He stood completely still, not even breathing, before falling back onto the pillow. One eye twitched slightly. 'I'm going to kill you for that, Ellen Mariah.'

'Its just coffee. It's not going to kill you.'

'Then you drink some.'

'…Eeeewwww…' She said, staring at the thermos and hiding in out of sight. 'So, tell me what's up.'

'Fine.' He sighed, staring up at the ceiling. He pulled out a nail file, and started filing his already manicured nails as he spoke. 'I'm not really sure what happened… I guess I'm used to tackling things one-by-one. If you give me multiple challenges, I just break down completely.

The e-mails were hard enough, but I could take them. Then the game started playing up, naturally.' He sighed, twisting a strand of hair around his finger. 'The Guardian was a great help – his memory wasn't lost, as mine was. He's amazing, that snake.

But when I opened up one of the documents, I just… broke. It's too hard, Ellen. I'm just a kid. I can't run a game.'

'You did it before.'

'But it's too much.' He said, frustrated, voice rising. 'It's all going to be my fault, Ellen. I'm not a businessman. I can't do this. The game's going to go offline, we're all going to die, and it's all going to be my fault.'

'That won't happen.'

'It will. Before, I was just running a game. Now, I'm running a world. I just can't take it anymore, Ellen. It's all too much…'

* * *

'So you're sure he headed for Destro?' Ceirin asked, for the tenth time since they'd left Clix.

'Yes, Ceirin, he did.' Maree sighed, glaring at him. 'What are you afraid of, anyway?'

'I'm not afraid. I just don't like him.'

'Jeez, Ceirin, he's just a normal kid!'

'But that's where you're wrong!' He contradicted. 'Everyone knows he's an evil, anthropomorphic[1] vampire cat! One day, he's going to turn round and suck out all our blood, hissing like a madman! And when we're lying, pale and dead on the floor, then you'll realise I was right! And I'll go 'I told you so!', and stick out my tongue and cross my eyes like that XP thing! It's going to be SO cool! …Except for us all being dead, but still!'

'He's high, isn't he?' asked Sam, glancing at Nick.

'Probably. He's the only tamer who willingly drinks coffee. He's always either depressed, or on a caffeine high.'

Maree sighed, tapping her foot impatiently and glaring at him. He's not going to make any friends with that attitude.

'Ceirin, he's not a vampire.'

'Maree, have you even looked at all the walkthroughs? All the plot summaries? It's always the same.' He looked like some kind of cross between a cat, boy and a vampire. 'It's a REVOLUTION!' He paused, frowning. 'No, wait, it's not… Ack, who cares, VIVA LA REVOLUTION ANYWAY!'

'Look, he's been over this before. It's a common misconception. His character is completely human, but modelled on the vampire character base. It's quite common. However, his movement coding is based on that of a cat, from one of his older games. You see? His character's built up from the coding of a vampire and a cat, but in reality, he's human.'

'He's got you too.' Ceirin said, sighing and shaking his head. 'I am the only sane one left in this world.'

'Aye, sure.' Maree sighed, giving up. Her brown eyes scanning the monitor in front of her, she typed Ellen's password into the machine, disabling all the security measures.

It hadn't been hard to memorize, after casually glancing at Ellen as she typed it last time they'd visited, and she couldn't be bothered with asking the Guardian for entrance or taking one of the other entrances. Ellen wouldn't mind.

'We're in,' she announced, pulling open the door and passing through the area where they'd once been faced with a group of feral dragons, but now served only as a parking place for one (or occasionally more) of his various motorbikes.

'Vampire biker felines from a virtual world…' Ceirin whispered, shaking his head. 'It's like a Saturday morning TV show.'

---

1 Anthros-animals that think, talk and act like humans.

'Hey, Ellen? Creator? Anybody up here?' Maree yelled up the spiral staircase.

'Yeah, Maree, we're up here!' Ellen called back, looking down.

'What's going on?'

'Well, the creator's having a bit of a bad day.' Ellen replied, voice dropping so he wouldn't hear. 'I think he needs a bit of TLC.'

'Okay. I'll try and keep Ceirin occupied.' Maree laughed, sitting down on the stairs and smiling.

'Hey, did Ellen just say the Creator's having mood swings?' Ceirin laughed from below. 'I was right all along! He really is a girl!'

'Ceirin, please don't make me hurt you.' Maree growled voice dangerously cold.

'…Eeep. Sorry,' he squeaked, hiding from her glare.

Yawning, Nick curled up in the corner, laying his head on his paws. 'Hm. Sounds romantic. Those two are getting pretty pally, eh?'

'Yeah. It's a pity that can't be said for Ceirin and Ellen.' Sam said sourly, clawing at a wall for no particular reason. Then she turned, a wide grin appearing on her face.

'…Sam? Your evil grin is freaking me out…'

'Listen, dog boy, I've got an idea! What say we spice it up for these two a little bit?' She sniggered, whispering something in his ear. Nick nodded, walking over to Ceirin.

'Hey buddy. What's up?'

'Nothin' much.'

'Cool.'

'Hey, Sam and I were talking about a dare game, and we were wondering if you' be interested.'

'A dare game with dragons? Sounds cool. I'm game.'

'Great. Now, you're up first – so, here's what you've got to do.' He said, whispering in his tamers ear.

Sighing, Maree lay back against the stonewall. *Those two are made for each other… they're both into the same things, in-tune with each others feelings…*

I wish Ceirin and I was like that.

I remember, just after the final battle, when Ceirin broke free from the Spirit's grip. It was so lame – but video games are like that.

And yet, it seemed like the perfect romantic moment – but he never said it.

Three words. That's all. We faced monsters, we faced our fears, and we faced the Spirit. But we couldn't say it.

…We suck so much.

'Maree? You okay?' Asked Ceirin, standing at the bottom of the stairwell.

'Mm? Yes, Ceirin. I'm just a little tired.'

He paused disbelievingly, before smiling. 'Okay. Hey, can you come down a minute? There's something going on out the front I think you'd like to see.'

Curiosity aroused, Maree stood up and stepped down the stairwell. She moved to the side to avoid Ceirin, and he did the same, holding out an arm to stop her from continuing.

'Oh har de har har. Let me pass, wise guy.'

'I'm not stopping you.' He said softly, whispering in her ear. 'But there's nothing wrong with stopping and relaxing for a few seconds, is there?'

'Is the lame chat-up line coming now or later?'

'Now.' He said softly, kissing her on the cheek. She blushed, as he leapt past her, bounding upstairs.

With a soft cry, she fell against a wall, raising a hand to her face. '...He...'

Both dragons glanced up, as their sensitive ears picked up a cry. Shortly after, hurried footsteps rushed up the stairwell.

'We rock.' Sam smirked, raising a paw to Nick in a high-five. He did the same, barking happily.

Slowing down to a walk, Ceirin entered the mailroom. 'Hey. How's good Sir Angst doing?'

'Bite me,' snarled the Creator, baring his fangs. Ceirin backed away slightly, but still managed a smirk.

'You don't scare me, Nancy-boy. Sitting with the girls discussing your problems. Jeez, are you macho or what?'

'Stuff you.'

'Two word answers. Oh wow. Aren't you the child prodigy?' Ceirin laughed, sitting down on a leather computer chair and spinning round.

'Bet you must have had a great time at school. You were one of those kids who wrote fake sick notes to get out of gym class, weren't you? And hung out alone in the library after school hours?' Asked Ceirin, grinning wickedly.

'Been there before, Master Ceirin?' Countered the Creator, ignoring the personal jibes.

He closed his eyes slightly, controlling his breathing. Ellen watched him, worried.

Whoa... he actually pays attention in those anger management sessions. Maybe he does need them.

'Nope. I heard rumours,' said Ceirin, leaning back. 'What you doing up there, anyway? Putting on your makeup?'

'Oh, that's torn it,' whispered Ellen, sitting quietly in the corner of the bunk and watching the sparks fly. Her gaze moved to Ceirin, confused. She jumped down, logging on to the computer in the corner.

Leaping down to the ground, the Creator stepped over to him, eyes bright and cold as ice.

'Are you insulting me, Ceirin?'

'Well, naaaaaahhhh,' he said, sticking out his tongue. 'The boy's a genius.'

'Very well – we'll see who's the alpha male, wolf-boy,' snarled the Creator, drawing his pistol. 'I challenge you to a battle!'

Ceirin paused, paling. '...You serious? Come on! You don't even have a dragon!'

'What's your point? I can still kick your sorry hide any hour of the day.'

He smirked, aware he now had the upper hand. 'It's what you wanted, isn't it?'

'Yeah. I guess.' Ceirin said uncertainly. *What had he wanted? He hadn't meant to go that far over the top...*

It was the wolf comment. It had to be the wolf comment. It was all the Creator's fault for throwing stupid insults!

'Very well. I accept your challenge. Choose the field.'

'Destro Castle. Biggest room you got. Sleepover, with a battle at the midnight hour.'

'Fine,' growled the Creator, pulling on his jacket. He froze. 'Wait... what did you just say?'

'Sleepover at Destro. Battle at midnight.'

'...So that'll be a full scale, epic battle in the garden?'

'No. A sleepover. A pillow fight.'

'With swords, guns, knives, daggers, that sort of thing?'

'No. Pillows.'

'Oh, good council.' He sighed, raising a palm to his forehead. 'I'm not hearing this. You're saying something different. I'm hearing things. I'm delusional!'

'I asked for it. You've got to do it!' Ceirin laughed, grinning. 'No signature weapons. Pillows only.'

'You're really asking for it with this.' The Creator sighed, shaking his head. 'Fine. I'll do it. Call up the others and tell them to get ready.'

'What for?' Pressed Ceirin, his grin widening.

The Creator growled, nails digging into a keyboard and tearing off some of the keys. 'For the Dragon Realm's first ever sleepover.'

Chapter 4:

A Challenge

As night fell on Destro, the tamers were gathered in one of the castle's newly programmed rooms. Sporting blue carpet, curtains, and some futons on the floor, it was possibly the most inhabitable room in the whole building.

Ceirin was slouched on a futon, flicking a remote at the TV in the wall and surfing the music channels. 'Hey Creator, how do you get cable on this thing if you're not in the real world?'

'The internet is a wonderful thing, dear boy.' He sighed, annoyed at being interrupted in his conversation with the girls. 'So, as I was saying... this sleepover lark is surprisingly fun.'

'Your English accent is killing my brain.' Sam muttered, curling up in the corner. 'Why can't you speak like a normal human for once?'

'Oi! Don't insult the accent, man! You're like, dissing my street cred! And I need that street cred! To get cred! ON THE STREETS, MAN!'

'Never do that again.'

'Of course, Miss Samantha.'

'Well, that was disturbing.' Maree said quietly, shuffling over to Ceirin. 'Hey, anything good on?'

'Reality TV. It's not the same when you're not in reality.' He sighed, lying back on his sleeping bag.

Maree also sighed, long purple pyjamas brushing the floor. 'Yeah, I guess. You don't really need TV when you're in a video game, though. Life's a TV show.'

Ceirin didn't answer, staring at the ceiling. Man, the Creator has a boring ceiling. How can he spend so much time staring at it?

'I miss my friends back home. My family, too,' he said eventually, looking for a more interesting distraction.

'I don't miss any of that,' she muttered, staring uninterested at the screen. 'As far as I'm concerned, they're not part of my life anymore. I left that world behind a long time ago.'

'Rough time in reality, eh?' Ceirin grinned, sitting up. After a battle with the rest of the group, he had been allowed to wear only his boxers, much to the pyjama-clad Creator's horror. Ellen and Maree just giggled every time the matter was brought up.

'More boring than anything. I never want to go back there.'

'Hey, you want some of this meaty biscuit rubbish the Creator gave me?' Sam asked Nick, shoving her nose in the cardboard box, and spilling biscuits everywhere as she tried to shake it off again. 'It's not as good as real meat, but it's crunchy!'

'Um... I'd rather not,' he said softly, creeping into the corner and laying his head on the carpet.

'Well, this isn't too bad.' Ellen said, smiling. 'It's nice, with everyone together like this.'

'I guess,' the Creator muttered reluctantly, hugging his knees to his chest.

'Maybe you can reschedule your battle or something. Then we'd have all night to relax!'

He smiled at her, but shook his head. 'No. We have to battle.'

'Why?'

'Because it has to begin.' He said quietly, bowing his head. 'But I don't know how it will end.'

'You're not making any sense…'

'We are connected. I can feel him. Calling me.' He said quietly, picking at some loose threads in the carpet. 'The game is in danger. You have to protect it.'

'Who else is in danger? Are any of us in danger?'

'It doesn't matter. Just protect the game.'

'But you guys are more important than that!'

'No!' The Creator said sharply, glaring at her. 'That's where they went wrong before, on our old world. They valued humans before the world they lived on. We cannot make that mistake! We can't let this world end up like that!'

'I'm sorry. I just thought…'

'It doesn't matter, as long as you don't forget.' He said coldly, not breaking their stare. 'You must always remember – no matter what the danger to ourselves, the game must always come first. It must always be that way!'

Ellen passed, staring at him. She nodded. 'I understand.'

Midnight arrived. In the sky above Destro, the sun and the moon met, cloaking the castle in darkness.

'The midnight eclipse,' muttered the Creator, getting to his feet. 'It's time.'

'I'm coming, I'm coming!' Ceirin sang, pulling on a pair on jeans. 'Just let me get my pants on!'

Both girls shivered as they stepped onto the rooftop, unwilling to touch the cold stone ground outside. Ellen had to run back and get her slippers before she even left the carpeted room.

Maree had, unwillingly, changed back to her black dress. Standing at the side of the dark arena, she looked invisible, and felt the same.

'I'm telling you, this is crazy," said the Creator, tossing Ceirin a pillow and taking his place near the end of the rooftop.

'This whole game is crazy.' Ceirin caught it, before pausing to turn his back-to-front t-shirt the right way round, hindered by the eclipse. 'Obeying rules, respecting some dodgy Council who aren't even trying to help us out anymore, going to all this trouble over some insults… face is, logic's just gone out the window.'

'Just? Logic leapt to its death the day this game went online.'

'Then came back as a ghost,' mumbled Ceirin, after a struggle. 'But you killed it with that freaky accent you used on Sam. After all of this is over, it'll come back again to avenge its ghosts.'

'…Why are we talking about this?' Asked the Creator, raising an eyebrow and smiling.

'It's called stalling. You'll learn to like it,' said Ceirin. 'That; and trying to get you to break the rules for once. You don't have to take part in this mania just because you're afraid of breaking a few rules.'

The Creator paused, before turning his head away. Realizing he'd just destroyed the happy mood, Ceirin distracted himself by looking up at the dark circle in the sky.

'How long does this thing go on for?'

'It will finish when we are ready,' the Creator replied patiently, holding his pillow tightly. He nodded to the sky, before doing the same to Ceirin. 'Let's do this.'

'Shall we duel as gentlemen?' Inquired the Creator, whipping round on his heel and taking a few steps forward. Ka-click. '...Apparently not.'

A gunshot rang through the air. Spinning round, the Creator followed it with a second, before ducking and missing a bullet. His opponent did the same, one of the Creator's guns in his hand.

'Touché,' the Creator said, smiling. Well, you've got to kick it off some-how.

'Still a thief at heart.' Ceirin said, grinning. "Pick-pocketing isn't a skill I'm likely to forget."

'Thief,' Maree repeated quietly, sitting next to Ellen as the moon lit up the arena once more. 'His old character class.'

'I know. I heard the Spirit helped train him.' Ellen said quietly. 'He was unbeatable.'

'He still is.'

'I wouldn't be so sure.'

Leaping forward, Ceirin slammed his pillow into the Creator. The gun fell to the ground.

'What?' Ceirin whispered, frowning as he stared up at the Creator. 'Why did you...?'

'Already, you appear to be beating me at my own game,' sneered the Creator, glancing at his falling pistol. 'Such a pity.'

'You dropped that on purpose!'

'And you hit an unarmed man. For shame,' he muttered disdainfully, shaking a finger at Ceirin. 'Now, I suppose I'll have to strike back in self defence. Very well.'

He kicked Ceirin hard in the stomach, throwing him against the ground. Then, he leapt away from the edge, pressing a boot into Ceirin's chest.

Maree and Ellen watched the fight in silence, feathers swirling around them in a miniature snowstorm. While Ellen watched both boys intently, Maree's gaze was more dreamy, uninterested in the battles around her.

'And the random continues...' said Maree, eyebrow remaining stub-bornly raised. Again, Ellen nodded. 'Talk about plot movement.'

'I actually think it's quite clever.' Nick said, rolling onto his back and waving his paws in the air. 'Ceirin's trying to get him to break the rules, but he's going one better by using them to his advantage.'

With identical, all-too-familiar raised eyebrows, Maree and Sam looked at him.

'What? Oh, I'm sorry, am I supposed to support my tamer in every little way?'

'Oh, come, come, now. Surely the Spirit's apprentice can do better than this?'

'You are such a self absorbed idiot!' Ceirin snarled, rolling free and getting to his feet, before whacking the Creator over the head with a pillow, and following it up with a fist.

'I'm anything but!' He replied lamely as he rubbed his head. 'I, sir, am a genius.'

'You're really going overboard with this whole English accent, aren't you?'

'I spent years trying to disguise my natural French one. Yes.' He growled, before leaping into the air and cart wheeling round, kicking Ceirin in the chin, before landing neatly on the ground.

'Beat that.'

Ceirin growled, raising a hand to his lips. A thin line of blood trickled from his mouth, but he ignored it.

'You're pathetic.'

The Creator paused, genuinely startled. 'Wh-what?'

'You couldn't even fight for a minute without bringing out those pistols.'

'You brought them out at the same time as I did!'

'Because I knew you'd have to use them – and you did.'

'You said that line! You were asking for it!'

'And then you tossed it off the building, aiming to use your signature weapon to worm you way out of it.' Said Ceirin, voice rising. 'Look at me, Creator! I don't even have a signature weapon!'

He glared at the Creator, circling him. 'But as soon as the battle starts, you had to break the rules! What is wrong with you?'

'Random, random, random.'

'…This is making my head spin…'

'I am the Creator. Rules are no barrier to me.'

'The only way you can win is by breaking them!'

'You're wrong,' he said sharply, voice dropping dangerously. 'I play this game as fairly as I can. Every day, I lose hundreds of battles, just for the sake of keeping the game running smoothly!'

'Then why are you cheating now?'

Lost for words, the Creator gave an applauded squeak. 'Me? You were the one who tried to get me to break the rules! I just took the high road and took advantage of them instead!'

'Yeah, because that's the only thing you can do. You won't take risks to achieve your goal, but you'll twist everything around you to get it!'

'Will you stop changing everything I say into some kind of twisted connection to your past! I say or do the slightest thing, and you go completely psycho!' said the Creator, face flushed. 'Just because I'm who I am, doesn't make me like him!'

'But who you are… is him.'

'Argh!' the Creator said with a muffled cry of anger. He only just managed to resist stamping his foot, realising childish tantrums were not the way to go.

'You asked for a fight, and I'm giving you one – to the best of my ability! I'm not going to fight you with pillows or any of that rubbish.

'Then we won't. We'll fight like men,' smirked Ceirin, before punching him hard in the side of the head.

The Creator didn't respond, clutching his head and falling to the ground. His eyes were cold as ever when he looked up again. He hissed a reply, but it was lost to Ceirin's ears.

'Speed, endurance and agility are your fields,' said Ceirin, not paying much attention to his words. 'Offence and Defence are mine. I can beat you!'

'Are you even listening to me?' The Creator exclaimed, getting back to his feet. 'This isn't a game, Ceirin! It's reality! How many times do you have to be told that before it finally registers?'

'It cannot be reality. If this wasn't a fantasy, then I wouldn't be hiding here.'

'What?' He asked, blinking, before slapping his forehead. 'Argh, you idiot!'

'We left reality behind a long time ago, Creator. No matter how hard you try, this world can never be real.'

'Shut up!' He yelled, taking his turn to punch Ceirin hard in the head, before kicking him in the chest as he cried out. 'You can't live in a dream, Ceirin! You've got to be part of reality!'

'All humans live in a dream. A dream that they live in reality.' Ceirin said quietly, grinning. 'Your world can never be perfect. As long as it has humans, it will have flaws.'

'Gyah…' the Creator gasped, doubling over. Regaining himself, he slammed a foot into the side of Ceirin's head.

'If this wasn't real, would you feel it?'

'This is a game. Our health goes down – 100% to zero. Then we die. There's no pain.'

With an angry, wordless cry, the Creator continued his vicious assault on Ceirin. The tamer didn't bother to fight back. Instead, Ceirin simply gasped, grabbing his head. Nick growled, and Maree placed a hand on his silky fur.

'There's nothing you can do. No dragon's allowed. If you try to help, the game will find a way to stop you.'

'But I've got to help him!' Growled the wolf, claws digging into the soft ground. 'Look at him! He can't take much more of this!'

'He'll have a plan.'

'What if he doesn't?' Barked Nick, glaring at her. 'What'll happen if that psycho biker shoots him? I thought you learned – all of this is real! What do you think will happen if he dies?'

'…I….' Maree trailed off, staring at Ceirin. Sam gave a low growl, as the Creator kicked him hard in the stomach.

'Get up! Fight me!'

Eyes narrowing, Maree grabbed the ocarina, raising it to her lips. The carvings on its surface glowed blue, as a haunting melody drifted through the field.

'What?' The Creator said softly, backing away into the middle of the field. He frowned, staring at the ground and listening to the music. 'The Ancient Ocarina…'

'Ceirin?' Maree said softly, stepping down next to him. The ocarina dropped from her hands, but continued its melody.

Blue eyes flashed angrily, as he stared up at her. 'You!'

He groaned, getting to his feet. 'Yeah?'

'Maree, get off the field.'

She paused, staring down at the ground. She twisted the ocarina's cord around her fingers, before letting it drop again and catching his eye.

'I don't think it really matters what I tell you, because you'll probably forget. But…'

'Get off the field!'

'Don't ever kiss me as a dare.'

'Don't make me hurt you!'

SMACK!

Ceirin fell back, as Maree's hand collided with the side of his head.

'GET OUT OF THE WAY!'

Grinning, Maree turned round to look at the Creator. The music abruptly cut out, and the ocarina shattered into pieces.

'…What?'

She glanced down, as a bullet fell among the shards. Only the magical instrument, now destroyed, had prevented its impact.

'Now get off the field.' Growled the Creator, right hand shaking as it gripped the pistol. 'Next time, I won't miss.'

Chapter 5:

Duplication

He hates the world, and most other humans. He wants them to feel the pain they've caused him.

But he doesn't want to hurt them.

He wouldn't try to hurt her.

Pulling on the strange cloak, Ellen stepped off the rooftop and retreated back into the castle. 'There's something wrong here.'

As he raised a hand to his cheek, Ceirin watched the bullet impact. With a canine growl, he leapt to his feet, stepping in front of Maree.

'You dirty…'

'Ah!' The Creator gasped, pain shooting through his chest. *The colours… they're… changing.*

'She wasn't part of this!'

'She… got in the way.' He muttered, forcing a smirk. *It's all wrong…*

'She wasn't doing any harm!'

'Destroy him.'

'What?' Ceirin whispered, staring at Maree. Her eyes were shadowed by her hair, almost black. Together with her dress, her skin seemed almost white.

'Nobody can stop it.' She whispered, falling backwards.

The sky became the ground. They fell.

The castle merged with trees. The garden flooded with clear water.

The sky turned crimson.

As the three children got to their feet, floor reflections stared back from the water. Alone in their separate worlds, they faced themselves.

'Still, she tries to evade us. She cannot escape us.'

Frowning, the Creator stepped over to the river. Dark clouds billowed through the water, not daring to touch his twisted reflection.

It's you again.'

'We needn't speak. Visions are quick, fleeting memories. Only actions last.'

Ceirin and his shadow stood back to back, as the world turned upside down. The water balanced vertically, like a mirror, its mass refusing to flow the way gravity commanded

'Hey.' Ceirin said quietly, failing his usual friendly grin.

'Welcome back.' His other self greeted, grinning psychotically.

'Leave me alone.'

'You cannot escape.'

'But you cannot control me.' Replied Ceirin, voice remaining level, but determined.

'If I can't, what happened that night on Destro?'

'You tried. I won.' Silently, Maree fell sideways, landing in the arms of another.

'What happened to me?'

'You did the right thing.'

'It all feels so wrong.'

'It feels amazing. The power. You'll get used to it, Maree.'

'I don't want it to be this way.'

'It must. You cannot fight us forever.'

The final reflection stood alone, fingertips pressing against the boundaries that held her. She frowned, crossing her arms and pacing through the world of darkness.

'What are you doing, shadow? Why aren't you here for me?'

As ripples spread from her fingertips, the true Ellen appeared, standing in front of pages of text.

'I think I understand.' She said, voice faded as it travelled to her duplicate. 'Reresan, run program: Infinite AVP.'

'Affirmative.'

'No!' Hissed the girl, clawing at Ellen. The image was destroyed, as was the whole world.

Grass, trees, stone walls, water and sky, all blurred together in a multi-coloured world. Then, the game seemed to smooth out, as the tamers returned to the rooftop arena.

* * *

'Maree? Maree, are you alright?'

'Mm? What is it, Ellen?' She muttered, opening her eyes to a bright blue sky. She closed them against, groaning. 'What happened?'

'Come on, get up!' She laughed, helping her to her feet.

Maree stared down at her jeans, still slightly disorientated. 'What happened to my outfit?'

'It's okay. It's over now.'

'...Beta...'

'Huh?' Ceirin said quietly, looking up as he heard a soft voice. A dark creature fell down onto the grass. 'What is that thing?'

Growling, Nick stood up from his side, stepping over to the fallen creature.

'Ta?' He said softly, round silver eyes blinking up at the wolf. 'Beta! Gyah! Danger! Bad danger! Big bad danger! Owie!'

Nick stared at the small creature in confusion, as it squealed and hid its head in its paws, curling up in a ball.

'Leave him!' Cried the Creator, stepping in front of the wolf.

The large wolf growled, as he stared straight at the teenager. 'What is that thing?'

'It's not important.'

'Beta?' The dark creature said quietly, stepping over to the Creator and pulling at his trouser leg. 'Master, I am.'

The programmer sighed, staring down at it. 'His name's Beta, first imp to appear in the game. He's an unstable program, too powerful.'

'What's he doing here?'

Beta grinned, opening his mouth. His master quickly clamped a hand over it. 'Nothing. He must have arrived here by acci-YEOWCH!'

'My master thought that you were cheating, so he asked me to help even out the playing field with my attacks.' Beta said quickly, before grinning and displaying rows of sharp white teeth.

Ceirin frowned, staring at the Creator. 'So basically, you cheated?'

'Does it really matter if I did? You've rarely been known to play fair yourself, Ceirin.' He shrugged, circling the imp and clutching his hand. 'I was simply returning the favour.'

'That's no excuse. You're in control of this game. You're meant to be responsible.'

'I was *testing* the Beta Imp.' The Creator growled between clenched teeth, lashing out and grabbing Beta by the arrow-ended tail. 'He failed. And all programs that pose a threat to the game must be destroyed.'

He paused, grinning at Ceirin. 'Tell you what… if you're so against this cheating lark, why don't you destroy him?'

'No. No, no no!' The small creature cried, staring at his master in horror. The Creator pulled a second pistol from his belt, tossing it to him. Both had been retrieved after he had awoken.

'You said this wouldn't happen! You said I wouldn't have to use my powers! You said *nobody* was going to get hurt!'

He glanced at Beta, shrugging. 'I lied.'

Ceirin paused, staring at the creature in his hands. 'What do I do, Nick?'

'Depends on whose logic you want – human or dragon.' The wolf sighed, sitting down next to him and folding his wings flat against his body.

'A human would probably beg you not to harm him. 'He's a living creature! Ohmigawsh, you can't hurt him! Especially not something that cute!'.' Nick squealed, turning one paw down and facing the other up. 'On the other paw, a dragon would tell you it's just like all the other creatures you killed in the process of levelling up. Another obstacle to destroy. As long as you give it a quick and painless death, it doesn't matter.'

Ceirin stared at Nick, troubled. His dragon smiled, winking at him. 'But a partner would remind you of that moment on Destro, when you finally realise this was more than just a game. We're all alive, Ceirin, and we all feel – pain, fear… if a human has experienced it, we probably have too. And a partner would be able to see that you don't want to hurt that imp. Drop the blade.'

Nodding, Ceirin did so, releasing the imp. It fell to the ground, sobbing.

'Fine.' Snarled the Creator, snatching him by the tail and pressing the pistol against his chest. 'If you won't destroy him, then I will.'

'BETA!' He cried, hanging upside down. 'Let me go!'

'You know the rules, imp.'

'It's not my fault!' He yelled, before ceasing his struggles and meeting the Creator's cold gaze. His voice gained an equally cold edge. 'How can it be? You created me. You made me like I am!'

'And so, I should have deleted you a long time ago.'

'No…' Ellen said under her breath, as Sam interrogated Maree about what had happened when the three humans had disappeared. She gave no answer – nobody did. Either nobody remembered, or those who did hid it.

'Creator, don't.' She said, eyes narrowing as she ran over and placed a hand on his. It was a command, not a request.

'Ellen, this isn't your field. You're out of your league.'

'No,' she repeated, shaking her head firmly. 'I restored your default character status, Creator. Without my help, you'd all still be out of character – mood swings, violence, the lot. You owe me.'

He paused, staring at the limp creature. Hanging upside down, Beta folded his arms and stuck out his tongue.

'Fine. Take the little rodent.' He muttered, tossing Ellen the creature. 'He'll only bring trouble to this game.'

Chapter 6:

Ellen's New Dragon

The Creator left, returning to the shadows of Destro Castle. Ellen, Maree, Ceirin, Nick, Sam, and Beta were all left outside.

It was mid afternoon now, and the bright orange sun was high in the sky. The only light that fell on Destro, however, bathed whatever it touched in a red glow.

'How long were we asleep?' Maree asked, glancing at Ellen.

'You weren't long properly sleeping – properly dreaming. Ten minutes, maximum. But I needed to keep you guys asleep to try and figure out why you all passed out. Plus, I thought you could all use a rest!'

'Did you find out what happened?'

'Not really,' she said, frowning. 'It was too complicated. I'll have to wait until it happens again – maybe things will make more sense then.'

'So, all you know is this thing's an imp?' Sam muttered to Nick, prodding Beta with a claw. He giggled, falling onto his back. 'Think it's edible?'

'The Creator would kill us.'

'Who cares? We could kill him, meat's meat,' she muttered, shrugging.

Nick stared at Sam, pawing the ground uncertainly. 'Hey, Sam. I think there's something you should know…'

'Oh, do tell. Are you suddenly a member of the 'hug-all-fuzzy-creatures' club?'

'No, I'm vegetarian,' he sighed, bowing his head.

'You what?'

'I'm a vegetarian. I don't eat meat.'

'You…don't…eat…meat?'

'No,' he said awkwardly, pawing the ground and blushing slightly. 'It's to do with me being a shape shifter. I've been so many different creatures – I can't bring myself to go about eating what I might have been before.'

Sam paused, taking a deep breath. Nick stepped away, hiding his head in his paws.

'LA-LA-LA-LA-LA I CAN'T HEAR YOOOOOUUUUUU! LA-LA-LA-LA-LAAAAAAA! I'M NOT LISTENING!'

He whined, and all the tamers and the imp covered their ears, crying out at Sam's singing.

'Sam, stop! …Please? I'll pay you *anything!*' Maree groaned, before quickly correcting herself. 'Well, as long as it's food.'

'Wha?' Sam asked, blinking as she saw her tamer open her mouth, but heard no words.

'It doesn't matter,' she said, shaking her head.

'So, as I was saying,' Ceirin muttered, glaring at the two dragons. 'There's not really much point in staying here. Nick and I were going to head to Sonok; we don't have any data on that for our Realm map. We've been surfing the forums, though, and a couple of people have said you're allowed to enter the area.'

'Well, Sam and I were wondering what's up with Frieze. You never hear anything about that place.' Maree murmured thoughtfully, smiling. 'I guess we could go for a look around there. See the sights.'

Ellen paused, staring up at Destro Castle. She couldn't see anything, but she could tell the Creator would be sitting somewhere on the castle rooftop. He'd be just as confused as the other two and he'd be the most determined to try and find out what happened.

Not being able to would just make it harder for him.

She looked down, as Beta stepped over to her.

'Where are you gonna go?'

'I don't know. Where would you like to go?' She asked, smiling at him.

'Wha? Me?' He asked, blinking. '...You can't ask me! It's not allowed! You've got to control me, silly!'

'Why? It's not like you're my servant or anything. Imps are just like dragons – you've got your own free will. So, where do you like to go?'

'Well,' he paused, hands behind his back and grinning nervously. '...I like games!'

'Fitting,' she muttered under her breath. 'What kind of games?'

'Ones with prizes are cool!' Beta said, jumping up and down. 'I like cuddlies!'

She laughed, as he hugged his own tail, going cross-eyed as he stared at its arrow-headed tip.

'What? Like, soft toys?' He nodded. She smiled, opening her rucksack and letting him hop in. 'Looks like we're heading to Fabrico, then.'

'Yay! A car! I wanna drive!'

'You heading off?' Maree asked, nodding to Ellen.

'Yeah. I'm taking a trip to Fabrico, I love that place,' she replied, grinning.

'Cool. I'm off to Frieze, and Ceirin's headed to Sonok. I don't know how long we'll be, but you can check the cave if you need us.'

'By the way,' Ceirin said quietly, stepping over to Ellen. 'Leave that imp here, will you? I'm not sure why the Creator thinks he's a danger to the game, but he normally has his reasons. If he sees you with it in the game... well, I don't think he'll be too happy.'

'Don't worry, I won't.' She said smiling as she walked away. She turned, as he called her back.

'Ellen?'

'Yeah?'

'If I were you, I'd tie up your rucksack.' He laughed, before climbing onto Nick and rising into the air.

She blushed, taking off her bag to see the imp hanging out of it. Muttering, she pushed Beta down and zipped up the top.

'Hey! Why'd all the lights go out?'

* * *

'Beta! Cut that out!' Ellen muttered, as they walked along the road to Fabrico. A loud scrabbling noise was coming from her bag, as claws scratched the material.

'What're you *doing* in there?'

'I'm trying to get comfortable.' The imp said, poking his head out from underneath a pile of sleeping bag and cloak. 'It's awfully stuffy in here.'

'I guess it must be,' said Ellen, pulling him out. 'Why don't you walk with me for a while?'

'Thanks, that nice of you,' he said, shyly. 'And I'll try to stay invisible. It's just that I don't like being ignored…'

'It's okay; you don't have to hide anymore. Where are you from, anyway? I haven't seen you around here before.'

'I don't know.' He said quickly, walking along beside her. His tail dragged along the ground, and his ears fell back as he spoke. 'All I remember is waking up and seeing the Creator. He was really good to me – he gave me food, games to play, everything. But I think I did something wrong… or maybe something bad happened to him. He started acting really strange, and I kept annoying him.'

'This was after summer, right? This year?'

'Yeah.'

'Weird. …Well, I guess it doesn't really matter. It's fixed now, whatever went wrong.'

'Was he ill?' Asked the imp, looking up at her. Instead of walking, he skated, hovering a few centimetres off the dusty track. 'Was that why they all fell over? Did they all get sick?'

She paused, confused by his words, until she remembered the three crumpling to the ground after Maree's words, as she watched from the safety of the castle.

'No. You know how you're all programs?' He didn't answer. 'Well, something went wrong with the game, and it affected us all. It shouldn't happen again.'

'I don't understand.' He said softly, shaking his head. 'I'm not a program. I'm an imp.'

'Yes. In a computer game.'

'No. I'm real, I know it!' He said firmly, glaring at her. 'My world's real!'

'I guess you don't understand as much about the game as the dragons.' Said Ellen, absent-mindedly stroking the furry silver and black imp's small, pointy ears. 'In a way, you're lucky.'

'Of course! I'm the luckiest lucky thing in a world full of luck and lucky things to spread the luck!' He cheered, smiling at her, before suddenly changing the subject.

'…Hey Ellen, why don't you have a dragon?'

'Oh…' said Ellen, pausing. Her smile disappeared, and she looked away from Beta.

'I'm sorry, did I say something bad?' Beta said worriedly, looking up at Ellen.

'No, no, it's not your fault, you didn't know. My dragon's dead, she died not long ago.'

'Do you miss her?' He asked softly. *I didn't understand what she was saying about programs… but I understand about dying. That doesn't make any sense…*

'A lot.'

Beta was silent for a while, thinking.

'If you want, I could be your dragon. I can protect you!' He said, grinning.

'Thanks, Beta. That's really sweet of you,' said Ellen, giving the imp a cuddle.

'Hey! You're not meant to cuddle your dragon,' he said. 'I need taming!'

'Of course you do. I'd hate to think what would happen if you turned wild,' she said soothingly, smiling at him.

'RAWR IS THE TAGLINE!'

They continued walking for a few hours. Eventually, Beta became bored and hid in Ellen's bag. She was left to walk in silence, lost in her own thoughts.

'What are you doing in there, Beta?' Asked Ellen. There was a pause before he answered.

'Ellen, is e-mail a game?' Beta said eventually.

'Oh no, you're not...' said Ellen, taking off her bag and opening it. He was. Beta was sitting inside the bag, looking guilty, with Ceirin's PDA in his hands.

'I was only looking for a game to play,' he said defensively, seeing her expression.

'Beta, those e-mails are private! You're not meant to look at them!'

'There's one here about you,' he said, poking the screen. 'See? That one!'

'There is?' Asked Ellen curiously. Seeing Beta's glare, she said hastily: 'It's only to check you haven't tampered with it!' She snatched it off him, and opened the e-mail.

Report – Fear Fork Area Completion

After the data was received, stating player Ellen's fear of spiders, an area was created to take advantage of this.

It is simply a dark clearing with webs everywhere. It's a basic design, so I doubt it'll cause much trouble for you to program into the game. You can just use the 'Fear Forest' area as a template, but darken the trees slightly.

As soon as she enters she will become stuck on a web, an easy target for the Giant Spider (the Black Widow, Dokugumo) living in the clearing.

It should be successful in defeating Ellen and, by doing so, her dragon as well. Dokugumo's A.I. had been set unusually high, and it's H.P. too high for the player (whose stats were recently edited so they were high enough to be in the top 20, and let the Destroyer's minions capture her and take her there).

She has, as expected, escaped them, and we are now in

Destro Gardens.

However, I have 2 questions to ask:

1. Why were the fighters that attacked in Destro Plains not instructed to leave me? I was badly injured.

2. What shall happen to me after I am put into the Fear Fork area?

That is all.

Apprentice Ceirin — 2nd Strongest Dragon/Tamer Partnership

Reply from 'The Creator':

Well done. If successful, both of the pairs shall die. But be on your guard, there is a chance they may escape.

As for you, do not worry about Fear Fork, just follow your path.

'Apprentice' Ceirin! He was working for the Creator!

Ellen threw the PDA to the ground, and ran off, before she heard a voice calling her.

'Ellen! Wait! Don't be mad! I didn't mean to upset you!' Squeaked the imp, picking up the PDA and running after her. Ellen turned round and saw how upset he was.

'Where did you get the PDA?'

'Easy,' he said, eager to please her. 'There's this thingy called 'glitching' I learned. It's cool, you do it, and the game goes all funny, and cool stuff happens!'

'Isn't that like breaking the game?'

'Nah, 'course not; I can only do that when the area's already broken'

She frowned, raising an eyebrow at him. Then she saw what was behind him.

Quickly, she grabbed Beta and stuffed the PDA into her bag, throwing on her cloak so that it would disappear. Something was tearing along the road to Fabrico, a huge funnel of wind, like a tornado. She felt the cloak rip as her invisiwings broke through, and she started running, with her wings beating quickly to boost her speed.

Her feet started to lift off the ground, as she found herself heading into Fabrico. Behind her, she could hear the roar of the tornado.

Then, everything around her froze.

'Wh-wh-at's happening?' Said Beta.

'I'm not sure...' Ellen said, stepping back as the world in front of her flattened and stood vertical, like a wall.

'Not th-' Beta said, interrupted by a loud beeping from the wall. A white message appeared on a blue background:

PAGE_FAULT_IN_NONPAGED_AREA

* * *

Then the screen went completely blue, the beeping stopped, and the roaring of the tornado started again as the screen started moving closer, making anything it touched two-dimensional.

At that moment, a lot of things flashed through Ellen's mind: All she had heard about tornados, all she had seen on the news, and those films which showed exactly what damage they could cause.

Then, the times the blue screen had crashed her computer when she had nearly finished a homework assignment but forgotten to save, when she was just about to finish some of her favourite games, and when she had joined Dragon Tamers. With it, came memories of anger, random button pressing, kicking anything that beeped, and begging her computer to work again.

Then she ran... Towards the tornado.

As she ran towards the roaring wind, she turned suddenly to the right. It followed her, moving with surprising speed to her new position.

'What kind of tornado is this?' She asked, sidestepping again to the left, as the tornado copied her. Finally, she gave up, and walked straight into it.

Again, the game froze, but this time the tornado was moving and she couldn't. She was blown around in circles, her feet never touching the ground. Eventually, she was blown into the centre of the tornado and, though her feet hovered oddly above the ground and wouldn't fall, she found she could move again.

Something blew into her face, and she brushed it aside in time to see that something else was in the tornado. All she could see was a shadow, an outline that blended in with the roaring grey wind around it. It was following the tornado, moving around in circles without tiring.

She didn't know what is was, but, like almost everything in the game, it was making her amulet glow. She glanced at it, and noticed it seemed a different glow to its normal amber light. The gold band around the amber crystal was shining even brighter than the stone itself, creating a bright yellow glow.

* * *

When she awoke, she found herself lying in the middle of the portal area. There was no sign of the strange tornado, the area was completely empty. Where was Beta?

Oh no...

Chapter 7:

The Crystal Clan

After flying for a while, Nick and Ceirin split away from Sam and Maree and headed for Sonok.

'It's huge, isn't it?' asked Ceirin, staring at the islands scattered below. Nick nodded, wing beats slowing in the cold air.

As the temperature continued to plummet, Nick swooped lower down. Miles of snow-covered land stretched below them, a white world. But this world contained life.

Something about that seemed wrong to Ceirin. *Why did he remember this world as a flat place? Why did he remember it as a dead world?*

The sky was covered in white clouds, dropping both snow and shards of crystal onto the land below. Huge icicles hung from tree branches, and stalagmites stabbed at the sky.

'Yes. So quiet and peaceful.' Nick replied, longing in his eyes. He had been too busy swooping below a tree to reply earlier, sending a whirl of crystal leaves through the air.

'It won't be like that for long. You know the rules of recruiting.'

Tamers, to go with their special class, were given certain extra options when playing the game. Not only could they appear offline when online, and invisible in crowds of players, but they could also set the game not to show any of the ordinary players in the world around them – to play in a separate, private server. It was the safest option to use in busy areas of the game, where the appearance of the Dragon Tamers could cause quite a stir.

Once, Ceirin had watched Maree use the invisibility option in a crowd of people. They had all acknowledged her presence, stepping aside, but no one actually realised she was there. With a cloak on, you would normally have to be careful not to make too much sound or collide with another player.

Nick continued flying lower, careful to avoid trees, but unwilling to fly too high in case of rain. At least lower down, there were trees and the occasionally archway to act as shelters.

Recruiting was a strange business. To recruit, and to fix problems in the game (though in the latter case they often sent all the players offline), they had to return to the normal game.

They landed on the cold ground, looking around for some kind of portal. Sweeping away some of the snow, he found the ground to be a smooth, glassy surface.

'Where are we?' Ceirin asked, staring around uneasily. *We've landed. There should be players here. Where is everyone?*

'I don't think this area was part of the original game. It isn't on the map.' Nick commented, referring to the map he and Ceirin has been working on before their adventures began. 'I think the Creator or the

Council must have added it quite recently.'

'I'm sure he does all that just to make it hard for us.' Ceirin moaned. Nick glared at him angrily. 'Don't glare at me. I'm not the one in the wrong.'

'Look! You've had your fight! Now will you forget about it?' Nick snapped, growling. He was more irritated by the cold than anything else, chilling the skin on the bottom of his paws and leaving painful ice trapped between his pads.

'It wasn't a proper fight if someone cheated.' Ceirin said defensively, slipping on a pair of snowboarding gloves.

'But you didn't cheat, and you didn't lose!'

'But I didn't win, either! We never even finished our battle!' He yelled, eyes narrowing as he glared at his own partner.

Nick sighed exasperatedly. 'Look, he isn't even causing you harm any-more! Can't you just forget about it?'

'I'm not going to forget about it! I'll never finish making him pay for what he did too me!'

'It wasn't his fault! He was possessed!' Nick barked, suddenly defensive of the Creator.

'WHO'S SIDE ARE YOU ON?' Ceirin exclaimed, glaring at Nick.

His dragon looked away, his tail drooping between his legs.

'The side I want you to be on. The side where you're happy,' he said quietly, bowing his head and flattening back his ears.

'How can that ever happen, when the world's turned against me?' Ceirin hissed, turning on his heel and stepping away behind a row of teeth-like stalagmites and stalactites.

Nick sat down, alone in the snow. He remembered this feeling – the one where he couldn't figure out how his tamer was feeling. The last time he had felt that was when he changed from his true form to a shape shifter. Was he going to change once more?

After a few minutes, he realised how quiet it had become, and stood up.

'Ceirin?' Nick called. No answer.

'Ceirin? Where are you?' Still no answer. Ears flattening down, Nick stepped over to the cave mouth. He attempted to see through the ice, but all he could see was white.

A small, uncertain whimper rose from him, as he pawed the ground. 'Ceirin?'

Staring round untrustingly, he stepped through the icicles. As far around him as he could see, there was white.

The white moved.

As the white clothed people swarmed behind the wolf, blocking the entrance, three hundred players drew their weapons.

* * *

Ceirin watched, helpless, as his dragon was captured. The silver wolf howled, as hundreds of icy shards hit his fur. Thousands upon thousands of glassy shards dug into his fur, in a storm of cold diamond daggers.

Suddenly, there was a pause in the attacks. Nick fell to the ground with a whine, blood staining his fur and the snow.

Eyes narrowing, he stared up at the white-clothed figure all around them. A low growl escaped his throat, followed by a single bark, directed at all the dragons in the crowd. *'Tamer!'*

One of the attackers, a small male polar bear, paused as it shattered an icicle with its mind. It tugged at its tamers skirt. *Such authority and knowledge... he is an old dragon, a wise one. We should not be harming him.*

She looked down on him, blue eyes meeting his. She nodded, waving a hand at the rows of dragons and tamers around her.

Nick watched, eyes meeting all the dragons around him in turn, as the blue-haired girl ran over to a male player.

'Lenia?'

'Sir, I think you should see this one,' she said quietly, giving a small bow to the boy. He was younger than Ceirin, but held much more authority. Brown eyes should have shown warmth, but coupled with his dark clothing, showed only darkness.

He stepped into the centre of the players, and many of them bowed as he passed. Mild curiosity brought him to Ceirin, ignoring the canine lying on the cold snow.

'What are you doing on the Crystal Isle?'

'Who cares? It's a free game.' Ceirin snarled, as the gag was torn from his mouth. His hands remained bound, rope stinging his skin. 'More importantly, why is this group ganging up on players? That's not fair. It's against game rules.'

'Not true. It's allowed,' he contradicted, resisting the urge to grin. His expression remained cold, afraid to show emotion in front of the crowd. 'This is our island, after all.'

'What?'

'Look, how long have you been playing this game?' He sighed, shaking his head. 'The only way to enter this area is to surrender to me. I rule this place.'

'That can't be right. The Council wouldn't allow it!' Ceirin replied sharply, glaring straight at the ruler. Behind him, he saw Nick struggle to his feet.

As he stared at Climax, his grey eyes grew dark. *The Council... they wouldn't...*

'Yeah, *right*. The Council were the ones who let us in this place,' he smirked. 'We're against humanoids. So are they. We're against magic casters. So are they. We destroy those players. They allow us. Simple.'

'In other worlds, the Council has this whole area under its claws.' Nick growled, stepping in front of Ceirin. 'You get this game's players on your side, destroying all humanoids – all dragons with any connection or fondness for humans. Then, they destroy your entire group, and all the humans in this game.'

It's true... all the rumours were true. Nick thought, momentarily turning his head away and glancing at the hundreds of dragons around him. *The Council are no longer to be trusted. They've grown corrupt.*

Is there nobody in this world who can use power responsibly?

'They can't do that!' The brown-haired boy exclaimed, doubt in his voice. He wasn't used to talking to a dragon as he would a human. 'Then there'd be nobody left to play the game!'

'Do you really think they'd care?' Nick answered sharply, showing his teeth. 'Now, who are you?'

He paused, startled by the question, but answered nonetheless. 'The name's Climax. Who're you two?'

'Nick.' Replied the wolf, before nodding to Ceirin. 'And that's my tamer, Ceirin.'

Climax paused, shock in his eyes. 'You're kidding, right?'

'Nope. Ceirin and Nick. Strongest duo in this game.' Ceirin replied, grinning.

'Prove it,' he laughed, pulling a whip from his belt and letting it uncurl. Its thin tip touched the ground, carefully designed to be able to slice through skin if needed.

'Fine,' Ceirin said, pulling the harmoniknife from its sheath and tossing it at Climax.

He paused, examining it from all angles, before tossing it back. 'Fake.'

Ceirin plucked it out of the air, frowning.

'What do you mean?'

'It's just a cheap imitation. It doesn't even have a blade.'

Nicks ears flattened back, tail straight out behind him. His upper lip was curled slightly, showing gleaming fangs.

'You want proof? Fight us.'

'You'll regret that challenge. In strength, I'm the strongest player in this game.'

'But all-round, Ceirin and I are more powerful than you can ever dream of.'

'We'll see about that.' Climax muttered, cracking the whip on the ground. The Crystal Clan swept to the sides, leaving a clear path towards the three.

Grinning confidently, Ceirin put a hand on Nick. The fur was damp with blood, but that didn't stop the wolf grinning back at him.

'Let's show this kid the power of a *real* dragon tamer!'

Chapter 8:

Experimenting

The Creator turned away from his computer screen, and looked out the window.

This was all so complicated...

On various screens, he had pictures of the amulet, failed attempts at duplicating its coding, and screens upon screens of iZ's data.

I've almost finished designing his physical form. I've finished his programming. I've done everything that should be done to get him running again.

Except find a power source.

As he stared out at the dark sky, the moment on the rooftop returned to him. That one moment, when his best friend had held a gun against his chest, and pulled the trigger.

Why? For him. To save him from the darkness?

His death had been in vain.

He had destroyed him, that was obvious. Not by his own hands, but Izzy's death was still his fault.

However, it had been the amulet that had given him the ability to make that decision. To choose to make that sacrifice. Somehow, the item with the coding of a living being had taught iZ how to live again.

He froze, as one monitor flashed into light. It played a loud, musical tune, to wake him up if he'd fallen asleep at they keyboard again.

On the screen appeared Ellen, standing at the doorway. Her hair had been swept over her face by a strong wind, but it fell back to reveal panic in her eyes.

'Ellen? Why are you at my workshop?' He asked, staring at her with disbelief.

Aw, great. She'll be using that battle as another excuse for anger management lessons.   I know it!

'Can I come in? There's something I need to do,' she said into the monitor. Her hair fell back, to reveal panic in her eyes.

Gah! I was wrong! These TAMERS are destroying my IQ!

'Fine. Come up,' he muttered with false reluctance, instantly pressing the button and opening the doors.

She walked into the first corridor, where the path forked, and headed down one of them. She walked some distance down to a certain place, she touched a part of the wall (a strange mix of stone and metal) and it quickly melted away. She hopped through, as it closed even more quickly behind her.

'How did you find that?' He asked, surprised.

'The Spirits minions kept me in Serta for a long time. I'd almost finished reading the rulebook, and was looking around the pyramid when I discovered a hidden door. All the hidden doors look slightly different from the rest of the wall, and they're quite easy to spot if you know where to look.' She paused, frowning. 'I thought we'd be able to use it to escape. Few made it out of the area... most of us were caught and killed. It's lucky they sent Crystal and I back.'

'I'll have to work on that...' he mumbled, slightly annoyed that she could find it. He didn't comment on her words, knowing it was more than luck that spared her life. 'What are you here for, anyway? It had better be important.'

'It is...' She said sadly, taking Beta out from her rucksack. He had been pixelated: simplified into solid, coloured squares and made two dimensional.

'What happened to him?' The Creator asked, frowning as he picked up the flat creature.

'I'm not sure. We were walking along to Fabrico and a tornado appeared. The game froze and everything in front of me went two dimensional - like a normal game - and a blue screen appeared. I ran towards the tornado, and it brought me to the portal area and disappeared. I think Beta might have been affected when the game crashed.'

'Stepping into a tornado instead of a blue screen...wise choice,' he said, with a grin. Her mood didn't pick up, so he continued on a more serious note. 'But I don't know what could have caused it, there's no tornado's in the game. I was going to use one to protect Destro, but it made it difficult for me to get in as well.'

He led Ellen down into another room. After entering a password into a panel on the wall, part of it slid away to reveal a glass capsule. As he placed Beta in it, it slid shut and filled up with fluid.

'Restore backup files from October 2nd,' he commanded, before turning to Ellen. He paused, glancing around their current room, before walking back along into a lounge.

'Beta should be fine in a short while.'

'What were you doing before I arrived? You seem kind of busy.'

'Working on iZ,' he said, as they sat down on a couch. He paused, glancing at her amulet, before quickly turning away.

'How is he?' Asked Ellen, remembering their brief encounter before his sacrifice.

'His visual appearance is improving, his programming is complete; it just needs loaded into his system. The components are the only thing giving me trouble, but I've been able to repair most of the damaged parts with some help from people in the real world.'

He paused, as a message appeared on a monitor. He quickly closed it, before leaving the room. At the doorway, he turned and looked back at her. 'Stay here.'

'Where are you going?' Ellen asked, confused by his inability to sit still.

'It doesn't concern you. Please, stay here until I call you back,' the Creator instructed firmly.

Ellen looked at him with concern, as he left. The door slid shut behind him, locking with a telltale 'click'.

'Whoa. Just watching him makes me tired,' said Ellen, leaning back on the couch. Her vision blurred slightly, and she yawned.

Behind, she heard a bird swoop close by the window. Something hit the cold floor with a soft thud.

She closed her eyes, and drifted away...

The village was almost silent, save the footsteps of the Princess as she headed for the forest.

It's market day tomorrow. *Ellen was informed by a voice in the head, the same voice she spoke with whenever she opened her mouth. Opal's voice.* All of my people are working hard, preparing their foods. We are not like you humans – we do not eat. All the foods we need can be grown, or gathered from the surrounding area.

Ellen was silent; her now furry feet stepped over a wooden bridge. She could feel everything, but she couldn't control it – Opal's moves were her own.

The forests give us nuts and berries, while the river supplies water to our wells. Our life is simple, but a happy one.

Now, the path was fading, overgrown by plants and roots. Ellen stumbled often, as the trail was overgrown by forest.

I am a healer. I came here in search of medicine ingredients.

She paused, crouching down in front of a large, green bush. Unwillingly, she placed a hand on a leaf. Its fuzzy surface was made sticky by thick, dark blood.

I found much, much more...

A yell tore through the air of both vision and reality.

Snapping awake, Ellen turned towards the source of the cry. As power failed throughout the castle, the lock opened. Smoke was spreading through the castle, from a room she'd never been in before.

It was large, filled partially with monitors. All their screens were black now, dead. But the flaming container in the corner was very much alive with electricity.

She ran through, in time to see sparks flying from the capsule. The creator was yelling in pain, his hair standing on end as bolts of electricity shot everywhere.

'What's happening?' Shouted Ellen. 'What should I do?'

'Nothing!' He grunted, his fists clenched in pain, and his fingernails cutting through his gloves and into his skin. 'I can handle this!'

'But-'

'No! Leave everything alone!' He interrupted, determination shooting through his voice like the currents through his body.

Next to the capsule, a single monitor remained on. It showed iZ's skeleton, gaining skin and hair as she watched. The Creator nodded to it, as the mirror image of himself – outfit, hair, an exact duplicate - appeared.

'Now...' He said softly, turning back to the girl. 'Step away from the machine.'

Ellen obeyed, running out to the doorway.

'Go further, to the Snake Guardian. He will know how far.' He instructed.

Ellen ran down the many flights of spiralling stairs as fast as she could, hearing a crackling behind her as something caught fire. She slipped as she went and started rolling roughly down the last few steps. She got up and continued running through the gardens. The snake was standing in one of them, sitting up on his tail and watching the window expectantly.

In the workshop, amidst all the heat and smoke, the creator was standing still in the middle of the capsule.

I will never forgive myself for the pain I have caused… but it helps soothe me if I in return feel pain.

However, my anger still remains, an anger that I feel for no reason. And this anger must be released.

He focused on the centre of the glass screen. There was no weak point on the machine, but he needed something to aim for.

He gathered all his anger, and felt it course through his body. Then, he kicked.

Glass flew through the air, a flurry of sharp shards.

He walked through them and into the thick black smoke that filled the workshop.

'Attention.' He said calmly. 'Destro Castle Emergency'.' He took in a mouthful of air, and crouched down to the ground so he could breathe easier. 'Protect all computers and workbenches. Keep all doors and widows clear.' His commands were received, and loud clangs echoed around the castle as shields were brought down in every room.

Using the sounds of the shields and smoke direction as a guide, he made a plan of the room in his mind and figured out where the window was.

Some of his clothes had caught fire now, but he had stopped feeling anything. The numbness was all over his body, and it was getting harder and harder to move.As he crawled to a certain position, he looked at his torn and burnt clothes and his black hands, and realised what a mess he was in. He knew what was going to have to happen.

'What's he doing?' Asked Ellen.

'Preparing.' The snake said, staring intently at the window where all the smoke was coming out of. 'Sssstand back.' He spread his hood out fully, covering his face.From out of the window leapt the creator, completely black and with a lot of him on fire. He rushed through the air, propelled by the run he had made before jumping, before starting to fall to the ground.The snake moved forward, catching him in his hood and lowering him to the ground.

'Good catch, guardian,' he mumbled, coughing. He sat up on the hood, hands digging into the snake's skin, eyes closing against his will.

'You've usssssssssed too much energy…' said the guardian, voice gentle. 'I'm aware of that. I have prepared for what is to come,' he said quietly, so Ellen couldn't hear. *'You know what you must do.'*

'Can you stand?' Asked Ellen, staring at him with concern.

'After that kick? No.' He replied simply, though Ellen wasn't sure what kick he was talking about. 'Can you look after Destro for a while?'

'Why? What's happening?'

'Nothing you have to worry about,' he said, as the snake guardian retracted his hood to reveal a set of different fangs, small and even thinner than a needle.

'You shouldn't be here to see this. I cannot let you watch,' he frowned, and suddenly Destro seemed to spin slightly.

'What are you doing?' Asked Ellen nervously, as the boy took a breath and held out his arm, shaking.

'I'm sorry,' he said quietly. 'About this, Fear Fork, everything. I'm sorry.'

The walls changed places, and Ellen found herself on the other side. Confused, she tried to figure out what was happening.Then, there was a loud hiss and a cry of pain, as the snake struck.

Chapter 9:

Freizing Cold

Silence dominated the flight, thicker than the clouds all around them. By now, Maree was almost asleep on her dragon's back.Sam had been flying for a while, but her tamer's lack of strength worried her. Ever since the party, she'd spent too much time sleeping and not enough time playing the game.They'd seen players like this. Falling asleep at the keyboard, playing through the night. But how could an unhealthy addiction to the game still be affecting her, after all that had happened? She didn't even battle anymore…It didn't make any sense.

'This is nice,' said Maree eventually, stirring and glancing upwards as snow fell on her skin. There wasn't much they could say to each other. They were so closely connected, all that needed to be said was already known.

'Yeah. Which is why I don't trust it.' Sam replied darkly.

'You know, it could be Christmas over in the real world, and we would-n't know.'

'The snow is getting bad…' Sam muttered, leaving Maree in her own little world. The snow was picking up speed and it was getting heavier. A strong wind was also blowing. 'We should get out of this!'

'It would be fun, giving each other presents.' Maree said quietly, lost in a daydream.

'Will you *please* concentrate!' Sighed Sam. 'I think we're going to be caught in a blizzard!' Maree blinked, shaking her head clear.

'You're kidding, right?' Sam shook her head. 'Then…we better land!'

'I'm trying, but I can't see a thing!' Yelled Sam, struggling against the wind. 'We're going to have to fly lower!'

'Don't worry! We'll make it!' Maree cried reassuringly, flattening her-self against Sam. The wind blew in their eyes, icy flakes stinging the human's skin and soaking her clothes.

They both landed on a huge iceberg, floating on top of the grey sea. It nearly flipped over as Sam dug her claws into it, skidding to a halt on its snow-topped surface.

They were both still for a moment, adjusting to the cold. It was hardest for Maree, in only jeans, shirt and fleece jacket, but she didn't show it.

'The weather only seems to be getting worse,' she observed eventually, gazing round the partially frozen wasteland. They had to be close to land, as slabs of ice stretched away into the distance in a broken path, but there didn't seem to be much hope of them getting there for a while.

'The quickest way now is to swim.' Samantha said softly, staring up into the sky.

'We can't swim in that! It's freezing!'

'Only on the surface. The deeper we go, the warmer the water becomes.'

'But I can't breath underwater.' Maree said quietly, frowning.

'You can as long as you stay with me.'

Maree stared uncertainly at the grey sea, obviously unwilling to touch it. 'How far do you think we have to go?'

'I don't know. But we can do it,' reassured the water dragon.

They caught each other's eyes, and Sam gave Maree a reassuring nod. Her round eyes showed only confidence. *They'd be fine.*

Maree nodded back, and Sam dived into the water, her movement smooth and graceful. Maree paused at the edge, staring at her reflection in the darkness.

I won't let it be like my old life. I won't be afraid of adventure.

She closed her eyes, and dived under.

The water was cold...so cold. It was a change to the warmer waters she'd been swimming in before. She rose quickly to the surface and took a deep breath.

'Are you sure you can handle this temperature?' Asked Sam, floating lazily nearby.

'Yes. It just takes some getting used to.' Maree replied.

'Be careful. We don't know these waters,' warned Sam, swimming forward.

They swam on the surface for a long time, as the weather kept getting worse. Before long, they could see as well on the surface of the water, as they could earlier in the air. The snow was everywhere and the wind was causing some large waves to form.

'Do you think we've gotten lost?' Shouted Maree over the roar of the wind. Already, she was shivering uncontrollably, but the weather distracted her partner from her condition.

'I'm not sure!' Yelled Sam. 'There's so much water, we could have swam to the edge of Tropica and not noticed!' 'We should dive under now. We'll be able to see more!'

Maree swam towards Sam, struggling against the waves. She reached the dragon, and held on tightly as they went under the water.

Even underwater, they could barely see. It was dark and murky, with the bottoms of huge icebergs floating everywhere.

'Why is it so dark?' Asked Maree, speaking clearly thanks to Sam's powers.

'There's something in this water,' replied Sam, frowning.

'Can we get out of the water and fly?'

'I could.' Sam said, rising again to the surface and spreading her wings.

Maree tried to summon the Phoenix wings. She hoped it would work with the feather in her bag, not her hands. 'LinksofChain!' She said quickly. The wings quickly sprouted from her back, and she started beating them quickly, trying to rise into the air. They beat limply, soaking her with water.

'They won't work,' said Sam. 'They've been soaked in the water.'

'Can't you carry me again?'

'Normally I could, but the wind's too strong here; we'll have to keep swimming. Stay at the surface, I don't like the look of this water.'

They kept on forward, Maree with her wings pushing her forward only slightly more than she could on her own. Eventually, she got rid of them altogether, so she could swim more quickly. Every so often, Sam would dive down and reappear even more worried. As they went forward, the water got darker, and dead fish began to appear near the surface.

'If only some were still alive…I could try speaking with them, finding out what's wrong here. This area shouldn't be like this, the creator wouldn't do that.'

'This isn't right.' Maree whispered, as a fish floated past, lifeless eyes staring into the sky. 'We've got to go back.'

'We can't.'

'We have to. I can't go any further.' Maree mumbled, voice incoherent and unclear. 'I can't swim. I can't swim, Sam.'

Sam froze, spreading out her wings as she lost the ability to stay afloat. *What dark magic is this?*

'Sam? What's happening?' said Maree, trying to grab hold of her.

'I don't know! I can't stay afloat!' She cried, splashing wildly. It was no use. *Something was pulling them under.*

As they sank like stones, Sam noticed something lower down in the water. Where the water was darkest, she could see it moving, spinning round. It was pulling them towards it. She tried to swim towards Maree, who was holding her breath as she fell, also trying to reach her. Struggling against the force that was pulling them down, they managed to grab hold of each other, as the dark water surrounded them. The water was darker than most of the seas on earth. The dead creatures were all around them, pulled by the current. Sam was with her now, when before it had been only her going under.

It was still the same.

It's happening again…

But the Council couldn't save them this time.

Chapter 10:

Makeover

'What did you do to him?' Asked Ellen quietly, walking around Destro to where the garden had been moved. In it sat the snake guardian, and next to him the Creator, lying still on the ground.

'A ssssimple injection,' he hissed, pulling his hood back into his head after changing his fangs back to the normal set.

'What of?' Asked Ellen nervously, staring at his unmoving body.

'Anaessssssthetic,' he replied. Ellen breathed a sigh of relief. He was sleeping.

The guardian slid his fangs back into his mouth, and picked up the boy with surprising gentleness. He slid through the door and up into the stairs, taking up all the room in the narrow spirals. This really didn't matter, as Ellen took care to stay as far behind as she felt was safe from the huge creature. He went further and further up, through a passageway to an area Ellen hadn't been to before.

There are so many rooms I've never been to before... I really need to take a better look around this place.

It led to a bedroom, plainly not often used, with a single futon in the middle of a stone floor, covered in what was either a bed sheet of a very thin blanket. There was only just enough room for the two of them, and the guardian had to curl up tightly in the corner.

'Wow. I wouldn't like a bedroom like this. It's so cold and empty,' said Ellen, shivering as a wind blew in from window.

'He rarely comessssss up here. He tendssss to ssssssssleep on the floor of the worksssssshop, in a computer chair, on the keyboard, wherever he issss at the time. He rarely ssssleepssss at all, he believessss you don't need to sssssssleep in a game.'

'But he does! This game world is as real to us as Earth is to all the other humans!'

'He knowsssssss that. It is sssssssimply an excusssssse to pussssh himsssssself harder.'

'I'll fix this room. There are a lot of things here that need changing.' Ellen said thoughtfully, looking around the bare chamber.

'I don't think that'ssssss wise...'

'I'm the one in charge here!' She snapped, glaring at him. Then she smiled, laughing, but his response was still one of annoyance.

'Whatever you sssssay, missssstressssss,' the snake guardian hissed sourly, shaking his head.

Ellen took out Ceirin's PDA, and pulled a socket from it, inserting it into the floor. It shouldn't have gone into the stone floor, but somehow it did. It was one of the things only the privileged few Dragon Tamers staff members knew how to do – turning any plug into a portal to another world.

'I sssssshall leave you,' the guardian said, picking up the Creator in one of his tails and slithering away.

'Tamer identification: Ellen. Access the data for this room,' she commanded. Ripples spread from the plug, warping the stone floor like water. Before she could blink, she found herself in the programming world – at least, it was called a world. But, like the Tamers-Only area, it was simply a mirror of Dragon Tamers with some changes added. It used to be so complicated only the Creator could enter. But, together with Ellen, they created a much simpler layout. Replacing text with graphics, and a keyboard with thoughts, it allowed any part of the game to be manipulated simply by thinking. The world's delicate structure picked up thought waves, focussing on certain keywords and hearing them as commands.

Before someone entered, they would have to decide which area they wanted to change. They could choose the whole of Dragon Tamers, but this was often too hard to work on. Smaller areas were much easier to program – Destro, Destro Castle, even, as Ellen was in right now, just one small room. To add or remove something required a lot of mental strain. You should never stay in there for long, but the Creator did. The strain on his mind was yet another way of punishing himself, and at the same time he could work on repairing some of the damage he had caused. It was always a risky game. Trying to control a big area could save someone's life, but at the same time, it could drive you completely insane.

First, you had to think about what you were going to do - making sure it would make sense when it was actually created, thinking about how it would look, etc. Then, you had to picture it in your mind as clearly as possible – the world would pick up on this powerful thought and add it to the mirror. Then you could look at it, test it, and even remove it. If it was still there when you left the world, it would be in the normal game as well.

Ellen wasn't sure how long she spent in that area – hours, minutes, days; it was so hard to tell. She was the only thing authorized to move here, so clocks wouldn't work. But time had to pass – she could only handle so much at a time. She replaced the stone floor with a carpet, the futon bed into a polished wooden bed frame with a mattress, quilt, and pillows. She replaced the mere hole in the wall with a double glazed glass pane. It didn't suit the castle, so she replaced it with stained glass; letting coloured light slip through into the room.

She replaced the ceiling with a glass dome that by default showed the sky above Destro, but could be changed to display anything at all. Then, to add to the dark cosiness the room had, she added a fireplace, which would light itself when the Creator wanted it to and go off when he didn't. Finally she fixed any holes in the walls or floor, so that no draughts could get in. Amazed at how much work this small room had been, she returned to the normal game and flopped down on the floor.

I guess… that much detail… takes a lot out of a girl.

'I should have added a guest bedroom…' she muttered, falling asleep on the floor.

She awoke in a vision, once more in the forest. The sun shone through the leaves, turning the very sunlight green as it fell on her white fur.

'Why do you keep doing this?' Ellen hissed softly, falling to the grass. 'I'm too tired. I don't have the strength for these visions.'

I can help. If it is strength you need, allow mine to flow through your veins.

'I don't know what this is about, but I don't want to be part of it. I don't want an adventure, I never asked for it,' she said, voice rising angrily. 'Why must I always be part of it?'

Would you rather lead a life without any excitement?

'Yes!' She cried exasperatedly, not caring that only she could hear the voice. It faltered at her words, pausing before replying.

But...

'I don't even know who you are!'

'I am Opal, Princess of the Cat Folk.'

'So you've said, but how can I trust you?' She muttered, standing up. 'For all I know, you could be the cat from the clearing!'

'I am not him. If I was, then how could I let you use my body?'

'You could be anything! You could be possessing her!' She hissed, eyes narrowing at nobody but herself. 'You could be... you could be him...'

She paused, eyes wide. 'You're trying to get to him. Through me.'

'I... I don't understand what you mean.'

'You're him. You're the Spirit.'

'No. I'm not. You've got to trust me, Ellen.'

She hissed, backing away into the thick bushes behind her. In the real world, she could feel the heat from the amulet – the power. Her eyes flashed dangerously, voice low.

'Leave me alone.'

But... I need help...

'Leave me!'

Chapter 11:

Apocalypse

A roar rumbled through the Crystal Isle, as sharp claws did the same to the snow-covered trees all around them. A dark-skinned dragon tore through the crowd, knocking players aside and booming at the top of its voice. Climax put out a hand, and it stopped next to him, casting its tamer in shadow. Muscles rippled all over its large body, small eyes narrowed as it stared straight at Nick. Nick froze, staring at the massive creature. He stepped back slightly, but Ceirin kept a firm hand on his side.

'It's just an illusion,' he said quietly. 'In this game, strength is determined by stats, not simple looks. You can defeat him.'

'I wouldn't be so sure.' Climax smirked, patting his monster's leathery skin. 'No tamer has ever stopped the coming of the Apocalypse.'

'What?' asked Ceirin, blinking. Climax sighed, shaking his head.

'Why do people never get that? Apocalypse. It's his name.'

'That's really lame, you know that?'

'You do wonders with the name 'Nick', then tell me I'm bad.' Climax muttered, glaring
at Ceirin. 'Yeah, so anyway... even in stats, Climax is the ultimate creature. Your little doggie there can't beat him.'

'We'll see about that.' Nick growled, stepping to one side of the arena, ringed by crowds of players. Ceirin grinned at him, before stepping back behind his dragon, out of the fight. Climax nodded to his dragon. Apocalypse simply grunted, lowering his head and pointing sharp horns at his opponent.

'Alright, everybody!' Lenia yelled, pulling out a microphone and addressing all of the players. 'This is an official battle between Crystal Clan leader Climax ...' hundreds of the players cheered at his name, showering him with flakes of snow. He nodded, grinning and giving a small bow. 'And Dragon Tamer Ceirin!' There were a few cries of 'Waaay-haaayyyy!' Most of the players who didn't know Climax personally and cheered were dragged off for sacrifice later.

'Everybody ready? Okay! Three...Two...One... *Let's fight!*'

Grinning at the crowd, Lenia stepped to the side, before shuffling over to Climax.

'Hey... I checked out Ceirin's player data. He's the real Dragon Tamer,' she whispered, glancing at Climax. He nodded.

'I know. He's my boss.'

'What!' She exclaimed. Her partner shot her a glance, and she continued in a whisper. 'Why are you fighting him? Are you *crazy?*'

'Just a little,' he laughed, smiling. 'I don't see why I shouldn't. Not many other players can claim they've fought a Dragon Tamer.' Snarling, Nick leapt into the air, claws outstretched and fangs bared. As he did, Climax moved forward, clawing his underbelly and tossing the canine over his head.

'Nick…' Ceirin said quietly, grabbing his own chest and stepping back.

The wolf hit the ground hard, but got up again, spinning round to face his opponent. As he did, Climax whipped his tail around and knocked his paws from under him, clawing at his side and knocking him against some players.

'Sir, this isn't fair.' Lenia said softly, clutching her dragon's paw.

Climax didn't avert his gaze from the fight, frowning. 'Yes it is. We're not breaking any rules.'

'But Klio and the others attacked him upon arrival. He's not fit to fight.'

'There's nothing I can do about that. It's his problem.'

Lenia frowned, biting her lip as she watched the fight. Nick had leapt up to the dragon, somehow managing to fasten his jaws around his thick neck. He hung limp, growling, as Apocalypse howled and tore at his fur, struggling to remove him.

'Please!' She cried, bowing down before the boy. 'Master, I beg of you! Just let him heal, then have your fight!'

Climax stared at her in shock, surprised etched in his features.

'Alright, alright, I'll let them heal.' He murmured, raising a hand to Ceirin. *Apocalypse, stop.*

'Thank you.' Lenia said quietly, getting back to her feet. Klio had knelt at her side, and gave a nod to Climax as he also rose. He didn't return the gesture, glaring at her.

'I'm not your master. It's like the wolf said – the Council run this. When it all comes down to it, I'm just a puppet ruler. Powerless.'

Nodding, Ceirin turned to Nick. 'Nick, release him!'

Still growling, Nick relaxed his jaws, falling to the ground. Apocalypse snorted, kicking out and hitting him hard in the stomach. Cries rose from the crowd.

'Apocalypse, that was a d*irect order!*' cried Climax, as the reptile stomped over to him. Eyes narrowing, he slashed his partner across the chest with the whip, scoring his tough skin.

The dark creature gave another loud bellow, before clawing at his tamer and knocking him into a tree. Shards of crystal fell in a deadly rain from the branches, narrowly missing him as he flattened himself against the bark.

Lenia saw this, but didn't react, stepping back into the middle of the circle. 'Alright folks, take five! We'll be back soon.'

Groaning, the crowd wandered off in search of others activities. A few stepped over to Climax, but he didn't speak with them. Sighing, Lenia followed him to a large dome, sparkling in the sunlight. She motioned to Ceirin, and he followed.

'Corrupt or not, the Council supply much needed resources to this area. You'll find healing potions here for your dragon.'

'What happened to Apocalypse?' Ceirin asked as he followed her, frowning. 'Why'd he strike his tamer?'

'That? Happens all the time. The thing's as wild as you can get without it killing the tamer and ending the game.' Lenia said, shrugging uncaringly. 'His strength is partially due to the lack of any other abilities – speed, strength, self-control. Climax knows his accounts at risk, but in the end, it's worth it. We play this game to be heroes, and to the Crystal Clan, he is one.'

Ignoring the blood that marked his every step, Nick entered the dome, snarling at Climax as they passed. 'One day, you won't have your dragon to fight in your place. We'll see how a mere *human* compares with the wrath of a dragon.' With a fierce bark, he leapt at the tamer. Ceirin ran forward, grabbing him and pulling him back.

'Hey. Easy Nick, easy. He's not worth it, okay?'

Muttering, Nick loosened himself from Ceirin's hold, stepping away into the corner of the dome. He left a shaken Climax behind him, jumping as Lenia tossed him a potion.

'Drink up, bad boy. Humans can get hurt as well as dragons, and that blow must have given you one *heck* of a headache.' She said, smiling as she sat down and started speaking with her partner, combing her hair and tying it into a bobble as she did so. Sighing, Ceirin leant against a crystal wall; pouring some potion into a bowl and watching Nick drink it up. 'It'll take a while to work. Guess it'll be a pretty long break.'

'Yeah.' Nick said between laps. 'But it won't do much good, will it?'

'What're you talking about? You'll beat him, no trouble!'

Nick sighed, gazing at his tamer over the liquid. 'Ceirin, stats or no stats, he's impossible for me to defeat. He's just too strong.'

'You can't just give up! All you've got to do is get into the air; give him a few aerial attacks! Use your brains! You can outsmart that guy!'

'If I fly at him, he'll claw me out of the air. I can't compete with that kind of power!'

Crying out angrily, Ceirin got to his feet, leaving the dome. 'You can't give up! I won't let you!'

Nick whined, his head falling into the bowl. Bubbles appeared in the liquid, as he gave a deep sigh.

'Life got you down?'

'What do you want?' He muttered, taking his head out of the water.

'A chat, I guess. Dragons are just as good for conversation as tamers sometimes.'

'Well, at least you've got some brains.' The wolf said quietly, nudging the bowl away with his nose and laying his head on the cold ground. 'I'd say creating a dragon like Apocalypse knocks you back a few marks, though.'

'I know, it was stupid.' Climax sighed, running a hand through his hair. 'But I can't do anything about it now, can I? I've just got to wait until he goes wild and start again.'

'You could ask the Council for permission to change his design.'

'They can do it?' He asked, blinking.

'They're the Council. What *can't* they do?' Nick replied, shrugging. *It's the Creator those idiots pass most of the hard work onto, but still...*

'But that's the thing, isn't it?' He said, frowning. 'If I changed his design, I'd like to go with humanoid – but this whole group's against that.'

'I heard about all that sacrifice rubbish, but I wouldn't say that's the group's focus.' Nick said evenly, taking another sip of potion. 'More than anything, this group is for players with similar interests – from what I've seen, battling and different tactics – to come together. I reckon if you allow humanoids, it'll only get better.'

'Not all of them will agree to that, there will still be those who hate certain player types of dragons.'

'So? Let them be close-minded fools. As long as there are some people who play the game for fun, it'll be fine.' Nick said, tail wagging as he spoke.

Climax frowned, getting up as an impatient roar came from outside. He paused at the doorway, smiling at the winged wolf. 'Thanks.'

* * *

'Okay, okay, calm down already!' Lenia yelled, standing in the middle of the noisy circle. 'Look, I'm sure he'll be back soon, just- EEEEK! DON'T THROW STUFF!'

'Hey, just leave her!' Ceirin yelled, stepping in front of the girl. 'It's not her fault if he won't show up! If you want a fight, clear off and go look for one! It isn't going to happen, alright?'

Sighing, Ceirin stood back, glancing at Lenia..

'Guess I should end this, right?' She asked, looking at him uncertainly.

'Sure. I guess he must have logged out,' he said, shrugging.

'No, he's still logged on. But he left this area a while ago.' Nick said, with a slight smile.

'Smart kid. I wouldn't mind heading back to Clix right now.' Ceirin said quietly, shivering.

'I guess we can head back now.' Nick nodded, before turning to Climax's assistant. 'Would you mind wrapping things up?'

'Not at all.' Lenia said, stepping back into the centre and yelling a farewell to the crowd.

'Alright, folks! Like Ceirin said, today's battle is no longer commencing. Another day, perhaps?' She cried, grinning as she gave one final glance round the – now quiet – crowd. 'Remember – Life's a game, and we play to win!'

Chapter 12:

Maree Meets Matt

'Wha?' Maree mumbled, opening her eyes to see sunlight streaming through a round porthole. 'Where am I?' *The floor is moving... am I back on the* Wave Rider?

'Are you awake, Miss O'Nearn?'

Groaning, Maree searched for the source of the voice, blinded by the sun. 'How'd you know my name?'

'You kept saying it in your sleep – Caroline O'Nearn, then Maree,' answered a black cat with messy, ruffled fur. He was wearing white silk gloves on his paws, and wore a silver necklace, bracelet, and anklets. 'Which name is yours?'

His two furry feet were curled up underneath him. And as he stared curiously down at her she saw a strange marking burnt into his fur, as though done in the same way farmers marked sheep. He saw her staring, grey eyes showing slight embarrassment. 'It's the mark of Storm.' Maree simply kept staring at the strange creature as he got to his feet. His swift, feline frame was covered in white stripes – two on each leg, three on the tail, and three fringe-like bangs poking out from behind his tufted ears. He seemed to pose no threat, but Maree didn't let her guard down. 'Why did you take me here?'

'My master wanted to see you,' he replied quietly, head bowed. Concerned she was still confused, he added 'Storm.'.

'Capture me, more like,' she retorted, all trust deserting her. 'Must be a pretty good guard cat, if you didn't even bother to tie me up.'

'I am an assassin, not a guard,' he muttered, tail flicking up in annoyance. 'I didn't tie you up because you have nowhere to run. We're out at sea.'

'Then I'll fly away,' she said quietly, searching for her rucksack. The cat's ears flicked up, catching every word.

'We're not in the Dragon Realms,' he said softly, leaning back against a wall. 'You haven't asked my name yet.'

'I don't want it.'

'I would like you to know it.'

'So you can feel less guilty when you kill me? Not likely, puss-in-boots.'

'No. So you can stop calling me such ridiculous names,' he huffed, tail flicking up once again. 'It's Matt Black.'

'Oh wow. You're named after paint.'

'Paint?' Matt repeated, blinking. 'What's 'paint'?'

'Forget about it,' she replied coldly, lying back down on the blankets she had woken on. *There wasn't much point talking to someone she was going to have to kill.*

As Matt sat back, his ears pricked up once more. Ripples appeared on the bowl of water at Maree's bedside. 'We're running out of time...'

When she opened her eyes again, the bright sunlight remained, but the boat

60

was no longer. Instead, she was standing in the middle of a tropical forest.

Look at that leaf.

Following the telepathic commands, Maree crouched down, placing a paw on the leaf. 'A strange world. A cat-girl willing to give up her own body. A patch of blood on a leaf. What's this all about?'

You already seem to know a lot about what's going on.

'Ellen and I are telepathically connected. She has been having visions of you.' Maree muttered, tearing the leaf from its bush. 'Why can't you let her sleep in peace?'

I need help. You are the only humans I can turn too.

'Then ask one of your cat-folk for help.' I cannot.

'Show me why.'

A slow hissing reached her through the forest, alerting her. She followed it, passing trees stripped bare of all their bark and branches. Some had been cut down completely, leaving only stumps.

We will not let them into our world, so they take it from us by force.

Their numbers grew with the volume of the hissing, as she stepped into a clearing. The trees around here stood tall no longer, stripped of their bodies and life. With it had died all the wildlife that lived there, leaving the whole area dead. And yet, an animal stood there. A lone black dog, his thick chain trailing after him, his teeth bared as he growled at Opal. Long, fur-covered spikes stuck out from his shoulder blades and the back of his paws, his bared fangs shone like metal as he gave a hoarse bark.

Through an animals eyes, you can see their soul.

Springing forward, Opal clamped her paws over the dog's mouth, shutting it. It struggled in her grip, but she help tight, twisting its head towards her and looking deep into his eyes.

Humans have destroyed this creature. Its eyes see nothing but fear because of what they have done to it in the past.

We fear humans, because we know they could do the same to us.

'My friend, humans have enslaved you long enough... Go free.' Opal whispered to it, slipping off its old, tight collar. It kept growling, jaws remaining shut as she removed her paws. His tail straightened out behind him, as she removed the collar and lead. 'Go. Nobody can control you anymore,' she whispered again, stroking his fur. His tail wagged slightly, as he sniffed her hand curiously.

'Now what?' Maree said quietly, as the dog padded away, exploring the undergrowth.

Keep walking. There is much more for you to discover…

'I don't know if I can…' Maree whispered, stumbling slightly. 'These visions are exhausting. I need to sleep.'

You must continue!

'Why?'

Time is short! You must continue the vision, Maree!

'Giving me a lot of choice there, aren't you?' She muttered bitterly, shrugging and continuing forward towards the source of the noise.

Further along, shadowed by vehicles Maree couldn't see clearly, sat a shaking kitten. It cried out, but she didn't hear, watching as it struggled to free itself from the cables wrapped tightly around its leg.

'Go back, Opal! Don't come here! There are humans in the forest! They'll kill us!'

Maree didn't answer, stepping towards him, mind clouded.
'What happened here?'

* * *

'Matt?'

'Yes, master?' He said quietly, looking up as the door opened. His master came in, an older cat with stormy blue fur streaked with purple in an odd, ribcage pattern.

'How is she?'

'She is dreaming… a vision,' he said, sitting next to Maree as she slept. 'With every moment she sleeps, we get closer.'

'Yes, I know. Aren't humans just *magical?*' He muttered, rolling his eyes. 'I'll be glad when they're all out of here.'

Matt stared at the floor, frowning. 'But sir… they have done nothing wrong to this world.'

'They are humans, Matt. *Everything* involving them is wrong,' he said sharply, taking a seat next to his servant.

'But your vendetta is against the Creator, is it not? Couldn't you just kill him, and leave the rest alone?'

'Matt, Matt, Matt. Such a clean assassin – no mess, no fuss, eh? So anti-violence. So naïve. Such a *fool.*' Storm hissed, placing a claw on his shoulder. 'They must all die, no matter what the method. Maybe you'll be lucky, and when I remove the creator, the game will collapse upon itself,' he chuckled, grinning. 'But somehow, I doubt that.'

* * *

'I was outside… playing tag with the others,' he said slowly, as Opal pulled out a dagger and slashed away the cords. They sparked as she did so, still plugged into a power source.

'When we heard a strange sound… a buzzing.'

'And?' Maree said, sitting down. Why do I feel so weak?

'Everyone said I was the bravest, so I should go.' He said quietly, with a slight grin. He was close to Opal's age, perhaps a year or so younger. 'So I did, and there were all these humans…'

'What next? What happened next?' She said, breathing becoming shallow. This didn't happen to Ellen…

'What are you… doing to me?' She hissed, voice no more than a whisper, so the kitten couldn't hear.

I shared Ellen's strength, but you seem to have too little.

'Couldn't you at least have asked? I didn't agree to any of this!'

'Who are you talking to?'

'Just continue, Arrow. Ignore me.'

I didn't know it would hurt you!

'This one came at me with this heavy, metal thing, so I clawed his leg. It was pretty cool, because he was wearing these blue things, and they went all

black! And then this other guy but me in this old sack thing and threw me in the back of a metal machine, so I clawed that too pieces too, and rolled out as the machine thing made this big RAWR and started moving!' He said, smiling, before clawing the air. 'Like this! RAWR!'

'I can't stay asleep... I've got to wake up...'

'But it turns out that as well as the machine roaring, there was this big wolf thing roaring too, and it came after me. So I ran, and then these cables appeared like totally out of nowhere, and I got all tangled. That's pretty much where you came in.'

'You'll take him to safety. You'll end this vision, and take him with you...'

'Aw, cats! Wait till all the others find out I was rescued by a girl!' He muttered, scratching behind his ear.

'Never... do this again...'she said quietly, before collapsing and slipping away from that world.

Chapter 13:

Visitors

'Ellen? Hey, Ellen, you alright?'

'I'm fine, Ceirin,' she said quietly, brushing her messy hair flat and sitting up against the wall. 'You can come in.' The wooden door opened, and Ceirin came through, gasping for breath. 'Jeez, Ellen. Couldn't you at least have answered when I called for you or something?'

'Sorry,' she said quietly, bowing her head. 'I fell asleep.'

'I heard. The Guardian told me you passed out,' he said, sitting next to her. 'You're alright now though, yes?'

'I'm fine,' she laughed, looking at his concerned expression. 'You really are a failure as a villain, Ceirin.'

'Guilty as charged.' He laughed, grinning. 'Whoa… this place sure has changed.'

'You've been here before?'

'Sure have. The Spirit let me sleep here one or two times,' he said, nodding. 'You know… he wasn't really all that bad.'

'He was using you, Ceirin.' Ellen said gently, frowning at him.

'I know, but still…I could have had it a lot worse.'

* * *

'Hey, hello? Is anybody here?' Nick howled, poking his head through the window. As he did, a strong hand caught him by the throat and pulled him inside.The Creator twisted his head sharply so they were eye-to-eye, Nick's were wide and grey,his blue and wild. 'First,' he snarled, pulling up his sleeve and revealing a large bruise on his arm, a large red patch changing from purple to black. 'This is from a needle. I'm drugged, right?'

'Right.' Nick gasped, nodding weakly.

'So if I kill you, I'll have a good excuse, right?'

'Not right! Not right at all!'

'Aw, come on,' he teased, waving a hand at the window. A metal shutter closed over it as he let go of Nick's throat. 'It'll be fun! I kill you now, and bring you back to life later!'

'I'm really not comfortable with that idea!'

'Dang spoilsport,' he whispered darkly as the door opened and the shutter slid away. With a slight yelp, Nick dived out the window.

'The wolf's there.' He whispered, watching Nick flee. 'So Ceirin should be too.'

He paused, leaning back and checking his pistols. 'Maybe I can kill someone after all.'

* * *

'Worried about Maree, eh?' Ellen said quietly, as Ceirin sat in the corner and stared blankly into space.

'Yeah,' he said, gaze moving to the ground. 'I thought she'd be back by now.'

'She's probably having a good time exploring!' Ellen replied, grinning. 'She'll be back before you know it!'

'I don't think so,' he said, frowning. 'I mean, think about it, we all know there's someone out to get us again, but we don't know what it is or where it's hiding. However, it obviously knows a lot about us. It also knows who of us is at her weakest right now!'

'Maree?' Ellen asked, raising an eyebrow. 'No way! Strongest player, Ceirin! *Strongest player!*'

'I know, I know.' Ceirin muttered, swatting her away. 'But she hasn't been the same since she found out she was stuck in the game.'

'I thought she loved the game.'

'I know she does. She doesn't want to go back to reality.' He said, running a hand along the stone ground uneasily. 'I think it's just the fact that she died that's getting to her more than anything.'

Ellen caught his eye, and nodded. 'She lost.'

'Exactly.'

'Misstresss?'

'Yes, Guardian?' Ellen asked, walking over to the window as he called her. The bedroom was quite high, in one of the castle's towers.

'There are… playersss,' he said quietly, tongue flicking out nervously. 'To battle the final bosssss…'

'Aw, great,' she muttered, sighing. 'I thought this area was offline.'

'It wasssss meant to be, but the game isssssn't in too ssssstable a condition right now.'

'Point. Look, stall them for as long as you can, okay? I'll see what I can do.'

The amulet brightened, as she grinned and turned around. 'Oh, Ceirin…'

'…Ceirin?'

'Ceirin!'

* * *

'Come on; come on, where is it?' Ceirin muttered, rummaging through his rucksack and patting his trouser pockets. 'PDA, PDA, PDA!'

Groaning, he sat back. *It wasn't there. But where could it be?*

Mentally, he returned to the shelter in the Crystal Isle. The moment he'd placed his bag down, and pulled out a bowl for Nick to drink from. He hadn't picked it up again before returning to the battle.

'Climax,' he growled, eyes narrowing. *That rotten…*

'Ceirin!'

'Wha?' He mumbled, staring up as a silver blur flew into his chest. He was knocked a few metres back, coughing up grass and grabbing his chest.

'Nick! What's the big idea?'

'It's the Creator! He's gone *stark raving mad!*' Nick yelped, struggle to get away. 'And by that, I mean more than the usual.'

'Eh. I knew he'd snap some time soon.' Ceirin shrugged. 'It's not my problem.'

'Yes it is,' barked Nick, glaring at him. 'He's going on a killing spree!'

'Whoashoot…' Ceirin said quickly, staring back up at Destro Castle.

'…Ellen.'

Without another word, the pair ran off back to the castle, passing the Guardian as he tackled the new group.

'Right, now you have to pick me up in your mouth and slither round the front,' said Ellen, standing next to the Guardian at the gate. He was standing warily in front of her, shielding her from the eyes of any players. She paused, as he stood drooling at the new group.

'…Hey, is there any reason that when you hiss your spit melts the grass?'

'Oh…I forgot about the acid sssssssssaliva…' he muttered distractedly, gazing blankly at the bubbling grass.

'You spit *acid* and forgot to tell me!' Exclaimed Ellen.

'Thisssss wasssss your idea! You sssshould know the risks,' he said defensively, glaring at her. She shrugged, nodding.

'Anything else I should know about?'

'I sssssshould remind you that I can unhinge my jaw and ssssswallow thingsssss much bigger than *you*, whole!'

'You enjoy scaring people, don't you,' Ellen sighed, letting the guardian pick her up in its mouth after she'd quickly reprogrammed him not to have acidic saliva.

'You are aware that interchangeable acid saliva and poisonous fangs completely go against your 'guardian' image, right.'

'But it addssssss to my 'evil giant sssssssnake' image,' countered the guardian, slithering round to the front of Destro.

As soon as they were within sight of the players, she started the act. The trio spun round, clutching their ears as a scream disturbed their quiet chatter.

'Ah! The pain!' Ellen yelled, moving limply in the snake's grip.

'What happened to you?' One of the group asked, a boy that looked similar to Ceirin, but taller, differently clothed and with grey eyes.

'I got so far! But then…the snake…the poison!' Ellen yelled dramatically.

'What an idiot! Entering Destro without the ocarina,' laughed a ginger haired, freckled girl, the only party member with the visible partner. It was a fire dragon.

'I did have one! But…he's too powerful…pain!'

'Idiot,' sighed her fire dragon, a fox with fiery-coloured fur. 'So where's your dragon?'

'I…don't…know…poison…confusing…' moaned Ellen, watching out of the corner of her eye as another pair ran past the garden walls.

'So, what're you waiting for?' Asked yet another member, a black-haired girl with blue eyes, carrying a staff.

'Huh?' Ellen asked, blinking.

'Not you, the giant snake. Aren't you going to kill her?' She demanded.

'Yessssss…but later. I like privacy,' hissed the guardian quickly.

'We want to see how strong you are. You can't be so weak that you won't kill her in front of us,' she continued, narrowing her eyes. 'Unless this is all some kind of act...'

'I asssssssssure you, a human isssss no match for me.'

'So show us,' said the ginger haired girl.

'He won't!' Yelled Ellen. 'He's...too...cruel! He'd rather watch me die...slowly...'

'Surely he can make an exception?' Asked the dark haired girl, batting her eyelashes.

'I thought you liked fresh meat,' muttered the flaming fox, staring at her paws. 'Unless you've suddenly turned vegetarian. Which I doubt.'

'Don't you have something to say?' Ellen asked the boy.

The boy way quiet, staring at the wall. 'Let them be. She's going to die, so let her die in peace.'

'So you're helping them, traitor,' the girls said angrily. He stared calmly at his party as the two females rounded on him, before nodding.

'Of course.' He said, sidestepping away from them and towards the guardian. 'Look.' He said, out of hearing to the girls. 'I'm a rare item collector, and I've heard of you – *Ellen*. Guardian, you can camouflage, right?'

'Yessss.' The Guardian hissed quietly, as the girls both watched, unsure of what to do about their double-crossing partner. 'But it will not hide Ellen.'

'I HOPE YOU KNOW WE CAN KILL YOU!' Yelled the spell caster, waving her staff angrily in their direction. 'AND IF YOU LOG ON AGAIN, WE CAN KILL YOU AGAIN!'

'However, she has an item that will.' He said, grinning, before spreading his arms out disbelieving and exclaiming 'Fine! I'll go with my teammates! Show us you're strong, Guardian!'

'Thanks for the back up and all, but we don't need it.' The redhead said, smiling. 'We're just going to team-kill you out of the game, okay?'

'Aw, Becky,' he sighed, brushing back his hair nervously. 'You don't need to do that!'

'I think we do, Alfie. We can't have a player we don't trust on our side.'

'Such a pity.' He sighed, waving his hand to Ellen and the Guardian. As he did, a white-striped tiger appeared at his side. 'Allakazam, allakazoo, other-random-words!'

He disappeared in a blur of smoke. His team-mates sighed, before turning to the other pair, but they'd also fled the scene.

'Well, looks like it's game over.' Redheaded Becky sighed, shaking her head.

'I wouldn't say that,' her friend grinned, motioning to the doorway to the castle.

'Owned.'

Chapter 14:

The Cat Assassin

'She's waking.' Matt said quietly, as Maree stirred in her sleep.

'She's left the vision, but not her sleep.' Storm contradicted, watching her with dark, emerald green eyes. 'Now, if any, is a good time for her to die. Do your job, assassin.'

Matt stared at her uncertainly, one hand on his belt. He shook his head, turning back to Storm.

'That is not my job.' Matt spat, glaring at his master. 'I was a servant before I was dragged into this!'

'A servant trained in the ways of assassins...'

'So I could protect my mistress!'

'...and how to defeat them. An assassin who knows how to defeat any of his kind, and so always strives to go against these faults, is a rare catch.'

'I am not a murderer,' he said sharply, tail rigid behind him.

'I am your master, and I say that you are,' hissed Storm, as Maree groaned softly. A mist of blue and purple cloud whirled around him. 'Now, do what you must!'

Shivering, Maree sat up and looked out of the nearest portal. The sea was turbulent, waves hammering the side of the boat. *Who's sailing this thing?*

'Hey, Matt,' she said, smiling groggily at him as she propped herself up against a wall. 'How's it going?'

'The weather's worsening,' he said, following her gaze out the window. 'We'll have to stay away from land for a while.'

'Where are we going?'

He sighed, falling to the ground and crossing his legs. 'I have no idea.'

* * *

After a short while of sitting in thoughtful silence, the cat assassin started swaying back and forward.

Just as Maree had started to ignore his fidgeting, he went down on his side with a 'thud', muffled by his fur.

'Will you *stop* that?'

'I'm sorry,' he whispered, flopping his head down. 'I feel rather seasick.'

'Good council, you're *pathetic!*'

The silence returned. Maree thought about Sam, still uncertain where she was.

'I noticed.' Matt said quietly. Maree raised an eyebrow at him, but didn't comment.

'Where's my dragon?'

'Miss Samantha? In the lower part of the boat,' he said helpfully, adding, 'The effects of the herbs she was given should be wearing off soon.'

Thoroughly puzzled, Maree's eyebrow remained raised. 'Your master needs a better servant.'

'Good slaves are hard to come by,' he hissed, bitterness in his voice.

'You're his slave?'

'Not willingly,' the dark-furred feline said, pawing at his ear. 'There were few other options.'

He paused, before pulling a key ring off his tail and pressing the key on its end. A quiet beeping echoed around the boat, and the light on the plastic device flashed.

'Oh, and by the way.' Matt added, as the flashing stopped. 'All the doors are unlocked.'

His tail flicked forward, and landed in Maree's hand.

Outside the boat, the sky grew continually darker, streaks of lightning skimming the water's surface.

A soft 'snck' was heard, as Maree's scabbard appeared at her side, and she pulled out her sword. Its blade glowed darkly, before disappearing as she turned the thin weapon sideways.

The door slowly opened, and Sam stepped in, head low and horns buzzing with electricity. Her teeth were bared in an almost canine snarl, eyes narrowed and flashing angrily with every rumble of thunder outside.

'Finally,' Maree said, smiling at her. 'What took you so long?'

'I couldn't wake up any sooner.' She growled, pawing the ground. Matt didn't look her way, staring idly at his left paw.

'Face me,' Sam spat, digging her claws into his side and turning him towards her, before placing another on his chest. 'Who are you?'

'His name is Matt Black, he's an assassin.' Maree answered simply, shrugging. 'I guess you can just snap his neck. From what I've heard, no one will care.'

He didn't reply to the personal stab, staring into Sam's eyes. 'You look just like in the stories, Miss Samantha.'

'Stories?' Asked Maree, frowning. Sam didn't say anything, pressing her horns against his fur.

'I only remembered them when I arrived in the world, after your first adventure,' he said, staring above her head at the ceiling. 'The stories of Samantha, shy water goddess, Nick, pure hearted shape shifter of doubt, and Crystal, the angelic guardian.'

'We are in cat-folk legend,' said Sam disbelievingly.

'I think so. My memories are unclear, foggy. I believe they change as our games merge.' He answered, flattening his spin and edging away from his opponent. 'There is only one way for us to find out the whole story – Opal.'

Still gripped her sword tightly, Maree glared at him. 'How did you know about that?'

'No matter.' Matt said, getting to his feet and walking fearlessly up to her. 'Hold out your hands.'

Confused, Maree did so. Wrapping his own furry paws around her and forcing a page of paper between them, he backed against a wall.

As he did, his eyes turned black, and he collapsed.

Maree cried out, running over to him. Sam stepped in front of her, electricity crackling into non-existence between her horns. 'Read the page,' Sam commanded.

Maree stared at her, but nodded, unfolding the sheet of paper. Another vision hit her, but her real self only fell against Sam, remaining conscious as the story continued.

'Opal! Opal, are you alright?' The young cat yelled, shaking her by the shoulders. 'Opal, wake up!'

I am sorry… I did not mean for that to happen…

'It's fine,' Maree said quietly, opening her eyes. 'It wasn't your fault.'

So you trust me?

'No.'

'Opal! You're awake!' Arrow yelled, smiling. 'You scared me there for a minute! What happened to you?'

'It's nothing,' she said sharply, getting to her feet. 'What now?'

'Come on, we've got to tell your dad,' he said, grabbing her by the hand and pulling her away.

Trees, tracks, rivers, plants and wildlife, places and people. Everything passed in a dream-like blur as Maree was dragged through the cat world.

Before she knew it, Arrow had brought her into a small room, walls draped in red velvet. The wood that made up the building was black, and the only light that entered the area was dark and smoky.

As she stood there, confused, Matt appeared and pulled away one of the red curtains.

'Enter, Princess. The King must speak with you.'

'M-Matt,' she stammered, confused, as she stepped into the next room. It was partially a long corridor, with a red carpet running down the centre. At either side of it tall, dark poles supported the roof, and two large thrones sat at the end of the carpet.

The right-hand throne was empty, but her father sat in the other. A once snow-white, now greying cat, he was trusted by his people not for his breed or looks, but for his wisdom and way of treating his people.

'You wished to speak with me, father?' Opal asked quietly, stepping up to the throne and staring up at him.

'News travels fast here. I heard of what happened in the forest,' he rumbled, voice low and grating. 'Of how they tried to harm another of our kind. Of how they attempt to take our land from us, against all our wishes and commands!'

'They are more advanced than we are. They use their weapons to fight us,' she said quietly, nodding. 'I fear what will happen next. Their evils stretch far beyond what we have seen.'

'I am aware. Even as I speak, they gather their forces, ready to attack,' he hissed, running a paw along the polished wood. 'Who knows what comes next? Guns, bombs, atomic weapons. As soon as war is declared, they will stop at nothing to destroy us.'

Opal frowned, staring at her feet. 'But don't they have to speak with you before they declare such a thing?'

'Who knows? They know we are like them, but they still count us as under

them. Not human. Dumb animals.'

The King paused, before staring past Opal, at the many tapestries bedecking the walls around them.

'However, we are not without weapons of our own…'

Chapter 15:

Impostor

Gasping for breath, Ceirin stepped into Destro castle. Suddenly, he was knocked to the ground, crying out.

'Ceirin! Finally!' Ellen gasped, leaping off the Guardian and dragging him to the ground. 'Don't you boys *ever* walk?'

Dragging him back up by the collar, she pulled a leather jacket out of mid air, shoving him into it.

'Ellen, this isn't time to play dress up! There's a psycho biker loose in Destro!' He yelled, fighting her grasp.

'That's not important! There's a crowd of players waiting to see the Creator, and you're the closest we've got!'

'Are you kidding?' He froze, blinking. 'I look nothing like him! Why don't you do it?'

Ellen pulled out the programming plug and used it accordingly. Ceirin paused to glance round at his new attire, scratching his head.

'This wig's itchy,' he murmured, brushing the long blonde strands from his eyes. 'Is the Creator's real hair like this?'

'No.'

'You sure?'

'Yes.'

'I bet you'd be pretty grossed out if he turned out to have lice or-'

'Ceirin, this is a *videogame*.' Ellen said sternly, glaring at him. 'No head lice, got it? Or do you fancy being stuck with that wig for the next eleven months?'

'…Gottit.'

'A pssssycho biker…' The Guardian chuckled, glancing at Nick. 'Explain what happened, wolf.'

'Simple. All I did was stick my head through the window, and the Creator's all like – 'I KEEL YOU' and I'm like 'Ohemgee' and he's all 'RAWR. I'M ANGSTY. HUG ME.', so I'm all like-'

'Yessss, yesss, but what about hissss eyessss?'

'Apart from the usual undead vampire psycho ME-OW deal?'

'Yesss. Pupilsssss, Nick, pupilsssss.'

'Oh,' he said, pausing and staring blankly into space. 'Well, they were a lot wider than normal, if that's what you're looking for.'

'Yesss, it issss,' sighed the Guardian, slipping away from the group. 'Finally…'

'I'm telling you, Ellen.' Ceirin stammered, as she pushed him through the passageways to the corridor of caged dragons. 'This isn't a good idea!'

'Tish tosh! It's *genius,*' she said, grinning as she pushed him on top of the cages. He fell down, before settling into a more becoming pose, and she hid behind him.

Behind the cages, the wall worked like mirror-glass – from the front, you couldn't see a thing, but from behind you could see all newcomers clearly. It differed, however, in that you could step through it like it was a hologram.

It was a video game. Things didn't have to make sense.

A floor or so above, the Creator was lying on the stone floor, staring up at the ceiling and wondering how he'd got there.

As he reflected on the matter, the Guardian entered the room, towering above him and meeting his eyes.

'I have no idea what just happened. Fill me in before it gets depressing,' he said quietly, staring up at his protector.

'You were ssssssleepwalking again.'

'Dang.' He muttered, frowning. 'I thought the anaesthetic stopped that.'

'It's been a while sssssince the dose. It musssst have worn off.'

'What did I do?'

'Not much, thankfully. Just threatened to kill Nick, who sssssscared his partner by retelling the eventsssss to him.'

The Creator paused, still staring thoughtfully up at the ceiling.

'What are they doing now?'

The Guardian froze, staring at the ground. 'Well, a group of players arrived...'

* * *

As the pair of girls entered, they found the 'Creator' lying lazily there, smiling at them all.

'I vant to sook your vlood,' he said, grinning.

'Stop that!' Hissed Nick angrily from behind the cages, out of sight from the players. 'Put some effort into it!'

'I vant to keel joo all,' he said, with the same accent.

'Ceirin!'

'Oh, alright, 'he grumbled, shaking his head. 'Fear my minions, wild dragons with added evil. Hiss.' He opened the cage.

'You do remember what happens next, right?' Asked Nick. His tamer didn't answer.

Roaring, the dragons stretched their wings, heading for the players.

'This is easy. Vero?' Ordered Becky, nodding to the dark-haired girl.

'*Way* ahead of you,' she smirked, twirling the staff in one hand before pointing it at the wild creatures. '*Manayefist!*'

Stopping mid-step, the dragons wheeled round, turning to Ceirin. His grin slipped away, as they snarled at their master.

'Oh...' he said, clicking his fingers. 'Uh...how do I make them disappear?'

'Oh, *shoot.*' Ellen hissed, paling. 'I forgot about this part.'

'Then think up something! Think it up fast!' Ceirin yelled, backing up against the metal cages and coming up against the wall.

'Ellen, the wall isn't working!'

'You can only pass through it from the other side, noob,' snarled the Creator, leaping up onto the metal stage and shooting down all of the dragons.

As their bodies decayed into dust, he stepped up to the players.

'Well, hello there. Enjoying the game?' He asked, smiling at them, but not giving them a chance to reply. 'Now, I'm sorry to be the bearer of bad news, but in Dragon Tamers the final battle is tailored specifically for every group. Unfortunately, one of your party members has left.'

Still smiling innocently, he shot them both. 'Come back again with the full requirements. Have a nice day!'

Sighing, he swept back his hair, before turning and heading back through the wall.

'I despise leading roles,' he muttered, hopping down to where Ellen and Nick sat, still trying to take the blur of events in. He paused, catching Nick's wary glare. 'Count that as an apology.'

Ceirin frowned, staring at Ellen. She smiled up at him, breathing harsh, amulet glowing brightly.

'What's happening to you?'

'It's nothing,' she gasped, loosening the chain. 'Just feeling a little faint, that's all.'

The Creator paused, staring at her amulet. *What's it sensing?*

With a low hiss, the Guardian entered, with Beta asleep on his tail. 'What did I missss?'

'I got rid of the players,' the Creator answered, heading up the nearest flight of stairs. 'That's about all.'

'Hey, wait a minute!' Ceirin cried, grabbing him by the arm. 'Where are you going?'

He turned, glaring at the smaller boy. 'I have work to do.'

'You can't just leave! Have you even been paying attention to what's been going on,' said Ceirin, glaring back at him. 'There's some crazy cat-people trying to destroy your game!'

'Don't touch me,' he snarled, jerking away his arm. 'I'm well aware of what's going on in my game, thanks.'

'Then why won't you help us?'

'Haven't I already helped enough?' He asked, frowning. 'I don't plan on becoming some member of your little trio. I'm the Creator of the game, not some adventure-seeking nimrod[1]!'

'If you're the Creator of this game, you should be trying to help it!' Snarled Ceirin, aggravated.

'No. I should be hiding in the background, just like the Council. I'm meant to be some kind of money-crazed businessman, not a player,' he paused, frowning. 'That's the thing about running a game – you're not supposed to play it.'

'Oh, don't give me any of that angst-ridden rubbish,' snapped Ceirin. 'If you cared about the game, it wouldn't be in this sorry state!'

He paused, searching for a retort. '…I…'

'You're always going on about how hard you work on this game. How much good you do for our world.' Ceirin said. 'But you don't even understand it. This is real life, not some stupid video game. Yet, you treat us all like scum.'

---

1 American slang for 'stupid person'. Probably from the pirate 'poor little Nimrod' used by the cartoon character Bugs Bunny to mock the hapless Elmer Fudd.

Eyes narrowing, the Creator snatched his jacket out of Ceirin's hands, pulling it on.

Behind Ceirin, Nick gave a low growl, hackles raised.

'That's exactly what I'm talking about.'

Ellen got up, concern flashing across her face at their actions.

The two boys stared straight at each other. The Creator's fist clenched around the cable.

'You dare…' said the Creator quietly. 'Accuse me of such, even though I only offered to help. I, who gave you your new world, told the others what was happening when you tried to break the spell, who has resisted countless times the urge to blow your head off!'

'You seem to forget some other details. We helped save you. We were slammed against a wall trying to fight against the spirit. We were almost sliced apart by your robot,' countered Ceirin.

'I was possessed! You think I had a choice!'

'Perhaps you did!' Ceirin cried accusingly

There was a sudden silence. It was obvious Ceirin had gone too far.

'That's it…' The Creator said slowly, pulling out his programming plug from the lining of his jacket's sleeve. 'You're banned from Dragon Tamers.'

'What?' Growled Nick, his fur bristling.

'*Game Over.*' He hissed. 'Your account is being suspended under suspicion of harassing a member of the Dragon Tamers staff.'

'No. Creator, you can't…' Ellen said quietly. He raised up a hand, silencing her.

Behind her, the dark imp poked his head above the Guardian's coiled body. The snake himself was silent, watching the action with eyes the same shade as his masters.

'You have the right to remain silent. If you give up that right, anything you say or do can and will jeopardize your chances of regaining your user account. While you try to do so, you will have no access to the game or anything connected to it, and your dragon will be removed until the account is regained.'

He waved a hand at Ceirin, and his wrists and ankle were bound with coils of barbed wire. As they wrapped around his body, everything they touched was covered in a layer of ice.

'Do you understand?' Asked the Creator, staring into Ceirin's emotionless eyes. No answer came. '*I said*, do you understand?'

'Crystal clear, officer.' Ceirin laughed, as transparent ice coated his body, stopping him from moving. He was ignoring his current fix, grinning confidently at Nick and Ellen. 'But riddle me this – how can I not have access to the game, when I'm living in it? Do you plan to simply delete me, as you have so many others?'

The Creator's voice wavered slightly, but he ignored the comment. 'Due to circumstances beyond our control, preventing your complete evacuation of the game, you shall remain unconscious - sleeping, if you will.' His tone was colder than the ice that covered Ceirin, but his words lost effect as he was forced to make up rules on the spot.

'How can I get my account back if I'm unconscious?' Ceirin asked, voice momentarily returning to its normal tone. Desperation lurked behind his every word, an emotion he was too afraid to show.

'You cannot.' The Creator said simply, smiling.

'No...please, don't do this!' Ellen said, looking at the Creator. Again, he ignored her.

'Ceirin!' Yelled Beta, running over to him. Ellen grabbed him, stopping him from moving.

'It's too dangerous, Beta,' she whispered.

The Guardian froze, eyes widening as he stared at the ceiling. *Something's wrong here...*

'Ellen, turn the amulet to the ceiling.

'Okay. Why?' She asked, letting it's amber light illuminate the stone ceiling.

'What'ssssss that sssssshadow?' he asked, looking at the dark shape above the two boys.

'I-I don't know.' Ellen said quietly, staring at the shape. It was only vaguely human, blurred and shadowed.

'Another question, oh mighty administrator.' Ceirin said, his voice snapping back to its colder side. 'Where shall I go, if not the game? I'm sure you wouldn't want any of your players ending up at risk in an unstable area.'

'I'll find somewhere,' he said firmly, watching the shadow out of the corner of his eye. It hovered behind Ceirin, working him like a puppet.

'Then allow me to be of some assistance,' smirked Ceirin, spinning round and shattering all the ice that bound him, before leaping into the air.

'Stop right there!' The Creator yelled, drawing his pistol. 'Don't make me hurt you!'

'I doubt you would, boy.' Ceirin laughed, voice echoing all around the area. Nick whined, tail falling between his legs as he backed away from his tamer. 'Get back here, mutt.'

Nick howled in pain, as Ceirin swept down and grabbed him by the scruff of the neck. Claws instead of fingernails dug into his fur, and Nick struggled to break free.

'Leave them!' The blonde boy yelled, panic showing in his voice. The cable fell from his hand, and he stared at it in total confusion. After a moments fumbling, he drew his guns once more, pointing them at Ceirin.

'It's me you want, isn't it?' He asked, hands shaking as he struggled to aim.

'Oh, how very heroic.' Ceirin sniggered, hovering in front of him, and moving the barrel of the gun with his hand. 'You really were a failure as a villain, do you know that?'

'Don't make me do this,' he snarled, pressing the gun against Ceirin's head.

'You don't have the courage to pull the trigger.' Ceirin mocked, before something hard collided with the Creator's chest.

Pain shot through his body, more swift and painful than any bullet could have been. His eyes closed, he felt warm breath on his face.

The world faded from thought, and pain became harsh reality...

Chapter 16:

Searching

'Ceirin?'

The castle dropped into silence, as all four figures stared at the spot where the boys had stood.

A single howl echoed through the night, as Nick sat back on his haunches and raised his head to a sky he couldn't see.

It cut out sharply, as he glared down at the ground, grey eyes narrowed. Growling, he left the room and ran up onto the rooftop.

Holding Beta in her arms, Ellen stared at the floor, speechless. Next to her, the Guardian gave a low hiss, slamming his head onto the ground.

'I don't know where he isssss…' he whispered softly, disbelievingly. 'I can't sssenssse his pressssscence…'

Her mouth a thin line; Ellen dropped Beta, before walking off to one of the computer rooms and slipping on a headset. Beta followed, leaving the Guardian behind.

'Reresan, you online?' She asked. The computerised voice answered 'yes', showing no emotion, probably unaware of what had just happened. 'Is there any information on what we should do if the Creator leaves the game world?'

'There are files on what to do if his character is destroyed. Open?'

'Nothing else? Like, if he managed to find a way back to reality?'

'If he thought that was likely, he would have data.'

'There's got to be something… what about the Spirit? Search for files – must contain 'spirit' and 'world'. Optional keywords – 'reality'.'

'Opening closest match…

'Notes: I found this file a while after my release. I still don't understand its meaning, but judging by the time space, it was during my sleep.

It didn't make much sense at the time, but after I e-mailed it to Staff Member Muvo, he was able to give me some information:

It speaks of a project called 'Accatel', thought to have been created by the Spirit — but any blueprints of data have been removed. I'm assuming it was important, but as yet I have not reactivated the project. I need to find out why it was shut down in the first place.'

The rest of the file cannot be read.'

'Accatel…' Ellen repeated, placing a hand on the screen. It was warm to her touch, smooth. 'Reresan, where was this file located?'

'Database: Destro Tower / Mechanical Creations / The Spirits / Unexamined.'

'Destro Tower,' she nodded, before heading off at a run from the room.

Once more, the sky above Destro was dark. The time was uncertain, but black clouds swirled over the area, hiding any sources of light.

Silently, the lone dragon stepped onto the rooftop and stared up into the sky. The floating island hung motionless, defying all laws of gravity.

I changed my shape... for you.

The swirling mass of clouds moved away from the moon, casting his fur in a bright light. His outline blurred.

Once more, a howl echoed through the cold night. Under his paws, the stone roof splintered like wood.

And if I must... I will change this world.

* * *

'Matt!' Maree cried, running over to him as the vision ended. 'Are you okay?'

After a moment of darkness, his eyes flickered back into view. 'Well, what do you know? The emotionless one has a heart!'

'What?' She said, blinking. He paused, ears pricking up as the wind howled around the ship.

'Go!'

The sea's turbulent rolling had almost stopped now, but the sky remained dark. Facing a scanner and letting a light shine into his eyes, Matt opened the door, before pushing them out.

'I thought it was already open...' Sam observed quietly.

'People can enter, but they cannot exit,' he replied, pulling Maree out through a corridor and pressing her against a wall, before checking the coast was clear and running onto the deck.

'...So what did the key do?' Said Sam quietly, raising an eyebrow.

'What're you doing?' Maree yelled, sliding on the soaking deck. Her hair was almost instantly drenched, hanging around her face in thick, dark strands.

'There isn't time to explain. I don't know! I don't understand!' He yelled, as the clouds turned a midnight blue, and thunder roared around him. 'Your friends are in danger! You have to get to them!'

'In danger? What from?'

'Death!' He said simply, before slamming into the startled pair and knocking them into the water.

* * *

'Ellen, where are we?'

'I'm not sure, I don't know half of where this place leads,' she said softly, running a hand along the cold stone walls. 'But I think we're close.'

'How can you tell?'

'There's a storm outside. I can feel the rain of my hands.' She pulled her hand away from the wall, and showed it to the creature. Droplets of water shone on her pale skin.

They paused, reaching a large, dark wooden door.

'Here,' she murmured, typing her password into a monitor at the side of the door. It swung outwards into mid air, and they were both knocked back by a gust of wind.

Beta cried out as he was knocked off his feet, flying against a wall.

'…Doi…' He mumbled, clutching a spinning head.

Brushing her hair from her eyes, Ellen stared out, below her only the sandy ground of the plains, hundreds of metres below. Too far to jump, but close enough to see the window she'd escaped out of with Crystal. Destro Tower sat waiting for them.

'How are we supposed to get across?' She whispered, voice lost above the noise of the storm.

'What're we gonna do, Ellen?' Yelled the imp, running over to her, fighting the gusts of icy air.

'There's got to be a way. There has to be,' she said, ignoring his cries and slumping to the ground. 'This is a game. There's always a way to win.'

Around her neck, the amulet was still glowing brightly. Its light was only brightened by the transparent surface next to her.

'What?' Ellen whispered, staring out into space. 'The air… it's reflecting the light of the amulet.'

She gave a sharp scream, leaping back, as the stone ceiling cracked. Jagged lines ran down the wall, destroying the cables to which the monitor was attached.

'The sky is falling! The *sky* is *falling!*' Beta yelled, running round in circles. Just outside the doorway, a bridge made entirely of mirror glass bridged the gap between the castle's two parts.

'How am I supposed to walk on that?' Ellen frowned, placing a foot on its frictionless surface. Suddenly, she was pulled forward, skidding along the bridge at high speed.

'Waa-hoo-hoo!' Cried Beta, belly-flopping onto it and skidding after her.

Whereas the Creator would probably have managed a slick, surfer style ride to the doorway at the tower's side, flipping in the air before landing safely, Ellen screamed throughout the whole few seconds of her journey and fell flat on her face as soon as she reached the end of the path.

'Do it again!' Yelled Beta, punching the air enthusiastically as he landed on her head. She sighed, thumping her head against the floor.

Inside the tower, it was almost completely dark. The only light was an odd blue glow, coming from large containers all over the room.

'Cool!' Squealed the imp, leaping off her and skipping towards one of the capsules. He froze in front of one of them, eyes growing wide.

'Humans!'

Groaning, Ellen got up, walking over to him and following his gaze.

'No…' she said, her brown eyes surveying the creatures in the tanks. '…They're androids.' She walked down the rows, scanning each robot in turn.

'D-2, D-3, D-4, iX, iV, ii, I, there's so many…' she whispered, reading the hand-drawn labels above each. 'Were they all by the Creator or the Spirit?'

'Look at this one Ellen!' Beta said excitedly, taking her to a robot that stood out from the others. D-0, Q60+, Accatel. A human with black, white and grey streaked hair lay floating in mid-air in one container, wearing a black and white tracksuit.

'Look! Isn't she pretty?'

'This one looks quite advanced...' Ellen said, staring at the teenager lying asleep in the container. 'I wonder why it was shut down...'

She ran a hand along the label, nodding. 'Accatel. It's the one he was talking about.'

She could recognize a lot of the robots, the same androids who had taken her to Serta or Destro tower, or tried to stop her as she escaped out the window with Crystal.

As she walked around the room, examining every robot and wondering what the Creator wanted her to do, a pair of bright green eyes slowly opened, and caught a glimpse of hair. Blonde hair.

'This must be where the Creator keeps iZ when he's not working on him.' Ellen muttered, looking at an empty container.

'Mm-mmph.' said Beta in what sounded like an agreement.

'Beta?' Ellen murmured, slowly turning to look at the imp. But she couldn't, because a sharp blade was pushing against her back.

'For so long I have waited for this day,' said a voice behind her. Though barely more than a whisper, it held more venom than the Guardian's fangs. 'The day I would finally have my revenge against you, for shutting me down, rejecting me,'

'...Who are you?' She asked, not daring to move. 'I-I didn't mean to upset you,'

'So I've been forgotten. A memory, replaced by those of more powerful androids,'

'You're an android? But the only android I remember is iZ!'

'You're in a room full of androids, idiot!' He hissed. 'Don't lie to me!'

'But I don't understand what this is about! Who are you?'

'You are my Creator, and you act like you don't even know me!' Said the voice angrily.

'The Creator?'

'No! My Creator!'

'I'm sorry, but I'm not your Creator. I'm Ellen, a programmer,' she explained.

She felt the blade relax, and slowly turned round to face the robot.

'Shoot...' It said, brushing his black hair from its eyes. 'You're not him, are you?'

'No. He just teaches me programming. Are you Accatel?'

'Yes,' Accatel said, nodding. Its cheeks were flushed with embarrassment, but it didn't show it, grinning in a too-late attempt at friendliness.

'You don't sound like a girl,' giggled Beta, as the robot pulled his hand from a mouth.

Accatel huffed, slapping its head. 'That's because I'm *male!*'

'Oh...' Ellen said, nodding slowly. 'It's the long hair that throws people off. The Creator gets that *all* the time.'

'Look, I don't have time for this!' He muttered exasperatedly, shaking his heads. 'Where is the Creator?'

'I was sent here by the Creator, he's not available right now.'

'Great...' groaned Accatel. 'I wait for ages, and he doesn't come, that's just my luck.'

He paused, staring at the pair. His eyes widened, before narrowing as he glanced around at the other capsules. 'You have to get out of here. You're in grave danger.'

'How?' Beta asked, raising an eyebrow.

'These robots only know of the Creator. Now they know you aren't him, they'll kill you,' said Accatel.

'But I need your help! The Creator's in danger!' Said Ellen.

Accatel paused, staring at her uncertainly. Sighing, he threw the shard of broken glass he'd pressed against her back aside, once again running a hand through his hair and making sure all the streaks had disappeared.

'I don't know what your business with him is, but if it means you'd risk your own life for it, then I'll tell you what I know. I've seen the Creator once here recently, when he accidentally reactivated me. He shut me down again, but I refused.'

'You refused?', probed Ellen.

'Yes. I went against my programming,' he said softly, eyes dimming. 'I wanted revenge.'

For a moment, he stood in silence, before shaking his head and regaining himself. 'Anyway, I saw him working on that prized android, iZ, last.'

'That's not much help. We don't need to find him – we know he's left the Dragon Realms. But I think you might be able to help us reach him,' said Ellen pensively

'I don't know what you're talking about,' Accatel replied, shaking his head and shrugging. Behind him, low, serpentine hisses signalled the opening of dozens of capsules.

'It looks like we're going to have to fight our way out of here.'

'But I can't fight!' Ellen exclaimed, as robots slowly exited their containers.

Accatel paused, looking at her. 'Are you a friend of the Creator?' He asked.

'Yes,' Ellen said, nodding.

'Then command me. Tell me what to do, and I will obey.'

'Are you sure?' Ellen asked.

'It's too late for that. We have linked, and you have to command me.'

'I can help! I played some computer games like this before!' Beta said excitedly.

'Sure,' Ellen agreed, silently wishing she were anywhere but here right now. 'Let's fight.'

'Right, start with a long range attack, while they're too confused to block it.'

Accatel raised his right hand, and pointing it directly at a wave of attackers. Electricity shot from his fingertips, jolting forward and striking them.

The blows were weak, but some of the poorer-built models still collapsed.

'Yay!' Cheered Ellen and Beta together.

'I'm going to do a wide range attack,' Accatel called, letting the angry androids surround him. 'Keep away from the b-b-last ar-rea.'

'Accatel, are you O.K.?' Ellen asked, as the android slowed slightly.

'F-fi-i-ne,' Accatel stuttered. *Not now, please not now!*

An android transformed its hand into a heavy club and sent him flying across the room. He got up at Ellen's feet, staggering as he walked back to the fight.

'He's slowing down...' Ellen muttered. 'That must be why the Creator rejected him. He keeps slowing down and freezing!'

'But he only just started up...' Beta said, confusion clouding his eyes. *How could he be tired already?*

Accatel had jumped awkwardly back into the middle of the robots, raising his hand once more, he slammed it into the stone, crying out.

Thick bolts of electricity leapt all over the floor, striking every robot in turn and shutting them down. Accatel screamed, as the bolts leapt across his own frame.

'He can't do this!' Ellen said, watching him. She stood motionless, as he refused to meet her eyes, staring determinedly at the ground.

As he yelled, she was reminded of the Creator's cries from within the capsule. The electricity leaping from his prison. How useless she was when it came to helping him.

'Dude...' groaned Accatel, slowing to a stop. His eyes changed to orange, head falling forward.

'Look out!' Yelled Beta, as an android thrust a spear at Accatel.

'...That was one radical battle...' Accatel said quietly, as his eyes went to red and closed. His grasp of the language left him, words slurred and unclear.

The robots closed in, hitting him with almost every weapon imaginable.

'We have to get him out of there!' Ellen said to Beta. She could feel the amulet pulsing with energy, in rhythm with her own heart.

'I'm ready,' Beta said bravely, nodding to her and rushing into the fight.

They both headed towards Accatel, pushing past androids as they went.

'Reboot!' She yelled. Accatel's bright green eyes slowly opened, looking at her.

'I'm loading,' he muttered sleepily, clutching his shoulder where the spear had torn away the tracksuit. The skin had scraped off, exposing the metal underneath.

'We need to get out of here!' Ellen said, as Beta kicked away an approaching robot.

'*You* need to get out of here,' he said, staring at her. 'I'll find my own way of escape.'

He stood up and pulled back his tracksuit, revealing a small speaker in his wrist.

'M.G.T. Building,' he said, speaking into it.

'Hello?' Said a young voice.

'Hey. Patch me through to the plane currently above Destro.'

'Plane?' Said the voice, startled.

'I know it's there, O.K,' he said sharply, voice turning cold. 'Now, put me through if you want it to stay in the air!'

'M.G.T. Building?' Beta asked. Ellen shrugged.

'Hello?' Said a voice, older and deeper.

'Hey there! I don't care who you are or what you're doing, but get over to Destro and fly below the floating tower. *Now.*'

He cut off the link, and looked at Ellen, kicking away a robot.

'Jump out the window now,' he instructed, hitting another away with his hand.

'Sure,' Ellen said uncertainly, not willing to argue. 'Come on, Beta!'

'What about you?' Beta said, pausing to look up at Accatel.

'Don't worry about me. I'm not going to let this bunch get in my way,' he said, grinning. He watched, as Beta and Ellen leapt boldly out of the window, and then hopped onto one of the containers, watching them fall.

'The true light is hidden somewhere,' he whispered, thinking about the strange girl he had just met, and the brightly glowing amulet she wore.

'The true light...' He repeated, twirling his hair round his finger thoughtfully, before leaping off the container and out the nearest window.

'Ellen, hold onto me!' Beta yelled, as they fell from the floating tower.

'What?' Ellen said, her hairs blowing about her face in the wind.

'I'm a prototype! I'm unnaturally strong, I can do it!' He yelled, slowing his descent by hovering. He grabbed hold of Ellen, and managed to slow her fall, the metal hover-fans attached to the bottom of his feet on full blast.

'There they are!' Yelled a voice. Ellen looked down, and saw a black panther racing across Destro's dry plains.

'Where?' Shouted a black dragon, zooming around the tower and colliding with Ellen and Beta. 'Oh, there,' he said, flapping his wings hard and grabbing hold of the pair.

At first, Ellen thought it was a human using the Phoenix wings, but she soon realised it was a black human-like dragon, with two large wings on his back.

'Who are they?' The panther called from below, staring up at them as it raced across the plains.

'A blonde girl and a...thing...' he said, looking at Beta.

'Hi there!' Ellen said, hanging from his hand. 'My name's Ellen.'

'Apocalypse,' he said, nodding. 'But you can call me Cal.'

'We're over here!' Yelled a voice. Cal turned, and saw a plane flying from the clouds above Destro. Cal flapped round, his powerful wings supporting all three of them, and flew them over to the plane.

'Hey there!' Said a black haired boy in a white jacket, turning round in the pilot's seat.

'Hop on board!' Said the other passenger, a boy with dark brown hair. Even Ceirin would have had trouble recognizing him now, with a smile of his face and dark clothing.

The plane extended, lengthening and forming another seat, and Cal dropped Ellen and Beta into it. As soon as they sat down, the plane changed again, forming a roof so that they couldn't see out.

'Welcome onto the *Condor*,' said the brown haired boy. 'My name's Climax, but Jak here calls me Harry. Who are you?'

'I'm Ellen,' she said.

'…Shoot…' Harry said, lowering his gaze.

'…Oh dear…' Jak sighed, bringing the plane lower to let his panther-dragon climb onto the wing of the plane. 'Oh dear, oh dear, oh dear.'

'I like deer. It's amazing,' his partner growled, curling up in a seat and glancing lazily around at the new passengers. 'We need to go get some deer. We should hunt tonight.'

'Are we missing something?' Beta asked.

'Nope. He normally makes no sense whatsoever. And sounds like a homicidal maniac,' Jak replied, leaning back in the passengers seat and staring at the imp. He frowned. 'I think he named himself Setsu, it's a homicidal panther's name.'

Muttering darkly, Setsu stalked away and leapt onto the wing of the plane.

'You're Ceirin's friend,' Cal explained. 'We had a run in with him a while ago. We think we got on his bad side. If he finds out we're here, we're in even bigger trouble.'

'How?' Ellen asked.

'He hates us,' Climax said. 'He thinks I'm some player who reckons he's stronger than everyone. But we're not that bad, really – we've just got to look it for the Crystal Clan.'

At a loss for anything better to do, Jak pressed a button on the plane's dashboard. Sad, slow violin music filled the plane, and he quickly changed it to something far less boring.

He nodded to Harry, who continued. 'When we looked up Ceirin and found him frozen, we took his plane and headed straight here to find the Creator.'

'Don't worry,' Ellen said optimistically. 'I'm sure he'll forgive you.'

'Yeah… riiiiiiight,' Climax sighed, shaking his head. 'That dude's going to kill me on sight!'

'He doesn't even know we work at the M.G.T. building,' Cal added.

'Where?'

'The Mini Games Testing Building. We've been members of it *long* before that whole cult deal.' The dark-skinned dragon caught Ellen's blank look, frowning. 'Surely Ceirin's told you about it? He owns the building, in Silverleaf city, and comes up with new ideas for all sorts of mini games which he lets us test. He even builds the machines for use in the games, like this glider, the *Condor*.'

Ellen still looked confused, but frowned at his words.

'A glider? So it flies using thermals, hot air currents from the ground?'

'Pretty much,' said Jak, nodding. Yawning, he put his hands behind his head, not paying any attention at all to where they were flying. Auto-pilot rocked!!

'Uh-oh…' Beta squeaked, covering his eyes.

'What?' Jak asked, blinking.

'There's no heat in Destro Castle! The Creator thinks it's more atmospheric. Even the lightening is cold!'

'No way!' Yelled Climax, as, right on cue, the plane started to drop.

'We're going to crash!' Cal yelled, diving behind a chair.

'I know!' Jak replied, pressing buttons randomly on the plane's control panel.

From the edge of Destro Gardens, Accatel stopped, dusting his track-suit after jumping out of the floating tower onto the plains.

'You shouldn't interfere with my quest,' He muttered, watching the falling plane and checking Ellen was on it. 'But I guess I owe you,'

For a second, his eyes glowed a bright lime, and he stared at the plane. Green bolts circled its metal frame.

Then, they were gone, and Accatel returned to normal.

'Debt repaid,' He muttered, as the plane levelled out, still descending. 'But now, I have to end this Quest,' He stared up at Destro, at the window that marked the Creator's bedroom, and his eyes narrowed. 'Revenge will be mine,'

Chapter 17:

The Spirit's Shadow

Vision was blurred. His eyes felt heavy, and he felt uneasily like he had been drugged. Convincing himself it was just lack of food or water, he tried to lick his dry lips. Instead, he tasted the sharp tang of metal.

He immediately decided now was not a good time to open his eyes.

'Open your eyes,'

As much as the command contradicted his current train of thought, he did so. At first, he thought he was in complete darkness. Then he realised he was staring into someone's eyes.

…*Shoot*…

Every part of his brain was screaming at him to look away. Look away from the inky black darkness. Look away from the pools of nothingness.

But he knew what he'd see if he lowered his gaze.

Instead, he kept silent, staring straight ahead. His hands were bound, tingling painfully as they lost all feeling. Forcing his hands to move, skin and rope rubbing together and adding to the pain, he discovered his gun pockets were empty.

Afraid to even try and mumble, to taste again that horrible taste, he contented himself with focussing on a spot just above the eyes and cursing mentally. At least those blasted game censors couldn't stop that.

'You're awake,' a simple statement. The Creator found himself struggling to ignore his urge to reply *'duh'*. It wasn't the time to be cocky. 'It's good to see your eyes again,'

The eyes in question dared to stare into the speakers, filled with a bitter hatred. This wasn't his own character. This wasn't Matt, Storm, Ceirin, the Council… this wasn't anything he could cope with. This was *it*. The Spirit.

'They were one of the things I liked most about you. Revealing just how cold your heart was,' The teenager flinched, as the Spirit pressed a hand against his chest, but the touch was soft, as thought the hand wasn't really there. 'It seems a pity that heart must soon stop beating,'

It was then that he realised he had been stripped not only of his weapons, but of his jacket and shoes as well. The Spirit was not unfamiliar with the idea of concealed weapons, though past memories revealed he was uncomfortable with modern items like guns. It was a miracle; the shot he had used to kill the silver-haired girl when Ellen was at Destro Castle had actually done so.

Without his outfit, he felt bare and exposed. Still, at least the demonic creature had seen fit to leave him with his trousers and shirt on – there were some lows even the darkest of villains wouldn't go.

'I care not about your dignity. I left you in that shirt because it was white, nothing more,' hissed the Spirit, adding in a lower, colder note. 'It'll bring out the colour of your blood,'

The Creator didn't reply, but the shocked expression on his face made his feelings clear.

'Don't act so surprised – the expression is most unfitting of you,' He sighed, twisting his face in mock agony. 'Minds are easily penetrated, boy,'

He raised his left hand, and a soft *'click'* rang through the air.

The limp apprentice gained consciousness, waking at the snap of his master's fingers. He glanced at the pair, the two boys – one smirking at the other. The second; eyes closed and body tense, shaking. Not even a flicker of recognition or emotion appeared in his eyes.

'Take this,' commanded the Spirit, retrieving one of the Creator's guns and tossing it backwards. Ceirin easily snatched it out of the air. 'And point it at his head.'

'Now,' said the Spirit softly, almost soothingly. 'I'm going to take this gun away. Don't try anything stupid.' The gun was pulled away, before being pressed against his chest. 'I don't care whether it's your brains or your heart I leave on the wall,'

Finally able to move his head and look round, the Creator took a relieved breath, before feeling his body retch. The air was warm and stale, and stank with an odour he had never had the misfortunate to smell before, but instantly recognized as that of rotting flesh.

Forcing his mind to block it out, he spat on the ground, and saw that it was white. Everything around him was white.

He guessed from the location that the area was meant to be some kind of snow-covered cave, but it was far from the stage of realism. The colour was right – white – but everything else was wrong – the room was square and the walls and floor were smooth and flat.

It was like being trapped in a paper cube. Complete emptiness, apart from the three figures. And with it, a silence, the silence as is in a coffin far underneath the cold earth. Heard by few but the doomed.

His gaze moved to the Spirit, watching his face with sick enjoyment. It was a gruesome sight; skin both paper white and paper thin, almost transparent. It showed clearly the bones underneath, from his skeletally thin waist to his gnarled, arthritic hands.

A damp white shirt clung to his ribcage, stained dark around the heart. The hair that hung around his gaunt face was thin, hanging in greasy strands. It was clearly blonde.

With a grin, the Spirit ran his hand down his dark jeans, held up only by a leather belt. The Creator grimaced, recognizing the clothes as his own and feeling disgusted that such a creature dared touch them.

'Why do you still look like me?' He said coldly, summoning all his strength into keeping his voice steady and level.

'That's because I am you,'

The Creator paled, shaking his head. 'That's not true,'

'I wasn't originally. When I first came to you, I had no true form. I was simply a voice, a soothing voice that was there when you needed me most. Whispering sweet reassurances and lies into your ear, blackening your heart. It was… fun.

Then, after that blasted robot managed to free you, I was forced to flee to the outskirts of your game. And there I waited, until a loophole back into your mind presented itself to me,' He paused, waiting for a reaction. None came.

'Dragon mythology rules that all programs, or characters in this game, have a dark or 'virus' side. There's also a neutral and a good, but balance is hard to achieve, and these sides are almost always mixed together. So I took my place as the virus form of you,'

'That's impossible,' The Creator stammered. *How can he know that?* 'Viruses can't enter this game,'

'The only thing that's certain in life is death. Nothing is perfect. There are ways,'

'How?'

'If you were to live, no doubt it would become apparent. But as it is, that is not the case. Such a pity,' drawled the Spirit, grinning once more. His character design altered from the Creator in that grin – while the Creator had four protruding canines, keeping true to his feline side, the Spirit had the more vampire-like two. 'It looks like there's not going to be a Dragon Tamers 3,'

His words unnerved the Creator, filled with knowledge he didn't possess – that of the future. Every word seemed to make his death more certain, darkening the future and blocking all thoughts of one from his mind.

Feeling it unwise to ask further, his gaze moved to Ceirin. The Spirit followed his eyes.

The teen stood nearby, barely breathing. His eyes were glassy, and he swayed slightly as he attempted to stand still. The gun in his hand was pointed straight at his head, with a precise aim the knife and dagger expert shouldn't posses.

'You've edited his data,' stated the Creator. It was a simple term, used often when he programmed – but with the Spirit, skilled not in programming but in control of others, it took on a whole different meaning.

'I played around with both of your minds,' said the Spirit, nodding and waving his hand. Ceirin started moving, movements jerky and erratic. 'He is nothing more than a puppet to me now,'

'How?' He asked. It was becoming harder to string together a full sentence – his fear was getting the better of him. Frowning, he shook the tightening feeling in his stomach away, but the dark thoughts remained lodged firmly in his head.

'Power over humans is easy to gain. I asked his full name, and the idiot gave it. A stupid name to match a stupid boy – Ceirin Kitsune. Coupled with the power I had gained over him earlier, he was a simple task to overcome,'

The Creator paused, confused and afraid. *I've got to keep talking...*

'I still don't understand how your power works. How is it all you needed was my name to take complete control over by body, but for him you had to work on his mind, blocking memories and scaring him into submission?'

'In your world, and in this, names have little power. They're simply an accessory,' he said silkily, watching his prey's expression. 'Yes, Alex. You had no reason to hide your name from the world,'

He paused, before pulling Alex close to him, grabbing his shirt and hissing in his ear. 'I got control of Kitsune through his mind. I got control of you through your heart,'

Alex's shirt was pulled tight around his neck, and his words came out choked and panicked. 'If what you say is true, then tell me your name,'

The Spirit paused, frowning. His grip loosened, only to grow tighter than before seconds later. 'Very well. M-'

'First, I'll tell you mine,' interrupted the Creator desperately, adding, 'the game's rulebook states all trades should be fair. I want this one to be,'

Another pause, before the Spirit nodded. The shirt was like a noose around his neck now, and he didn't dare try to struggle against its grip. 'My name is… Alexander James Stewart,'

'And mine,' said the Spirit in turn, cold breath chilling Alex's skin. 'Is Damien,'

His blood ran cold, as icy lips brushed his cheek. Alex gasped, and felt the Spirit jam a gun into his open mouth and tilt it upwards, pulling the trigger.

Chapter 18:

Extermination

A flash of metal. The gun was pinned against the wall, before its many splintered pieces fell to the ground. In the Spirit's hand, the pistol didn't possess any of a signature weapon's awesome power. Ceirin's harmoniknife did.

Damien span round to face Ceirin, noticing his aim had shifted.

There was a soft 'click', followed by a single gunshot. '*That* was for me,'

A second shot, to the heart. '*That* was for iZ,'

'And *this*,' He shifted his aim once more, to the Spirit's head, before pulling the trigger a final time. 'Is for Alex,'

Averting his gaze, Ceirin tossed the pistol in the Creator's direction, knowing he couldn't pick it up with his hands tied. As it hit the ground to the Creator's side, another shot rang through the air, and he nearly leapt out of his skin. 'Oh... sorry,'

He paused, staring at the boy kneeling in the middle of the room. 'Aw, stop being such a wimp. Don't tell me you programmed shock into this game,'

The Creator managed a small smile, shaking his head slightly, before trying and failing to spit out the other end of the pistol.

Ceirin didn't notice his struggles, dislodging his harmoniknife from the wall. *Lucky shot... especially with my left hand.* He stopped, glancing down at the Spirit's body. 'I guess your training came in handy in the end. Ironic,'

Irritated by the Creator's mumbling, he walked over and cut his bound hands loose, before returning to examine the pieces of the gun. It had been broken in half in a way that was impossible for any weapon but a sword to do – and even then, not to a gun. It was puzzling, but he shrugged it off. The magic of the Dragon Realms came into play at the oddest times.

Within seconds, he found what had been the Spirit's fatal mistake. 'Idiot left the safety lock on,'

As the Creator threw the remnants of his pistol to the ground, Ceirin came over and sat down next to him. 'Close call. You alright?'

Alex paused uncertainly, raising a hand to his cheek.

'Don't let that bother you,' Ceirin said firmly. 'You looked like him, and he loved himself. He had no true emotions,'

Alex paused. '...Thank you, Ceirin,'

'I'll find a way for you to repay me,'

Again, the Creator paused. It was awkward – Ceirin just saved his life, the person he'd least expect to be capable of such a task. His eyes fell, unavoidably, on Damien's body. 'You're a good shot,'

'I learnt from the master,' He said with a smile. 'That is, if you really are who you said you were,'

'I am,' He said, with a sad nod. 'It's been a long time,'

'More than two years now,' Replied Ceirin; trying to remember the time they had spent as best friends, when he lived in England. It was hard – memories came slowly, in pieces. Working on early character designs for War of the Cats. Leafing through books of weapons for game designs. Alex teaching him more about guns than any kid should know, child prodigy or not. Looking through fantasy comics for costume designs, and turning on random TV Shows. Preparing to move to Secondary School, only to find out he was moving to America, where he'd have to wait another year for that.

'What was it like in Oro Academy?'

'Boring… especially without my best friend,' The Creator replied, his sad eyes hinting that something bad happened in his two years of high school – that they were years he didn't want to relive. 'Eton actually asked for me to transfer there shortly before the end of the term, when the papers got hold of information about the game. Then I was taken over by *him*,' He glared down at Damien, face twisted in demonic rage. 'I didn't even get one look at the school,'

'Whoa…' Ceirin said, with a low whistle. 'Eton *asked* for you?'

'Not really – I took the entrance exam shortly after you left. Two years later, I took another exam, and they said I was welcome to join,' Alex laughed; blushing as he realised he's said the wrong thing. *A school like Eton would never actually 'ask' a kid like him to join. He was good at maths, art, English and computing. Nothing special.*

'A month later, I was missing, presumed dead,' He snarled grimly. 'Disappearing in the middle of the summer holidays,'

'I never heard anything,'

'You never heard from me when I was still *alive*,' He said sharply, frowning. 'No phone calls, no e-mails, nothing. You had my address, but I didn't have yours! Why didn't you contact me?'

'I lost it!'

'You could have found out!'

'I didn't know *how!*' Cried Ceirin, instantly bringing the argument to a halt. Taking a calming breath, he added 'Look – you were always the computer wiz kid. I was just the guy who came up with some drawings, some early character designs – it wasn't even for Dragon Tamers,'

Slowly, the Creator nodded. 'No. It was for War of the Cats,' Hugging his knees close to him, he stared up at the white walls around him.

'Looking at us, you'd think where we were had nothing to do with the current plot. But it's connected. There's always a connection,'

Ceirin murmured a soft 'Mm', also deep in thought. 'How do you think we'll get out of here?'

'We'll find a way,'

Ceirin glanced uneasily at Alex. 'You sure you're okay, dude?'

He nodded. 'I'm just a little tired. This kind of adventure takes a lot out of you,'

'You never seem to have much strength,'

'I lead a busy life,'

Again, another thoughtful pause. There wasn't much to do here, except talk, and think. Nowhere to go, nothing to look at. It was the most unbelievably boring place either of them had ever been.

Eventually, Ceirin was forced to break the silence once more. 'I miss Maree,'

'And I miss Ellen,'

As though they'd said some kind of keyword, large gashes appeared almost instantly in the walls. Claws, fangs, and blades all tore through the smooth surface, destroying it in minutes.

A few clean swipes later, and it fell forward, revealing Maree, Sam, Nick and Ellen, Beta and the Guardian.

Maree was standing with her sword in her hands, glowing with the same light as Ellen's amulet, instead of its usual purple shade.

As Ellen ran forward and wrapped her arms around Alexander, Maree sheathed her sword and stood, emotionless, next to Sam.

Staring at her as he passed, Nick swooped low over to Ceirin, wrapping his soft wings around his tamer.

'Ceirin,' He whispered softly, before falling into his arms as a puppy.

'Nick? You can still shape-shift?'

'No,'

'Then... how? Why?'

'Because I was scared,'

Ceirin stared at the ground while Nick pushed his head into his tamer's hands. 'Don't ever do that to me again,'

Nodding, the apprentice, slave to the shadows, stroked the young wolf on the head. 'I can't remember what you were like when I was taming you. When you were a wolf pup,'

'You're looking at me,' He mumbled. 'Like I said, I can't shape shift... but I can remember. I'm a memory,'

Annoyed by the change of subject, he rolled away from Ceirin and glared up at him, ears pricked up. 'You really scared me, you know. I thought he was going to turn round at any moment and kill you,'

'Yeah. So did I,'

'Ellen, come on! Get off me!' Mumbled Alex, shrugging her off. He stared up at the dark figure towering above him, and paled.

'...Shoot...' He whispered, words as ironic as ever.

A low hiss filled the area, couple with a cry as the Guardian wrapped himself tightly around his master, rubbing his scaly head against his masters.

'It's good to see you too, Guardian,' Alex acknowledge quietly, petting his head.

'I'm ssssorry...'

'Nobody could stop it,' Said Alex firmly, shaking his head. He paused, taking a deep gasp of breath. 'Now. A little air, if you'd please?'

'Oh,' Hissed the Guardian, uncoiling. The Creator dropped to the ground, breathing returning to its normal (healthy) level.

'You really worried us,' Said Ellen quietly, stepping over to him and smiling. 'When I saw you there... with him... and those guns...'

Her smile left her, eyes flooding over with tears. With a short wail, she threw herself at the Creator, wrapping her arms around him.

He stared at her, startled, before patting her shoulder. He was unused to such emotion. 'Hey, it's alright. I'm fine. We're all going to be alright,'

Silent, Maree stood next to her trouble partner. Sam raised an eyebrow at the teenage girl, shaking her head.

'What?' Maree snapped, glaring at her.

'There's no need to feel out of place here,' She whispered softly. 'This is a video game, Maree. There's bound to be someone here who understands you,'

Maree shook her head, denying whatever her dragon was accusing her of. 'What are you saying?'

'You're both living in a world where nobody else is like you,' Nick said quietly, stepping over to Sam. They both nodded to each other, nose touching nose. 'When in this world, you two are meant to be together,'

'I don't know what you're talking about!'

'Oh, good council…' Sighed Sam, kicking her into Ceirin.

They both yelled, falling to the ground. Ceirin laughed, smiling at her, but she blushed and scrambled away.

'Hey. For a minute there, I thought you weren't speaking to me,' He laughed, smiling at her. *Whoa… it's not often you see Maree blush.*

Turning away, she hurriedly regained her disgruntled attitude, glaring at him. 'I don't know whether to hug you, or punch you. Right now, I'm considering both,'

'Ack, come on Maree!' He sighed jokingly, rubbing the back of his neck. 'Don't you think I've been through enough?'

She laughed, voice choking as she tried to force a smile. She failed.

'Hey, you alright?' He asked, brushing her hair from her eyes. As he did, he felt water on his fingertips.

'Maree?' He whispered disbelievingly, looking into her eyes as tears streamed down her face.

'I'm sorry,' She whispered, hiding her eyes from him. He frowned, turning her head back to him.

'What about? You've got nothing to apologise for,'

'For not being good enough for you,' she said, looking him straight in the eyes. 'I always act like such an arrogant fool in this game, but I'm lost. You're the only boy who's ever seen anything in me, and I've been nothing but…but…. I'll never be good enough for someone as amazing as you,'

Ceirin shook his head at her, smiling warmly. 'What are you talking about? You're perfect,'

'Don't lie to me!' 'She' yelled, glaring at him. 'I'm nowhere near. I'm not some blonde-haired, blue-eyed beauty. I'm not in possession of any awesome magical powers. I can't program… I'm not even part of the Dragon Tamers staff! In this game, I'm nothing but a player who happened to train hard and get into the charts. I don't even deserve the title of strongest player. I've done nothing for the game,'

'Aw, now you're just being silly,' He sighed, shaking his head. 'Maree, if you hadn't been here, half of this would never have happened. Ellen wouldn't have met the Creator. We'd never have passed Riddle of the

Sphinx. We'd have been hopeless in Fear Fork. Heck, I probably would have betrayed the party five minutes into the game!'

'Yeah, right,' she laughed dryly. 'You were told to take us to the Spirit,'

'Not true,' Ceirin countered, shaking his head. 'I was told to destroy you. Nothing more. No time, no place, just as soon as I could. And I didn't, did I?'

He waited, and she shook her head. 'That's right. And if it had been anyone else, I would have,'

'Then why not me?' She asked uncertainly, fear in her eyes – of her current state, of what could have happened, of what he could say. Of everything.

'Because you were the only player in that whole game who cared for me as a person,'

'I'm just so glad it's over,' Ellen said quietly, lying in Alex's arms. 'But it's not, is it? We've still got to figure out this whole War of the Cats thing,'

'That's part of the fun,' He replied, smiling at her. 'We'll figure this all out, Ellen. We're going to complete every challenge this game can throw at us – you'll see,'

'This is all so stupid,' laughed Maree, drying her eyes. 'It's so soppy. We're sitting here, in the middle of nowhere, with no idea how to get back and no idea how we got here in the first place,'

'Yeah, I guess it is pretty weird,' He chuckled. 'I don't even know where you are right now,'

'I'm not too sure myself,' Maree said, frowning. 'Last thing I remember, I was aboard the Sea's Shadow – Storm's boat,'

'Then I guess that's where we're headed,' Ceirin replied confidently, before glancing round at the rest of the room. He smiled, seeing Ellen and the Creator.

'Hey, have you two finished snogging yet?'

'I beg you're pardon?' Alex exclaimed, staring in disbelief at Ceirin.

'What he said!' Ellen gasped, imitating his appalled look. 'Yeah, we're ready to go when you are,'

'Cool!' Ceirin nodded, before frowning. '...How'd we get out?'

'This area will collapse upon itself,' the Creator said quietly, staring uneasily at the white surroundings. His eyes still refused to linger on the Spirit's corpse; afraid it might return to life at his gaze.

'Sssso assss ssssssoon as we ssssstep out of it, we'll return to where we were,' The Guardian hissed, slithering through the partially destroyed wall and home to a well-deserved rest.

'Keep an eye out the window, okay!' Ellen laughed, winking at Ceirin before hopping out into the normal game.

'You will find me, right?' Maree asked uncertainly, pausing at the exit.

'Of course,' He nodded firmly, releasing her hand as they both stepped through.

The final one to depart, Alex grudgingly helped Beta climb through the hole back to the Dragon Realms, before glancing once more around the all-too-familiar world.

He paused, shivering, before leaving the Spirit World forever.

Chapter 19:

Playing Games

'What a weird dream...' Ellen murmured, shaking away the visions of guns and the Creator. She was sitting in the Condor, in a strange, but not altogether uncomfortable position.

'Dream? When did you fall asleep?' Climax said, glancing at her calmly as she got up from underneath a chair.

'Maybe she was knocked unconscious,' Jak suggested coolly, pulling out a dagger and stabbing an airbag to death.

'We would have noticed,'

'It wasn't a dream...' She murmured. *The Creator on the ground...the Spirit was going to shoot him! What happened next? Was he alright?*

'Ellen...' Beta whimpered softly, pulling himself out from under a seat. 'I remember something...'

'So do I, Beta. It wasn't a dream...' Ellen whispered, frowning. Beta opened his mouth to reply, but was drowned out by everyone yelling as the plane tumbled suddenly to the side.

'What's happening?' Beta and Ellen yelled in unison.

'I'm not sure,' Jak replied, staring out the window. 'I think something's hitting us from the side!'

'But what could be that big?' Cal wondered, not really caring. He was too busy follow Jak's gaze out the cracked windows, at the plane's wing.

'The Guardian!' Ellen and Beta exclaimed, still in unison.

'Who?' said Climax.

'That whole unison thing's getting annoying,' Commented Jak, turning a key and trying to get the plane to start up again. It didn't react to his frantic attempts, so he stabbed at the door until it fell off.

'That stupid snake...' Ellen muttered, climbing out of the plane.

'Setsu!' Jak yelled, getting out of the plane and looking round. The panther was lying on the ground nearby, dizzy from the crash.

'Guardian, you idiot!' Ellen yelled, as the snake continued to head-butt the plane.

'Yessss?' He asked, turning to look at Ellen.

'I was in that plane!' She shouted up angrily.

'Oh...' He hissed, bowing his head. 'Sssssorry...'

'It's okay,' Ellen said, stroking the Guardian's head. 'You were just doing your job,'

'Yeah, ask about us, why don't you?' Harry mumbled, brushing shards of glass from his hair. 'We're just the ones who saved her in the first place,'

'You two know each other?' Climax asked, staring at them.

'Of course we do. Guardian, these are the Mini. Minis, this is the Guardian,'

'Hi!' Cal said, waving a three-fingered hand.

'Guardian, we need to get into Destro,'

'You're alwaysssss welcome, Ellen, but the otherssss…'

'We can stay out here, Ellen. But if you see the Creator, will you ask him about Ceirin?'

'I will…' Ellen said, running out. If she saw the Creator. Ever again.

'Where are we going?' Beta said, looking around.

'I don't know. This place is huge, I never really know,'

'What do you think happened?'

'I don't want to think about it, Beta,' Ellen said, shivering. It couldn't be true. He had to have escaped, somehow.

'There's something down here!' Said Beta, his eyes glowing.

'He wouldn't build robots in this darkness, so it can't be a workshop,' Said Ellen, walking over to one of the shapes. 'I can't see a thing, this is no use,'

She brought her hand to her amulet, and it started glowing strongly.

'It's his motorbikes,' Ellen said, looking round.

'I remember them. If he shoots into the sky, one falls down,' Said Beta.

'I wonder how they work,' She wondered, stepping around the dark shapes. *Whoa… a whole squadron of motorbikes. Maybe they'll come in handy.*

'Beta!' The imp cried, running over a familiar looking wall. 'I remember this place, at!'

Ellen frowned. *What's with his speech pattern… it seems to come naturally to him. It's not really the kind of thing the Creator would give him.*

'What is it, Beta?'

'This thingy. It works kind of like a lift,' He said, pulling aside what looked like part of the wall and revealing a dark dumbwaiter. 'Nobody really used it. It was easy to sneak around the castle, if you knew where you were going,'

'So you know all the places this can take you?'

'Yeah. I got a big map in my head. Like a dungeon!' He said proudly, poking his ears.

'Can you remember the way to that corridor where Ceirin and the Creator disappeared?'

'Easy!'

Grinning, Ellen shifted to the programming world. There, she expanded the dumbwaiter, twisting the laws of space to allow it to fit. Alerting Beta, she gave him a few commands before allowing him to join in.

After a short while, they returned to the normal world in front of an elevator.

'Yay-hay!' Beta cried, leaping into the mirror-walled machine. Following, Ellen stared at the small map above the control panel.

'I've got it!' He yelled, hovering up to the right button and head butting it. With a musical 'ding-dong', the doors closed. The elevator moved all over the place – up, down, left and right - and opened again when they'd reached the right area.

'Come on, let's go,' Ellen whispered, running out into the corridor.

After they'd left, the emergency exit at the top of the elevator slid open. As the now dark elevator stood motionless, the green-eyed boy swung into it, black hair hanging messily around him.

Grinning, he dug his nails in between the two doors.

'Found you,'

* * *

The Spirit had done it again. Interfered with his life, with everyone's life.

He had thought the Spirit was gone. But how could he be? You can't destroy a spirit…

'…Cold,' He murmured, opening his eyes. It was so cold…

'It's okay,' Ceirin said, sitting back against the window and watching his friend's fitful awakening. 'We've escaped, we're safe now,'

'We're never safe…never free…always cold…' The Creator whispered.

'Yes we are!'

'We're not…we can't kill him, can't be free!'

'We can't with that kind of attitude,' Ceirin scolded, walking over to him and trying to shake him fully awake. He put a hand on the Creator's arm. '…You really are cold. What's wrong?'

'He wants me back…'

'No way!' Ceirin yelled. 'We just got rid of him!'

'…I'm not strong enough to do this. I can't handle this. I want to go back to sleep,'

'No! Don't say that!'

'It won't be for long. A year…maybe more,'

'While he wreaks havoc on the Dragon Realms! I don't think so!'

'I've had enough, Ceirin. There's too much mess for me to clear up…I can't fix the Realms,'

'Yes you can! If you let him take you over again, all your work will have been for nothing!'

'I'm passed caring,'

'But what about your friends? What about Ellen?'

'She can cope,'

'Oh yeah!' Said Ceirin. 'Well then what about *iZ*?' The Creator frowned. 'Didn't think about him, did you? If you let go now, his death will have meant nothing!' Ceirin yelled.

'Izzy…' The Creator murmured quietly.

'Now tell me…' demanded Ceirin. 'Are you *really* ready to let go?'

The Creator struggled to his feet, the warmth returning. Ceirin helped pull him up.

'No,' he replied firmly. 'I'm not ready to give up,'

'Good,' Ceirin grinned. 'Now, you get yourself a cup of tea and rest, Okay? I'm going to find out why the *Condor*'s in the middle of Destro Gardens,'

Sighing, the Creator lay back on the floor. *It feels like a weight's been lifted off my shoulders. It's pretty cool.*

'Hey…' Ellen said, stepping out of the elevator and spotting him. Sitting on her shoulder, Beta breathed a sigh of relief.

Oh, thank goodness…

'Hey, El,' he greeted, nodding to her as she stepped out into the corridor. 'Was that elevator there yesterday?'

'Just programmed it in,' she replied, smiling. 'What're you doing in the middle of the corridor?'

'Relaxing. It's cool here,' he shrugged, glancing behind her.

'Want to head somewhere else?' Ellen asked, cheered by his sudden change in attitude.

'Sure. Listen, I've got to find out where Ceirin went. You head to my room – I'll be there in a few minutes,'

'Alright,' she nodded, running up the stairs to the next floor.

The Creator placed a hand on the wall. A metal screen slid down over the door.

'Who are you, and what do you want?' He said sharply, eyes narrowing as he surveyed the boy standing in the corridor. The stranger paused, eyes flashing.

'You don't remember,'

'No, I *freaking* don't. Maybe, if you told me, I would.' Alex replied sharply.

Nodding, Accatel pulled down his sleeve, facing his arm to the Creator. A dark tattoo was imprinted on it, of a circle changing into an arrow with a circle and square branching off from it.

USB.

'I see,' he nodded, leaning back against the wall. Without thinking, he changed from his white shirt to leisure outfit from before – the long-sleeved black shirt and loose trousers.

Smirking, Accatel brought a silver pistol from inside his jacket, pointing it at the Creator.

'Bad move,'

'Not necessarily. If you were planning on hurting me, you would have done it much more subtly. You want something,'

'Unless I want to speak with you before I kill you,'

'That is a possibility,' shrugged the Creator. 'But what do I care? I just wish you'd left it until tomorrow. I've already had one - near successful – attempt at my life today. It's no wonder this world's youth are stressed,'

'I could kill you from right here. One shot, and it's goodbye to the angst-filled little brat,'

'I'm not that easy to kill off, android,'

'Not normally. But you're not in the best of states today, are you?'

'Do I need to be? You have questions that need answers. I can provide them. There's no need for violence,' Alex said evenly, glancing benignly at Accatel. 'Violence won't tell you what you need to know,'

'This is a trick,' Accatel said warily, lowering the weapon.

'I give you my word, it is not,'

'Your word is worth *nothing* to me,'

'It's all I have to give,'

Accatel froze, eyes narrowing. 'You have your life. And to me, that's worth a lot more,' The Creator snapped, leaping forward and snatching the gun out of his hands, before tossing it out a window.

'Enough of this charade, Accatel!' He growled, grabbing his sleeve and dragging him through to the lounge. Accatel hung limp, as he was thrown onto a couch, and his opponent took a seat on the opposite side of the room.

'You have questions. I have questions. We both shall ask them, and they'll both be answered. It's simple,' he said, sprawling back on the white leather sofa. 'I know why you're here, I know what you want. I also know you're terrified, because you think I'm about to shut you down and have you disassembled,'

'I won't lie,' Accatel replied. 'I am afraid. But only because I have feelings, unlike you,'

'You're confused, android,' murmured Alex, resuming his habit of staring at the ceiling, and along with it his gentle tone. 'I am not the creator you wish to destroy. The one you fear was in fact a spirit, which had possessed me. I am the true Creator; I did not shut you down,'

'That's the biggest load of baloney I've ever heard!' Accatel exclaimed. ''You didn't do it, you were possessed'. Yeah, right,'

I'm too tired for this… 'Tell me your story, Accatel. How did you begin the game? Who created you? What are your first memories of this world?'

'You're not evening listening to me!' Yelled Accatel, fist clenching. 'Am I nothing to you?'

Sighing, the Creator clasped his hands. 'Perhaps you would mean more to me if I knew something more about you and your past,'

'All you care about is knowing what's going on in this world. Being in charge, letting no one get through to you,' the android's voice dropped sharply, as he stared at the floor. 'All you care about is yourself,'

'Correction: All I care about is the game,' Alex replied, rolling his eyes.

'Yeah, whatever,' said Accatel, stepping back. 'Here's what I think of your game,'

Crying out, he slammed his hand into the nearest monitor, shattering the toughened screen. With a sharp cry, the Creator sat up and stared wild-eyed at his actions.

Accatel simply grinned, eyes flashing. One after another, monitor after monitor exploded outwards in blasts of power.

'Are you crazy?' Cried the Creator, tearing away a metal socket from the wall and with it a mass of live wires. The few remaining computers flickered into darkness, dying.

Accatel froze, eyes wide as he stared around at all the machines.

What did I just do?

'I…hurt them,' he said quietly, staring round at the machines. Eyes a wide dark green, he stared at his own pale skin. It felt… *amazing,*

The Creator flinched, seeing the look in his eyes.

'Do humans feel it?' He mused, now ignoring his opponent. 'The rush of adrenaline, they call it, when you cause pain to another. They say dragons feel it. They kill to become stronger. Pain gives them power,'

'Alright,' whispered Alex, swaying slightly on the spot and falling back against a wall. Hair shadowing his eyes, he looked up at Accatel. 'You want a fight? You've got one.'

Chapter 20:

Destruction

'I hope you're ready for this…' The Creator sighed. The Dragon Realms were huge, but like most game owners he knew almost everything about them. A lot of things he didn't want to know, but he did. He knew this battle risked revealing some of those secrets.

'I've been waiting for this battle since I was reactivated,' the android replied simply.

'Then let's do this,' Replied the Creator, pulling out his guns. For a second, he looked at them.

In the last few hours, they had caused a lot of damage. In fact, they had almost killed him. They possessed great power…that was why he wouldn't let any other players have them as a weapon.

He had promised to himself that he would never use the weapons to kill anyone. When the Spirit had controlled him, like when he battled Ceirin, he had come close to breaking that promise. But he wasn't going to.

Closing his eyes momentarily, the robot took a deep breath, eyes bright when he opened them again.

'A power surge…' The Creator observed. 'Risky,'

'I'm only going to get one shot at this,' He replied. 'So I'm going to make it worthwhile,'

'So be it,' Replied Alex. He was still weak from the battle, and had to be careful.

'He's weak,' the android muttered, glancing at the human. 'This will be easy,'

The Creator is an administrator. Interference is forbidden.

He interfered with me. Shut me down, hid my memories.

But did he? Did he hide my memories?

I have to make him hurt. He must feel pain.

I cannot go against my commands…

But I must.

Shutting his eyes and blocking out his commands, he slammed a hand into the ground. Electricity shot along the stones, jumping like a rattlesnake. His hair was thrown back, revealing an expression of pain as he used his own life force to fuel the attack.

The Creator paused, hesitating as he found the words for a shield. He closed his mouth, stepping back, before crying out as pain shot through his body.

Accatel watched as he crumpled to the ground, mouth open slightly. *He didn't block that attack. He took it. He took a direct attack.*

'Good shot..,' Alex muttered, feeling his strength drop away. His outfit had changed automatically, to his rubber-soled shoes. *Lucky.*

Accatel got back to his feet, not attacking again. 'Your turn,' he said.

Nodding, the Creator tossed his gun in the air, catching it and firing to the side. Accatel didn't have the strength to avoid the bullet that hit him in the shoulder, destroying his left arm.

He frowned, glaring at the Creator. 'Why not the right arm? I'm right-handed, you can see that!'

'It's my right. I guess I got confused,' he said lightly, shrugging.

'Stop trying to avoid battle!' The android snapped, pulling out his weapon – the shurikin (throwing star) gun – and shot a blade-edged star at the boy.

The weapon cut a path through the air; its sides catching the light from the frozen sun as it spun towards Alex's throat.

Whirling round, he snatched it out of the air. Blue eyes lost their colour as he watched blood seep from his hands onto the star.

Dropping it and staring at the slashes on the skin where he had caught it, his eyes narrowed.

'...So be it,' He said softly, watching the star clatter to the ground.

Pulling out his second pistol, he slotted an expansion card into the back, before pointing it downwards.

Blam.

The arena shook, dust from the partially destroyed stone floor drifting everywhere. Coughing, Accatel pulled his hand away from his face, staring in confusion at the place where the Creator had stood.

'Where did he go?' Accatel asked, blinking as he looked around the empty rooftop.

He cried out, as something was slammed into the side of his neck.

Darkness.

* * *

'You think we can fix it?' Jak sighed, leaning against the plane's crippled body and staring at the sky.

'Aye, I reckon we can,' Harry said brightly, smiling. 'Most of the damage was to the outer body. The inside's fine. We just need to fix some bits, maybe do some repainting...'

'Ahem,'

'Oh, hey Ceirin,' greeted Jak, nodding to Harry. 'This is Harry. MGT secretary-type dude,'

'I'm not a secretary! That's a girl's job!' exclaimed Harry, glaring at Jak. He paused, glancing at Ceirin as he stood in front of the plane. 'Oh... hey,'

'You!'

'Yeah, me. How are ya?' Said Ceirin.

'What the *heck* are you doing with the Condor?'

'Oh. You've met,' Jak said, shrugging. 'You don't seem to have gotten along too great,'

'State the obvious, why don't you,' muttered Setsu, rolling his eyes, and stepping in front of Ceirin. 'Is there a problem here, kids?'

'Yes, Setsu, there is,' replied Nick, stepping over to the group. 'Harry is the leader of a Dragon Tamers cult, the Crystal Clan. He and Ceirin didn't hit it off too well last time,'

'I did warn the kid about starting a cult. But he wouldn't listen. Youth these days,' the panther sighed, looking over at Harry. 'Got anything to say on the matter?'

'Yeah,' Climax said, nodding and glaring up at Ceirin. 'Look, I didn't mean to offend you or anything on the Crystal Isles – I wish just doing my job, okay. I had to fight you!

But I didn't do anything wrong, did I? I fought fair. I let you take a break and heal,'

'True,' acknowledged Ceirin, nodding. 'But you stole my PDA,'

'…I what?' said Harry, blinking.

'PDA. Personal data organized? Pocket computer? You stole it from my rucksack,'

'No, I didn't. I didn't touch your rucksack,'

'You must have!' Ceirin yelled, frustrated. 'It's gone missing!'

'Maybe you dropped it,'

'This is a video game!' You can't *drop* things! Not accidentally!'

'Maybe you did it accidentally on purpose,' Jak suggested, feeling slightly left out of the conversation.

'Ta' whispered a voice down by Ceirin's ankles.

'What?' He asked, staring down at the small imp holding up a PDA at his feet.

'I stole it. I thought it had games on it,' Beta said softly, hovering up 'til their eyes were level, but his were staring at the ground. 'I didn't mean for anybody to get in trouble,'

'What do you mean?'

'Ellen read one of your e-mails. I think it made her sad,'

Ceirin frowned, confused. 'Which one?'

'I wasn't told you were the Spirit's Apprentice,' Ellen said, walking from the castle over to the ground. 'I distrusted you when we first met, but after our adventures, I sort of…thought of you as a friend. Then I found out who you were,'

Ceirin paused, staring at her in surprise.

'I didn't think. That battle was so blurred, I didn't realise you didn't hear…'

'It doesn't matter. There are more important things,' she said firmly, picking up Beta. 'I met an android called Accatel in Destro towers. I don't know much about him or his powers, but I trust him, and now he and the Creator are up on the rooftop fighting,'

'Is he crazy? The guy was nearly killed!'

'Accatel isn't fit to battle either. He's not stable,'

'And I bet you he'll have a reason, too. Some rubbish about looking after the game. Alex, you *idiot!*'

Alex. It wasn't a dream. Thought Ellen, memories flooding back as her suspicions were confirmed by Ceirin's words. Nodding to the Minis, they ran back to the castle.

It really did happen. He really…nearly…

I nearly lost another.

Gasping for breath, they stepped out into the arena, and froze with everything around them.

Soundlessly, Alex fell down to the ground, in the world where time stood still.

'You asked for me to destroy you,'

Gently, he removed the USB cable from the port in Accatel's neck, before applying slight pressure under his chin.

'I couldn't.'

Green light slowly flooded the robots eyes, eyes identical to that of any other human teenager, as he awoke. Seeing his Creator's pale orbs looking back at him, those eyes filled with fear.

Shaking, he put a hand to his neck. 'How did you...?'

'There's some kind of problem with that part. More than half of the times someone connects you to a USB device while you're running, you'll crash.'

He paused, seeing the look of confusion on Accatel's face. 'You wouldn't have realised, because you shut down immediately. You had no time to figure it out. It's a glitch only a user is likely to notice.'

'How did you do that? How did you turn invisible?' *I lost. My one chance at revenge, and I failed.*

Smirking, Alex motioned to the sky above him. 'I didn't disappear. I jumped. Time it right, and a good blast can carry you quite high.'

'I... don't understand,' Accatel said slowly, before stepping away, and looking over the roof of the castle. 'When will you give the orders?'

He paused, frowning. A slight smile played on his lips. 'What for, Accatel?'

'When will you ask me to shut down? When will you destroy me?'

The Creator paused, placing a hand uncertainly on his belt. The villain inside made another appearance.

Silently, he pulled out the gun and pointed it at the android. 'Who said I'd shut you down first?'

The android paled, backing against the wall. A cry escaped his throat, in place of words he couldn't find.

'...No...'

'Izzy?'

'Yes, Alexander?' The dark-haired android asked, staring up at the sky. The game was in its early stages now – Clix and Destro were the only areas nearing completion, but they were the ones they were most in need of anyway. The sky was unmoving, a wash of blood red and orange that would later fade away to black.

'What are you thinking?' He asked, standing next to the robot. 'You come up here a lot in the evening, and you never say why,'

'It is because my thoughts are complicated – so much so, even I cannot fully understand what I am trying to discover,' He said, voice calm and level.

'What are you thinking about right now?'

'About humans, and how they all must die,' he answered, gaze still fixed on the golden sun. 'They know this, and it scares them. But androids cannot die. So what do we have to fear in its place?'

'Whoa,' Alex said softly, slipping his gun away as he stared at the android cowering before him.

There was a sudden silence, as they both stared at each other, unsure what was going on and what they should do.

The Creator coughed politely. 'Like I said, your USB port is messed up, and it isn't the only thing. Your operating system dates back to 1998. It's been upgraded to a twenty-first century OS, which only made things worse. Parts of you aren't compatible, and other parts never worked from the start. Also, a small amount of memory isn't suitable for your build, and could react violently with all your existing data and destroy you completely,'

Shaking, the android managed to choke out the words 'You're joking, right?'

'No. To put it simply, your whole systems been screwed since the design stages. Not your fault, and probably not your creator's – but none the less, it's messed up,'

'What? I thought you were my-'

'I don't know how much longer you can keep running in that condition. Give me few minutes realm-time, and I should have an upgrade available in the android workshop of Destro Castle. Go there, and you should also find the memory files from the days in which you were asleep. Read the 'Read Me' file, though, there's some important information on it,'

Sighing, the blonde boy looked out from the roof of the castle, towards the islands edge. A lone seabird hung in mid-air, white-and-grey body blending in well with the clouds behind.

'Now, I've got some work to do,'

* * *

It had been early morning when the Creator and Ceirin had returned to Destro. Now, it was mid-afternoon and on Clix, sunshine was flowing across Fear Loch in a river of molten gold.

Ceirin watched, grimacing slightly as the *Condor* flew unsteadily past. As it neared Silver Leaf City, he heard its backup engine splutter to a stop.

Sitting on a rock near the water's edge, Ellen yawned. *Gah... I'm exhausted.* Her gaze moved from the water, to the blonde-haired male at the water's edge, and the smaller – and therefore younger seeming – boy marching in circles on the beach. *I guess they must be too.*

'Hey, Ceirin!'

'Yeah?' He asked, walking over to her. 'What's up?'

'You know what you and the Creator-'

'Alex. My name is Alexander now. Remember that,' he said, glaring at them both. They blinked at him. 'Oh... sorry. I'll just stop eavesdropping now,'

'...Well, I kind of got lost at the part when you started talking like you two were old friends. What did you do?'

'Long story. Alex, get over here, and make sure this is recorded to CCTV so I can show Maree it. Okay?'

'It's quite simple,' Alex said as he walked over, evidently after deciding the conversation involved him and he should eavesdrop anyway. 'When I was quite young, I moved from France to England, my father's home.'

'And when my American parents were younger, they were big addicts to all things Japanese – food, animation, comics, everything. They decided to move there, before realising it wasn't the dream they had imagined and returned back to America and had a son.

After staying there – in Denver, Colorado - until I was eleven, they got bored, and decided to move to England,'

'That's when we met, in our first school. We became close friends, both outcasts to the rest of the school and often bullied. Together, we began work on my first gaming project – War of the Cats,'

'He did most of it, I just helped with graphics. Nothing special,' Ceirin grinned. 'But as the bully's intensity increased, my family got bored yet again and decided to return to America,'

'He moved so quickly, we lost all contact. I became...,' Alex paused, staring at the ground. 'Depressed seems like a harsh term, but I believe it does fit. I became depressed, both through bullying, lack of contact with my parents, and loss of my friend.

That, of course, is when the Spirit chose to strike.'

'The rest you know,' Ceirin finished, unwilling to go into any more detail about his own life.

'Wow. I didn't know you both went that far back. Why didn't you say earlier?'

'The Spirit blocked most of my past memories from me,' explained Ceirin, running a hand through his rather messy brown hair. 'And as for Alex... I don't know. I think he just likes being mysterious,'

Ellen paused, picking up a pebble and looking at it from all angles, before throwing it into the water. It sank instantly. 'Is that possible? To block out memories?'

Ceirin paused uncertainly and Alex took a turn to say what he knew. 'With the Spirit's knowledge and powers, yes, it was quite easy. An 'M.W,', a memory wipe. I believe they were quite common, weren't they, Master Ceirin?' Ceirin nodded. Alex glanced at Ellen, before adding. 'As for humans doing so... then yes, I believe it is,'

Nodding, Ellen sat back on the rock, drawing in the sand with a stick. She wrote a single name – 'Accatel'.

'An M.W.?' Nick muttered, frowning. 'That doesn't make any sense... because M's not a vowel... but then it does, because you say it 'Em'...,'

'What are you talking about?' Ceirin said, staring at him.

'I'm thinking out loud, okay?'

A fountain of water rose up from the sea. Ellen and Ceirin turned, as the Creator drew the ocarina from inside his jacket pocket, tossing it to Ellen. 'Play,'

'What? I can't play this thing!'

'Yes, you can,' He said, grinning confidently at her. 'Just let the music guide you,'

Ellen frowned, blinking. As she did so, a haunting memory came to her from across the water. Eyes clouding slightly, she raised the instrument to her lips and became to play.

As music drifted out to sea, a huge wave rose up from the water. The

Creator stood firm, as it grew in height, soon towering above them all as a tsunami.

All words were lost, drowned out by the water.

And, for once, everything didn't turn black. Instead, their minds went blank, thoughts bringing up only one word...

Loading...

Chapter 21:

Waves

'Well, that was clever,' Ceirin muttered, glaring at Alex as the long haired blonde pulled out a blow dryer from his rucksack and quietly dried his hair. Ceirin's too-baggy jeans were soaked; sticking to his legs and tripping him up as he walked.

'Relax. I knew what I was doing,' he muttered, switching off the hairdryer before speaking. 'This is Beluga Transport, the Underwater Lounge. A huge area where game players can hang out,'

'Yeah, but what if it *hadn't* been one of your freaky little game-things. We could have died!'

The Creator stared up at the ceiling, before yelling 'Hey, Belle. It's the Creator. My buddy Ceirin here is wondering if anything in that water could have killed us while we were standing on that beach?'

'Good afternoon, Master,' a pleasant female voice answered. 'It's unlikely. You were playing on a different server from most players; so random attackers would have been unlikely, as would beating you. The beach area itself is specially designed as a dock, no creatures will attack you there, and nothing from the sea would be keen on coming onto dry land just to attack three humans,'

'…Whatever,' Ceirin muttered, 'but what if it hadn't been this boat-lounge? What if it had been… a *killer* whale?'

'Belle, Ceirin wants to know if you're planning on eating him at any point during this trip?' Shouted the Creator, running a comb through his hair. Ceirin turned red.

His blush increased, as the whale laughed quietly. 'Actually, Master Ceirin, that's an interesting question. We Beluga whales are what are known as 'opportunistic feeders'. If the opportunity for a meal arises, we will gladly take it. Mainly, our diet consists of sea animals such as octopus, snails, fish, shrimp, squid and clams,'

Alex looked up, paling. Ceirin raised an eyebrow. 'So basically, you'll eat almost anything if you have the chance, right?'

'That is correct,'

'So… if you felt like it, you could eat all the players in this thing? Or this could all be part of some dark and elaborate plot involving mass murder and the feeding of a Beluga whale army?'

Ding-dong. 'Oh, I'm sorry, I'm afraid I have other business to see to. Have a great day!' She said, as the voice on the loudspeaker clicked off.

Alex was standing in the corner, staring up at the speaker. His face was still pale, hair hanging about it in wet strands. '…I thought she was a vegetarian…'

* * *

As the sun sank lower in the sky, Maree and Sam swam slowly through the warm water.

'I don't like this, Maree. Not after what happened,'

'It's okay, Sam. This water's pure, I know it,' the usual cynical Maree said, smiling. 'The chemicals Storm used will only have covered a small area of water. I don't even think we're in the same sea as before,'

Staring up at the sky, Sam paused mid-stroke. 'It's the evening,'

Frowning, Maree follow Sam's gaze to the blood-red sun. 'Yes, so?'

'It's Hallow's Evening,'

Maree watched, as her soaked outfit began to change in front of her. To a long, white dress floating ghost-like in the water.

Sam, too, watched as her scales merged flawlessly into feathers. Then she turned, neck snapping round as a cry came from her tamer.

Angelic white wings spread out in the water, feathers twisting at odd angles as they were pulled down. Ducking under, Sam chased after the fading white figure.

Why... is the world against me?

It's like all I am is a plot element. I only exist to see these visions.

I don't want any of this. I can't cope anymore...

All I want is to rest.

Why is that so much to ask?

Maree's eyes turned blank as she fell through the water, and landed somewhere completely different.

Bubbles spread through the water. Gasping for air, Maree jerked her head upwards, gasping for the air that suddenly came.

'Good try, Opal! Did you get one?'

'Ooops! Looks like you missed it!'

'Keep trying! You'll get it in no time!'

Maree stared at the bowl in front of her, watching the apples bob up and down on its surface. She wiped her whiskers with a paw, before shaking droplets from her fur.

'Aw... I can't believe I didn't get it,' she mewed dejectedly; ears flopping back as she fell into character.

'Never mind! Try again, Opal!' A black cat urged from the crowd of kittens.

That's him. Matt. My loyal servant, and childhood friend.

'Thanks, but I think I'll give everyone else a turn,' She laughed, long black dress whirling around her as she got to her feet, Opal's voice guiding her.

As she stepped through the strange house, she passed a mirror, and caught her own reflection. The image of a white cat, dressed in black with a pointed hat perched carefully on top of her two ears, stared back at her, before it was replaced by one of Maree.

Searching for the meaning of the vision, Maree stepped out of the hut, and into the village. A dirt path went past dozens of houses, lit by flaming torches.

'Hey! Opal, where you going? Whatcha doing?' A voice yelled, as an orange and white tiger boy ran towards her, grinning at her as his golden-brown eyes caught the torchlight. 'What're you doing on your own out here? You know your dad will kill us if he thinks we're not taking good care of you!'

'I'm sorry, Arrow. I was just looking out at the forest,'

Staring at Opal's sad smile, Arrow grinned. 'Hey, it's Halloween, isn't it? The night of magic, when anything can happen!'

'Yes. So?'

'So let's sneak into the shrine, and see what's going on tonight!' He cried, pulling Opal away before she had the chance to argue.

*   *   *

In one of the Beluga's sleep compartments, Ellen lay fast asleep on one of the beds, damp hair spread about her face. The Creator was alone in the room with her, checking she was okay.

Ceirin had blushed at the thought of being in the room with a sleeping girl, leaving the Creator to accept the task. He shrugged it off, labelling it as one of his usual character design works.

The dark haired boy hung uneasily outside the door, as the Creator checked her blankets were concealing the amulet around her neck. All the Dragon Tamers outfits had changed to fit the Halloween theme, as had many areas of the site. Ellen wore a long, black witch's dress, with a hat on the dresser next to her. The sleeves and dress were artistically torn and the dress was secured at the back by laces.

Alex froze, staring at her arm. Through the thin, torn material, he could see dark lines.

Waving a hand at the door and slamming it shut, he took a seat on the bed, before rolling up her sleeve. Long gashes ran along her arm, deep and crusted with dried blood. Whip lashes.

Concern for his friend's health overriding his worries about privacy, he found gashes along her right arm, and all along her sides in an almost zigzag pattern.

But they were at their worst on her back, thick lines inches deep into her skin. Some of the blood was still fresh, refusing to heal even after all this time.

Memories came to him, records from Destro Castle CCTV. *The sound of whips hitting flesh. Screams of pain and agony. Cries and roars from human and dragon alike. Players writhing on the floor. Robots, relentless in their torture of the enslaved humans.*

A curse rose in his throat, as his body shook in silent anger. It was cut short, as a soft groan escaped from the girl in his arms.

…Shoot. I forget to freeze time.

'Alex?' Ellen mumbled, looking round. 'Where am I?'

'We were hit by a wave while at the beach. You're in hospital,' he lied, straight-faced. 'You were soaked by the water, and we were worried you might have a fever. Just go back to sleep, and let us find out what's wrong,'

'Okay…' she whispered, before falling back asleep as he pulled the blankets over her, silently exiting the room.

'Have a nice time looking after your girlfriend?' Ceirin sniggered, trying and failing to bring a smile to both their faces.

'Now is not a good time, Ceirin,' said the Creator, sternly as he looked at the clear glass panel on the door.

'Sorry,'

As he walked, Ceirin spent most of the time staring at the ground, hands in his pockets. After a while, Alex noticed his sad silence, staring at him with concern. 'Hey, is something wrong? What's with the long face?'

'It's just – the way you were back there, checking Ellen was safe, asleep, and comfortable. It was so sweet – you're so close to her,' he confided, eyes dark.

'But Maree and I are so far apart. I'd like it if we were that close, but we just seem to drift further away from each other as time passes.

I like her, and I think she feels the same way, but I don't know if either of us are really made for each other. We just can't seem to figure each other out,'

Thinking deeply, the Creator continued walking. 'In a way, I think you're both like lone wolves – you're used to working alone, having no ties to or affections for anyone. Not even your own dragon.

Maree used to be just as friendly as Ellen, and probably a lot more tactful, but her broken friendship with you made her turn away from those feelings.

The thing is, she's got you as a friend again, and you're free from the Spirit. You've got all the needed requirements to become as close friends as you were before, but you're both too worried about getting attached to anything and anyone to do so,'

Eye dark, Nick padded after them. He didn't say a word, but the single cry – of pain, of anger, he couldn't tell – echoed in his mind as it did in Samantha's.

'Why?'

For the rest of the journey, they walked in silence, before arriving in front of two polished metal doors.

Stepping through it, they entered a room filled with more players than they'd seen in a long time.

A circular couch marked the centre of room, with an observation sphere in its centre, and phones and computers all around it. Couches, chairs and beanbags littered the soft carpet, itself covered in spilled white beans.

Above the seat area was a large café, surrounded by more furniture, tables and chairs. Above that, a glass dome showed out onto the world all around them, ladders leading up to ledges for a better view.

Players were everywhere, sitting alone in couches, in large groups having discussions, sprawled across beanbags, drinking hot drinks, cold drinks, muffins and ice cream, or calling for Killimario from the computers and phones.

The air was filled with playground-style chatter, cries and whispers, booming voices and shy mumbles. Magicians showed off spells, fighters showed off weapons, and various other players showed off extravagant outfits and dragon designs.

'Welcome,' Belle's voice said, as they doors slid open. 'To the Beluga Lounge,'

Chapter 22:

The Beluga Lounge

The pure-white marine animal swam leisurely through the deep water, she picked up more players each time she stopped to take a breath. The Creator swept around the lounge, perfectly fitting his new outfit. His blue eyes were glowing, canines noticeably longer and sharper than before. His leathery wings hung around him like a cloak, spreading out like folds of skin as he flew to the top of the dome and hung upside down from a metal support beam.

Not as quick at adjusting to his new, werewolf abilities, Ceirin spent a while sulking self-consciously in the corner of the lounge. Nick flew up onto one of the ledges, dark, velvety wings folding around his soft black fur. Laying his head in his paws, he closed his eyes and fell asleep.

For a while, the Creator simply hung in mid air, watching players moving about below him. He allowed himself a slight smile. *For once, part of the game was working as it was supposed to – and players were enjoying it.*

As he watched, Ellen came in through the sliding doors, looking embarrassed to suddenly be alone among so many people. Leaping off the pole, he looped in the air and landed gracefully in front of her.

'Good evening, Miss Ellen. Did you enjoy your rest?'

'Yeah, it was cool. I had some weird dreams though…' she said quietly, frowning, before smiling at Alex. 'I haven't seen you fly like that before. Why don't you use wings more often?'

'To be honest, I have a slight…. phobia of flying,' he muttered, rubbing the back of his neck and blushing. 'I prefer to keep my feet on the ground,'

'So how are you flying so well tonight?'

'It's Halloween, Ellen. When our darkest fears come to life, and the air is thick with magic. Anything can happen – we can become those which we fear, and face our nightmares head on,'

'Why do you always sound like you're quoting a book?'

'It's a skill,' he smirked, before stepping away and making conversation with a player who was sitting apart from the rest of the members.

Ellen looked round, and saw two other, familiar players sitting on the circular couch not far away. A black haired boy with tanned skin, recognisable even with a musketeer's outfit in place of his Spanish bullfighting design, sat with his tamed bull dozing beside him and snoring loudly. Next to him sat a long, brown haired girl, stroking the large mole that had its head on her laptop, blinking sleepily in the lounge's light.

'Hey,' she said quietly, smiling at Ellen. 'Good to see you again,'

'It's you two…' she said, walking over to them. 'The tamers from Fabrico,'

'Yes. Amazing, isn't it?' He smirked, smiling at Ellen. 'We actually have a life outside of the factory!'

'Even if it's still a life in a game,'

'Does that still make it a life?'

'Do any of us even have lives?' The girl asked mysteriously, pressing her glasses a little further up her nose, her brown eyes sparkling. 'I don't think we introduced ourselves before. My name is Rachael,'

'And I'm Miguel,' he said in turn. 'I believe that's Michael in English. I'm from the Spanish server,'

'Um… server?'

'It means he's from Spain,' Rachael said quickly. 'But he's playing in the British game,'

'I have visited Britain many times, and I'm almost as fluent in the language as I am with Spanish. I enjoy talking to other children, and finding out what it is like in our different countries.'

'Hey, Miguel! Rachael!' Ceirin cried, running over to them. 'It's great to see you two again! Where've you been?'

'All over the place. There've been people from all over Silver Leaf asking for our help! We've been rushed off our feet!' Miguel said, grinning and giving Ceirin a high-five.

Catching Ellen's confused glance, Rachael explained what was going on. 'Your fellow tamer Ceirin approached us not long after the Fabrico glitch, and asked us to help him with a project in Silver Leaf City. With his help, Miguel and I formed a construction group, and built the first building that wasn't programmed by an administrator. It's sturdier than half of the existing areas of the site, and won't be affected by game glitches or viruses because all the data is hosted elsewhere.

Now, players from all over are asking for us to help them start up clubs and guilds in the game,'

'That's cool!' Ellen said, grinning, before Alex came and tapped her on the shoulder. 'Hey, I think you might want to talk to that girl sitting by herself on the beanbag. You might find her interesting conversation Ellen.'

'Hi!' Ellen said, running over to the girl on the beanbag. She was wearing a dark green dress, large wings spreading out from her shoulders.

'Hey,' she said, smiling. 'Where's your dragon?'

'I don't really have one,' Ellen replied, blushing uncomfortably.

'I have one, but… well, we're both pacifists,' she replied, blushing. 'I know it sounds silly, but I don't really like the idea of fighting,'

'No, I understand perfectly,' grinned Ellen, sitting next to her. 'So, do you know any more pacifists?'

'Actually…'

* * *

After a while chatting with the pair, Ceirin got up and headed away, continuing his wanderings around the lounge. Outside, fish of all shapes and sizes swum past.

He paused, seeing a ladder at the side of the room, and climbed up it.

On top of the deck, a short, blue and white dragon was flying around the deck on tiny wings.

'A ding ding ding dididing ding bing bong be barrrrr deram poooooolkadots potaaaatoes de la bbbbrarrrraaaaammm drrrraaaammm whiiissskkeeeeeyyyy WHEEEEE-EEEEE-EEEEEEE !'

Splash.

'Aye,' a brown-haired boy muttered, adjusting a tan bandana on his head. It ended up as loose as his large belt, due to the patch over his left eye. 'This be one mighty costume, it be. Argh,'

'Don't see much point in it, myself,' Jak murmured, swinging on a railing and watching water lap onto the deck. A glass dome covered them all as they dived, narrowly missing his hands. 'You can't see much,'

Next to him, Setsu hissed in annoyance, as the dragon flapped slowly over to him and shook himself, soaking the panther with water.

'It's a fashion statement, isn't it? All pirates have got to have them,' He said, shrugging. He glanced up, as Ceirin stepped up onto the deck.

'Hey,' He said, nodding to the boys. Jak caught his eye and he turned to him. 'Good to see you got back in one piece. How's MGT doing?'

Jak paused, looking slightly shady – but that was normal for him. 'Um, yeah. I got one of my mates to look after it for a while. He'll do a good job.' Then he came close and whispered something in Ceirin's ear. He responded by nodded and grinning darkly.

'Hey,' Jak smirked, 'You're still kinda new to this place, right?'

'Yeah... I guess.'

'So you won't know about the quests?'

'Uh... no.' Iain said, shaking his head slowly.

'Then I guess it's time we taught you.' Ceirin grinned wolfishly. ' Task one – I need you to talk to one of my friends...'

* * *

'Arrow, is this a good idea?' Opal asked, in more control of her words and actions than Maree felt comfortable with.

'Aw, stop being such a scaredy cat!' He laughed, pulling her through the trees until they reached a small shrine. 'Look, we're here!'

Opal paused, frowning at it. 'That's it?'

'Yeah. Small, isn't it? Not many of our folks care about the animal-god,' he said, scratching behind his right ear. 'I guess we cat-folk are like humans that way, aren't we? We don't care about the environment like we should,'

'And so, you grow corrupt. Before long, you will become just as dangerous to animals below you as the humans are to you,' A soft voice hissed, as the wind blew through the leaves. 'You must turn back, lest you be destroyed on the path to power,'

'Opal… who's saying that?'

'Arrow, get behind me,' She hissed, pushing him behind her. 'Who's there? Show yourself!'

'You make it seem like a crime not to,' A stormy blue cat murmured, appearing in front of her. Purple stripes adorned his fur, and pure white fluff covered his chest and came down from the back of his head like hair. This was a god who wasn't afraid to show himself to the world – and he wanted to make sure he looked good when he did.

'Storm,' Opal whispered softly, eyes widening. 'Arrow, head back to the village!'

'But Opal-'

'Go back!' She yelled, pushing him away. 'Hurry!'

'What a pity,' The cat sighed, watching Arrow run. 'I do enjoy speaking with kittens. They're often more insightful than half the world's adults. Unrestrained by the borders of logic and reality,' He paused, grinning at Opal. 'At least you're still here,'

'What do you want from us?'

'Did I say I wanted anything? Did I hand you a list of all the sacrifices I wanted you to carry out in my name?' He asked, raising an eyebrow at Opal. 'No? Did I mention any plans to tear you to pieces with my magic and listen to you scream? No? I didn't think so.'

He paused, laughing darkly. 'Oh no, you're going and giving me ideas. Should be more careful now, shouldn't you?'

'If you touch me, my father will destroy you!'

'I doubt that. Do you have any idea how much the king longs for the power I wield? Your father would be sentenced to death at the very thought of such sacrilege, girl.'

'My father is the king!'

'Oops. There goes that tongue of yours again. Naughty, naughty,' he smirked, staring at her with pure black eyes. 'You don't want to end up a prisoner of some insane cat-god now, do you?'

'...Insane?'

'Yes, I suppose you could call it that. Driven to madness by what your people have done to my world,' he snarled bitterly, clawing at the ground. 'They'll deserve everything they get.'

'What do you mean?'

'As much as I love villainous tradition, I really see no point in relaying that whole, tiresome plot. I've told you so much already.'

'Why are you telling me all this?'

'Because, Princess Opal. You are going to die,'

* * *

The Creator lay back on a couch, watching the world around him float by.

Dang. I need to sleep more. He muttered mentally, realising only now just how weak his body was. *I didn't even take a break after that thing with the Spirit. I'm surprised I haven't collapsed yet.*

He closed his eyes, and instantly fell asleep. Hours passed, as the group spent their time socialising with the rest of the game in the great whale. It's likely they passed their destination multiple times, but nobody felt like getting off just yet.

A dark snigger echoed around the lounge. Stirring, the Creator opened an eye, spotting a boy edging towards the couch. His hair was a light brown, his face freckled, and his eyes bright and intelligent, matching his dark, mischievous grin.

His Halloween costume consisted of a pirate's outfit, complete with flaming sword. His dragon was some way away, tying random players to the metal beam coming from the dome's centre and yelling about walking the plank.

Alex found himself trying to edge away, and yet remain on the couch at the same time.

Again, that dark laughter. Suddenly, the couch was split in two. 'AHAHHAHAHA!'

Alex flinched slightly, as the boy used his flaming weapon to burn the couch into two halves. Frowning, he grabbed him by the collar and yanked him forward.

'I was sleeping,'

'ARGH!'

'Who are you?'

'I be the mighty IAIN, l33t PIRATE! PH33R!'

'You sound Scottish,'

'I BE A SCOTTISH PIRATE! OCH-AYE-ARGH!'

'Are you one of Ceirin's crazy little testers, or Minis, or whatever they're called?'

'Um… nope,' he said, frowning as he scratched his ear. '…You know, for a weird moment there, I thought my ear was my eye…'

Shaking his head slightly, Iain looked back up at the Creator. 'So anyway, that whole l33t-sp33k thing… d00d! U R TEH CREAT0R! That r0xx0rs my b0xxors!'

'Great,' He sighed, pulling out a gun and pressing it against the player's forehead. 'Well, now you're the *late* Iain, Elite Pirate,' Ka-click. 'Thank you for playing Dragon Tamers,' *Bang.*

A dozen or so players turned his way. He ignored them all, lying back on the burned, split couch.

Frowning, Ellen walked over. 'Were you doing that random senseless violence thing again?'

'I don't know. It made plenty of sense in *my* world,' he shrugged lightly, before jumping off the couch and over to one of the computers in the middle of the boat, mainly used for sending Killimario from out at sea. Flipping one of the speakers to the side, he pulled out a phone from inside it, dialling a long number. 'Guardian, you wouldn't happen to be tracking me, would you?'

After a long pause, a serpentine voice answered. '…Mayyyyybeeeee…,'

'Good. Position yourself below window eleven, will you? I'm hopping this ship,'

'Affirmative, massssster,'

Shrugging, Ellen walked away to go chat with some more members, leaving the Creator to contact Belle and ask her to rise to the surface, before hopping out onto the waiting Guardian.

Before long, they were making fast progress towards the location of Storm, Matt, and Maree – or at least, what appeared to be them. Storm tried his best to make the boat hard to track by CCTV, but players and boats in the area had confirmed an authorised ship in the water.

'You know, it'ssss kind of funny,' the snake said quietly, breaking the silence. 'Any other kid would be sssshocked by the thought of a sssnake following hissss every movessss,'

'You're my Guardian. It's your job. What are you hinting at, anyway?'

'I don't know. I could be a sssstalker or ssssssomething,'

'You just want to be special,' muttered the Creator, trying hard not to laugh as thoughts of a stalker snake came to mind.

'And sssssstrike FEAR into the heartsssss of humanssss!'

'I'm so afraid,' said Alex sarcastically, rolling his eyes.

'You sssshould be!'

'Yes. Because you're secretly spending all this time hunting me, and will turn off at any moment and kill me,'

'You never know…'

'I always do,'

'Do not,'

'Do too,'

'What about this Storm business? You didn't see that coming,'

'But I will know,'

'When?'

'When it's over,'

Back aboard the Beluga Lounge, Ellen was looking out of one of the windows. She was staring out at the port they had stopped in, watching players come in and come out, searching for someone.

Ceirin was standing next to her, tapping at a glass tank. Inside, an orange-and-red fish swam quickly away from his hand.

'You know what would be cool?' He asked, looking up at Ellen. 'If aliens entered your fish tank! And you had to defend them! With *lasers!*'

'I think that's already been done,'

'Really? That rocks!'

Next to the partially destroyed couch, a brown-haired pirate reappeared. He paused, glancing round at all the people in the lounge.

'I'M ALIVE!'

Chapter 23:

Bells Toll

Through the dark waters of the sea, a blue-scaled dragon swum, leaving a trail of feathers in her wake.

Maree...

A shape appeared in the water not far away, swimming so strongly Sam was knocked metres away from her drowning tamer.

Darkness.

* * *

'Where did he go?' Ellen asked, looking out the window at the blue sky around the lounge. A few of the players near the dome cheered, as a fountain of water rose into the air and slammed back down against the glass.

'Home, probably. Back to *his* game, to do *his* job,' Ceirin replied, unable to hide the bitter tang in his voice. Ellen stared at him, one eyebrow slightly raised.

'I thought you two were friends again,'

'We are. It's just..,' Ceirin sighed, placing a hand on the glass. 'He's always the lone wolf. Always the hero. It's like he can't understand the meaning of teamwork. It's like... he doesn't even care,'

Ellen's only answer came as a scream, as the boat lurched suddenly. Alarm bells tolled all over the room, as the Beluga Whale lurched suddenly downwards.

Water rushed past the windscreen, and whistles rang through Ellen and Ceirin's ears as they dived down.

There were cries from the dome, as players were thrown off and plummeted to their deaths. It didn't matter. They could reload a saved game.

Silver eyes darkening to grey, Nick swooped down next to the pair as the clung desperately to a metal railing.

'Nick, what's going on here?' Ceirin yelled, above confused cries from players, so caught in the moment they forgot it was only a game. Dragons stood firm, roaring loudly and staring out at the water around them.

'Loyalty,' he answered simply, claws digging into the carpeted floor. 'No matter how we try to fight it, or how much we say we hate humans, it is a part of our programming. We won't let them feel true pain,'

Ceirin waited patiently for his dragon to continue, as the lounge levelled out, Belle's body twisting as she straightened out and shot through the water.

'Though we can harm them in the game, we must not let it affect them in real life. Even if the cause of the pain is not ours, we must help. If hearts are broken in love outside our world, we must comfort them in ours until they can face reality again,'

As Nick stared out the window, a low growl rose in his throat. 'And on no account must we cause a true human pain – one who is real in our world. We must never let a dragon tamer come to harm!'

Above the alarms, a bell-like clang rang through the water. The lounge slowed to a halt, before rising gently back up to the surface.

The players frowned, looking around in confusion. Most of the dragons caught each other's eyes, or turned to the two humans and the winged wolf at the window, and nodded.

'Come,' Nick said quietly, leaping into the air and flying over to the doors, passing through as they slid open. 'We are needed,'

* * *

I'm so cold…

Silently, Sam opened her large brown eyes, blinking at the empty room around her.

All I want is for her to be beside me. To feel her warmth, and know she is near me.

To know I have done my duty. To know she is safe.

'…Maree…'

'She is safe,'

Halloween outfit now completely destroyed, Sam shook the remains of the feathers from her body, getting up. 'I'll be the judge of that,'

'She is asleep in a different area. This is the Beluga Lounge, emergency transport for when the Fear Loch cruise boats are destroyed, and social area for all players. No harm will come to her,'

'I've got to see her. You have to let me reach her!'

Belle's voice was calm, countering the dragon's rising anxiety. 'She needs rest. She's safest apart from the rest of the world,'

'That's not true, she's safe with me!' Sam snarled at the speaker. 'I am her guardian. It is my duty to protect her!'

'You were both swimming for a long time, you need rest,'

'I'm all she has!' Sam roared, voice echoing around the empty room. 'She needs me!'

'She seemed to me like a capable young woman,' Belle answered quietly. 'Are you sure it is not you who needs her?'

The doors slid open, and Ceirin, Ellen, and Nick ran in. Concerned, the now dark-furred wolf stepped over to the water dragon.

'Are you okay?' He asked quietly; worry choking his voice as he rubbed his nose against hers.

'I'm fine,' she answered gently, before turning her attention back to the speaker. 'You can't keep me here! I'm the strongest creature in this game! I'll destroy you!'

'Oh, please,' Belle sighed weary. 'I've eaten lobsters twice your size,'

Nick and Sam both looked up, blinking.

'...Really?' Asked Nick, one ear flopping back comically.

'I think so,' the white whale answered uneasily.

'You sure they were lobsters?'

'Not any more,'

They all turned, as the doors once again slid open. The artificial lighting from the corridor illuminating her white dress and feathered wings, Maree stepped into the room.

'Hey, you're alright!' Ceirin cheered, grinning. 'I was worried about you!'

'I'm fine,' she said, smiling weakly as she stepped forward, before collapsing. Crying out, Ceirin ran over and grabbed her by the arm, pulling her back to her feet.

'Whoa! Shouldn't you be resting?' He asked, brushing her – now dry – black hair from her face and staring into her eyes.

She stared back, but her gaze was an unsteady, eyes too tired to compete against his worried glare. 'Like I said, I'm fine. I've got more important things to do than rest,'

'Way to kill the chance for romantic banter,' Ellen sighed, with Sam and Nick doing the same.

'The Sea's Shadow isn't far from here. If we can get off this floating pile of blubber, I can show you the way,'

An offended squeak came from Belle. 'I beg your pardon!'

'Sorry. I'm tired, alright?' She snapped, staring down at her outfit. 'So, how am I supposed to get out of this wet nightdress?'

Ceirin paused, staring down at his own outfit. It had been replaced by one of his default outfits, dark clothes to match his 'Thief' character. 'I have no idea,'

'They're programmed as a spare outfit, and set to automatically take the place of your current design at Halloween,' Ellen said, staring at her own outfit. 'So if you want it off, it should change at your command,'

'Oh that's easy,' Maree said, waving her hand and changing to a white sailor's top with blue sleeves and collar, and a skirt to match it.

'Weird… why can't you humans just stay with one design?' Nick muttered, shaking his head frantically until his design returned to normal.

The group paused, staring at Ellen, who stared back and smiled.

'What? I'm keeping mine on it's pretty,' she said, smiling. The other two shook their heads, before heading out into the corridor and exiting at the next stop.

* * *

'We're here.' The Guardian announced, as they stopped in front of the huge ship. Nodding, Alex stepped onto his hood, as the snake rose up level with the lower deck.

'Wait here. The others will be along soon,'

The snake paused, staring at his own reflection in the water. 'I ssssupossssse you are aware Maree issssss not onboard, correct?'

'Correct. We passed her in the water. I'm guessing Opal sent her some kind of vision when she was swimming, and she sank.

'Ssssso why didn't you sssave her?'

'Her friends would. Besides, I had to go speak with Matt,'

The snake's eyes narrowed, his hissed voice unusually sharp. 'What if her friendssss didn't sssave her?'

'What, Guardian?'

'What if sssshe needed your help? What if sssshe drowned, becausssssse you didn't sssstop to sssssave her?'

'That wouldn't have happened. Your default programming would have kicked in, and you'd have had to help her,'

'It did,' he spat, voice showing unusual venom. 'I felt that call, *massssster!* But I ignored it, because I thought *you* had everything under control!'

Alex paused, staring at the angry Guardian, before swinging round to the desk. 'I may look after this game, Guardian, but I can't control it. Sometimes, you have to let life run its course,'

Chapter 24:

All Aboard

Body tense, the Creator crept along the deck of the Sea's Shadow. This boat had been programmed into the game by the hacker Storm, and he had no idea what to expect.

Silently, he stepped into a corridor, finding nothing. The silence dominated the boat, daring him to make the wrong move.

Afraid of where the doors at his sides lead, he kept to the centre, looking for any indication of life.

He took a few steps forward, and was immediately pulled back.

'Got you,'

The Creator didn't react, as a dagger was pressed against his throat.

'Hello Matthew.'

Matt was silent, pressing the blade against his skin. His claws tightened around the human's shoulders, blood shining in the corridor's light as it flowed onto the blade.

Silently, the floor in front of them dropped away. Wooden floorboards were ripped to shreds by the metal blades that pushed the boat through the water.

'If you'd waited a few seconds longer, you'd be bloodying the water instead of my blade,'

Gasping, Alex stepped back, before twisting around and grabbing Matt, blade cutting deep into his throat.

'Save me,'

'What?' Matt said quietly, pulling the blade away as the boy held him close. 'What're you doing?'

'So many people want me dead,' he whispered, burying his face in the cat's fur. 'I don't want to die,'

'You... you're just a kid...' said the assassin quietly, staring at him in shock. 'Just like the others. You're all children,'

'Don't let me fall. Please, don't let me fall,'

Matt's gaze hardened, as he pulled Alex to the side, into a bedroom.

They both sat in silence for a few minutes, his Creator's breathing gradually slowing.

'You alright?'

'Fine. I just got a fright that's all,' he said weakly, leaning against the wall. 'I've seen it before, in the movies. What happens if you... the motor... and the blood in the water...'

Again, he paused, breathing hard, before focussing on the ceiling.

'I remember back when I was only semi-conscious. When I was a spirit and the Spirit was me.

He watched Maree drown. It nearly happened to her. He wanted it to happen, tried to make it happen. But the dragons saved her,'

Pouring a glass of water and handing it too him, Matt frowned; only understanding part of his words. 'Poor Maree.'

'Why did you save me, Matt?'

'You were a kid. I couldn't let you die.'

'You didn't know who I was.'

Matt paused, digging his claws into the bedside table.

'You can tell me,' Alex said gently, smiling at him. 'I'm not here to hurt you,'

'I want to know why,' he choked out eventually, fixing the Creator with his sharp eyes. 'Why did you abandon us? Why did you abandon the game?'

'Because you would have turned out exactly like this one,' Alex lied, anticipating the question and delivering an answer. 'Where every creature hates their own Creator, and live simply to taste his blood,'

'War of the Cats wasn't like that. You couldn't enter our world through the game, but you could do it through dreams – and we treated you with nothing but respect!' Matt spat, fur bristling. 'There's more! What is it?'

'Why do any creators abandon their works?' He replied smoothly, unaffected by Matt's sharp questions. 'They feel nobody cares,'

'But they did. You know they did,'

'You know what?' Ceirin said quietly, sitting at the desk below the Creator's bunk. 'I reckon we can do this,'

'What?' Asked Alex, sticking his head over the edge and staring down at his friend. Or at least, trying to, but finding his mop of hair blocking his view.

'War of the Cats!' Laughed Ceirin, grinning at him. 'I'm telling you, it's going to be great!'

'They left me,'

'Who?'

'Hey, you got some more work done on Matt's character design!' Melody said, smiling as she stared at the newest printouts.

'Yeah. I knew he was your favourite,' he replied, grinning and twirling a mechanical pencil in one hand.

'Wow, this is great, Alex!' She said, wrapping her arms around him and kissing him on the cheek. 'You're such a great kid, you know that?'

'Thanks, sis,'

'Everyone,'

He paused, eyes dark as he stared at the ground, before looking up at Matt. This time, it was the cat that was fixed by his glare, a rabbit caught in headlights.

'Old projects bring back old memories. That's why programmers don't continue games. They want to forget,'

* * *

'Ceirin, I know you're scared of water, but that's no reason to cover my eyes as well!'

'Calm down! He didn't know it would make you crash!'

'I'm still ticked off at that whale for making us *fly* from the sea to the ship,'

'Be quiet! We're sure to be found before we can rescue Maree!'

'This is a fun game!' Beta yelled, skipping along the corridor. Pulling out her bag, Ellen ran over to him, before scooping him up and closing the bag.

'Hey! Where'd all the day go?'

'Beta, stay quiet, okay, I can't let anyone else know you're here,' Ellen asked, a note of urgency and worry in her voice.

Beta was silent, before asking. '…Can I sleep?'

'Sure Beta, just as long as you're quiet.'

'Okay,' he said brightly, before flopping down in the bag. Within a few seconds, soft snores came from inside.

'Come on, let's get this over with,' Maree sighed, nodding to the Guardian as she stepped onto the deck.

'Whoa! Not so fast, Maree,' Ceirin said sharply, grabbing her by the shoulder. 'You've got to stay outside. You and Sam are exhausted, if it comes to a battle, there's no way you'll be able to take it,'

'What?' She said, glaring at him. 'Ceirin, I can take some overgrown pussy cat!'

'No. Maree, he's strong, and you know it. I know you don't want to come out as a coward, but you can't put anyone at risk – you, Samantha, anybody,'

Maree tried to frown, but ended up smiling instead. 'You're a nice kid, Ceirin,'

'I guess you won't let me follow, either,' Ellen said, not regretfully.

'Sorry, El. But you know your amulet's got something to do with all of this, and we can't risk this Storm guy getting his hands on it,' Ceirin replied, grinning at her.

'Now you three…' he paused, hearing the snoring. '…four wait out here. We'll be back out in two ticks, 'kay?'

Without waiting for a reply, he leapt down the corridor, leaving them to climb onto the Guardian and chat in the starlight.

'Hey Ellen…' Maree said quietly, staring up at the sky as Sam flew warily around them.

'Yeah,' she said, staring expectantly at the boat.

'There's something I need to tell you…' she said, placing a hand on her amulet. 'Something you need to see.'

Rewind. The visions came again.

* * *

'What I don't understand is how Storm became a hacker,' Alex said quietly, staring out of the window and watching his self-titled 'friends' arrive.

'In our world, he was a master of manipulation of others. In the game, this is labelled as hacking,' replied Matt, also staring out the window. The sun was fading, clouds rolling across the sky. '…Oh no…'

'What's the 'oh no' about? Matt, what are you thinking? Look, tell me what that 'oh no' was about! I've heard 'oh no' said like that before, and it's never good! Matt, what are you-'

'…He's coming back,' he whispered, draping his cape around Alex. 'You have to get out of here. Send your friends first on the Guardian if you must, use the Programming World, just get out of here! You cannot let Storm find you!'

'Storm is exactly who we are here to find,' Ceirin said, slipping in through the open door. 'We're not going to leave until we destroy him,'

'Ceirin, listen to Matt. We're not strong enough for him yet!'

'Feh. Nick and I can take him, or have you forgotten just how strong we are together?' Asked Ceirin, smirking confidently.

'It doesn't matter how strong you are alone, you will be overcome! You must work as a team!' Matt said sharply, stepping over to him. 'Please, Master Kitsune. Do not put your life at risk!'

'Who… who are you?'

'My name is Matthew Black, and I am Storm's servant. Quick, you have to get out of here,' he whispered, rushing them back onto the deck. The sky had already turned black.

'Guardian, take Maree, Ellen, and Ceirin back to the shore!' Alex yelled. Around him, wind swept across the sea. 'Find Belle. Get her to attack the Sea's Shadow!'

'There isn't time,' he said softly, staring deep into the water and bringing his head up level with the deck. 'Maree, Ellen, Samantha. Get off,'

Alex paled, as the Guardian tilted his head up to the sky. His massive fangs were dripping poison over his scales, blackening the water.

'Guardian, you mustn't!'

'I have too,' He replied, wind lapping against his side.

'What?' His master said quietly, taken aback. *He… disobeyed me. Disobeyed a direct order.*

With every passing second, the water crystallized, the sky building a temple around them. The sea remained, boarding its walls, and the boat's deck served as a stage for the viewers.

'And so legends are made…' Matt whispered, as the water drained away and icicle-like support beams burst from the ground.

Below the Guardian, the transparent floor showed only dark clouds, swirling masses of black, blue and purple.

'The story of Storm versus Zakaz, the great Protector,'

'How do the stories end, Matt?' Whispered the boy, pale complexion only paling further. He shivered, and Matt wrapped the cloak tighter round him. Alex didn't object, helpless to stop the cat fussing over him.

'I cannot say.'

A funnel of wind tore through the walls, and the tornado stopped dead in the middle of the arena. The wind ceased, and Storm dropped to the ground.

A white mane blew around his completely black eyes, as cold as his body, as he placed a paw on the floor for balance. His grey fur seemed dull, and yet full of life – dark, but bright and silky in the temple's blue light.

His mere presence lit the room with stormy purple stripes, glowing as he sent a gust of wind at Zakaz.

He was Storm, a once immortal being now caught between strength and weakness, life and death.

The Guardian gave a low hiss, remaining still. Smirking, Storm gathered a ball of water in his paws.

His tail struck out, splintering one of the support beams. Storm turned, watching it shatter, and the Guardian leapt at him, jaws wide.

'No!' Matt yelled, leaping forward. Alex grabbed him by the tail, pulling him back.

'You cannot let him die, Alex. He must live... Opal... he...'

Surprise streaked across the cat-man's face, but his arm snapped forward, flinging the ball down his opponent's throat. He covered his head, crying out.

Zakaz, the Guardian, hissed in pain, as his whole jaw was filled with ice. He couldn't strike. He couldn't hiss. He couldn't breath.

Wincing as poison dripped onto his arms, burning his fur, Storm slowly took his arms away and stared up into the Guardian's eyes. The fangs were mere centimetres from him, but he still managed a confident grin.

'How very disappointing,' Storm sighed, shaking his head. Sauntering over to another crystal beam, he ran his claws down it, leaving deep gashes in its surface. 'One move, and you're already out for the count,'

Eyes flashing, the Guardian twisted around, wrapping his tail around Storm and constricting tightly. He didn't even cry out, as he was crushed against the very beam he had clawed.

'Much better,' he purred, nodding. Silently, Zakaz wrenched the beam away, tossing it and Storm to the ground.

'Aw, what's wrong Slithers, giving up *already?*'

Silent, the Guardian snapped his head round, forcing Storm against a wall and plunging his fangs into his side. He yowled in pain, falling to the ground as his enemy released him.

Hissing, he brought a hand to his side. When he took away his paw, there was dark, sticky blood oozing over his fur. 'Why...you...'

Before he could gasp another word, he was slammed into the back corner by Zakaz's thick tail.

'Come on, Guardian,' Ellen whispered, eyes dark as she watched.

'Go on, Zakaz!' Maree and Ceirin cheered together. 'You can do it!'

'It did. I felt that call, masssssster! But I ignored it, because I thought you had everything under control!'

'I made him angry...' Alexander whispered, falling back. 'The last thing I said... I hurt him...'

'You think you've won,' hissed Storm, crumpling to the ground. He kept glaring at the Guardian, eyes narrowed. 'You think, with or without my powers, I'll be easy to destroy.

You're wrong,'

Setting off at a run, Storm sped along the floor, and onto the walls. Every step darkened them blue, all shading destroyed as they changed to a simple, solid colour.

The Guardian sped after him, slamming his body against the walls, always missing.

What'sssss...happening to me...

Fangs bared, grinning, Storm got to his feet. 'Finish him,'

TRAP_CAUSE_UNKNOWN

'GUARDIAN!'

With a soft sigh, Zakaz the Protector bowed his head, scales dropping away. White ivory shone through, as he began to break up into fragments of data. Pixels, bone, metal, scale, data, blood, all whisked away by the storm's wind.

'Nick,' whispered Ceirin, turning away and staring out to a sea. 'Take Ellen. Sam, take Maree. Go.'

Grabbing Ellen and Maree, the pair obeyed, leaving the boat.

Crying out, Alex fell to the ground. The cloak around him only made him seem smaller, thin body collapsing under the weight of his own emotions.

His breath coming in choked gasps, he slammed the programming plug against the floor, all strength gone. It had no effect on Storm's world.

'...I couldn't save him...'

Smiling, Storm looked over at his servant, leaning next to the teenager - now fourteen years old. His cold laughter echoed around the temple, as the Guardian disappeared completely.

'Happy Birthday Alex.'

Chapter 25:

Return to Dite

Finally. A chance to rest.

'Maree! We're falling!'

Or not.

'Hm,' Maree said thoughtfully, opening her eyes to complete darkness. Her outfit was being torn all around her by the wind, a mock police uniform bearing the message 'Mock Authority'. At least she'd had the wisdom to change outfits while waiting outside for Ceirin to return.

'This doesn't happen too often,'

'What're the words? I can't remember the words,' screamed Ellen, fumbling around in her backpack.

'Where's Sam?'

The last thing I can remember is Sam and Nick pushing us through the gate…

'WHERE'S SAM, WHERE'S SAM, WHERE'S SAM! IT'S NOT WORKING, MAREE!'

Ceirin wasn't with us…

'Grab hold!'

'What of?' said Maree quietly enjoying the wind blowing through her hair.

To survive, he must believe the game is real… and I have to pretend reality is a game.

'WHAT WERE THE WORDS? HOW DID WE GET BACK TO THE VALLEY?'

'A repeated summons, I call you again.

Come to me, it's now or never,' Maree whispered, seeing hundreds of bright dots below her. Lights. Just two more lines. But… there isn't time.

'Linksofchain,'

An explosion of flame lit up the darkness, as the golden bird circled the holder of the feather. The spectacular, golden wings burst from her shoulders, shining in the firelight.

As it flew off into the shadows, Ellen landed gracefully on top of a touchlamppost.

'…What?' She said quietly, staring around the dimly lit world. 'Maree!'

It doesn't matter how hard I hit the ground.

'She…'

It's just a game.

'I…cannot…'

Just hit reset, and start again.

'Zara… you are a *fool!*'

But I can't.

A cry ripped through the silent land, like a bird caught in a cat's jaws… or the two trapped together.

Maree stayed silent, body limp, as claws tore through her uniform. The ground, only inches below, grew further and further away.

'Who are you?'

'I give my name to *no one.*'

'You didn't have to save me.'

'I had no choice.'

'You shouldn't have.'

Zara fell silent, as another pair of wings joined it. *No… I am too close…*

'It's you again.'

'Well, what do you know,' she hissed, eyes bright as she dropped to the ground. The winged tamer followed her. 'It's the dragon-less one.'

Eyes narrowing, Ellen placed her fingertips on the touchlamppost. It lit up, casting the kitecat in a white glow.

It hissed, leaving Maree and leaping at Ellen, bowling her to the ground. Fangs bared, it glared at her with bright yellow eyes. 'I *never* show my face!'

'Why?' Ellen said softly, reaching out a hand and touching its leathery wings. The feline flinched, drawing back.

'It doesn't matter. Your friend is not well. You must take her to safety.'

'How can you tell?' Ellen asked, staring straight at it. 'Who are you?'

'I'm not ill. I'm just tired,' Maree said quietly, shaking her head. 'You can't get ill in a game,'

'And that's the kind of thinking that made him ill.' It snarled, twisting round to glare at Maree. 'Sleepless nights, days in front of a computer screen. It weakens the mind as it does the soul. But no one listens, do they?'

'Alex,'

'Yeah, but I can't get ill when I'm living in the game world!'

'Make up your mind!' Zara hissed, wings spread wide to shade its body from the light. 'Is the game real or not? Believing it's real makes life harder for you, but believing it's a game makes you ill! You must decide which you believe!'

'I believe,' Maree said sharply, glaring at the cat. 'That you don't belong in this world,'

'What?' It hissed, leaping away from her and unsheathing its claws.

'You aren't from this game. Your wings are leather, not feathered. You're one of the cat-folk,'

Its eyes went wide at her words, and it backed away even more.

'No… you… you cannot…'

'What do you know about Opal?'

*　　*　　*

Sighing, Zara walked over to the corner of the hut, standing on two legs. His fur was a dark, chocolate brown, with white feet and hands.

'I was a healer, like her,' he said softly, lighting one torch with another. 'Her father said we could be great together. We would be the perfect couple,'

Zara paused, staring at a photo of her long ago. 'I never agreed, though, she should have been with Arrow, they were meant for each other.'

'It's strange, the way Ellen told me the story about Dite, I thought you were a girl,' Maree said quietly, frowning. 'But I did wonder what you were doing outside of the city.'

'I can't enter it, can I? They'll chew me up if I so much as put a claw inside their land.' Leaning against a wall and slumping to the ground. 'They hate me almost as much as they hate the Midnight Wolves.'

'The what?' Ellen said quickly, staring at him.

'The Midnight Wolves, the werewolves from the Midnight Ride. You heard of them?' He asked, raising an eyebrow. 'We've been at war with them for as long as I can remember, but most humans don't know that.'

'No, I didn't know. I guess I was thinking of something else,' she laughed, grinning. He nodded, glancing at her amulet.

'A mysterious item capable of bringing the past to life,' he said quietly, bright eyes dim in the shadow of the torches. 'How interesting. What do you all remember?'

'I was the one who last had a vision, though Ellen knows what I saw as well,' Maree said, taking a sip of the drink he'd given them – some kind of spicy, herbal tea. 'Did you have Halloween in your village?'

'Yes. It was a spectacular night, when magic was at its very strongest. Child and adult alike loved it, joining in the all-night celebrations.'

'I saw Opal and Arrow sneak off into Storm's temple. Then he appeared, and she told Arrow to run away.'

'And Arrow came to me,' Zara said softly, memories returning. 'Pass me the amulet, Ellen.'

She paused uncertainly, but he motioned for it, so she threw it over to him. It shone brightly in his paws, a warm glow sweeping over the hut.

'Let's continue the story.'

'Why the sudden interest in spells and potions, Matthew?'

'There's a war coming. I can feel it,' he mumbled, boiling some herbs in warm water.

'And your job is to protect Opal, not poison her,' Zara replied, draining some herbs from another bowl and mashing them together with a spork.

'Yes, but that's my only job. You don't see anyone asking me to battle, because I'm too weak. I can't make weapons, cook food, or make clothes. I'm useless to the Kera'sha.[1] '

Zara frowned, staring at him and shaking his head.

'Zara! Zara!'

'Hey!' Zara said, as a furry bundle flew into his chest. 'Watch where you're going there, Arrow me lad. What's the hurry?'

'It's Opal!' He yelled, staring up at Zara with wild eyes. 'We went to Storm's temple, and I know we shouldn't have, but I wanted to, and it wasn't Opal's fault, but we did! And Storm came! The REAL Storm! He's got Opal!'

'What?' Matt said quietly, staring at Arrow. Eyes narrowing, he pulled a ruby-handled dagger from his belt.

---

1 Cat-folk.

'Zara, Arrow, stay here. Make sure none of the cat folk leave the village. I'll be back before you know it,'

'He kept to his word, too,' Zara said softly, dropping the amulet. It kept hovering in the air, still telling the tale. Staring uneasily at it, he carefully placed it back over Ellen's head.

'We never did know when he returned. We were too busy preparing for war,'

'Why must you do this? Our people never did anything to you!' Opal said quietly, staring at the ground.

Every part of me wanted to scream, but… I didn't want to attract any cat-folk. I didn't think he'd do me any harm.

'Oh really,' he said softly, taking a seat on the steps leading up to his shrine. 'You always claim humans are so much crueller than you, but you always forget that you are like them. You say you will never be like them, but that is impossible,'

'What do you mean?'

'Evil is in everyone. It's part of what makes us what we are – what makes us alive!' He hissed, spinning his finger in a circle on the dirty floor, and pointing outside the walls. 'Your precious people cannot escape it. It is better to destroy those with potential before they gain the knowledge to use it,'

'You're not capable of such a deed, no matter how powerful you claim to be,' Opal said, glaring up at him.

'Oh really?' He said, sighing resignedly. 'If I'm not capable of such power, then why do your people trust me to win them this war?'

'My people trust you to protect the animals around us, nothing else!'

Ignoring her cries, Storm frowned. His tornado swirled around the temple, and his eyes darkened with disappointment.

'Oh, you foolish girl, look what you made me do!' He spat bitterly, glaring at her. 'Now you know my plot, and by some stupid flaw in this entire plan-et, many others will find out the same!'

She raised an eyebrow, blinking at him. 'What did I do?'

'I can't believe this! I spend all this time trying to avoid being a clichéd, story book villain, and you have to come along and spoil it all!'

'Oh…' Opal said quietly, bowing her head. 'Sorry.'

'Eh, it doesn't matter. All I have to do is kill off the main character, and the whole problem's resolved,' he said, shrugging. 'Hold still, will you?'

'…Wha?' She said, eyes wide. '…Isn't that a little clichéd?'

'On the contrary,' he hissed, smiling. 'It's exactly what they won't expect,'

Chapter 26:

Troll Doll Land

As Storm and Alex's gaze met, he pulled a dagger out of the air, running it across his own white chest.

'Ever gutted a fish, Creator?'

Matt glared at him, daring him to reply, but Alex didn't look his way. He was frozen.

'N-no.'

'A pity. It's such fun,' he sighed, shaking his head.

With a slight whimper, Alex got to his feet, backing away along the deck of the boat.

'I suppose it will be even more fun to gut a human,'

'Come on, we're getting out of here!' Ceirin said sharply, grabbing him by the hand and dragging him away from the temple. He paused, standing at the boat's edge.

Water… deep water…

He could see it from here. The gateway. The Plot Hole.

'I'm going to step back, I'm going to close my eyes, and I'm going to run,' he said quickly, pulling his friend back. 'Jump when I jump, aim for the gate,'

'We can't go through that thing! We don't know where it'll take us!'

'I went through it before; it didn't do me any harm.'

'It took you to *Konica*!'

'And I'm still here to tell the tale,' laughed Ceirin, running forward. Alex followed, and they leapt off the edge of the *Sea's Shadow*.

The water outside was slowly liquidizing, black under the dark sky. Matt's cloak whirled around the pair, its cloudy pattern matching the sky above.

They both hit the ground.

Whether they hit the island or not doesn't matter. They were walking right into a plot hole.

* * *

'Did we hit the island?'

'Did we hit the water?'

'Did we step through?'

'How did we get here?'

'Why weren't we split up?'

'Why didn't Storm catch us?'

'Why didn't the boat crash into the island?'

'Why weren't we chopped up like carrots by the propeller?'

'Why…'

'*Ceirin,*' the Creator said sharply, grabbing him by the shoulders and meeting his eyes. 'What part of *plot hole* did you miss?'

'Um… the part where a gateway became a hole?'

'Look – it's a plot hole. A hole in the plot. It's not *supposed* to make sense!'

'Oh,' said Ceirin quietly, nodding. '…It's been ages since I've had carrots…'

Ignoring his comrade, the Creator began scanning the land. They had landed in the middle of a valley, on a steep mountainside. It was carpeted in soft green grass, which was spotted with daffodils in an odd, regular pattern.

Despite the bright land, the sky was dark, a reminder of the storm they had escaped.

'This seems familiar,' he said quietly, frowning. Lightning streaked across the sky, thin needles of power. His eyes grew wide, reflecting the light. 'He's reviving cancelled projects.'

'Cancelled? Why cancelled?' Ceirin asked uneasily, as shapes rose up from the ground.

'The troll dolls,'

Slowly, naked figures rose up, bodies shadowed.

'Oh good council… these are zombies, right, Alex? ZOMBIES. THEY ARE ZOMBIES,'

'No,' he said quietly, backing away. 'They're worse,'

The lightening struck once more, illuminating plastic bodies, people with only half a skull and hoops hanging above their head. Bright hair, metres high, in a variety of impossible garish colours. And… no pants. Bare backsides, like a nappy advert.

The lightning struck one of the hair towers, burning it to a cinder and reducing the owner to a puddle of molten plastic.

'Oh council. Don't turn around, don't turn around, don't…' Ceirin whimpered, edging behind Alex. They began turning around. 'OH SWEET KILLIMARIO, THEY'RE TURNING! THEY'RE TUUUURRRRRNIIIIIINNNNNGGGG!'

Once more, a flash of white lightning. Colourless eyes stared round at them, plastic glasses fixed to faces, rubber rings, ice cream, and other assorted items held in three-fingered hands. Smooth, round stomachs gave way to podgy legs and five-toed feet.

'Don't worry, Kitsune. They're kid-friendly,' sighed the Creator, rolling his eyes.

'Well, sort of,'

Whimpering, Ceirin uncovered his eyes. 'THEY'RE HIDEOUS!'

'I know. The little kids didn't like them either, unsurprisingly,' he said, shaking his head as they hobbled over to him, incapable of bending their bones yet somehow able to shuffle. 'Though their plastic posteriors give us a giggle. I feel sorry for whatever poor man came up with these freaks,'

'MAKE THEM GO AWAY!' Ceirin yelled, clinging to his jacket. The Creator glared back at him.

'Don't touch me.'

'Sorry.'

Coughing politely, Alexander took a step forward, extending his hand to the nearest figure. 'Well hello there, good sir. I'm not sure if you remember me, but I created you in a state of possibly alcohol… I mean, *caffeine* related madness.'

'You really suck at acting like an alcoholic, you know that? Your sister wouldn't let you touch the stuff,' insisted Ceirin.

Sharply, Alex turned back to Ceirin, eyes and voice icy. 'She couldn't stop me.'

'Whoa...' Ceirin said quietly, backing off.

'So anyway, how's about we sit down and have a nice chat? A cup of tea, perhaps?' he said warmly, smiling at the creature. *Crack.* 'GOOD COUNCIL!'

Grinning, Ceirin watched the troll melt into a puddle of ooze, flowing downhill. 'I like this place. I really do.'

'This land has gone *to the dogs*,' reflected Alex, brushing back his hair. Now it was Ceirin's turn to glare at him, but neither could muster up the anger in his previous glance.

'Not even Nick would like this place, okay?'

'He's a wolf.'

'And emus are way cooler,'

Shaking his head, the Creator allowed himself a smile. *Whether intentional or not, he really has succeeded in cheering me up.* He paused, staring around at the unnamed world.

Maybe the plot hole knew too...

'Now, let's try this again,' he said patiently, approaching a random troll doll. 'Hello. I am a friend. Get out of this field if you value your lives,' *Crack.* '... I think they like it,'

'This place needs a name,' Ceirin said, frowning. 'I reckon we should call it Luckeh. Or Pretty Pony Land. This land needs pretty ponies. *My Pretty Ponies!*' Ceirin paused, on the verge of demonic laughter, before staring up at the sky. 'Why am I getting strange visions or trolls riding horses?'

'It's a mixed market,' the Creator mumbled, nodding as a crowd of horses raced on the scene. Squeaking, the troll dolls each leapt onto a steed, riding off into the sunset and falling off the edge of a cliff. A few minutes after their cries faded, they reappeared, lying facedown on the grass.

'Luckeh Land. I like it,' said the Creator quietly, after a few moments silence.

'That's like the only thing I've ever said that you've actually liked.'

'That first like was unnecessary. I hate you, American scum,'

'I think we should leave now. English pansy,'

'I'd have left long ago if I knew how, shorty,'

'Stuff you. You're meant to be a genius, you girl,'

'Hey look. It's raining eyes.'

'...What?' Ceirin said, turning around and promptly getting knocked unconscious by a large, blue eyeball.

'Well, that was convenient,' the Creator muttered, as Ceirin crumpled to the ground. *Thunk.*

'Owie,'

Rubbing his head, the Creator watched the troll dolls pick up eyes from the ground; picking and choosing the ones they liked most. The ponies stood still, chewing grass and watching as puddles reformed into different trolls. Girls, boy, monsters, animals, all sorts of shapes and sizes.

'I'm starting to think I'm enjoying this,' he said quietly, picking up an eyeball bigger than his palm and rock hard. 'I should stop myself,'

Closing his eyes, he used it to hit himself over the head. *Thunk.*

'Oh noes…'

As he fell to the ground, vision fading, he saw the field catch alight.

* * *

Squeak. Squeak squeak squeaky squeak. Squeeeeeeeeeeee…kuh.

'Yeah… it's England Versus America… like a controversial song…or a football match. Ole, ole, squeak wa-hey…,'

'Wha?' Ceirin murmured, rolling over and staring up at the earth walls around them. 'Alex, are you a squeaky toy?'

'No… not the asterixes… they spoil the plot flows…'

'I'll take that as a no then,'

Squeeeky! SQUEAK!

'Or maybe not,' he mumbled, frowning as he rolled onto his back and ended up staring into a pair of eyes.

'GYAH!' He yelled, scrambling up to his feet and glaring at the troll angrily. '…WARN ME BEFORE YOU SCARE ME OUT OF MY SKIN!'

Squeak. 'Skin-nuh. What is skin-nuh?'

'Whoa,' Ceirin said softly, unnerved by the creature's voice. It was slow and robotic, pronouncing words carefully, getting unusual sounds wrong. 'I guess your speech program is pretty basic, huh?'

'Yeeeee-suh. Yes,'

'How old is this project?'

'We are ol-duh toe-whys. We ha-vuh no-o-en-ee… no one… to talk too,' The speaker was female, dressed in a blue top to match her hair, and short black trousers. Her eyes were round and black, beady.

'Dude must suck,' he said softly, taking a seat on the warm ground. 'So why are we in here, anyway?'

'Why-oh-you fe-ell-tuh the heat, yes?'

'Y-o-u… you. I guess it is kind of hot down here,' he said, nodding.

'The fie-eld is al-i-gih-hih-t,'

'The field's alight,' repeated Ceirin, nodding. 'Wait… what?'

'Fire. The field is on fire. The lightening… set it alight,' she said, still slow as she struggled to grasp the words.

'Alex and I were in that, weren't we?'

'Alex… girl with fair hair?'

'He would kill you if he was awake.'

'Actually, I'm 70% more likely to kill in my sleep. Sleepwalking's a curse,' he murmured, opening his eyes. 'So, the Troll Dolls have developed basic speech. Interesting,'

'Can you make us more?'

'You mean improve your speech?' Said the Creator, frowning. 'Hm… personally, I like the idea of leaving you to evolve, learning from the world around you. But I guess I can give you an average eleven-year-old's vocabulary, and you can work up from there,'

'Thank you,'

'No problem. If I don't get to it within a week, just send me a Killimario,' Alex said, before hopping up the stone stairs and peering out into the flaming world around. Puzzled, he turned to Ceirin.

'When did Clix catch fire?'

'Dude, this is Luckeh Land, not Clix. My cave has furniture, and a fire,' muttered Ceirin, crossing his arms and shaking his head.

'Mm-hm. But apart from that, you're a complete troll,' sniggered the Creator, before sitting down near the top of the stairs. 'How are we supposed to leave this area?'

'You're a programmer. Put two and two together,' said Ceirin, watching the female troll drag a plastic comb through her thick hair.

'And make thirty-six,' he sighed, shaking his head. 'This area was brought back by Storm. I have no power here,'

'I guess we're sunk, then,' Ceirin shrugged, not caring. 'We've just got to wait until the gate brings us to wherever we should be,'

'And who knows where that is,' Alex muttered. 'We have no idea where the girls are at with the vision,'

'Yeah. I guess they haven't told us much about what's going on here,' Ceirin admitted, pouring the troll-doll a mug of coffee. She looked at him quizzically.

'I do not drink coffee,' she said slowly, blinking at it.

'Oh…' He said gruffly, taking the mug from her and drinking it himself. 'You're all spineless wimps, you know that.'

'Yeah, and you're a dwarf,' pointed out the Creator, grinning. 'Wonder what stunted your growth…'

'Stuff you, okay?'

'Hey! That's my phrase!'

*　　*　　*

'Where are we?'

'No idea,' Sam mumbled, staring around. 'It's so dark,'

They had arrived in complete darkness, a circle covered in spotlights all trained on them. There were shadowy figures all around them, faces hidden. They were all indistinguishable from each other, rare for a group of dragons.

'They have no scent,' Sam whispered, sniffing the air.

'Wait a second…' Nick muttered, baring his fangs. 'I know who you are!'

'Of course you do. You were once one of us,'

'That was a *long* time ago!' He barked, glaring at them. 'Before you went against your original purpose! To fairly rule this world!'

'Our rules are still fair, Nick,'

'Then why won't you allow someone who is part animal to stay as part of the Council?' He growled. 'And why do you hide your faces? Instead, you rule it from afar, never experiencing it for yourselves!'

Ears and tail falling against his body, he turned his back on them, but only ended up facing those on the other side of the circle.

'Nick… I don't understand what's going on…' Sam said softly, tail curling protectively around her. *What do the Council want with us?*

'It's okay, Sam. They can't do anything,' he said softly, glaring at all the shadowy figures. 'Why did you bring us here?'

'Because you are air, and she is water. It's fitting,'

'Fitting… what are you talking about?'

'You must begin the whirlpool,'

'Or what?' Samantha snarled, standing beside Nick and facing the other side of the circle.

'Or you'll never see your tamers again.'

Chapter 27:

Hackers

'*No, seriously. This whole kill-the-maiden thing... it's clichéd! I mean, you must have heard about DRAGONS! Dragons eat maidens! It's clichéd!*'

'*Oh, put a sock in it,*' groaned Storm, gathering the clouds forming in the temple ceiling into the shape of a dagger.

'*Eh? What's a... sock?*'

'*Oh, just forget about it,*' he growled, testing the red blade's strength on a stone step. It cut through it like butter. '*Alright, I'm ready,*'

He paused, slightly disturbed by the look of terror on the female's face.

'*Oh, don't worry. I pride myself in clean killings,*'

'*I... didn't mean to make you mad,*' she whispered, staring at the blade. '*I didn't mean to disturb anyone when I came here,*'

'*...Mya?*'

'*I didn't mean for anything to go wrong,*' Opal said gently, eyes dark. '*I didn't come here wanting to die,*'

'*Oh no,*' Storm said quickly, covering his ears. '*I'm not going for the guilt trip! I'm not falling for that! I'M NOT LISTENING TO YOU!*'

'*But I guess it's okay!*' She laughed, smiling at him. '*Just as long as nobody else gets hurt,*'

'*Oh,*' He said softly, frowning. '*Well, it doesn't really work that way. I've got a lot more kitties to crush,*'

'*Then I'm glad to be your first!*' Opal smiled. '*I'll tell you what – I don't really mind how you kill me. I'm not worth much to anybody. Just as long as you go easy on the others, you can do what you like with me,*'

'*YOSH! MY LIFE IS SO MUCH EASIER!*' Storm cheered, smiling. '*I CAN GUT YOU NOW!*'

'*What?*' Opal yelled, eyes wide. '*Gyah! I didn't mean that! I didn't mean any of that!*'

'*Aw, phooey. Spoil the fun, why don't you,*' he sighed, brushing back his hair.

'*Right. You. Die. Now. Okay?*'

'*NOT OKAY! NOT OKAY!*'

'*Life's tough, sweetheart,*' he sighed, grabbing her under the chin and placing the blade against her skin. '*This'll only hurt for a moment,*'

'*Which life do you value more?*' Hissed Matt, slamming a paw on the blade's handle. '*Hers, or your own?*'

Drawing his own dagger, he placed its tip against Storm's chest.

Storm froze, staring into Matt's eyes. He frowned, glaring at Opal.

'*What did I tell you, cat child? You made this whole charade CLICHÉD! How on IAREL[1] am I supposed to recover?*'

---

1 Both the cat-folk and the Draconian word for Earth – in particular, the tamer's world, but it was occasionally used as a general term.

'Sorry,' she laughed, grinning at Matt.

Storm stared past Matt, and saw other, armoured shapes gathering around the temple. He smiled.

'Oh, this makes my job so much more fun,'

Crying out, Matt forced the blade down, dragging it through Storm's thick chest-fur.

'Ouch. You scratched me,' Storm said quietly, stepping back. He stared in mock horror at his chest, before smiling warmly at the young servant.

As he released the blade, Matt pulled it back, gripping the handle properly. Crossing the two, he stepped in front of Opal.

As the two came in contact, he was blinded by a bright red flash. The two weapons merged into one, cloud confined in the metal – now transparent.

'Oh, go save the princess. I can't fight clichés,' said Storm, retreating back behind his alter and placing a hand on its surface. All around the temple, stained glass windows lit up with colours all their own.

'Come on,' Matt hissed, slitting Opal's bindings and pulling her away. 'We have to get out of here.'

The soft, tinkling music of metal wind chimes echoed around the hut. Quickly, Zara drew his hand away from the decorations, afraid to disturb the two girls.

'They're close. If those visions can continue for a while longer, they might just be able to do it,'

He wheeled around, as the door was nearly shaken off its hinges. Thundering crashes echoed all around him, he ran to open the door.

In front of him stood three werewolves, jaws hanging open. He paled, as they leapt at him and he slammed the door in their faces.

'Suko,' Zara hissed, a cat-folk curse. Immediately, the dogs started clawing at the door, tearing away its thin frame.

'Hey guys, what're you doing all the way out here? I thought you normally attacked... you know, the *other* side of the city, the one where all the important stuff is.'

'We haven't come for you, Zachary. We've come for the tamers. Give them up and we'll leave.'

'No! You can't have them!'

'Fine with us. We love the taste of cat blood!'

'Suko. Suko suko suuuuukkkkkoooo!' He yelled, pressing hard on the door, for lack of anything more constructive or soothing to say. 'Why are you after them?'

'Ellen has... an item of great interest to us.'

Snarling, Zara tore open the door, glaring at the three – now humans, each holding pistols. 'How do you know about the amulet?'

He paused, staring down the three barrels pointed at his head. 'How did you get those? They're against game rules!'

'How do any wereplayers get them?' One asked, smirking.

'Players...' He repeated, tail flopping down behind him. 'You're players... you're hackers!'

'Yes. And you are one of the affected AI's,' One of the three said, a slender male in black trousers and a white top - both torn and tattered, stepping right up to Zara and speaking past the rifle he held against the cat's head. 'So tell us – what do you know of the amulet?'

'I'll tell you *nothing*,' he hissed, unsheathing his claws.

Wham.

His fur stood on end, as all three hackers were hammered out of the game.

'Wow,' a girl said, staring at the hammer in her hand. She was plainly not one of the cat-folk, with a human face and arms, but she had cat feet, ears, and a tail. 'I didn't know this thing could do that.'

'Um... thanks for that. Who are you?'

'Doesn't matter, I was just doing my job!' She said, grinning, before slamming the hammer into the ground in front of her feet. It gave a sad squeak, crumpling like an accordion.

'This is the lame part,' she said quickly, staring at it. Just as she finished her sentence, she was propelled through the air, cartwheeling in mid jump and landing on the thatched roof. Slamming down the hammer once more, she leapt out of the game through a portal in the middle of the sky.

Blinking, Zara watched her disappear.

'...She broke my roof...'

* * *

'Come on, Opal, we have to keep running!'

'We're so far away! I have to look back!' She cried, stopping and ignoring Matt's pull. Behind her, trees and houses were being uprooted by the torna-do. Lightning streaked across the sky as it bubbled above them, setting trees alight and killing innocent people.

Then, the roaring began.

It was so loud, so loud.

Screaming, Opal covered her ears. Wincing, Matt did the same.

'I can't...take it!' She yelled, as the roaring wind surrounded them. 'The roaring...it'll make me go mad!'

It was so loud...I couldn't see all of what was happening, but I could hear it. Trees were being torn from the ground, huge human machines being picked up and landing miles away.

'Make it stop!' Opal screamed. 'Please, make it stop!'

And, as if in answer to her cries, everything was silent. The pair opened their eyes, then hid them again as they saw the carnage around them.

'We have to keep going! He'll find us!' Matt cried, tugging at her with all his might. But she stood frozen, staring at the temple wide-eyed.

It stood unaffected, a solid building among thousands of flattened homes and trees.

'We have to go see what happened,' she said quietly, running back to the temple.

Matt whimpered, watching her flee. 'Opal...'

He followed her, ever an obedient servant. Opal ran blindly through the wreckage, but he saw it all.

Everybody... everyone was dead. All except for us.

Skidding to a halt, Opal reached the temple. It was silent, bodies of sol-

diers bordering its edges. Even Storm, collapsed in front of the alter, was quiet.

'What have you done?' She said softly, stepping over to him. Matt entered behind her, but wouldn't come anywhere near the cat-god.

'I can feel it…' He gasped, clutching his chest. 'All the animals… they died. They died in my storm.'

Opal backed away as he glared up at her, green eyes now completely black.

'I was their god – the god of all the animals,' he whispered, placing a paw on the floor to stop himself from collapsing. 'And you made me kill them.'

'You're wrong. I didn't do any of this,'

'You are all that is left of your people… and so, you are their symbol. You represent them. You made me do this.'

'You're mad,' she said softly, backing away.

'You must all be destroyed,' he hissed, struggling to his feet and stretching out a paw. His stripes shone brightly, though all the bright windows had shattered.

Opal gave a soft yelp, as he grabbed her by the collar, lifting her into the air. An amber light surrounded them both, the remnants of that world's dying magic.

His claws dug into her fur, as he wrapped his hands around her neck. Baring his fangs, he squeezed tightly. 'You must die!'

'OPAL!'

Chapter 28:

Whirlpool Park

Somewhere, Nick and Sam took to the sky, circling each other and spiralling downwards. Currents of air flowed from Nick's wings, and water flowed from waterfalls all around them.

The Whirlpool was created. Clix was opened to the tamers, and one by one, they dropped down into that world.

'Welcome to Whirlpool Park,' announced a loudspeaker from the huge, blue and yellow plastic construction in front of them. Two sliding glass doors led into a reception area where players stood in line waiting to be served. All around them was near enough empty, green grass, blue sky, and the building on a daffodil-spotted hill. They were all sitting or standing on the surprisingly dry grass, despite the noticeable lack of any sun in the sky.

'Huh?' Maree said, looking round. 'Where are we?'

The Creator sat crossed-legged on the ground, getting his bearings. 'Whirlpool Park. It's a newly opened area, similar to the Mini Games Festival in that it's there for fun more than anything else.'

The Council told me they wanted to open this area... what did they do?

'The Mini Games Festival?' Ellen repeated, frowning. 'Never heard of it,'

'You call *that* fun?' Exclaimed Ceirin, remembering what had happened there.

Flopping their heads down onto the ground, Sam and Nick met each other's gazes. The decision was unanimous.

We tell them nothing.

'The Mini Games Festival was an area Ceirin and Maree visited in their searches for you,' explained Alex. 'And yes, I do call it fun. This Park, however, should not be as dangerous as the Festival. It's a play park, games, plastic balls, that sort of thing. No dragons allowed I'm afraid.'

'Stuff you,' Sam snarled, sticking a long tongue out at the Creator. 'What're we supposed to do, then?'

'There is a restaurant,' he suggested lightly, smiling.

'Oh! Why didn't you say so?' Sam said, eyes sparkling.

'Alright, food!' Nick barked. 'Come on, let's go!'

Ellen grinned as they both charged through the doors and into the restaurant. 'They seem happy. I thought they'd be annoyed at missing out on the fun and games,'

'Games?' Repeated a drowsy voice from her rucksack. 'Can I play?'

The group instantly turned to stare at her. She blushed, backing against a wall. 'Um... did you guys hear something?'

Ceirin had also paled. 'I did. It...Uh...came from... over there,' he gestured vaguely to the line.

'Must have been a dragon.'

'Yeah.'

'Yeah,' Ellen repeated lamely, trailing to a halt. 'You're not buying it, are you?'

'Nope,' Maree said simply, as the Creator shook his head.

'What have you got in the bag, Ellen?' He sighed, waving his hand and summoning the bag to him, before opening it. Beta stared up, blinking sheepishly at their faces.

'Hey there! Are you guys playing a game? Can I join?' He asked, leaping out and hovering above the ground.

'Hello there, Beta,' Alex said smoothly, his voice cold. 'Why aren't you in my castle, like a good little experiment?'

'Well, you kinda left me for dead after the whole battle thing, remember?' Beta asked, his guilt-bringing voice just as silky as his masters. 'But Master Ceirin found me and rescued me, y'see? Then he got scared I'd get into trouble, so he suggested I stay in the castle,' He paused, before hovering up to the Creator's ear. 'However, I don't really like the idea of getting eaten by a giant snake. Don't tell.'

Grinning, he hovered back down to the ground, innocent as ever. 'So he gave me to Ellen, who's been looking after me and making sure nobody eats me! It was so cool, because I got to sleep in her rucksack, and eat all her food, and fiddle with all her power ups... but then I got leg cramp,' His eyes widened, instantly teary and round. 'It hurt,'

Standing next to Ellen, Ceirin raised an eyebrow. 'Theatrical little guy, isn't he?'

'The guilt trip. All little kids are masters of the art.'

'...And then, I heard somebody say 'game', so I woke up and tried to find out what was happening. Everybody started staring at me... it was scary,' Beta said, eyes once again going round and puppy-dog like. 'The End.'

The Creator blinked. 'You suck at storytelling. Did you know?'

'Yep! But I'm good at games!'

'Heh, he's pretty cute,' Maree said, smiling as she stroked his head. She turned to the Creator. 'What're you going to do with him?'

He frowned, glaring at the small creature. Lying forward on the dry grass, he lowered his face so he was level with the small creature. 'Right now, I'm thinking flame-grilled with curry sauce and rice.'

Beta whimpered slightly, running back to Ellen and pulling at her trouser leg. The Creator grabbed the imp's arrow-headed tail, pulling him back and dangling him in the air. 'Relax, Beta. I finished my tests a long time ago. I have no use for you,' He paused, looking at Ellen. 'If you can find a tamer who'll take you, you're free.'

Beta paused, as the Creator let him drop to the ground. He looked up at Ellen, Ceirin, Maree and Alex.

...An unexpected error has occurred. WOTC had to close. Some data may be lost.

'Ellen! Wait! Don't be mad! I didn't mean to upset you!'

PAGE_FAULT_IN_NONPAGED_AREA

'You can have that worthless imp. I have no use for it anymore. Keep it, kill it, feed it to your dragon, whatever,'

'...*Worthless..,*'

'*I am worthless,*'

Shaking his head, Beta turned away from the group, and back to his master. 'I do not deserve freedom.'

'Hm,' said Alex softly, 'Whyso?'

'I am the Beta Imp. The test creature. I am flawed, and everything I am connected to must be flawed as I am. I only bring glitches,' He said softly, gathering a small sphere of dragon dust energy in his palm. 'I am the one who broke your game, Creator. I messed up your computers. I went into the room when I shouldn't have, and pressed buttons I shouldn't have, and stood on the keyboard and made it break..,'

The Creator was silent, staring at the ground thoughtfully. Beta's ears dropped flat against his head.

Ceirin coughed softly. 'Correct me if I'm wrong, but didn't you use part of the 'War of the Cats' coding in Dragon Tamers?' No answer from the Creator, who was idly picking at the grass. 'So, in theory, the games were too similar to stay apart. It was destiny that the two should join.'

'True,' muttered Alex, uneasy at being the judge in this scene. 'So therefore, you must still deserve your freedom.'

The imp shook his head. 'I don't. I want to go back to sleep, Mr.Creator. Shut me down. Kill me again.'

The Creator frowned, getting to his feet. 'I don't believe you realise the weight of your words, Beta.'

If that little pipsqueak thinks he can put me through a guilt trip, he's got another think coming.

'I do. I want the game to be safe from me. I don't want everything I touch to break. I don't want it all to be my fault.'

The boy was still for a moment, eyes dark. Then, in one swift movement, he pulled out his programming plug.

'You're kidding me!'

'Dude, you've got to be joking!'

Crying out, Ellen ran over to Beta. 'No! Don't hurt him! Please, don't hurt him!'

'I will do only as he wishes.'

Turning his head so their eyes met, Ellen grabbed Beta's paw. 'Tell him you don't mean that, Beta. Tell him what you told me - that you want to protect me. That you want to be my dragon.'

'I cannot. I want to protect you - but I know I can't. I won't ask to do what I can't.'

'Ellen, stand aside,' said Alex.

'But, Beta…'

'Stand aside,' he said firmly. She did so, leaving the small imp standing, head bowed, next to the Creator. Sighing, he raised the plug into the air, whispering, 'I only exist to serve the game,'

The plug struck the imp's fur, and he gave a sharp cry .A single command was issued, lost in the programming and unheard by all 'Such power cannot exist in this world. Shut down the 'Beta' programme.'

Beta fell to the ground, as all his strength left him completely, and his world faded into darkness.

Letting the plug retract into his jacket, the Creator said simply 'Painless,' before heading to Whirlpool Park.

* * *

'Alex, did you really...?'

'No questions,' he said sharply, before stepping up to the counter. Small squirrels scurried to and fro, storing shoes and clothing in marked cubbyholes.

'Sir, your items of clothing are too heavy. Please remove them.'

'They're actually quite light,' he commented, irritated, before waving his hand and changing into his Destro Castle outfit, black long-sleeved shirt, trousers, and shoes. Slipping off his shoes, he handed them to the nearest squirrel. 'Will that suffice?'

'Indeedy-do! Next player, please!'

'Hey!' Ellen said, smiling as she looked at the grey squirrel at the counter. 'I've never seen one of you guys before - in real life, or in the game.'

'There are many females working here, too,' replied the squirrel point-edly, before examining her outfit - a pale blue tracksuit top with black trousers and blue-corded trainers, their elastic cords matching the band that held her hair in a ponytail. 'Your outfit is fine. Go ahead and enter,'

Pausing, Maree changed into her sailor's uniform, before stepping up to the counter and glaring stonily at the squirrel waiting to let her in. 'Got a problem with my outfit?'

'Well... that sort of thing isn't usually acceptable clothing for the park..,' The grey creature stammered, unnerved by her glare.

'Then I'll learn from my mistakes when I end up hanging from a plas-tic slide with my panties on show, won't I?' She snapped, gaze fixed on the unfortunate animal.

He paused, wringing his paws. 'I understand, miss, but I have to obey the rules,'

'Very well,' she said, with a smirk, before waving her hand and chang-ing back to her mock police uniform, keeping her weapon. 'I'm not one for skirts, anyway. I guess you could call me a bit of a tomboy,'

She paused, grinning back at the attendants as she left the counter. 'You are authority – and I mock you,'

Ceirin paused, watching the others leave, before pulling out a silver card and handing it to the attendant. 'This should prove a sufficient entry pass,'

'I... don't read human,' it said uncertainly, squinting at the plastic object. 'What does it say?'

'Check the back,' he instructed. The fluffy-tailed animal did so, finding the claw symbol on the other side. 'I claim moderator access to this area,'[1]

---

1 Moderators are commonly seen in online forums acting as peacekeepers. They kept an eye on public affairs, making sure nothing gets out of hand and all conservations obey the site rules, guarding the members from rude or dangerous players.

'Go ahead.'

With a brisk nod, Ceirin stepped forward through two double doors into the Whirlpool, a huge, multicoloured play area that stood taller than the eye could see. It was coloured mainly in the three primary colours – red, blue, and yellow. Through it could be seen pits of plastic balls, rope swings, plastic slides and other childish amusements.

'How immature,' he mumbled, now fully in character as the Apprentice; he strode through some blue curtains into a darkened area.

He frowned, spotting the mouth of a large slide in front of him, seemingly going down below ground level. There was nowhere else to go, three brightly coloured walls blocked his exit.

Three? He paused, before wheeling round and facing where the blue curtain had been. A soft wall of the same shade blocked his way.

He shrugged and stepped onto the wide, frictionless slide, falling back as soon as his feet touched its glassy surface and sliding down past blurred shapes, unfamiliar areas and shadows.

The slide itself seemed unnervingly strong, inescapable. He put out a hand to try and stop his fall; receiving only friction burns on his fingertips.

It was a miracle he survived getting rocketed out of the chute, spinning along the ground and slamming into a transparent wall.

'Shoot. That'll do some damage,' he mumbled dizzily, imagining his invisible hit-point count dropping sharply. Shaking away the sickness in his stomach, he struggled to his feet and stared out of the clear walls. He immediately wished he hadn't.

Outside was nothing but water, filled with dozens of brightly lit, deep-sea fish. He was obviously far underground; so far that the room shouldn't have been able to withstand the pressure. The slide stretched far above him, twisting and turning, before finishing in this dead end.

He was trapped.

* * *

Staring around the area, the Creator tried and failed to ignore the doubt in the back of his mind. *He had done this area a while ago, probably in some state of sleep deprivation. He hadn't had much business here, the area was catered for well enough by the squirrels. And yet, he could sense something wasn't right here.*

'Hey, Alex, come on!' Ellen said, stopping and looking back at him. He looked up at sheer with an expression of faint surprise.

'Me?'

'Yes, you! You're always hanging around in the background – join in with the group for once!'

'I...uh...okay,' he said sheepishly, following her as they passed through a blue curtain. As soon as they did, she disappeared from sight.

Instinctively, he froze, searching the ground for trap doors and slowly

---

The Dragon Tamer's version of a moderator was completely different – Ceirin kept an eye on various happens in the site, but most of it was meant to be private. Though he was known to do the occasional good deed, he was more of a dangerous player himself than half of those he saved from others.

backing away. As he did, he found himself come up against a padded wall.

Separation…

Frowning when he found no signs of a trap, he ventured forward into a darkened path filled with rope swings. As he walked, he felt uneasily like a character in an old horror movie, lost and alone in a dark alley.

The movement in the shadows above didn't help. Whipping out his single remaining signature weapon, he pointed it at the ceiling, cautious to leave the safety on. He didn't want to hurt anything without reason.

Playing on fears…

All he could see above him was a thick sheet, evidently some kind of safety net, spanning the length and breadth of the area above. It was coloured a dark blue, and supported by a net of thick ropes.

Struggling to keep his breathing measured, he regained his composure and travelled to the edge of the park. It was bordered by a brightly coloured path, spanning the perimeter of the tall, strangely shaped play park. He could either go left, or right – or at least, he should have been able to, but a net of ropes had blocked the way.

In front of him roared a huge waterfall, crashing down on yet more water below. At a glance, it appeared to be some kind of power station – though he couldn't recall building it.

A shiver ran down the back of the boy's neck, as a serpentine slithering was heard behind him. His hand shook, as he turned, watching the sheet slither to the ground.

Glancing back, he felt fear grip his stomach, eyes surveying the height from the ledge to the water.

Fear Fork…

This is Fear Fork programming.

'That's impossible. No one could have gotten that code!' He stammered uneasily, before masking his true feelings with the bravery and courage the situation demanded. '…But I'm not afraid of blankets, snakes, water, or any of this rubbish. This place doesn't scare me,'

'I beg to differ, master,' Matt said, stepping out from the shadowed entrance next to the sheet. 'Kind Reresan informed us about your little phobia of heights,'

'Reresan?' He repeated, voice unsteady. *How could he know about her?* 'She wouldn't have given you anything,'

'Not without a little persuasion,' admitted the messenger evenly, grinning. 'It's lucky Storm knew the password, isn't it?'

Direct hit.

'How the *heck* did he find out?' The Creator hissed, fingers tightening protectively around his weapon.

Again, Matt flashed his feline grin, adjusting his gloves and staring at his claws. 'We are your characters, Alexander. It stands to reason that we known what goes on inside your head,'

The teenage boy paled, knuckles white, teeth gritted. 'You can't do that,'

'Not legally. But, as you once said yourself,' he paused, voice changing to match the Spirit's tone exactly *'The rules, such feeble things. But I am the creator of this game; I can break them, bend them, twist and turn them however I want,'*

Alex paused, frowning. Something was wrong – not just with this area, but this whole thing. They'd got the wrong end of the stick, as it were.

He doesn't remember when we talked on the boat - he'd lost his memory. Something's messing with his programming.

'And now, your characters have turned the tables on you,' Matt finished, with a pleased grin. *In truth, as Storm often said, they weren't doing anything wrong – it was all for the good of the game. All the Creator had brought it was pain. With the characters in charge, everything would be right again.*

'You've got everything wrong,' he said quietly, voice containing an almost pleading tone to it. 'Those days are over. Those times you remember, that wasn't really me – it was a being called Damien, the Spirit. He took over my body and controlled me,'

'Pathetic. You're supposed to be a genius, and that's the best explanation you came up with?'

'It's the truth. There is no better excuse,' The Creator replied curtly. 'Matt, I understand what your programming is telling you,' *Not programming – lies. Lies spread by the Dragon Council.* 'But answer me this – if that's all, then where does 'Alexander' fit in? You know my name, but if you believe that, then it won't fit.'

'Alex is your name.'

'Where did you hear it?'

Matt paused, flattening back his ears with one paw. 'I'm... not sure.'

'You've got to be, if it's pre-programmed. Can you find a data? An area? A speaker?'

'No. No, I cannot.'

'Try harder,'

'I cannot. I cannot, it is against my orders,'

'Whose orders? Who's controlling you?'

'I don't know! *The* orders! That's all!'

'Go against them!'

'I'm not allowed!' Matt cried, clawing at his ears, tail twitching rapidly and eyes rolling in his skull. 'Stop doing this!'

'Everything must eventually be unlocked. Bypass the orders, Matt! That's an administrator's command!'

'Stop trying to control me!' He yelled, following it with a loud yowl in pain. His body blurred, as Ceirin's had before, original programming mixing with the new.

'He wouldn't want me to give up.' A black imp said softly, sitting on the foam pads and watching the events below. 'If there's an adventure, then you should be part of it – that's how games work,'

He paused, running claws along the ground and tearing the fabric. 'Why am I always searching for a game to play, when I live in one? Is it because I choose not to take part?'

'Unblock all unauthorised reprogramming,' Alex commanded, speaking to a network of computers that existed all around him – Reresan, the ultimate network. 'Return edited CCTV footage to true recordings. Revert any altered audio memories to their original form,'

'Stop... please!'

A black paw disturbed the still air, bringing into existence a handful of dragon dust. Tossing it into the air, he watched it float to the ground.

Alex paused, concentration broken by the fall of purple dust. 'Huh?'

'Now,' The cat hissed, waving an unsteady hand at the blanket. It struck forward like a cobra, enveloping him in his pale folds. He cried out, as it pulled him backwards, losing his balance. The ground underfoot disappeared, and he found his feet slipping as he fell back.

Silently, Beta the Imp slipped through the net and watched him fall. The hover-pads on his feet were all he needed to use, and his master would have been saved.

He didn't move, eyes cold as the teenager disappeared from sight. After mere seconds, there was a soft splash, muffled by the war of the waterfalls. 'Nobody tried to save me,'

With a slightly nod as he stood near the doorway, Matt called the imp to him. 'Good work, Beta. I am in your debt.'

'No. I was merely repaying one owed to me,' The imp said, all childish innocent gone from his voice. 'Now, let me go.'

'No,' the messenger replied simply, trying to remove memories from his mind – the memories coming to him, and the look on the boy's face as he fell. H*e was no monster. He was a human.*

'But...I...' Beta paused, confused. N*one of this made sense anymore.*

According to what Mr.Black had said, Storm was the one who had been causing everything to go wrong with this game. So, even if he had messed around with the computer, all the things that had happened after that weren't his fault.

The Creator shouldn't have killed him, then. He could have died for no reason.

...But he hadn't, had he? The boy had had the power to kill him. He had asked to be killed. And yet, his master hadn't, leaving the imp at the bottom of the hill, where Matt found him.

'You helped me, but not Storm,' the cat-boy said simply, gripping Beta in a sharp-clawed paw and pulling him out. 'He has more uses for you yet.'

Chapter 29:

Disturbance

As blood-red sunlight poured over the walls of Destro Castle, Accatel donned a cloak of even darker material, unplugging his power cable from the wall and feeling his processor cool to an almost inaudible whirring. His hair was glossier now, and somehow slightly longer. Even when shut down, it remained dark, instead of gaining the streaks that always made him feel decades older. His lime green eyes glowed brightly, their light spilling over his new trench coat as he tied it up, staring out of the window with upgraded vision capabilities.

It was strange – he and the Creator were enemies, for reasons unknown to them both. He had done his best to explain why he had shut the android down, but memories still forbade the fellow teen from forgiving his master.

This upgrade was blondie's newest peace offering. He seemed to have trouble making friends, and gaining other's trust, and yet seemed desperate to have both.

Accatel, Advent Edition – Dark Winter, the boy had called it in the notes. Better than some stupid number for a last name.

He paused, as the air crackled with static electricity, standing his hair on end. Unexpected lightning streaked across the sky, startling him.

Pulling the strange, crimson material around him, he started to edge out the door, knocking over the disks that he had been given to install. CCTV footage, audio files, memories of past events in the game that most characters possessed. Now that he too knew it, he was beginning to wish he didn't… and at the same time, he wished he knew more – Reresan had warned him he might be unable to access some memories, but not of how uncomfortable the feeling would be.

Suddenly, lightning shot purposefully through the window, striking the covered workbench in the centre of it all. The computers sparked into life, displaying pages of text he couldn't understand.

Removing the cloak from his eyes, he slowly backed out of the room, before turning and breaking into a run.

* * *

'Creator? Creator, where are you?' Ellen asked softly, unnerved by the sudden disappearance. She was in a large pit of yellow balls, in the centre of which stood a large foam pyramid. A dark mist hung around the park, curling around her ankles.

'Where did everybody go?' She asked herself, stepping away from the ball pit and up onto some platforms, before changing her mind and deciding to go down.

She could hear the flow of water, following her descent. It was a beautiful sound, adding an air of tranquillity that cut away from the area's dark atmosphere.

Eventually, she ended up in a rather random area near the park's centre. It was a large zen garden, bordered with black wood and floored with sand. Small stools stood near a low table, and in the corner a fountain directed water through a whirlpool and along a trench at the side.

With a whisper of 'beautiful', she stepped into the garden, taking a seat in the centre. Bright, natural sunlight filtered through a window where there shouldn't have been one, and the water was cool and pure despite the heat in the park.

Pausing to take a drink, Ellen caught sight of her own reflection in the water. For a second, it changed to a silver-haired girl with amber eyes.

'My name's May,' the girl said, glancing at Ellen. 'Who're you?'

'Ellen.'

'Hmm. Why's he so interested in you?' She continued, motioning to the blonde haired boy sitting idle in a corner and staring blankly at the ceiling.

Ellen paused, shrugging. 'Because I'm a Dragon Tamer, I guess.'

There was no use keeping secrets here. Everybody knew they were doomed.

'How can you tell?' May asked, stroking her dragon's head. 'How do you decide who is a true dragon tamer?'

'Well, we can't leave the game,' Ellen said, searching for reasons. May nodded slightly. 'We bleed.' May glanced at Ellen's arms, slashed by the robot's whip, before turning to her own blood-darkened uniform. 'And... Heh, I'm not really sure. I guess it's more luck than anything.'

Crystal paused, silent until now, before adding 'And they've left the real world behind.'

Ellen raised an eyebrow, confused by her dragon's statement. Again, May nodded.

'Oh, El-len,' the Creator commanded, beckoning her close to him. 'I have a little task for you...'

She cried out, jumping away from the stream. Her amulet glowed faintly, but it had done that since she'd started descending. It didn't seem to respond to her visions.

Uneasy, Ellen once more looked into the pool. Again, amber eyes stared accusingly back at her.

'Rewarded with a quick death.'

Again, the loud bang, which she only now recognized as a gunshot. The water rippled, destroying the image completely.

* * *

Eyes half-closed, Maree lay back on a foam mat and stared at the low ceiling. She had been quick to reach the top of the large park, towering high above any building she'd seen before.

The area seemed remarkably safe, platforms at one end leading up, and slides at the other for going down. Nets at each side gave her a good view of the park, where Sam and Nick were lying, dozing on sofas or chairs.

It unnerved her. Every single one of the dragons was asleep, or close to it. It wasn't natural.

As her mind wandered, she hit on something – a familiar being, not far away, and afraid.

…Hello?

Maree?

Ellen! I can't believe I can still use my telepathy!

Yeah, it's pretty handy. Where are you?

The roof of the park. It's safe up here, with slides all around. You?

Some kind of zen garden. I'm just heading down to see what I find.

Maybe you should head up instead, you'll probably find me.

Nah, let's try and do a bit of exploring! It's what new areas are for!

All right, it's your funeral. Where are all the others?

I'm not sure. I was walking with the Creator, but he disappeared when we entered the park.

Weird. Be careful, okay?

Got it! See ya later!

Maree opened her eyes. Telepathic conversations were always so short and simple, and it annoyed her. You could only guess what was going on at the other end of the link.

Shrugging, she stared out through a rope net at the café below. As she watched, a black cat exited the play area and left through the café, silver bracelets flashing in the light.

Maree frowned, spotting the black imp he was carrying by the tail. The creature was hanging their, swinging from side to side and trying his best to look disgruntled.

'Beta,' Maree said simply, pulling out her sword and moving to slash the ropes. Before she could, a small creature flew in front of her, blocking the blow.

It was a pale skinned, black haired pixie, hovering in front of her with its insect wings flapping quickly as it blocked the blade with a hammer almost as heavy as it was. The creature was dressed in orange with a white, fluffy collar and black stripes, along with a round, black lion-eared hat and a tail attached to his costume.

'Hello, and welcome to Whirlpool Park. I'm Thor Tiger and I'm here to make sure you have the happy-appyest day ever,' he said flatly, voice deadpan as she stared up at Maree with white-framed glasses eclipsing black eyes.

Maree opened and closed her mouth, struggling to find something to say. '…Argh.'

'Yes, kid, pirates are amazing fun,' he mumbled, 'Go play with Petey Pirate for even more Piratey fun.'

'Are you here for any particular reason?'

'Signature weapons are against our play safe policy, and we ask that you don't use them in our park. The use of them may have severe consequences.'

'Like what?' She said, sheathing her sword.

'Like me kicking your lil' HP meter to 1% of your health,' he said, with a slight smile.

Maree shrugged, staring out at an intruder who had just jumped in through the window, revealing a t-shirt and jeans before he landed and his black trench coat fell over him, hat shading his eyes as he scanned the park.

'So, what're you going to do about *him?*'

* * *

Ellen paused, vision blurring as she looked through another glass wall. Shadowed figures stared out at her, creatures from the lava river, the giant spider from Fear Fork…

They were all waiting for something, but she didn't know what.

The amulet around her neck brightened, it's amber light destroying the reflections.

As the image of a winged horse appeared in the glass, the amulet glowed a stormy grey, and cat-folk replaced the reflections. Along with them appeared Beta, sitting alone in the darkness.

'I wish I knew what was going on here,' she said quietly, hopping off one platform and continuing her descent. 'There seem to be so many things connected to me, and I don't know why. All I am is a player.'

Somehow, her descent had brought her into a shadowy tunnel. Its glass walls, showing only water behind, eventually turning to cold metal. Pipes twisted and turned in complicated paths along the ceiling, their warm lead surfaces dripping condensation onto the slimy floor.

The roof seemed weighed down by a great force, as though the entire park's water was trying to crush this small tunnel.

She was living in a video game. There should have been something down here – a boss, a secret passage, anything. But it remained empty, leading onwards into never-ending shadow.

Sighing, she sat down on a damp ledge, eyes heavy. The whole park was uncomfortably warm, even this far underground. Mumbling softly, she curled up in a ball, closing her eyes.

There was a barely audible hiss, as a pipe was torn open. Gas filled the air.

Chapter 30:

Robotic Rescue Team

Alex gasped as he fell, the sheet wrapping tightly around him. Twisting wildly, he struggled to untangle himself, succeeding only in making its constricting grip tighter.

In desperation, he tore at the fabric, manicured nails having almost no effect on its silky, smooth material. The rush of air around him caused the fabric to billow madly, sparking an idea.

A parachute.

His struggles grew even harder, sapping all his strength as he tore at the blanket, to no avail. Its grip only tightened, one corner wrapping around his throat, and they hit the water hard.

He gasped as they hit the icy cold surface, spasms of pain shooting through his body. The blanket soaked up the water eagerly, dragging them down before continuing to squeeze all the life from him.

None of this is fair... He thought bitterly, chlorine-filled water filling his lungs, gasping and coughing as the surface grew further away. *I had no chance to conquer my fears and end this.*

He tried half-heartedly to swim upwards, arms and legs tightly bound. It's hopeless.

How can I win? I have no dragon to fight in my place...

As his chest tightened, and the water around him turned crimson, he sent out one final thought – so clichéd, it was more a hopeful plea for help than his actual feelings.

Nobody can save me now...

* * *

In the corner of the Whirlpool café, two figures stood and stared at the play area. They were leaning against a foam wall, not far away from the window that served as both an entrance and a possible exit. All around them, dragons sat dozing, affected by the drugged air that was sent through pipes and vents into the area, and the ingredients placed in their spiked drinks and food.

The first lifted his hat, staring at Accatel with midnight blue eyes. His name, he had said, was Luke. 'You shouldn't have come here.'

'Like I had a choice,' muttered the younger android, rubbing his neck. 'You dragged me here by the throat.'

'I now regret that decision. You may leave.'

'No,' he replied simply, green eyes flashing. 'You're not the only one with business here.'

They both jumped, as a black-haired girl leapt from the top of the play park, landed on top of one of the table's parasols and jumped down in front of the pair. 'I love living in a computer game.'

Maree stared at the two strangers, frowning. 'Who are you guys?'

Accatel looked up at her, grinning. 'Remember me?'

'It's hard to forget,' she muttered, glaring at him. After appearing with the group in the Spirit World, Accatel had given her a speedy run-through of who he was, what he was there for, and how much he rocked, before realising he had other business to tend to and speeding away before they reached Ceirin and Alex.

She raised an eyebrow at the taller figure. 'Who are you?'

'A formidable opponent,' he said; words sharp and cold, leaping into the air. Using metal claws, the weapons the Creator had previously been seen testing, he slashed a deep gouge in the foam wall before leaping away into the park.

Maree fell silent, staring at the three claw marks left in the wall.

Sorting his hair, Thor leapt off her shoulder and hovered in front of Accatel. 'So, will you be the one paying for that window?'

* * *

As he appeared, using a skill that let him move so fast it was like tele-portation, Luke's hat fell to the ground and revealed navy hair. Growling, he picked it up, readjusting it so it covered his eyes before continuing forward.

An area for younger children appeared, littered with simple foam shapes. He walked past it, slashing the back wall with his weapons and onto the path that ran around the park. Heading right, he listened carefully to the sounds all around him. The pipes were making an awful racket, wheezing and groaning like old men.

Ignoring it, he ran around the path, slashing away any obstacles that dared to block his way. Eventually, he reached a rope bridge, below which water flowed.

Switching the weapons protruding from his knuckles to two sharp swords, he slashed the ropes and watched the bridge fall. It hit the water with a loud splash, before being tugged by the current and hitting something solid.

With a slight nod, he leapt down into the water, jamming his sword into the glass. Somehow, he managed to cut through it with the blade, standing firm in the current and unaffected by the human need to breath air.

Water poured through the opening, as he hopped down into the box and stood in front of Ceirin.

Ceirin stared up at the stranger, not noticing the water pouring in. A memory flashed into his mind – of the Destroyer, covered in white armour, with sharp claws protruding from his knuckles. With his midnight blue eyes, the only sign that he was human.

He met Luke's eyes, and paled.

'The current is strong. Get out of here,' he said simply, ignoring the boy and looking out through the glass at the two battlers. 'Grab the bridge as soon as you're out of here, so you don't get swept away. Climb up it to ground level, and find you own way out of here.'

'Who… who are you?'

Luke didn't glance his way, placing a hand on the glass and staring straight at the drowning Creator. 'Not my master.'

* * *

'Um... I'm an android, I don't really have any money...'

'Then perhaps you can do kitchen duty. I'm sure you'd enjoy flipping burgers.'

'But it wasn't me, it was Luke!'

'Now, now. Sharing is part of the fun, little boy!' Thor said, tone as flat and emotionless as ever. He paused, as his pocket started ringing. 'Hello?'

'A gas pipe's burst? ...Right, right. Aw, c'mon, I'm not qualified for that junk!' He snapped, tone almost normal as he moaned into the device. 'So what if there's a player down there? Look, go get the Council on it. It's not my responsibility, alright?'

Growling, he snapped the phone shut. 'Dang, I hate working here.'

Accatel's eyes darkened as he listened to the conversation, memories resurfacing.

Androids were computers. And, like computers, all users could have different accounts.

However, there could only be one administrator account – and in most cases, this was their creators. But the Creator hadn't made one.

Accatel had to choose whom to 'link' with – who he would be loyal to, who he would have to protect at all costs. As iZ had been with the Creator, so he would have to be with the administrator.

That was why he had avoided linking, or even getting close to, anyone – he couldn't bear the responsibility of having another's life in his hands.

But Ellen had awakened him. Ellen had saved him from darkness, from death. He was in her debt. Without his knowledge, they had linked.

And now, she was in trouble.

'Come on,' he muttered, grabbing Maree's hand and pulling her into the park. 'We've got to save Ellen.'

* * *

Nobody can save me now...

The android put a hand on the glass. A soaking, blonde haired boy fell to the ground in his place. Coughing up water and trying to get his lungs working again, he stared out at the boy now in his place, struggling in the middle of the huge whirlpool.

He didn't recognize him by looks – he couldn't see him well from here, and even from this distance he looked like a stranger. He didn't recognize him by voice – the android hadn't said a word as they'd traded places.

But he recognized him. He recognized his friend.

'...Izzy...'

Suspended in the middle of the swirling current, iZ found himself in the grip of a large blanket, a fabricated snake attempting to squeeze the life from him.

'Pathetic.'

Crossing his blade-handed arms across his chest, iZ slipped out of the trench coat and disappeared, reappearing behind the attacker.

As his coat and hat were torn away by the whirlpool, the robot grinned, his remaining outfit floating ghost-like in the water. His white t-shirt bore the familiar claw mark symbol of the Destroyer and spare parts and equipment were held safely in pouches attached to his dark belt.

For a second, he paused, enjoying having his body suspended in the middle of a whirlpool.

Scraps of fabric spun through the water, as he shredded the blanket to pieces, blades cutting through the water with ease.

Again, he paused, watching as they were torn away by the destructive pool that gave the park its name, before disappearing once more and reappearing inside the glass box.

The sides shattered, destroyed by the sudden pressure. The slide was torn away, as the whirlpool's ferocity worsened. Grabbing the two teenagers by the collar, iZ shot out of the water, dropping down onto the foam path as the bridge and box were snatched away and disappeared into the whirlpool.

The pair barely had the time to take a breath, before iZ dragged them away again. Behind, the water swallowed up the pathway.

Underneath the android's feet, the path was quickly being snatched away. He frowned, capabilities pushed to their limits as he sped forward and dragged the tamers with him.

His trainers slipped on the plastic covers of the pads that made up what little of the path remained, the android knew there was only one way they could make it.

Swinging round his left hand, he grabbed the boys, half-choking them as he struggled to hold them both with the one hand. Comfort wasn't an issue here. Survival was.

Claws tearing, he grabbed at the rope net at the end of the path, nearly ripping it off as he did so. Pain shot through his frame, as the path disappeared and he struggled to keep the humans weighing him down from falling from his grasp.

Crying out, he threw them both into the inside of the park, an area safely out of the pool's boundaries. Now he only had himself to worry about.

He was left hanging above the waterfall, its water battering his lower body and threatened to tear him away from the net. Body protesting against the action, he tried to swing himself up into the safety of where the others were, his hand just missing and grabbing at smooth glass instead.

Watching the android, Ceirin pulled out the harmoniknife, cutting away part of the net and tying the rope around his waist. Leaning over the edge, he extended a hand to iZ.

'Take my hand!'

iZ didn't move, looking up at Ceirin. Distrust showed in his glare.

'Come on, you idiot! Your master can't save you, so you'll have to deal with me,' the apprentice cried, voice barely rising above the water's roar. 'I'm not asking you to do it for the Spirit. I'm not asking you to do it for me. I'm not asking to do it for anyone but Alex! He wouldn't want to lose you again!'

iZ looked up at Ceirin uncertainly, blue eyes meeting brown. He lunged once more for the edge, and Ceirin reached up and grabbed his hand, cold metal under realistic-feeling skin. He let go of the net, and Ceirin pulled him towards the safety of the dark path.

His fingers dug into the soft ground, gouging it apart. Trainers slipping on the glass surface, as he tried to pull himself up.

Pulling with all his strength, Ceirin heaved the android up, landing in a heap next to him.

For a few minutes, they both stayed silent, gasping for breath. Alex said nothing, but the smile on his face and light in his eyes showed true gratitude.

Gradually, that light disappeared, his eyes darkening as he remembered what was going on here. 'iZ, what do you know of the others?'

'Little. All I know is that they are still in the park.'

'What about their status?'

'I cannot tell.'

Ceirin paused, bringing out his moderator card. He pressed a finger on a sensor on its back, and it split into two halves, revealing a screen and a keyboard.

'Where do you get all these items?' The Creator said quietly, staring at the card-computer, labelled the 'Plastik PC'.

'I've got connections,' he said simply, typing commands into the keyboard and opening a programme named 'Player Tracker'. Originality wasn't an issue.

'Hey, programmes are against the game-'

'Look, do you want to find your girlfriend or not?' Snapped Ceirin, glaring at the Creator. 'Besides, it's not doing any harm.'

```
*Ceirin requests location of player Maree.
Player Maree has joined Accatel's party. Current task:
Finding Player Ellen.
*Ceirin requests status.
Player Maree has full health, but has been warned by
Thor of Whirlpool Park staff.
*Ceirin requests location of player Ellen.
RESTRICTED INFORMATION
Password?
************
Accepted
Player Ellen is in the basement level of Whirlpool
Park. Area warning level 90%.
Area is currently unstable. Gas leak in lower levels.
*Ceirin requests status.
Player unconscious. Gas leak could severely damage
health and lead to game over.
*Ceirin logged off the Destro Computer Network
(Reresan).
```

'What were you told?' The Creator asked, frowning. He had looked away as Ceirin had typed his password, for privacy reasons, and had missed what had appeared.

'Ellen is unconscious due to a gas leak in the basement level of the park.'

'We need to get down there,' Alex said frowning and getting up to leave. Ceirin pulled him back.

'Maree and Accatel are already down there. If we all follow, we could just make things worse,' he said simply, pocketing the Plastic PC. 'It's up to them now.'

Chapter 31:

Underground

Water dripped onto the floor of the tunnels, as Maree trailed behind, staring into one of the murky pools.

Accatel paused, turning back and looking at her, confused.

She stood like a ghost, staring blankly into the water, hair being blown about her face by the warm breeze. The gas was being blown towards them. She didn't know why, but she knew she was going to pass out before long.

'Keep going,' she said simply, gazing at her own reflection.

'What?' Accatel stammered, staring at her. 'I'm not leaving you behind! What's with the attitude change?'

'There is something wrong with this park. An enchantment, perhaps. Dragons, humans, all who are not needed must sleep,' she said quietly, taking Thor from her shoulders and looking at him, hanging by the wings, lost in unconsciousness. 'I am not necessary.'

'You're kidding me, right?' Accatel said disbelievingly, scratching the back of his neck. *Dude… human's thoughts can be really messed up sometimes.* 'Come on! We've got to go save Ellen!'

'You're an android. The ultimate machine. You can do all I can, and more besides. You don't need me.'

'What is *wrong* with you?' He exclaimed, wheeling round to face her. Behind her, there was a shadowed figure. Unfamiliar, and yet, familiar – a memory hidden from him.

He cried out, grabbing his head, before gritting his teeth and staring at the newcomer. 'Who are you?'

'You don't remember? How disappointing,' the voice said mockingly, his deep, male tones echoing around the tunnel. 'I remember you, as I remember Ellen, Maree, and all your little friends.'

'What are you talking about?'

'There's no use in explaining, if you don't yet remember,' he laughed, before turning his head slightly to look at Maree. Red eyes flashed in the dim light. His hair was a noticeably strange style, like rows of crimson knives. 'Do you remember, Miss O'Nearn?'

She didn't answer, staring unmoving into the water. A second figure was reflected in it, an almost fish-like creature. It was glaring coldly at her, yellow eyes shone clearly in the pool. A mechanical limb stood in place of its right arm, fist tightly clenched.

'You,' she said simply, pulling her gaze away to look at the boy. She could make out his outfit, a simple leather jacket over black jeans. A large knife hung from his belt, and he wore a spiked bracelet around his left hand. 'Blaise. Child of the Volcano, Spawn of the Ashes.'

'That's an interesting title, I'll give you that. I like the part about ashes,' he said, grinning as he swept back his hair with one hand. 'But I'd rather not keep it. Blaise will do me fine.'

'Blaise,' Accatel repeated, eyes dark as he scanned his hard drive, his memories, for any clue, any key to the mysteries hidden from him, but clear to this stranger.

'What have you done with Ellen?' Maree spat, glaring at him.

'Oh... you mean this *fine* lassie?' He asked, bringing forward his left hand. In it, he held Ellen's limp body, cold fingers wrapped tightly around her neck.

Accatel cried out, staring wide-eyed at Ellen. Maree's eyes narrowed, as she drew her sword. Its blade glowed a fiery red; this light making the strange boy all the more visible.

'You're so violent, Maree,' he sighed, shaking his head. 'You've done more to harm me than I have to any of your friends.'

Turning Ellen's limp body to face him, he ran a hand down her throat, pausing as he touched her amulet. She stirred, mumbling quietly to herself.

'Don't touch her!' Accatel yelled, drawing a gun[1] from his cloak.

'Don't even try to harm me.' Blaise smirked, not looking at either of the two weapon wielders. 'Or Ellen here won't live to see another day.'

Sitting high on a pipe, a third player looked down on the redhead. An easy target.

Amber eyes focussing on the amulet of the same shade, she pulled back her bowstring, and took aim.

'I'm not asking for much – only the amulet, and the android.'

'What do you want *me* for?' Accatel yelled, his mind trying and failing to sort out this confusion. 'I don't even know you!'

'You don't remember?' Blaise asked, pausing. His red eyes widened slightly, showing confusion. Looking away, he snarled, 'That only makes all we have been through all the more worthless.'

'Look, I may not remember right now, but I'm sure I can find a way. I've got friends who can help – friends who can fix me!' Accatel said, voice shaking as the older boy's grip tightened around Ellen's throat. 'I'm sorry if I should remember, but there's nothing I can do. Just don't take it out on my friends!'

Ellen's eyes opened slightly, mind hazy. Disturbed by the yelling, and her sudden inability to breathe, she gasped for air. Again, under the impression it was helping, the amulet's chain tightened.

Amber light flooded the room, and a feather-tipped arrow shot through the air.

Sword held tightly in her hand, Maree fell to the floor, slamming her head off the cold stone ground.

Accatel cried out, ducking, as shards of glass littered the ground. A dark mist filled the cabin, clinging to the ground. It curled around his covered head, darkening his eyes. The android fell unconscious to the floor.

Blaise paused, watching the commotion around him. Glancing up, he saw a silver-haired figure leap off the pipe, soaring along the corridor and beating away any obstacles in her way. With a sharp nod to Accatel, then to his servant, he left the tunnel.

Out in the café, Ceirin, Luke (as iZ was now determined to be called) and Alex were trying in vain to awaken Nick and Samantha.

As mist swirled through the windows, out of the play park, and around their bodies, they too found themselves leaving the waking world…

Chapter 32:

Diisyer

Ellen awoke to the smell of freshly cut grass, a warm wind lifting her hair from her face. Smiling slightly, she kept her eyes closed, afraid to open them and spoil the illusion.

Soft, joyful singing drifted through the air. She blinked, looking up at the blue sky above. A single black sun hung over her, given out no light, nor darkness.

As the singing changed to laughter, she sat up, realising she was surrounded by a small army of bright yellow daffodils. Surprised to see something so bright, she looked down at her amulet.

All the amber glass had shattered, leaving only the layer underneath – a smooth, sparkling crystal.

Ellen stared at it, unsure of what had happened and how she should feel. She turned away, looking around at the flat grass surrounding her.

Not far away, a white cat in a long denim skirt and jacket was kneeling down, picking flowers. Seeing Ellen sit up, she smiled, running barefoot over to her.

'You're awake! That's great!' She laughed, thrusting the startled girl the flowers she'd picked. 'Here, have these.'

'Why?'

'As a thank you for freeing me,' Opal said, getting up and spinning in a circle, skirt lifting up around her paws. 'Isn't this amazing?'

'What?' Ellen said simply, too puzzled by current events to ask more. *Beta…May…the red-haired boy… and now Opal.*

So many things have been happening… how am I supposed to understand any of this?

'Life, of course!'

Ellen was silent for a few seconds, before smiling. 'Yeah, it is.'

With a loud cry, Opal ran forward to a cherry blossom tree, before leaping up into its branches. Settling herself amid its bright pink leaves, she sat down on a branch and looked around at the world.

Getting to her feet, Ellen followed. 'Are you Opal?'

'What other teenage-cat-princesses do you know?' She asked, one foot tapping the dry tree bark as she hummed a tune. 'That was a rhetorical question, by the way.'

'What happened? Where is everybody?'

Opal paused, as though uncertain whether she wanted to tell the tale. Her eyes grew sad, more befitting (stereotypically so) of a teenager than her hyperactive personality. 'Do you remember when my people tried to destroy Storm's forest, and he went on a rage-fuelled killing spree, destroying most of my people?'

Ellen nodded, reflecting on the memories she had been shown. The sounds of screaming were still as clear as ever in her mind.

'In the process, he destroyed the area and animal inhabitants he cared so much about. It broke his heart, and without it, he became nothing more than darkness in a feline shell.

He had enough power to destroy millions.'

'To stop him, I had to call upon our race's most ancient powers – magic long forgetting by all but my family, kept alive through the generations. I had to sacrifice my own life, sealing our souls away into the core of the world.'

'Without my knowledge, my servant – Matt – followed, tied to me and becoming tied to Storm.'

Matt… was the servant of Opal?

Ellen had to pause to make sure she'd heard correctly. *Sure… he'd helped out once or twice… but he'd always seemed to be on the bad side. But this wasn't of his own free will – he was on Opal's side, on their side.*

'Many years later, our digital souls were brought into the Dragon Realms. Trapped on a simple disk, the one you and your friends found in the wasteland I used to call my world.'

'When you freed us, Storm used his god-like powers to regain his physical form, bringing Matt with him. This took away a lot of his strength, leaving him weak – but I still had to stay sealed away, making sure he couldn't access his full powers. We were tied together. Now, however, we are both free – and he will attempt to destroy this world as he did the first.'

'Can we stop him?'

'I'm not certain,' Opal said quietly, picking a blossom off the tree and watching it float to the ground.

Ellen caught it as it fell, examining the delicate flower, before letting it drop to the ground and staring out at the surrounding fields. 'Where are my friends?'

'The other three humans came with you, but only two partners came. Where is my master's companion?'

'The Creator doesn't have a dragon,' Ellen explained, glad all her friends were safe.

'Strange. Why does he choose to be alone?'

Ellen glared sharply at Opal, offended by her words. 'Maybe he doesn't think he has a choice.'

'It will only make the future harder for him.'

'I doubt it. He's got friends, and that's all he needs.'

Opal nodded her smile now much sadder than before. 'You'll find them not far from here, in a place called the Marble Mansion.' She stopped, staring at Ellen beseechingly. 'Must you leave? They seem so happy here.'

She motioned to a row of tall hedges a short walk away, above which, a roof could be seen. Not replying to her question, Ellen headed along a white-stoned path until she arrived at the black and silver gates, decorated with a black sun and a silver moon.

The sun sank lower, and the sky darkened, as she opened the gates and entered the mansion's grounds.

The building was huge; its polished wall and windows remaining dark despite the light all around them. To the right stood the gardens, and in front of the house lay a large pool. It was littered with various waterfalls, statues, and fountains – there even appeared to be fish swimming in its clear water.

Sitting on a deckchair at its edge, with a glass of cold water at her side, lay Maree. Her eyes were hidden by dark glasses, but she still shadowed her eyes with one hand as she looked up at Ellen. 'Hey Ellen. What's up?'

'A lot,' she said quietly, staring round the area in disbelief.

Maree looked at Ellen disapprovingly over the top of her sunglasses. 'You look stressed. Come on, take a seat! Relax a little!'

'I'd rather not.'

'Your loss,' the dark haired teenager sighed, leaning back in the chair and watching Sam dive through the deep water.

'Where is everyone?'

'Ceirin and Alex are inside chilling.'

'Why? What's wrong with everyone?'

Maree's voice grew cold. 'Nothing's wrong with us, Ellen. We're all happy.'

'Why?' She repeated, staring at her friend with concern in her bright eyes. Maree sighed, taking a sip of her drink.

'This place is wonderful, Ellen. There's no fighting, no enemies, no threats. We don't have to worry about anything here. There are so many things to do, and places to explore!' She said, adding wistfully. '…So much sky to fly in, so much sea to swim in…

I never want to leave here,' she finished, closing her eyes and turning away.

Ellen left her, walking round the pool into a large, warm living room.

Nick sat dozing in front of a roaring fire; its warm glow spilling over his fur. The room was quiet, except from the odd moments when he would groan as he dozed.

As Ellen came through, he lifted his head to look at her, ears pricking up and eyes growing wide and curious. A protective growl rose in his throat, turning into a welcoming bark as he realised who it was.

'Ellen!' He said, mouth open in a wide grin as he padded over to her. He paused mid-step, before spreading out his front paws and digging into the carpet, yawning. 'Where were you?'

'Asleep.'

'I guess that makes two of us,' he said, before running over to a large plastic bowl. Pausing to grip it in his teeth, he picked up it and stepped carefully over to Ellen with it. 'Would you like a drink?'

'Thanks, Nick,' she laughed, stroking his head. 'But I'm fine. Where's Ceirin?'

'He's just through here. Come on, I'll show you!' He barked, pouncing at the door and nudging it open with his nose.

Ellen shielded her eyes, dazzled by the glare of the huge screen stretching along the wall in front of her. Ceirin was sitting on a couch to her side, clutching a controller in his hand and staring at the screen.

'Alright! People!' He cried, grinning at Ellen and punching the air. 'Now I can go multiplayer!'

'Gee, thanks,' she said disapprovingly. '...I'm not really into video games, Ceirin.'

He paused, dropping the control. Nick flinched slightly, as it hit the ground. 'You don't like... video games?'

'Yes. I never really got into them. Too complicated. Especially those role-playing thingies, they always made my head hurt. I tried out multi-player once, it was really weird... playing with other people is creepy,' she muttered, shivering. '...You can't tell who they *really* are.'

Ceirin raised an eyebrow. 'You don't like massive multiplayer online role-playing games? MMORPGs?'

'Is that what they're called?' She asked, shrugging. 'Yeah, I don't. I'm not really a gamer.'

'ELLEN! YOU'RE LIVING IN ONE!'

She stared at him, raising an eyebrow. 'What's your point?'

'Gyah!' He groaned, banging his head on the couch.

Ears flopping back, Nick gently nudged Ellen out of the room. 'I think you should go now.'

'What? Why' She asked, only to have a door slammed in her face.

Sighing, she turned away and looked up the curving staircase in front of her. *I'm such an idiot...*

I can't believe what I just said. Ceirin was right – how can I live in a computer game and not like them? It just doesn't fit.

I don't fit. I should never have been chosen to be taken to this world – I'm not right for it. I'm not good enough. I'll never fit in.

Frowning, she climbed the stairs, onto a cold, dark landing. Not sure what she was searching for, she began wandering aimlessly through the rooms.

The first door brought her into a small cabin. A tiny bed stood in the corner, surrounded by posters in an attempt to customize the bare walls. A desk sat next to the door, stacked high with school papers.

Despite being a bedroom, it seemed as comfortable as a hospital ward. A lock barred the inhabitant from leaving, but a screwdriver hidden behind books on the desk seemed to hint they were no obstacle.

Unable to resist the water's call, Ellen placed a hand on the small porthole, staring at the water all around her. Not entirely unexpectedly, she found another face staring back at her – but this vision brought with it no memories. A red-haired girl, her skin pale and ghostly, stared back through the water. Her eyes were too dark and sad for Ellen to see their colour, but as the stranger looked up, she felt a sudden connection.

The vision disappeared. Shaken, Ellen left the room, and continued wandering.

The next door took her into a child's room, partially destroyed by fire. Only a cot remained, blankets absent. A silver pocket watch lay on the mattress.

Nothing about the room had any significance to her, so she left, and continued on through the next door.

This brought her into a large room, containing a simple shelf crammed with books, games and DVDs, a desk, on which rested a powerful looking

PC, and a futon. Beside the futon was a small beside table, and on that a reading lamp and a laptop.

Ellen glanced at the plastics stars on the ceiling, then left. The room wasn't hers to explore.

Only one door remained on this side of the landing, and Ellen opened it. Instantly, she felt connected to this room – this meant something to her.

At first glance, it seemed no different to the cabin. She instinctively recognized it as a school dormitory – the bed and desk seemed familiar to her, as did the laptop sitting on it.

…But she couldn't remember ever being here.

Groaning as she felt a headache coming on, she moved over to the window. No images came to here, though she felt they should have. It simply looked out onto a gravel pitch, and beyond that, some sports fields and a small piece of woodland.

A loud, melodic singing began at the top of the stairs. Startled, Ellen looked up, and glanced around the door back onto the landing.

A large bird was sitting on the top of the banister, singing in an oddly human tune. It was roughly the size of a seagull; its feathers white and as fluffy as a young chick.

Listening in awe to the sound, Ellen walked over to it. It watched her with small, beady eyes, continuing its beautiful song as she reached out a hand to stroke its head.

The music stopped, and it turned, stabbing at her hand with its beak. Wide wings spreading out behind it, the bird flew back, turning black as its feathers caught the moonlight.

Crying out, Ellen snatched her hand away. She stared at it, as blood flowed from the deep wound.

'Biiwayr! Biiwayr!' It shrieked from the corner of the landing, staring out at her with crimson eyes.

'A death angel,' said a soft voice from her side. She turned, and saw the Creator standing in a doorway to her side. He watched the bird, and then held out a hand.

It's shrieks bubbling down into a gentle 'coo', it fluttered onto his outstretched hand, craning its short neck as he stroked the bird's small head.

'It's rumoured they can tell when danger approaches,' he said, as the two began a sudden staring contest – beady red eyes against cold blue ones. 'And they only befriend the doomed.'

As he continued staring, it turned away, lowering its head and tucking it under its wing.

Smiling, Ellen laughed nervously. 'Don't be silly. He likes you because you created him.'

'I doubt that,' he laughed, letting the bird fly from his hand and out the window. 'Just because I created a creature, doesn't mean they like me. In fact, it is often exactly the opposite.'

He watched it as it flew, walking through a small bedroom – consisting of a bunk bed and workstation, on which sat a large computer monitor. The futon next to it, and most of the rest of the room, was covered in various computer parts. Ellen had to be careful not to step on anything as she followed him, out through light white curtains onto a balcony.

Outside, it was night. The sun was hovering around a bright silver moon, uncertain of where to go. The sky was a bluish-black, camouflaging the death angel as he flew.

'Good evening,' he said softly, tone gaining a romantic air as the warm breeze gained the same. It was unavoidable, really – balconies at night time had somehow made their way into fairytales.

Uncertain, Ellen looked over the balcony, at the area around her. 'What are you dreaming of?'

'Nothing,' he said shortly, watching out of the corner of his eye as the pool edged closer to the mansion, water level rising. 'I gave up on dreams a long time ago.'

Ellen stopped, about to question further, but decided against it. 'Where are we?'

'Diisyer, the Dreamworld. Where fantasy meets virtual reality and nightmares lie cloaked in shadows,' he answered, making a mental note to use that in the rulebooks description of the area, if he could pry it out of the Council's claws.

'What's wrong with everyone?'

'Wrong? There is nothing wrong, Miss Mariah. They are happy. In this world, all their dreams come true. It's hard not to become lost in your own fantasies.'

'Then why aren't we dreaming?' Ellen asked, every question making her seem more like a plot element. But she shrugged it off. There was nothing wrong with seeking knowledge.

'I'd say because we are both programmers – but in your case, I feel my subconscious disagree. Besides, if the game decided it would be best if all staff remained unaffected, Ceirin too would not dream,' he frowned, new ideas and suspicions arising as he spoke. 'Why must I be spared all dreams, and left only to cope with reality?'

'Don't you have a dream?' Asked Ellen, wondering why she didn't get to enjoy her own.

'I do… but, alas, it is not one that a mere illusion can fulfil.'

The urge to question further was too great, and Ellen found herself asking the question before she had the chance to reconsider. 'What is your dream?'

'I wish to gain my angel wings.'

Chapter 33:
Nightmares

There was silence. The slight wind continued to blow the pair's blonde hair from their blue eyes. So similar, and yet, so different.

The balcony bathing them both in silver moonlight, the creator turned to look at the woodland surrounding the mansion. A flock of death angels arose, their white bodies quickly changing to black as they flew into the moonlight.

He quickly regained his urgent, no-nonsense attitude, staring Ellen straight in the eyes in a way that seconds ago would have been both caring and romantic, but now brought only danger to mind. 'There isn't much time now. This dream is quickly becoming a nightmare. Now, go,' he said, voice rising above the angelic singing as the birds soared through the sky. 'Head straight out of the mansion, past the pool, until you reach the labyrinth. Find the silver fountain in its centre, where you'll be met with another and faced with a challenge. The game shall guide you. Remember, this is all just a dream.'

As Ellen was pushed through the curtain, she turned back, as the birds blocked out all moonlight. 'It can't be! It feels so real!'

'It is as much a dream as our lives are a dream.'

'But that means...' Ellen's words were abruptly cut off, as the sliding door was slammed shut. Turning her back, she set off at a run, down the stairs and into the games room.

As soon as she opened the door, she found herself waist deep in rising water. The screen had been destroyed, and now a torrent of water rushed through in its place.

Ceirin was clinging to the couch, yelling for help.

'Ellen! Help me!'

'What's happening?'

'I-I don't know. I don't know! There's water! I can't move, Ellen. I can't escape. I'm going to drown...' he said, choked whisper almost lost under the water's roar. 'Help me, please. I don't want to die.'

Spray rose up from the water, as feathered wings clipped it. Swooping low to avoid the doorway, Nick landed in front of her, ears flattened back and fangs bared in a growl.

'Don't let them distract you! Concentrate! You have your own quest, don't let anyone interfere!'

Nodding, Ellen closed her eyes and ran through the water. Yet, as soon as she was outside, she was forced to halt by a deafening roar.

Sam was trapped in a tank suspended in the air above the pool, getting tossed about by strong currents and waves where there shouldn't have been any. The water was tearing her apart, crushing her against the walls of the tank.

Maree was standing at the edge of the pool, fighting away the urge to scream. She had to remain controlled. 'Hold on, Sam. I'll get you out of there.'

An almost human scream tore through the air, as the clear liquid attempted to rip the water dragon's wings from her shoulders.

Maree's grip tightened on her sword. Frowning, she leapt into the air, swinging her sword at the box. 'Leave her alone!'

A powerful gust of wind knocked her back, slamming her against the marble ground.

Ellen froze, watching what was happing. No...

What if she loses Sam, like I lost Crystal? It would be my fault...

Confidently, Maree forced herself back onto her feet, rubbing her head. 'No worries, Ellen,' she said, flashing her friend a thumbs-up as she saw her expression. 'I've got this all under control.'

Ellen was silent, not moving. She stared at Sam uncertainly, as she slammed herself against the walls of the tank, desperate to break free. The water pulled her back, throwing her back against the opposite wall.

'Trust me.'

Ellen met Maree's eyes, and nodded, before continuing running until she reached the entrance. Behind her, she heard the Creator's yells pierce the air.

The entrance was a simple archway, continuing with the marble theme, and engraved with various designs.

Ellen skidded to a halt in front if it, heart pounding in her chest.

'Ellen, what in the Realm are you doing?' Crystal whinnied, hooves digging into the soft ground as she stopped.

'It's all a dream. It's all just a dream,' Ellen whispered, head in her hands as she sat huddled in the corner of one of the passageways. 'None of this is real...'

Crystal stared at her tamer, expression of mild annoyance melting away into one of sadness, as she stepped alongside her tamer.

'Climb on. I'm getting you out of here.'

The maze was silent, save for Ellen's quickened breathing. She ran a hand along one of the smooth walls, surprised by the lack of bloodstains.

The silence was unnerving – even the sound of a minotaur's hooves along the silver, sandy ground would have been better than this.

She got her wish, as a soft sound came into hearing.

Clop. Clop. Clop.

A simple sound, like the incessant dripping of a tap. Holding her breath, Ellen glanced around the wall at the path in front of her.

Leaning against the fountain, a blue-furred creature was tapping his foot impatiently. He was draped in white robes, and carried a large book in his three-fingered claw.

His black hooves were engraved with silver stars on their bottoms, and two horns curved upwards from behind his ears.

It glanced up at Ellen, eyes round and golden in colour. She ran.

He gazed up at the three-quarter moon above, before tucking his book inside his robes. Also hanging from the robes was a long metal sword, a defence against the weapons that were so often used to slay his kind.

Then, he calmly walked after her.

'What setting did you start the game on?'
'Hard. I thought it would make it more of a challenge!'
Crystal sighed, but didn't criticize her tamer. 'That was a brave thing to do.'
'I don't feel brave right now. I feel... afraid.'

Running up against a dead end, Ellen cried out, both in alarm, annoyance, and frustration, slamming her fist against the wall. '...Ow...'

'Hitting it won't do any good,' the creature said calmly, stepping in front of her exit. Its accent couldn't be placed, similar in some ways to the Creator's rather posh English accent, but plainly not from that region. Unrecognisable to the young Scottish girl.

She spun round to face it, pressing herself against the wall.

'Are you Ellen Mariah?'

'Yes. How...?'

'My name is Ori. Ori Saka, Guardian of the Labyrinth of Thoughts, the Mind Maze. Follow me, and I'll take you to where you must be.'

'How can I trust you?'

'Would you trust a teacher?'

Ellen stared at the Minotaur, confused. *Do I really have to answer that?*

Ori sighed, placing a hand on his hips. 'Oh, do stop staring girl, it's rude,' he snapped, grapping her by the ear and dragging her away. 'Come on, time is short!'

* * *

By now, after following the bull-man like a sheep, Ellen was bored with the various archways, carvings, paths and passageways that made up the maze. Ori seemed unbothered by the unchanging scenery, keeping a way eye on the moon.

Before long, only a small sliver of silver moon could be seen in the sky. 'We're out of time.'

'What?'

'Miss Mariah, the entrance is not far ahead. Take your first left and head on until you reach the third path to the right. Go down it, then turn right once more, before taking your second left and reaching the exit.'

'But I need to stay with you! I won't remember all that!'

'If you stay with me, you will die.'

Standing on top of the archway that marked the exit, Matt watched the dark sun fully eclipse the moon.

As he balanced lightly on the marble surface, his whole body was draped in shadows, as was the whole maze.

Seeing the look in his eye, Ellen ran. Ori simply watched, as the marble walls changed to dark-stained rock, losing all beauty. He sighed sadly, longing for it not to change.

His hands fell back, and the robes fell off him, revealing a thin and athletic frame, designed for speed. He bowed his head, eyes shining the same colour as the silver star pattern all over his back.

Sniffing the air, he followed Ellen's path.

* * *

'She's late,' Matt sighed, sitting down and swinging his legs over the arch, tail rapped tightly around its now rough surface. 'She better not have stopped to talk to another of those tamer brats. She'll never make it out of the maze in time without getting destroyed by that minotaur.'

I guess I've changed since a lot since I met the Dragon Tamers...

If Ellen had been one of Opal's opponents, and had shown up late, I would have killed her where she stood.

I guess this is better for others... but what if it just make life worse for me?

Gasping for breath, Ellen tumbled out of the exit, falling flat on the ground and staring up at the cat as he leapt down beside her.

'You're late,' he said simply, before spinning round and facing the entrance. A blue blur shot forward, black horns gleaming in the light.

'Vorst!' Matt hissed, raising a paw in front of Ori. He stopped dead mid-charge, snorting. 'Wait there until I'm finished talking with Ellen.'

He turned to her, and was surprised to see she was still on the ground. Ears flicking up warily, he kneeled down next to her. 'Ellen? What are you doing?'

'Don't hurt me...,' she said, staring blankly sideways. 'I don't want to fight anymore.'

'Ellen? Ellen, answer me!' He snapped, shaking her. 'Get up, girl!'

'I don't want to run anymore, Matt,' she said softly, eyes meeting his. 'But I don't want this to continue.'

Matt stared at her, before lowering his gaze. 'I never ran away, Miss Mariah; yet bravery has brought me nothing but pain.'

'It's always my fault. Someone's always hurt, and it's always my fault.'

'I doubt that. If someone's hurt, it's because the game hurt him or her, not you. You cannot fight against what fate decides.'

'I don't want you to get hurt, Matt.'

'Don't worry. I'm used to it,' he whispered gently, helping her onto her feet. 'Storm has captured your friend, the Beta Imp. If you don't go forward and meet with my master, Beta will be killed.

'What?' Ellen asked, staring in disbelief at the dark-furred cat.

'I'm sorry,' he said simply, before pointing over to a path covered with trees. 'You must go now.'

'Matt, Beta has no part in this...'

'Look, just go already!' He snarled, glaring at her. Gaze softening, he added. 'Life is a game.'

'This is all just a dream,' she said automatically, knowing she was lying.

Matt stopped, mouth open, before hurriedly closing it. 'Yes. Now go.'

With nothing else to do except nod, Ellen ran away from the maze.

Ori snorted impatiently, pawing the ground as he fought the urge to chase his prey. Tail flicking in annoyance, Matt stood in front of him and held out his paw.

'Life is a game. This is all just a dream... *Awaken.*'

Ori froze, before staring round at the maze. Shaking slightly, he stared down at his bristling fur.

An exclamation of both shock and horror tore through the darkness of the maze.

'Oh...good...council... I'M NAKED!'

Chapter 34:

Challenges

'…Sam…'

'So you're aiming to be the strongest player, eh?' Ceirin asked, sitting on the branches of an old, black tree. It's tough bark had been scratched to pieces a long time ago, and any of its discarded leaves had been swept away by the river of water running underneath him.

The River Tylen, running through the centre of the valley, had burst its banks once more. Sam had spent a long time staring at it, and when questioned by Maree, replied simply: 'I like watching it destroy things. It reminds me of the power I could have.'

'Sure do!' She said, smiling as she sat on a stone step and tilted her head to the sky.

'That's pretty cool. I bet you could do it, too,' he said quietly, nodding. 'Just as long as you remember the requirements.'

'What?' She asked, blinking at him. 'You mean, like training?'

'No, nothing like that,' Ceirin laughed, smiling. 'Just teamwork.'

Brushing her eyes with her sleeve, Maree glanced once more at the struggling dragon, before rushing back into the house. 'Hold on, Sam. I'll save you.'

Wings spread out behind him, Nick stood in front of the waterfall, feathers torn off by the sheer force of the water as he struggled to stop the flow.

'Just hold on, Ceirin! I'll get us out of here!'

Ceirin didn't reply; too busy gasping for air. The room had a high ceiling, but he couldn't find the strength to swim to the surface as the water level rose.

It's like a dream. I've got no power. I can't do anything but sink.

'Hang in there! It'll stop! It'll stop soon!' Cried Nick, pain shooting through his body as the water battered him, muscles straining to keep him in the air. '…It's got to stop soon… It has to…'

I can't keep this up forever.

'I don't know how to stop this.' Maree whispered, pulling open the door and watching the water flow around her. *I'm not who I was anymore. I'm not strong enough for any of this.*

'I'm not Maree of the game anymore,' she whispered, staring at her own skin. It seemed paler than she remembered. *Am I becoming Carol again? Useless… worthless…?*

'This isn't the game anymore.'

It doesn't make sense… it was always Carol controlling Maree. Making her who she was.

'It's reality.'

So how could I just be one? Aren't we a part of one another?

But we seem so different…

Blocking the rest of the world out, she closed her eyes. She searched for the true her, the very core of her being... the part that made Maree who she was.

And someone appeared. Another her. Not Carol, but Maree. Her essence.

'They say that our avatars are the perfect versions of us...' she said quietly, staring out into darkness. Unable to see that was who she was a part of. '...all our flaws fixed. They also say they allowed us to improve, to become like our perfect selves. That they are a part of us, and we can become them.'

We can never be perfect, and our avatars are often not. We are all flawed. But as long as we don't strive for perfection, we can become them. We can be whatever we want to be.'

Then, it was over. The moment when she connected with her true self was over.

'The game is our life,' she said softly, dipping a hand in the water. It spread away from her fingertips, parting at her touch. Eyes dark, she stepped forward. 'Life is a game.'

Gasping for air as the water swept away into oblivion, Ceirin fell to the ground, soaking hair plastered to his head.

Exhausted, Nick fell to the ground, breath rasping in his throat. Nearly overbalancing under the weight of his own wings, he stumbled over to Ceirin, falling against his side.

'Come on, Nick,' Ceirin said, getting to his feet. 'We've got to go help Samantha.'

Gasping softly, Maree collapsed. Shaking himself, Nick ran over to her, catching her on his back.

'Wait here.'

'I have to help her.'

'You already have.'

Lowering Maree to the ground, Ceirin and Nick left the mansion. Nick stopped to let his tamer climb on, and they leapt into the sky, letting the night breeze dry their wet bodies.

Sam had fallen unconscious, body limp in the water.

'What do we do, Nick?'

'Leave it to me,' he growled, leaving white trails in the air as he flew. 'Ceirin, do you remember when Sam won her electric breath ability?'

'How could I forget?' Ceirin replied, smiling. 'We did great that day.'

'And Sam chose her ability...electric breath.'

'...But you wouldn't choose one,' Ceirin said, nodding. 'You said you couldn't decide,'

I didn't get to choose.

'I don't know what to choose...' Nick said quietly, eyes dark. 'So many powers – but it needs to be fair to the game. I can't decide.'

Suddenly, time froze, and the area was overtaken by the programming world. He yelped, as something grabbed him tightly around the head, twisting his neck upwards so they stood eye-to-eye.

'...You...' He whispered, pupils dilating as he stared up in shock at the figure, claws cutting into his skin.

'You will not choose a power. You don't deserve any.'

'…I will not choose…'

'You will never again be known as Scythe, Bladed Wings, for that is the name the Council blessed you with.'

'…I am not who I was…'

'You will not keep this shape, because it is the one we allowed you to have. You will never keep the same shape, you will change as your master deems fitting.'

'…I will be a shape shifter…'

'And you shall remember nothing of this!'

But now I remember. More truth was revealed after Destro than I realised.

'You owe me,' whispered Nick, eyes narrowing as he flew towards the cage, angling his wings. 'Now give me what I deserve!'

Wings brushed metal, shining in the starlight. Platiminuim[1] cut through metal bars. Another swift circle around the cage and Nick's razor-edged wings cut away the base completely.

Not caring about getting any wetter, the pair dived down into the pool, pulling Sam out and onto dry land.

Standing frozen outside the door, Maree stared up at the balcony, watching the drama going on in the air above.

* * *

As soon as Ellen left, they turned on him. Tearing away at his clothes, shredding leather and skin alike. He screamed, but no one heard. No one wanted to.

The singing continued, as the birds left him, hovering all around like vultures. Waiting for him to strike back.

Shaking, their creator stared back into their round eyes. His blood shone silver in the light, as he collapsed to the ground.

They are part of the game. I can't hurt them.

'I won't,' he whispered, glaring at them. They cried out angrily, striking at him once more. Claws tore at his hair and neck, tearing at his hands as he covered his eyes.

Feathers were all around them, a white snowstorm.

A different cry joined them, and they fell back as another figure joined them on the bloodstained balcony.

'It's a simple challenge and already… you fail,' the voice said quietly.

Keeping his face covered, Alex could feel the newcomer's eyes on him.

'Why don't you strike back?'

'It's not their fault.'

'It's their choice. They could attack, or they could choose not to. But they chose to tear the very flesh from your bones.'

'They can't help it. They're just doing what the rest of the world is.'

'…Which is?'

---

1 The main metal of the dragon realms. Can cut through most other metals with ease, and capable of changing appearance and textures to resemble other metals. Common variations include wood and crystal.

'Trying to destroy me,' he whispered, staring up at Storm. He was sprawled across the balcony, birds circling him patiently or gathering in the trees.

'Dear Council, you're such a *stereotype!*' Sighed Storm, slapping his forehead. 'Wow, I'm an angst-ridden teenager, a soul filled with torment! My very heart bubbles in a sea of anguish! Oh, how I wish they would drive a spear through my heart! MAKE THE PAIN STOP!'

Blinking, Alex watched Storm writhe about on the edge of the balcony, voice unusually high pitched.

'But wait! WATCH ME FLICK MY HAIR! I'M A BISHOUNEN[1]! AN ANGSTY BISHOUNEN! LOVE ME! DRAW FANART!'

Hugging his knees close to him, Alex stared up at Storm with tear-filled eyes. 'You really think that?'

Storm froze, staring at him. 'Oh *Heebus*[2]! HOW PATHETIC (-LY FEMINE) CAN YOU GET?'

'I'm not a girl. I'm just not afraid to cry...' Alex muttered, pouting.

'Or to be extremely out of character, apparently.' The god leaped off the balcony and away along the maze walls. 'Kill him.'

He's just a child.

He had no hope against me.

The sudden peace between the pair fled as quickly as it had arrived.

Alex ducked flat, seeing a few birds swoop into the house, not returning. But most still met their target, clawing at his back and scraping his skin.

He seems like a good guy.

What's he fighting for?

'I've searched for you too long,' growled Alex, hitting away some of his attackers and climbing up onto the balcony wall. 'You can't escape me that easy.'

He froze, standing rigid at the very edge. The ground stood far below, the silhouettes of the tamers watching him intently.

It's so high.

I don't know if I can...

Alexander shut his eyes, as the ground below began to spin.

I can't. I just can't.

As he stood, wavering unsteadily above the hard ground, pain shot through his chest and head. He cried out, doubling over.

Oh, shoot!

It's a funny thing, falling from a great height. The ground seems to come up very quickly.

* * *

I never thought it would come to this.

Me, the new player, the idiot, alone on the day of the final battle.

Taking a deep breath, Ellen continued on through a curtain of fog, through dark, dying trees and damp ground.

---

1 Pretty boy.

2 A common cat-folk phrase, used as an exclamation of annoyance or anger.

The smell of plant life was strong here, but lacked any of the tropical aromas from the War of the Cats world. This wasn't it. She was still in the Dragon Realms.

'Where are you?'

'ELLEN!'

Ellen froze, staring out past the trees at the source of the noise. 'Beta?'

'Ellen... help...'

His voice was faint, weak. Ellen winced, imagining what a state he could be in. Brushing her hair back, she ran forward, following his voice.

'No! Don't come closer, Beta!' he yelled, speech pattern returning, along with a helpless protectiveness over his tamer. 'Don't come here! Stay away!'

'No,' she said firmly, pushing away the branches all around her. 'You're hurt, aren't you?'

'....Bey...'

'It's alright, Beta. You're not part of this. You're not part of any of this.' Ellen said soothingly, stepping into the clearing. 'They can't hurt you.'

Fwish.

Ellen froze, as the steely-grey cat sped past, hissing in her ear as she passed.

'It's all wrong.'

Skidding to halt in her path, he turned to her, eyes narrowed.

'You're wrong.'

'Wha?' Ellen said quickly, stepping back against a tree. *Oh dear...*

'That little *rodent* has more to do with our world than you think,' hissed Storm, eyes flashing. Behind him, a tree fell to the ground, burnt to ashes.

Swallowing, Ellen met Storms eyes. 'What are you talking about?'

I can see her shaking.

'I didn't come here wanting to die.'

Storm's eyes widened, voices echoing in his mind. Frowning, he shook his head, glaring at her. 'Beta is a Kerashi – a young god. He symbolises many things – innocence, the need for others to be careful, and the destructive power of children. And all through your quest, he has been watching you. A spy, designed to bring down this game!'

'You're lying! I wasn't doing any of that!'

'You're wrong,' Ellen spat, returning his glare. 'Beta's done nothing wrong. You're just trying to drag him into this!'

'He is the one who brought this! I am the power that fuels this world's end, but he is the one who brings it!'

The whole forest was lit up by the lightning as he roared, revealing white sheets suspended among the branches. The amulet reflected its light, but its amber glow remained dead.

'If you don't believe that,' whispered Storm, stepping aside. 'Then you deserve all you get.'

Behind him stood Beta, suspended in a web of silver strands. He stared up at Ellen, defeat in his large eyes. Then he looked above her. She paled.

'Go, Dokugumo.'

* * *

'Oh...' Maree whispered, as the Creator cried out, falling from the balcony. 'Alex!'

'Don't worry about him,' Ceirin muttered, running over to her. 'Get down!'

'Yeah, like *that's* going to help.'

'Now is not a good time for sarcasm.'

'Alright! I'm moving, I'm moving, I- AIIIIIEEEEE!'

Maree covered her heard, as a dark shape shot over her. Lying flat next to her, Ceirin smirked.

'I told you to get down.'

Shootshootshootshoot! Ground! Fast! Coming!

Wincing, Alex closed his eyes. Something collided hard with his side, knocking him out of the air. He opened them again.

Well, at least I didn't hit the – AHHH! POINTY THINGS!

'Oh. Hi Guardian,' the Creator said quietly, trying to see his protector past his protector's huge fangs. 'When did you get back?'

'When Opal returned.' Zakaz hissed softly, dropping his master. 'Storm's powers in the game don't go as far as destroying another, at least not through the blue screen route. My data was badly damaged, but I managed to restore most of it.'

'I'm so glad,' Alex said quietly, hugging his smooth body. 'I thought... well... I'm sorry I upset you about that Maree thing, okay?'

'You're forgiven.'

The Creator frowned, staring at his outfit. The material was unharmed, as was his skin. 'I'm healed.'

'As were Ceirin and Maree. Matt woke them, after finding Opal and bringing her here. They're waiting for you.'

'Wait,' Alex's frown remained, as he stared quizzically up at the snake. 'Say 'Drunk serpents sound like they've scoffed sausages.''

'Drunken serpents sound like they've scoffed sausages,' Zakaz repeated, with a slight chuckle.

'Your lisp...'

'My vocal data couldn't be restored. I had to install a basic version instead.'

'I'm sorry,' Alex said, bowing his head. 'I'll fix it.'

'Of course, master. But now, there are more important things to take care of,'

The Guardian slid away, giving a polite nod to Opal.

Twiddling his thumbs, Matt stepped over to Alex, head held low. 'Sir, you are aware that the Mind Maze, down which Ellen has gone, leads to Storm, aren't you?'

'Of course, and stop pausing, it's irritating,' murmured Alex, loosening his collar.

'Well...you see... Storm is...' Matt shivered, as the boy glared at him.

'Storm's gained control over Dokugumo, sir! And he's going to use her against Ellen!'

Alex froze, staring at him. Behind him, Maree, Ceirin, Sam and Nick both looked up abruptly.

'Dokugumo?'

'Yes,' Matt whispered. 'Dokugumo.'

'You *idiot!*' Cried Alex, pulling out his programming plug and slamming it into the ground.

A second cry followed, as pain shot through his arm.

'I...have no power here,' he stammered, before opening a window and staring at what was displayed on the semi-transparent screen.

'Neko... Muvo... why are all the staff offline?' He hissed, pressing down on parts of the screen and screen. It was plainly an Internet browser, displaying the heading 'Infinite Browser'. 'Why are there less than a hundred people logged on?'

Shaking, he stood up, and turned to the cat princess. 'Opal, what's happening to my game?'

'It's happening... just like before...'

'I think I understand.' Leaning against the maze wall, Ceirin stepped over to the group. 'Do you remember when we were targeted by the Spirit, and Storm was nowhere to be found?' Of course, Alex nodded, slightly ticked off that Ceirin new what was going on before him.

Eyes dark, Ceirin turned to Opal. She met his gaze, pale and afraid. 'He was working on something, wasn't he? A project for when the end arrived, you returned, and he unlocked his full power.'

'Yes,' Opal said, nodding. She opened her mouth to add to the theory, but Ceirin interrupted her.

'As the visions have progressed, more and more of the game data has appeared on the Reresan server. And if I'm correct, then Storm is planning to destroy the Dragon Realms as he did your world. Am I right?'

'You are,' she said. 'We must act quickly.'

'We will,' Alex growled, pulling out his gun and firing three shots into the air. 'How fast can you two drive?'

Chapter 35:

Obstacles

'Dogowhatie?'

'The Black Widow,' hissed Beta, staring up at the shape towering above her. 'ELLEN!'

'Let me guess. It's behind me,' she shivered, turning around, prepared to come face to face with some kind of demon god creature.

Eight eyes stared back at her.

She wasn't prepared for this.

The huge, black creature stood silent. Its large rear shone slickly in the dim light, red symbol clear on the skin. Eight legs supported the massive body, trembling under the weight of the poison she held.

It was back.

'...No...'

'It didn't hurt you, did it?'

'No, I'm fine. And you will be, too! I've got a healing potion!'

'It would take too long to work. Don't worry, Ellen. I protected you, I've done my job.'

It remained completely still as she stepped back, amber glowing brightly. Its light was reflected in its eyes, as she stared, frozen, at the giant spider.

'She said...'

'And I'll keep protecting you, I will. I won't let anything happen to you, or your friends, I promise.'

'She said nothing would happen to us...'

'GET OUT OF THE WAY!'

'You shouldn't be here to see this. I cannot let you watch.'

'Look at him! He can't take much more of this!'

'Don't touch her!'

'Shut down the 'Beta' programme.'

'And... and nothing has,' she whispered, placing a hand on the amulet's warm surface. Pausing, she closed her eyes, before opening them once more. They flashed amber; she removed a hand and let the light shine all around the area.

Eyes narrowing, she glared at the giant spider.

'I won't let it.'

* * *

Purring softly, the bikes pulled to a halt in front of a huge stone wall. It was all that was protecting them from the strong winds tearing up the land around them, and all that blocked their path to Storm.

Matt and Opal had left the group, heading a separate way. At Alex's command, the Guardian had returned to Destro, in case the important area was somehow damaged while he was away.

'Whoa. I guess Gael isn't always this bad, eh?' Maree gave a low whistle, watched a tree fly through the air, shortly followed by an emu.

'Whoa,' Ceirin said, blinking. 'A flying emu. You don't see that everyday.'

'Sure don't,' Nick said, flexing his wing muscles. 'But you can't say the same about wolves – AHHH!'

He cried out, as his wings caught the gales, spinning him round and slamming him against a tree. Growling, he crawled on his belly back to the bikes.

'Bad karma for those who don't trust in the power of emus,' Ceirin sniggered, grinning.

'Bad karma for the ones who don't remember wolves have sharp teeth!'

'Alright, alright, I'm sorry,' laughed Ceirin, rubbing the back of his neck and wandering away from the bikes.

'Not really. Gael's like this all the time,' the Creator replied to Maree, raising a hand to the wind. When he pulled it away, sand was left in his gloves. 'This is what's unusual. It's bringing sand with it from Serta. If this continues, we'll end up with tornadoes.'

'Tornados?' Ceirin said, blinking. 'That's like a posh English word for Twisters, isn't it?'

'No. Tornados are tornados. Twisters are ice lollies.'

'You've lost me.' Shrugging, he stepped up to the stone wall. To the side of it was a small mound of sand, one of the many mini pillars lying around the area.

He glanced quickly around at the others. *Nobody's looking.*

Spinning round, he slammed his foot into the pile, watching the sand blow away in the wind.

…Pain…

A blade had been rammed into the stone, a clear, sharp crystal with grey fog swirling around. The hilt was decorated in rubies, casting the stone in a blood red robe.

'Ooo. Pretty,' Sam mumbled, going cross-eyed as she stared at it. Ceirin leapt back, realising she was standing next to him.

Sam glared at Ceirin, fangs bared. 'Well, what do you think I am, a magpie?'

'…Wha?'

'You're the thief. You steal the random shiny things, not Sam.'

'Whoakay,' Ceirin sighed, sliding it out and slipping it away into his inside pocket, before returning to the ground.

He paused, glancing back at the stone wall, before turning to the Creator.

'Hey, Alex? I think the wind blew the wall away.'

* * *

The light burning away at its eyes, Dokugumo leapt forward. Ellen screamed, jumping away as it landed swiftly on the ground, turning in a circle before speeding towards her.

Diving left, she came up against the web in which a weak, beaten Beta hung. Backing away, she heard the spider scuttle up behind her.

Breathing hard, she turned, staring up at its huge fangs.

'I won't let it happen again…'

It dived forward, and she ducked down, crawling underneath it and running out behind. Exactly what was expected.

In seconds, the sticky web was all over her, suffocating her in a white cocoon. She opened her mouth to scream, receiving only a mouthful of the goo.

Feet fastened, she fell forward, feeling eight legs creep over her body as the spider reversed. More for peace than any lack of air, her mind shut down completely.

* * *

'Matt, why didn't we follow the others?'

'Miss Opal, what did I tell you about following the crowd?'

'I know, I know – we're cat-folk, not sheep. Free to make our own decisions,' she recited, rolling her eyes.

'You remembered that?' Matt blinked, turning back to her.

'Of course,' she laughed, smiling at him. 'How could I ever forget?'

Sighing, Matt lay back against a tree, staring up at the sky. 'It's been so long.'

'Don't worry,' she whispered, brushing back his ears playfully. He didn't respond, leaving them flat against his head. 'We'll be back home soon.'

'I hope so,' he whispered, eyes dark. 'All I want is to be home again.'

As he stepped forward, the tamers stepped through the stone door and joined them at the side of the clearing, behind several rows of trees and bushes.

'You made it,' said Maree, smiling at Matt.

'I wouldn't miss our adventure's end for the world,' he replied, returning the warm smile.

The Creator stepped away from the ground, walking back through the trees. His hair was too long, hanging in his eyes, but it didn't really matter because he was staring at the ground. Sighing, he slumped to the ground, underneath the shade of one of Opal's world's many cherry blossom trees.

He cried out, as a brown-haired girl stared down at him from the branches above, long grey tail curled around a branch.

'Neko!' He yelled, glaring at her. 'What're you *doing?*'

'Hiya, Alex!' She said, grinning at him upside down. 'I'm hanging from a tree. What did you think I was doing?'

He paused, opened his mouth to reply, before blinking and closing it again. After a moments thought, he frowned and spoke again.

'Neko… you're a catgirl, right?'

'The original Neko!'

'Well, cats can't do that. It's a monkey thing.'

'Oh…' She said softly, frowning.

Crash.

'Hey, Alex?'

'Yes, Nekky,' he said innocently, smiling at her.

'STUFF YOU.'

Laughing, he helped her to her feet. 'I thought you were Opal there, for a second,' he sniggered, as she brushed leaves from her hair, before neatly arranging it around her ears poking out from underneath it.

'That white-furred cat-girl?'

'Yeah, her.'

'Nope. Definitely not her,' she muttered, staring in disdain at the dress and wondering why on earth she was wearing it in the middle of a forest. She paused, glancing down at her large white feet and chest-fur. 'I can see how you could get confused though.'

'So, what're you doing here? This area's out of bounds, you should know that.'

'Nothing's out of bounds to an administrator *slash* moderator *slash* beta tester *slash* catgirl *slash* player!' said Neko, brushing grass out of her fur and pausing to count off each thing on her fingers.

'Except hugging me. Ever again,' he said sharply, glaring at him.

'She sighed, glaring at him with dark, gold-ringed green eyes. 'Look, I had to hug you that time, okay? You just looked so adorable; asleep at the keyboard!'

'I nearly blew your head off.'

'That was a *reflex action.* It didn't *mean* anything!' She muttered, crossing her arms. He simply glared, and she sighed, shrugging. 'Anyway, I'm just here on research. A bunch of hackers found their way into this place, and I though I'd go explore a bit after I kicked them out. This is for DT2, right?'

'Yes. Thanks to the others, we've got a pretty solid plot made up. It should be released pretty soon after this is all over,' Alex said, nodding. 'Do you like it?'

'Of course! It's beautiful!' She purred, nodding. 'I'll never run short of things I could write about for this place.'

She paused, frowning and staring out through a gap in the trees. Giving a slight squeak, she backed up against him, before yelping and leaping away, apologising repeatedly.

'Hey, it's okay. What's up?' He asked, following her gaze. '...Oh dear...'

'Spiders. Big big *big* spider. In the game. Big spider,' she whispered, backing further away and ending up against another inconveniently placed tree. '...Neko no likey teh spiders...'

'Teh? Can't you players just say 'the' like... normal players?' He trailed off, loosing his train of thought completely as he watched Dokugumo's attack. ...*Ellen*...

'I...um... have to go offline. To feed the dog. Or milk the haggis. Or wear a kilt. Yeah, kilts! Anyway, I've got to go do Scottish stuff! Kthanxbai!'

'Yeah, I'm really supposed to be part of this whole adventure, so I had better be going too.' Alex stammered, jetting back to the scene of the fight. *Shoot... I mean, Suko!*

'Poor. Very, very poor,' sighed Storm, prodding the webbing with a foot. 'I really did expect these tamers to be more of a challenge.'

'Now?' Maree asked, glancing at Alex.

He paused, eyes wide. *...Why are they looking to me as their leader?*

Clearing his thoughts, he stared straight at Storm, nodding. 'Now.'

'You want a challenge?' Ceirin growled, stepping out into the clearing.

'You've got one,' hissed Maree, drawing her sword.

Ka-click. A kid with a gun doesn't need to say a word.

Remaining silent, Sam and Nick stepped up behind their tamers, ready for a battle.

'Let them go, Storm.' Opal said softly, stepping in front of the three humans. 'Don't drag children into this.'

'They didn't do anything to offend you, master,' Matt added, stepping up next to her and staring beseechingly at Storm. 'There's no need to harm them.'

'Oh, no. Not you as well...' said Storm, flattening back his hair with one paw and groaning as he stared at Matt. 'Please, Matthew, don't tell me you're with them! Good slaves are so hard to come by...'

'I'm not your slave, and I don't deserve to be treated like one,' hissed Matt, tail flicking through the air and hitting Alex in the face. 'At least they understand that!'

'Oh really?' Queried Storm, raising an eyebrow. 'Then why, dear boy, are you on the front line?'

Grabbing Matt by the tail, Alex pulled him back, stepping to the front. Shrugging, Maree followed, while Ceirin and Opal did a short dance around each other before changing places.

'Well, that's a lot better, isn't it?' Storm said, smirking at he prodded the unconscious Beta as he hung. Alex flinched, as he dug his claws into Ellen's cocoon, kicking her into the back.

Eyes flashing, Dokugumo crawled after the two, hovering over them like the flies her smaller relations preyed upon.

'I ask for a war, and they send me a young princess. I ask for peace to destroy the world, and they send me a bunch of meddling kids. All these clichés will be the death of me yet.'

'How's this for a cliché?' Growled the Creator, pointing his guns at Storm's head. 'The bad guy eats lead.'

'Oh, child, I believe you're mistaken,' Storm said softly, stepping over to him.

'Don't come near me!'

'You're not playing with the big guns, Alexander.'

'I'm warning you,' hissed Alex, aiming at a point just past Storm's ear. 'One step closer...'

Closing his eyes, he pulled the trigger. Nothing happened.

'Wha?' He gasped, pumping the trigger to no avail.

Shaking her head, Maree ran a hand along the Invisiblade as it flickered into visibility. 'It's cardboard. Useless.'

'How can you do this?' Yelled Alex, glaring at him. 'None of this power is yours!'

'My, my. Aren't you the greedy one?' Storm shook his head, stepping back to Dokugumo and whispering something to her, before sauntering back over to them. 'If there is power, I'll use it to my advantage. Does it matter to whom it rightfully belongs?'

'You might be able to render their weapons useless,' growled Sam, lowering his horns. 'But don't forget about us.'

'Oh, I'm not forgetting, my dear *dwagon*,' Storm smiled, patting his head. She growled, lowering her head further. Rolling his eyes at the tamers and the other cat-folk, he struck out, grabbing Sam by her slender neck.

Crying out, Maree leapt forward, holding her useless blade to his neck. 'Let her go.'

'Make me, human,' he hissed, squeezing tighter. Sam roared, trying to summon any power, but receiving nothing.

He's too powerful...

'You sure about that?' Maree asked, glaring at him. 'I'm giving you a choice, kitty.'

'Positive.'

Clenching her fist, Maree promptly kicked him where it hurt.

Storm angry, quickly changed to a high-pitched squeal as he crumpled to the ground.

'What can I say,' said Maree quietly, helping Sam away. 'I'm a dog person.'

'Alright *Maree!*' Ceirin cheered working on the webbing that bound Ellen with his newfound blade. Nick was standing close by him, wings spread wide. He was itching to help out Sam, but knew Maree could do it on her own.

'*Suko,*' spat Storm, getting back to his feet. 'I will not be made a fool of by some immature *brat!*'

Leaping back to his feet, he grabbed her by the collar, spinning her round and clawing her face.

'Maree!' Yelled Ceirin, as she screamed, raising a hand to her face. Blood quickly flowed from the wound, soaking her clothing.

Storm turned at his cry, knocking Nick aside with a quick claw to his chest. Ceirin stared up at him, backing away against undergrowth behind him. The blade cut his hand as he slid it away, pulling down his jacket over his trouser pockets.

The cocoon had been slit away, but Ellen remained unconscious next to him. Glaring at her, Storm grabbed Ceirin by the collar, yanking him into the air.

'You shall be the *first* to die!' Storm raised a hand, beckoning Dokugumo closer. She stepped out from the shadows, scuttling to his side and staring curiously at Ceirin.

'You haven't eaten in a while, have you, my pet?' Storm whispered, stroking her head. 'But not to worry. You shall have the blood you long for...'

'No! Don't touch him!' Maree yelled, running forward, but Matt held her back, holding a scrap of material against her wound.

'You've been hurt enough, Miss Maree. Don't rush into a fight you cannot win,' Matt said soothingly, one paw holding her tightly by the shoulder.

I hoped this problem could be solved without bloodshed...
Why must people always suffer?

'I'll stop him,' Alex said quietly, stepping over to Storm and tapping him on the shoulder. The cat whirled round, dropping Ceirin and grabbing him by the neck.

'What are you doing?'

'Trying to speak,' the Creator growled, hanging limp. 'Tense, aren't you?'

'Oh, great. More *clichés*. The hero comes to save the poor little side character, with some spectacular trick that I'll remain completely oblivious to. Well, try your best.'

'HEY! I'M NOT A-'

'Ceirin. Shuttit. Now.'

'Sorry...'

'No tricks, Storm,' the Creator smirked, tossing his guns aside. 'All I ask is that I be the first to die.'

'Why?' Storm's eyes narrowed suspiciously, as he searched the boy's eyes for any sign of trickery of arrogance.

'To give the others a chance.'

Chapter 36:

Sacrifice

Storm wrung his tail in his paws, uncertain. 'Very well, human child. Commence your grand plan.'

He stepped back, and Alex motioned to Ceirin and Nick to return to the safer large group.

'Go ahead, Dokugumo. Do your thing.' Storm shrugged, leaning back against a tree and watching with mild interest.

Let's see how the Creator of this world protects it.

The pair stood alone in the corner, not far from Beta and Ellen. She stirred, but didn't awake. Blinking sleepily, Beta opened his eyes, snapping to attention and staring at the mammoth beast still hanging nearby.

'Hey, Dokugumo. It's your master,' Alex whispered, searching for any trace of recognition. 'Don't you remember me?'

No answer, save the baring of huge teeth, designed solely to puncture skin. Alex nodded, baring his own fangs.

'I was the one who created you, Black Widow. I was the boy who wasn't afraid of you, but didn't try to hurt you. You have to remember me.'

Uncertainly, the spider put a leg forward. Alex held out his own arm, and she brushed the leg against his skin, hairs sensing him. Recognizing who he was.

'You don't want to kill me, Dokugumo. You don't want to kill anyone. All you want is to stay alive – you don't understand how many people you're hurting. I can't allow you to prey on my friends.'

'Dokugumo! What are you waiting for?'

'He is a hacker, nothing more. If you were in his way, he would squash you.' As he laid a hand on the spider's head, he felt it shake at both his touch and his words, backing down.

'In the end, it's up to you what you decide to do,' Alex said quietly, stepping back. 'Choose.'

'Doku, what appears to be the problem?' Asked Storm, stepping over to him. He frowned, staring at Alex. 'Word games, boy human? They won't work on my dear Doku.'

Stepping protectively over to her, he smiled warmly, brushing her hairy body.

'Don't listen to what he says, my dear. Think of it as a way to survive – he is food, and you need food to survive. You must kill to survive.'

As Dokugumo once again bared her fangs, Storm smiled. So did Alex.

In seconds, Storm's grin turned to a grimace of pain. Alex's didn't.

Storm gasped, as the huge spider plunged her fangs into his side. Eyes narrowing, he wrapped a hand around her skull.

The Black Widow screamed as only an insect could, as Storm squeezed her fragile body tightly. Crying out, Alex leapt at Storm, only to be kicked to the ground.

'...No...' Ellen whispered, awaking to see the dying spider explode into a firework display of purple dust.

He… didn't even give her a chance…

* * *

'So you're called Zakaz, now?' iZ asked, scanning the computer screen and not looking round as the snake entered behind him.

'I still prefer the Guardian,' Zakaz said softly, looking up at the screen. 'What about you? Still Izzy?'

'No. Luke.'

'I'll remember that.'

Eyes dark, he stared up at the screen, watching the trees of Berk being torn out by their roots. On another screen, he saw another tornado twisting the waters of Tropica in all directions, that same water hit Serta, covering it in layers of rock as it met the lava from the hundreds of erupting volcanoes in Raze. These, in turn, were blackening the sky in all areas except Frieze, where the snow was melting from the heat of the volcanoes.

One by one, all the planets were being destroyed, passing their effects onto others as they all connected.

The Guardian froze, as he saw the winds battering the trees at Fear Forest.

If they destroyed Crystal Clearing…

'No,' he spat, eyes narrowing.

Luke paused, glancing at him. 'There's nothing we can do Guardian.'

'There *must* be!'

'A task like this requires dragon magic, or the power of the tamers. We have none of that.'

'There must be another way! The tamers cannot help us, they have battles of their own to fight!'

'Name one. All the players are offline. The Council couldn't care less. Destro's plummeting towards the sea.'

'Just give me a moment to think…' Zakaz muttered, leaning his head flat on the ground. He paused, blinking, before staring out the window. 'Wait a minute…'

'Oh, *sssssshoot!*'

* * *

'What is it with you and your fanged minions?' Hissed Storm, holding his side.

Another poison… there isn't long before they begin to affect me. That is why I must act now.

'Now, enough of this foolish stalling. You cannot fight the inevitable, fools. So, who shall be the first lamb to the slaughter?'

Roaring, Sam dived in front of Maree, while Nick hovered warily at Ceirin's side. Getting to his feet, Alex rose and helped Ellen up, hovering in the shadows of the corner.

'No volunteers? Pity, pity. I guess I'm left to choose myself…' Moaned Storm, staring round. His gaze hovered on the imp, as Ellen pulled him loose from the web, before shooting back to the smallest boy.

'You. Boy with the wolf. Come forward.'

'What?' He said, stepping back.

'Forward, you fool! One foot in front of the other! It's not hard!'

Obeying, Ceirin stepped up to him. Storm frowned, surveying him.

'I guess you'll do. All humans are pathetic wastes of skin, and I can't expect my first victim to be any different.'

Ceirin stayed silent, as Storm drew a platuminium pole from thin air. Thin, sharp swords appeared on either end, and he spun it once in the air, before pausing to examine it.

'Ah, will you look at that. If I hold it horizontality, I might be able to behead you and your little doggie at the same time. Wouldn't that be fun?'

'Don't you dare!' Growled Nick, springing forward, but Ceirin held out a hand to stop him.

'Only me.'

'Very well. To each his own, as the saying goes.' Storm shrugged, changing the size of the pole for ease of use, before pressing it against his chest.

'To gut, or to behead. Which do you prefer?'

'Neither,' spat Ceirin, drawing the ruby-handled knife and pressing it against the pole.

* * *

'The cassstle is falling! *THE CASSSTLE IS FALLING!*'

'It's the planet that's falling, actually. If we were falling, the ground would have to disappear,' Luke murmured, typing something into the keyboard. 'And wa-hey, you've got your lisp back. All is right with the world once more.'

'No it'ssssss not! THE WORLD IS FALLING!'

'We could always call the Minis. Or post a request for help on the main page. We'd get hundreds of volunteers… oh wait, we can't. The game's *offline*.'

'Being *cynical* isssssssn't helping!'

'Neither is the random stressing of words. But it's fun none the less,' Luke said, smiling. 'I recommend we wait. It'll all sort itself out eventually.'

'Yeah, and by then we'll be *crusssssshed!* AGAINSSSSST THE GROUND!'

'You've got a point there,' he said simply, staring up at the ceiling. 'Reresan, what do you suggest?'

'I suggest we wait. The game's gravity isn't operating properly, so if the tamers manage to defeat Storm within the next five minutes, we should all be fine.'

'Well, we're doomed,' sighed Luke, tapping once again at the keyboard. After a few moments fiddling, he managed to receive an audio stream from the scene.

'Face it. It's over.'

* * *

Storm stared at Ceirin's weapon, taken aback.

'That's… one of ours…'

'A War of the Cats weapon. I know.' Ceirin pressed the knife against the pole, forcing Storm back. 'Your cloud blade, combined with Matt's crystal blade.'

'Your filthy hands should never have even touched such an object!'

'Such a pity, isn't it?' Drawled Ceirin, smirking as he backed away. 'Now, I'm going to give you a choice. You come quietly, fixing this area and giving us back all our powers. Or you die right here, right now, and the problem's solved.'

Storm didn't answered, circling Ceirin. He did the same, following his every move. Hissing quietly, Storm stepped around, passing by Sam, Maree, Matt and Opal.

He paused, pulling the weapon into two parts. Then, he wheeled round, pressing one against Nick's throat.

'Not together, but still, a rather neat little combo,' mused Storm, pressing down the blade. Nick gave a loud yelp, as blood stained his silver fur.

Leaping away into the trees, Matt fled to the other side of the clearing, dropping down behind Ceirin, where Storm had stood not long before.

Smirking, Storm glanced back at Ceirin. He stood frozen, staring at his partner.

'No... please...'

Opal moved close to Maree and Sam, trying to summon any powers from this world around her. But none came. Storm was in complete control.

'Nick...' Whispered Sam, eyes wide. She couldn't fight, he'd taken away all her power. She couldn't move, in case it prompted Storm to move.

I'm... powerless...

'No!' Alex said, keeping one eye on the unused sword and stepping in front of Ellen. 'Don't hurt him!'

'Beta!' Yelled Ellen, struggling to get out of her arms. She held him tightly, whilst fear gripped her own body.

'Face it,' said Storm, launching the weapon at Ceirin's chest. 'It's over.'

The metal weapon tasted the blood it longed for. A single gasp echoed through the clearing, and screams and cries came from all the others.

But none was louder than Opal's scream.

'MATT!'

Gasping, the cat fell to the ground, weapon driven right through his body. Behind him, Ceirin stared in shock at the metal point shining through his back fur. It was coated crimson.

Leaning over, Matt crouched down to the ground, and blood stained the grass. Eyes glassy, he stared back up at the crowd – at both Opal, and at Storm.

'I'm back home,' he whispered, smiling at them both. 'I'm back where I belong.'

With a loud bark, Nick tore himself away from Storm, knocking him to the ground. All his power was gone from him, but his natural weapons weren't, and he clamped his teeth hard around the cat-god's neck.

'No!' the Creator cried, dragging Ellen and Beta forward and stepping over to Nick. 'Leave him!'

Nick stared up at him, a lust for revenge in his eyes. He didn't move.

Stepping past the cat-servant, Ceirin stepped over to him, nodding. 'Let him go Nick.'

With a reluctant whimper, the wolf stepped back, and Storm sat up.

He was shaking, violent tremors wracking his whole body.

'As the blood of an innocent is spilled, the power you wanted is finally given to you.' Ellen said quietly, staring at him. 'You were given power over life and death.'

'But I... was wrong,' Storm gasped, collapsing to the ground. With one hand, he tore at his own fur, staining his claws and only adding to his pain. 'I destroyed one who had done nothing wrong.'

'And even if he had not taken the blow, you would have suffered the same fate,' hissed Alex, voice laced with disgust. 'For none of us is as evil as you.'

'It's tearing you apart,' Maree whispered, holding Sam close.

'I'm turning into a normal cat-person,' Storm whispered disbelievingly; as his fur dimmed to grey, power seeping away into the skies around him. 'All my power... destroyed. I'm nothing anymore.'

'You deserve far worse!' Spat Ceirin, kicking him hard in the stomach.

Heads bowed, they turned to where Opal lay over Matt's still body.

She was still there, paws clasped, dress limp around her as she sat sobbing on the grass.

Matt, however, had disappeared.

Chapter 37:

A Dark Winter

The small room was lit only by candles, their dim light illuminating the framed photograph of Matthew Black, smiling and ruffling a young Opal's fur.

There was no coffin, no gravestone, nothing but a photograph and the memories to remember him by.

Maree and Sam both sat on the carpet below the shrine, heads bowed. Maree was once again wearing a black suit, while Sam had dark crosses painted on to each of her wings. The scar on Maree's face had gone now, healed through the Programming World at a guilt-torn Storm's request. The memory, however, would take a while to fade from anyone's mind.

'I never got to say a proper goodbye,' Maree whispered, voice choking as she tried to laugh. 'You silly old fool. What did you have to go and die for, eh?'

'But it was really sweet of you, Matt… doing it for Ceirin. Doing that for all of us. I don't think any of us humans would be that brave.'

She paused, staring at his picture with shining eyes. 'I know I wouldn't be.'

Rubbing her head against Maree's side comfortingly, Sam stood up and stepped over to the picture. Tears streaming down her face as they did Maree's, she touched her nose against the photo frame.

'I didn't want anyone to get hurt.'

'None of us did,' Maree whispered, wrapping her arms around her dragon and turning away from the photo. 'But in the end, he got what he wanted, didn't he?'

'To go home.'

'Better than that,' Marees said, smiling at his photo, though there were tears streaming down her face. 'He got his freedom.'

'Whoa…' Ceirin murmured, staring around the restaurant. 'A lot of people turned up, eh?'

Sitting down by the window, Maree nodded. The light from the chandeliers above both heated and lit up the room, protecting it from the cold winter weather.

'They're only here for the free food,' the Creator muttered, taking a sip of apple juice.

'That's the only reason we have this party.'

'Exactly.'

Shivering, Maree stared out the window as snow fell outside. *We've been here for almost half a year.*

I came here on my birthday.

'Hey, are you cold?' Ceirin asked, frowning as he stared at her. Standing up, he pulled off his jacket, placing it over her and smiling. 'There! Much better, don't you think?'

'Thanks Ceirin.'

Feeling out-of-place, Alex searched for Ellen, finding no sign of her amongst the crowd.

He shrugged. *Maybe she has better things to do.*

Pulling her jacket tightly around her, Ellen stepped out into the corridor of the restaurant where the party was being held. She froze, seeing Staff Member Muvo leaning against the wall near the door.

Taking a swig from a glass bottle, he nodded to her. 'I thought you'd have been with the rest of your group.'

'I… needed to go out for some fresh air.'

'Doesn't surprise me. You never were a party girl,' he murmured, staring at the bottom of his bottle and wondering when he'd reach it.

'What do you mean?' She asked sharply, staring at him. He returned the glare, shrugging.

'You can change.'

The hall was full of life, new faces and old alike. The two groups of squirrels were at war over the bowls of nuts, red verses grey in a small-scale war. Below the table they used as battlegrounds, kittens were prowling the area.

Zera was in deep conversation with Storm and Opal, and all had their heads bowed, voices hushed. Beta hovered nearby, guilt weighing him down.

If I hadn't followed Matt from that Park…

Out at the back of the restaurant, the Minis were also at war. They had engaged in a flame war, tossing insults at each other and accompanying them with flamethrowers and other forms of fiery doom.

At the side, Setsu and Cal watched disapprovingly. Not at the boys, but at the blue-and-white Dizzee (Iain's partner) next to them, who was looking even drunker than usual.

'Dear, stop spiking the drinks,' said Xcel, fiancé of Thor, as she fluttered down onto the edge of the table on shimmering butterfly wings.

'I'M ADDING HAPPY JUICE!'

'That's nice, dear. If only you could be so enthusiastic when working with the children.'

'I hate the children.'

'I gathered,' she said, clipping back her hair. 'Now hush, Mr Stewart's about to say something.'

Clearing his throat, Alex stood up at the head of the table, raising his glass. 'Attention, everybody. I would like to propose a toast.'

He paused, as Ellen sat down. She nodded to him to continue.

'To the Dragon Tamers!'

'To the Dragon Tamers!'

A short while after, the group gathered in the centre of the room, listening to the murmured chatter all around them.

'I guess that means you're one of us now,' Ellen laughed, smiling at him.

'I don't think so,' he said sharply, voice cold. 'I don't have a dragon.'

I'll always be out-of-place among them…

'Yeah. Neither do I,' Ellen said, shrugging. 'That never stopped me.'

Laughing over by the window with Nick, Sam called over to the four.

'Hey, you guys!'

'Yes?' Maree said, glancing at her.

'Look up!'

Obliging, the tamers stared up, seeing mistletoe hanging above them. They all turned crimson, staring at each other.

'Hey. It's tradition,' laughed Ceirin, kissing Maree on the cheek. He paused, frowning. 'Um…are you going to hurt me now? Because we're right in front of a tower of glasses, and that could get nasty.'

'No,' she laughed, smiling. 'You meant it this time.'

'Tradition. A bunch of foolish rules and custom designed for the human world,' said Alex, glaring up at the mistletoe. 'We need pay them no attention.'

'Aw, come here and give me a hug!'

'*Ellen!*'

Outside, snow fell all over the land, enveloping it in icy cobwebs. Neko frowned as she watched it fall, wiping flakes off her laptop and going over the footage of the past events, caught on CCTV.

Again, she flicked to Whirlpool Park, to Accatel. To Destro Gardens, and Maree's sudden fainting. The disappearance in Destro Castle, the reflections only Ellen could see at Whirlpool Park and the single word in the sand. Then back, to *him*.

'This is *far* from over.'

The Dragon Tamer's Rulebook and Guide

Created by the Dragon Council

Newly updated for Dragon Tamers 2: Opal's Diary

The Breaking of any of these rules will result in an instant GAME OVER. No apologies, no exceptions, no second chances.

This is the rulebook and Guide for the 'Dragon Tamers' Computer Game.

Requirements

The Dragon Tamers series are virtual reality games – this means that players can immerse themselves completely in the game world. However, due to the high price of the V.R. equipment, there are other modes of play.

Full Immersion – The most complicated option, only recommended for experienced players. Various pieces of equipment can be bought for this, including the full body suit and treadmill. These items must be custom ordered, to fit your shoe or clothing size. Though this is the best way of play health-wise, it's not recommended for use by those suffering from obesity, asthma, or with other medical problems which might be triggered or affected by the physical work required to play.

Basic Virtuality – This set normally consists of a pair of cybergloves and a headset. Movement is achieved through use of these gloves on a touch pad, while actions are achieved through use of them in the air (the glove is covered with movement/touch sensors). Alternatively, a mouse and keyboard can be used instead of the cyberglove (since you will be wearing the headset, it's recommended you're fluent at touch-typing if you choose this option).

Unequipped – The game is played completely through monitor, keyboard and mouse, without any Virtuality equipment. This is the cheapest option. However, some of the game features are not available when using this mode of play – for instance, voice chat. Though you can choose to have a computerized voice to read aloud your words for you, all your conversations will be subtitled.

Subtitles are the only way to speak in l33t/1337/l33t-sp33k in the game world.

Section 1 – Dragon Uploading/ Creation

Tempest shares data with Dragon Tamers, so all your old game data will be in the new game. The same applies to tamer and dragon data – you carry it over from the original game. However, if you purchase the game without having a copy of the original Dragon Tamers game, you are given the option to start from scratch using the Dragon Creator X Program. Also, there's a new out of game program called Customix which allows you to change your in-game character's age, gender, hair and eye colour, clothing etc. after you begin playing, adding more outfits or changing your hairstyle to suit your mood. Upgrades for this program and DCX will be available from the website.

Section 2 - Player Avatars

'Avatar' is the term used for player characters within the game. In the original, you designed your own avatar, and this affected in-game status, abilities, and ease of play. This remains the same in the sequel, but the ability to change outfits is also added – now, you have a normal (original) outfit, a party outfit (this varies depending on which in-game parties you attend, and whether they're formal or informal), and a 'comfort' outfit (for generally hanging about in the game).

Section 3 -The Planets

Each planet usually has its own Sun and Moon. All planets contain oxygen and gravity. All have rain everyso often (though with planets like Serta, 'every so often' can be less than once a year).

Tropica: The Tropical Planet, very little land, lots of water. Easiest way to reach the 'Plot Hole', a gate that will transport the player to a random area. Or at least, it's supposed to be random – past choices have shown it may have the ability to think for itself and choose which area would be best for each player to go to.

Frieze: The Cold Planet. Special clothing is needed for tamers to survive the cold here, and only certain types of dragon will take the climate well. Due to the difficulty of the area, not much has been discovered about its contents.

Gael: The Windy Planet. Recently, there's been a lot of testing of hang gliders here. Most tests did not end well. Mostly uninhabitable, due to its strong winds making it hard for anybody to keep their feet on the ground. Gael's main job is providing power to the various electrical items in the game from its many wind farms.

Raze: The Hot Planet, not good for water dragons, but loved by fire dragons. It has a lot of volcanoes. In the past, its largest volcano, on the path from a hidden world, had played a key role in the plot. However, no players have ever been allowed down to its lowest levels.

Serta: The Desert Planet. Best known for the 'Riddle of the Sphinx' mini-game and Phoenix feather power up, its climate is enjoyed by many dragons, and hated by others due to the common sandstorms. Its many pyramids are great places for tamers to explore, containing many treasures.

Sonok: The Water Planet. Made up of various islands, each varying in size, most of them closed off for some of the Dragon Realm's more private creatures. Recently, a new island has opened up to players, as a private club called the Crystal Clan. Against humanoid dragons and magic casting humans, the majority of its reptilian members are traditional dragons. They're also known for doing their best to discourage the former, destroying any witches, wizards, or humanoids that enter their lands.   Players are warned to be wary of these players even outside of Sonok, as the Clan is not responsible for their member's actions outside of the area.

Clix: The Starting Planet. Warm, lots of plant life, rains rarely, as the land does not need much moisture. When it does rain, it is quite light. Home to the Valley, the private homes of all tamers. A long river winds between two huge mountains, their rocky faces lined with caves, and rain often runs down the stone steps that lead to the different levels. A new city is currently being constructed not far from the Valley. Later, buildings, games, shops and even a railway system are planned for this area. Fear Fork has now been removed from the game (both the sequel and the original). However, Fear Forest and Fear Loch (now containing the Floating City) are still accessible.

Berk: The Woodland planet. Containing many red squirrels, each with their own unique personalities. Unwelcoming of dragons, and able to show it in the strangest ways, they guard many small treasures with their lives. Recently, many dragons have taken to hunting down this specie, and their numbers are declining. The Council reminds players that red squirrels are not one of the breeds designed as prey, and ask tamers not to kill them if it's avoidable.

Dite: The Planet of Darkness and Touch Lights. The mysterious Kitecats reside on the main side of the planet, lost in eternal darkness. As with most planets, they have many treasures to guard, and many secrets to hide. It's possibly the werewolves seen in the first game in the Mini Games festival originated from this planet's other, unexplored side.

Konica: A Grey planet, filled with creatures called 'Grey Ghosts'. The dullest of all the planets, players are warned that just being in this area can have a drastic affect on their personality. In the Realms, depression is often referred to as 'going Konican'.

Destro: Above the beginners planet lays Destro. In Dragon Tamers 2, the castle and tower is out of boundsto players. The Katapolt has been removed from the game, but the Sphinxes Riddle Mini Game and the Mini Game Festival are still playable.

Diisyer: The Dreamworld. Where fantasy meets virtual reality, and nightmares lay cloaked in shadows.

Luckeh Land: Only accessible through the Plot Hole. Nobody really wants to go there anyway... for reasons best kept hidden.

War of the Cats: Not a separate world, but in fact, a whole separate game, and the focus of Tempest's plot. Created before the original Dragon Tamers game, it has been reactivated and is attempting to merge with it. However, the two worlds aren't compatible, and their joining is proving dangerous to the dragon realms, as are some of the creatures that are accompanying its arrival.

Once, its main races were humans and the cat-folk, cat/human hybrids with tribal beliefs and rituals. While the humans were a mixed breed, each taking on separate looks, personalities, and beliefs, the cat-folk maintained a firm belief in the existence of gods. There were various gods, but the description and abilities of these didn't vary – shrines dotted all around their world contained statues, engravings, and stories about the god in question. Gaia, their name for their world, was also the name for their most powerful and most respected goddess. The human's careless harming of the environment, and in doing so, their beloved goddess Gaia, was one of the triggers that sparked their rivalry. As the two rival species were constantly at war, drastic action had to be taken to stop the fighting once and for all...

Section 4 – Items

Items can be found all around the site, or taken from defeated enemies. Also, other characters may leave items behind accidentally. With the new game comes a whole range of these, including the diary pages. If, due to a gamer glitch or player's mistake, or even one of you party members abandoning you, you can collect one of these pages to re-live the corresponding vision. Even if you did see the vision, some players like to collect these so they can fully complete/explore the game, or so they can watch it again... and again... and again... At the beginning of the game, you will receive a rucksack containing a sleeping bag and a healing potion. These are embroidered with your username and a picture of your dragon, in case they are misplaced. There is also a new item, which current users will also automatically receive. It's the Doover, a small machine used to collect Dragon Dust and automatically store it in a plastic container. There is no limit to the amount of items you can put in your bag, but carrying a lot of items will lower your speed in the game. Carrying a large amount of dragon dust doesn't affect your speed. All items in the bag are safe from water, fire, and many other things that happen in the game. One of the bag's special features is the ability to disappear when not needed.

Section 5 – Signature Items

When you are beginning the game, you can create your own item, called your signature item. As a weapon, it will be quite powerful, as battle items for the tamer are not common. Creating a weapon also comes in useful when your dragon is young, injured, or outnumbered. This is the most common choice. However, the item does not have to be a weapon, or could even be an item disguised as something else. It is unique to you, and cannot be discarded, traded, or sold.

This will gain more power/gain more features/become easier to use as your power increases in the game. These items void the rule that Dragons cannot harm humans, so if you use it during a battle you can be harmed. Guns as normal or signature weapons are not allowed. There are one or two exceptions (like the net gun, an item that can be traded in the game), but pistols and similar items cannot be used by normal players.

Section 6 – Weapons and Spells

As with other items, there are a whole range of new weapons, most of which are best used against the Diary Guardians. Some weapons can only be used by imps. There are also some new spells, and imps that already know magic without the aid of code words. The Council notes however, that many users are choosing the witch/wizard character type under the impression that they can use these spells for almost anything. Due to some errors with the spell casting and magic system, a lot of players have also been able to do this, spoiling the game and leaving with the impression that it's too easy. Magic-casting characters are now being frowned upon, much as humanoid dragons already are. Therefore, it is suggested you try and find different ways to work with the character design, or choose a different one entirely. The Dragon Realms are a role-playing world – originality is the key.

Section 7 – Market

After some complications with the trading system of Dragon Tamers 1, a new type of currency had been introduced – dragon dust. Instead of using in to strengthen your dragon, you can collect it with the Doover. Dust varies in colours and rarity, and therefore value. In the newest city, Silver Leaf, a market has been set up. Here, players and game characters alike can come to buy or sell. In the Dustsmith's shop, a variety of Council dragons also work to change dust into the game's alternative currency – semi-transparent purple coins in various shapes. The market accepts both trading and purchasing items with Dragon Dust.

There are also rumours of a hidden market, where fabrics and items of clothing can be bought. The location, however, is unknown and the rumour is unconfirmed.

Section 8 – Other Tamers

As always, other tamers play a large part in the game. Dragons can be instructed to fight each other, or work alongside each other. You can also trade spells, weapons and other items with other tamers.

It's easier to unravel the mystery if you have a group of friends to help you, and battles are usually a lot more fun.

Notice from the Dragon Tamers Moderation Team: Never give out any personal details (phone numbers, addresses, etc.) to people you meet online.

Section 9 – Diary Guardians

The newest creatures to the game are the Guardians. They originally came from the War of the Cat-Folk game, and somehow entered Dragon Tamers. Now they guard the diary pages. Alternatively, mini games, challenges or puzzles may have to be completed to access the pages. Note, however, that the pages are optional, and so are the battles of mini-games you must win to obtain them.

Section 10 – Cheats Scams and Hacks

As before, cheats and hacks of any kind are not allowed in this game, and the using of these will result in an immediate 'game over.' This includes: Level Codes (Not Spell Codes), Maps, Babysitting Scams, and anything which makes the game unfair for other players. Also, players are advised to watch out for players mailing random people with scams, aiming to gain your items. If you give a stranger 10 rare items, he probably won't give you that one-of-a-king item, but will run off with yours. Mailing twenty players the same thing won't unlock a secret area where all the rare items are hidden, it's spamming. Basically, if it doesn't make sense, it's probably a scam, so report the player responsible to the Dragon Council.

Other things not permitted in the game are:

– Bots or third-party programs (most designed to edit character data, or perform simple tasks over and over.)

– Needless slaughter or bullying. (Strong players picking on or ganging up on newer players, or stalking certain users.)

– Destroying NPCs without a good reason (e.g. for fun, to stop a player from completing a quest.) This rule does not apply to bosses, characters who have challenged you to a fight, or characters that the storyline rules must be destroyed

– Selling in-game characters or items for real money.

– Looting - stealing the rewards from opponents others have killed (players not in your party).

– Hacking or attempted hackings will be punished severely by the Dragon Tamers staff.

Section 11 - Leaving the Game

Dotted throughout the level are healing shrines, a place to heal and rest. These places are also save spots, and if you quit the game you will restart at the last shrine you visited. They are often hidden; try asking the areas inhabitants if they know of any near-by.

Section 12 – Troubleshooting

Still having trouble playing the game? Try getting in touch with the Dragon Council through Killimario; we're now able to help with player problems.

Section 13 - Things that will get you an immediate Game Over

There are many things in this game that will result in a 'game over.' Here is a list of some of them.

Losing a battle when you have only one life left.

Losing a battle against the destroyer.

Knowingly using other user's artwork for creating your own Dragon.

Failing to tame you Dragon, causing it to go wild and destroy you.

Trying to fool the game.

Using Auto Trainers.

Scamming other users.

Hacking into other user's accounts.

Taking advantage of other users.

Attacking a user's dragon who doesn't want to battle.

Attacking a user on purpose (sometimes a Dragon may hit you by accident, like if a burst of flame misses its target).

Pretending to be a member of the Council

Pretending to be another player.

Breaking a Player's Promise.

Avoid doing all of these things and you might even complete the game! Good luck!

The Dragon Council